IN EVIL TIMES

D0766433

Also by Melinda Snodgrass and coming soon from Titan Books

THE HIGH GROUND
THE HIDDEN WORLD (July 2018)

IN EVIL TIMES

THE IMPERIALS SAGA

MELINDA SNODGRASS

TITAN BOOKS

In Evil Times
Print edition ISBN: 9781783295845
E-book edition ISBN: 9781783295852

Published by Titan Books
A division of Titan Publishing Group Ltd
144 Southwark Street, London
SE1 0UP

First edition: July 2017
10 9 8 7 6 5 4 3 2 1

A CIP catalogue record for this title is available from the British Library.

Printed in the USA.

This one is For Eric Kelley.

My Garrus and an invaluable source of late night brainstorm sessions.

1

FOR YOUR OWN GOOD

"We *wouldn't* want to make you *uncomfortable*. Put you in a *situation* where you might find yourself issuing *orders* to one of your *betters*."

Ensign Thracius—Tracy—Ransom Belmanor stared down at the Lieutenant Junior Grade bars. They glittered against the black velvet that lined the clear Lucite box. The box itself sat in the exact center of the desk belonging to Vice Admiral Duque Maximilian Vertrant, the Commandant of the High Ground. A small man, the massive furniture seemed to dwarf him.

When Tracy had started school three years earlier, Vice Admiral Vasquez y Markov had led the Solar League's preeminent military academy. Big and burly, Markov had dominated the room and the academy, but the admiral had been forced to retire at the end of Tracy's first year. The ever useful *spend more time with his family* being the stated reason. The real reason was that Markov had missed a plot against the emperor of the Solar League and his chosen successor— his daughter, Mercedes—that had been going on right beneath the commandant's aristocratic nose.

In contrast to Markov's rumbling tones, Vertrant had a rather high-pitched voice complete with a prissy upper-class accent and an annoying habit of stressing random words. Vertrant never forgot his title and never let others forget it either, and he had all the characteristics of the Fortune Five Hundred that Tracy most loathed and despised. The commandant finished by saying, "*Especially* given the *high station* held by *one* of your *classmates* in *particular* and you a *mere* scholarship student…"

Tracy and his fellow scholarship student Mark Wilson had endured countless such snubs and less than stellar assignments during their three years at the High Ground. That had certainly been the case for the shipboard trials that had occupied part of this, their final year. Tracy wished that he and Mark could have shared beers and bitches, but the other scholarship student had never forgiven Tracy for receiving the *Distinguido Servicio Cruzar* for his service to the Infanta. They had barely spoken beyond what was required for the past two years.

And now, mere days before the graduation ceremony, another insult. Instead of graduating as a newly minted first lieutenant like every other ensign in the senior class he was one step below his classmates. Except for one. He hoped. Tracy couldn't help it, he blurted out, "Is this being done to Ensign Wilson as well?"

The thin brows snapped together in a sharp frown and Vertrant's nose wrinkled as if confronted by a particularly noxious odor. "*Nothing* is being *done* to you, Belmanor. I *do* this as a *favor*, for your *own good*."

"Oh, of course, sir, how could I not have realized that."

Unfortunately Vertrant wasn't stupid. He stood and leaned across the desk, his small body almost vibrating with rage. "*Only* your *stellar* academic achievement is preventing me from responding, Lieutenant Junior Grade, but be advised—*school is over*. You are an *officer* in the *Orden de la Estrella* and insubordination can and will be *punished*. *You* are dismissed."

Tracy slammed his boot heels together, snapped off a perfect salute, swept up the now tainted emblems of his new rank and left the office. He wanted to find Davin or Ernesto and vent, but everyone was busy overseeing the batBEMs who were clearing out their quarters.

The person Tracy most wanted to talk to was Mercedes, but he knew that was impossible. Their closeness during freshman year had ended with the announcement of her engagement to Beauregard Honorius Sinclair Cullen, Vizconde Dorado Arco, Knight of the Shells, Shareholder General of the Grand Cartel and heir apparent to the 19th Duque de Argento y Pepco, known as Boho to his friends and as Asshole to Tracy. The wedding of the Infanta and her dashing fiancé was set for one week after graduation. Tracy was very glad he'd be aboard a ship and hopefully far away from Ouranos and Hissilek, the planet's capital city. He just prayed his future captain wouldn't insist the crew watch the royal wedding. Maybe he could arrange to be on duty or something.

He entered his room. Donnel his Cara'ot batBEM was snapping shut his holdall. Tracy threw the Lucite box at him.

The batBEM caught it with one of his four hands, the six fingers closing tightly on the box.

"Here, get these on my jacket."

The Cara'ot stared at the bars then looked up at Tracy, the four eyes blinking at him. "One last kick in the nuts before you leave the hallowed halls, I see."

"I'm sure it won't be the last," Tracy replied sourly.

Donnel's three legs propelled him quickly to the closet where Tracy's O-Trell—*Orden de la Estrella*—dress uniform jacket hung waiting for the graduation ceremony. "Wish we knew where we were heading. Big capital ship gives us more space. Small frigate and we'll need to leave some things with your dad."

"We'll know by three o'clock Saturday when our postings get announced."

"It'll be good to be in space again," the alien said.

"We're in space."

"*Moving* through space. Not stuck on this stationary behemoth. New worlds. New stars."

Tracy dropped onto his bunk. "You've missed it."

"Yeah. We Cara'ot are by nature gypsies. We spend most of our lives on trading ships."

"And stealing and manipulating the DNA of other races," Tracy shot back.

"We *traded* in DNA until your people came along and put a stop to it."

"And a good thing we did too. You're a goddamn horror," Tracy said, eyeing the alien.

Two of the four eyes rolled down the length of his squat

body, and Donnel gave himself a pat with all four hands. "Made to order for a specific purpose," he said in tones of satisfaction.

Tracy shuddered. "Like I said… a horror."

"You don't give a shit what we do among ourselves. It's just your own precious human DNA that's *so* sacred. Sir." It was added as an obvious and calculated afterthought.

"Our League, our rules. If the Cara'ot don't like it they can leave."

"Not really an option. You humans would go bugfuck if we tried to leave and kick the shit out of us again."

"Yeah, you're right. We know we can't trust you. Any of you."

"You know all of us aliens," three of the arms gestured widely, "got along just fine until you guys showed up."

"You startled us. We really had thought we were alone in the universe."

"Well God help us if we ever actually scare you, if this is how you react when you're just startled."

"Why are we even having this idiotic conversation? Get the bars on my uniform!"

"Yes, sir. Right away, sir. Boy, somebody's in a mood." Donnel's expression softened and he dropped the mocking tone as he said gently, "You let them get to you, sir."

The sudden kindness broke Tracy's control. "I'm second in our class behind Ernesto. I've got *that*." He pointed at where the *Distinguido Servicio Cruzar* glittered on the left breast of his jacket. "But I'll never rate. Not unless the FFH gives me a title."

"I'd say that's highly likely given your… connections."

Tracy gave a violent gesture. "Don't. Don't bring her up. I can't... I can't bear it."

"You knew it was impossible," the alien said in even gentler tones.

"I know. But knowing doesn't help."

Mercedes Adalina Saturnina Inez de Arango, the Infanta, stood on a riser while three Isanjo seamstresses knelt at the hem of her dress. The claws on their clever, long-fingered hands were retracted so only the soft pads arranged the flowing material over the stiff petticoats. Occasionally one of them would look up, large eyes set in a fur-covered face. Mercedes could read nothing in those eyes. No hint of what they might be thinking. The human designer stood back, fingers at his lips, eyes narrowed, a frown between his brows, evaluating the wedding gown. Tiny diamonds covered the dress, glittering and flashing. More jewels formed a pattern on the bodice, the symbol of the Solar League. Mercedes drew in shallow breaths because said bodice felt like it was trying to crush her ribcage. The only good thing about it was the deep V of the neckline that made her neck seem longer and displayed her décolletage, one of her better attributes.

After three years spent wearing primarily an O-Trell uniform complete with trousers or battle armor, Mercedes found the elaborate wedding gown to be confining and uncomfortable. She dreaded how the stiff netting of the petticoats would feel on the back of her thighs when she finally did get to sit down at the reception banquet. Tall as she was, she felt like the enormous belled skirt and lace flounces made her look dumpy.

Señor Vasilyev was approaching, holding a cloud of lace in his hands. He shook it out and it chimed as the tiny crystal bells kissed each other. The twenty-foot-long train was attached to the shoulders of the gown. He stepped back and beamed. Mercedes realized that his eyes were sweeping across his creation. He didn't even see her. How absurd she looked.

"Lovely. Lovely. His Majesty wishes you to wear your grandmother's tiara. I'll complete the design of the veil after I've seen it."

Mercedes held her breath and repeated the mantra— *courtesy, respect, civility*. Qualities always to be remembered and applied, particularly when dealing with a person who was not a member of her class. But the reminder of her grandmother's tiara, delicate twisted leaves of platinum, diamonds, pearls and moonstones brought into focus how much she hated this dress. Only two weeks until the wedding. How could she say anything now? She should have spoken up months ago.

"*Madre de Dios*, you look like an over-decorated bonbon," came a new voice, a light soprano with sarcasm dripping off every syllable.

Lieutenant Lady Cipriana Delacroix leaned against the doorjamb, one booted foot cocked over the other, completely at ease in her O-Trell uniform. Once one of Mercedes' ladies-in-waiting, she had joined Mercedes at the military academy. Smarter than she pretended, Cipriana was also an accredited beauty with jet-black hair shot through with strands of red, dark eyes, ebony skin and perfect features. She also lacked even a vestige of tact when it came to members of the lower class.

Her blunt assessment of the dress had Vasilyev puffing and bristling. Mercedes found a reserve of diplomacy. "I'm certain that Señor Vasilyev's goal is to make me look like a fairy princess, and I appreciate his efforts despite the deficiencies of his subject."

"Well, then he's an idiot." Mercedes again cringed. "You're damn near six feet tall, Mer, and you've got a figure. There's nothing fairy-like about you. Now Dani, she could have pulled this off..." Cipriana's voice trailed away into sadness.

"I don't want to die. Mercedes, help me!"

Lady Danica Everett's agonized words just before she was pulled away by agents of Seguridad Imperial. Mercedes shuddered because she hadn't, in fact, helped her one-time friend and lady-in-waiting. She hadn't even tried.

"Sorry. Bad memories. I shouldn't have brought her up," Cipri said, contrite.

Of the three ladies-in-waiting who had accompanied Mercedes to the High Ground three years before, only Cipri remained. Sumiko had been allowed to leave after the traumatic events of that first year with the fig leaf that she would someday return. That wasn't going to happen because Sumi was married, had a child and was pregnant with her second.

As for the third girl, there would be no return. Lady Danica Everett had died, but not, as Cipriana believed, in a tragic Foldspace accident. Something had indeed gone wrong when her parents' ship entered the Fold but it had been no accident. The Conde de Wahle's ship had been sabotaged by SEGU agents on orders from the Emperor. It was punishment for their involvement in the plot to discredit Mercedes, and undermine the Emperor's rule. The parents had accepted the death sentence in return for their youngest children being spared, but Dani had foolishly gotten herself secretly engaged to a claimant to the throne so she suffered the same fate as her plotting father.

"It's just the two of us now," Cipriana concluded and pulled Mercedes back to the present.

Mercedes pushed away the guilt and the residual anger that she still felt toward Dani, waved away the Isanjo seamstresses and Vasilyev, and stepped off the riser. She tucked Cipriana's arm under hers.

"Yes, but we made it, and the good news is that you won't have to be my chaperone after Saturday."

"But who's going to chaperone *me*? Oh wait, I won't have one. Just me… posted to a warship with all those lovely men. And did I mention… just me?" She gave Mercedes a droll look.

"You are impossible," Mercedes said, giving the other girl a slap on the arm. "And you won't be alone for long. There are two second-year women, and a whole four females in the freshman class."

"Who knows, maybe we'll break into double digits some day," Cipriana replied. "Though I doubt it."

The doors closed behind the designer and his minions. Mercedes gripped Cipriana by the upper arms. "Okay, tell me truthfully. How awful is this dress?"

"Awful doesn't begin to describe it. Try ghastly. Horrendous. Maybe monstrous—"

"Okay, okay, I get it." Mercedes clutched at her hair and took a turn around the room. The petticoats crackled and rasped against her legs. "Oh God, what am I going to do?"

"Get a different dress."

"I'm getting married in two weeks."

"You're the Infanta. An army of seamstresses will sew night and day, and what designer wouldn't love the chance to craft your wedding gown? Frankly I'm wondering if this clown is trying to undermine the succession by putting you in this... this..." Words failed her and Cipriana just gestured helplessly at the dress.

"Get me out of it," Mercedes ordered.

Cipriana's fingers were cold on Mercedes' back as she unzipped and unhooked. The yards of material puddled around her feet as Mercedes yanked off the stiff petticoats. It seemed to form a scratchy wall, trapping her inside. She stepped over it, padded over to the bed and sat down. With the tight bodice she wasn't wearing a bra. She found herself contemplating her bare breasts and wondered what it would feel like when Boho finally touched them without any intervening material. Despite every governess and duenna's objection there wasn't a girl in the FFH who didn't read the romantic novels—"little bonbons" as they were called—and dream about dashing space pirates or FFH nobles in disguise who fall in love with innocent *intitulado* girls.

Strange there aren't any books about FFH noble ladies who fall in love with intitulado *men who are anything but sweet but*

rather prickly and opinionated and who love her and save her and
whom she rejects—

Mercedes forced her thoughts away from Tracy Belmanor and back to her fiancé.

"I want to be pretty. It's my wedding day, and Boho is so handsome."

Cipriana joined her on the bed. "Mercedes, you are pretty. No, that's wrong. You're dramatic and that lasts. Pretty fades. And Boho loves you."

"Well he certainly loves the Infanta."

"Same thing." Cipriana hesitated then asked, "Mer, do you love him?"

They stared at each other for a long moment while Mercedes wondered if Cipriana had suddenly developed telepathy. She groped for a pillow, clutched it to her bare chest. "I… think so? I don't feel for him the way I felt for—" She cut off the words as if saying his name was dangerous, because it probably was. She took a breath. "We understand each other. We grew up together. We know our duty and he's what I need. What the crown needs." She gave Cipriana a quick smile. "And did I mention he's handsome."

"He'll be a good ruler."

Mercedes stiffened. "He won't be ruling. I will be."

Cipriana looked startled then embarrassed. "Right, of course, I just meant… I mean, do you really want all that on you? You'll have children, and look at Sumiko. She was the most ambitious of all of us, but she seems so happy with her daughter and a new baby on the way."

"Which brings up another problem. I can't get pregnant

too soon." Mercedes stood, crossed to the closet, pulled out a dressing gown and shrugged into it. "I've got to do at least one rotation on a ship to satisfy the old guard. Otherwise they'll never accept me." Mercedes frowned. "I'll need to discuss that with Boho. We'll be serving on the same ship, but we'll need to be careful."

"Use birth control."

"I can't do that. I thought I was hemmed in when I was a princess. Now that I'm the Infanta it's much worse." She sighed. "I never thought I'd say this, but I miss the High Ground. I had a lot more freedom there. Anyway, if I got a pill or a patch somebody would find out, talk, and God what an uproar there would be."

"IUD?"

"And who's going to insert it? No human doctor would agree."

"So go to an alien doctor."

"You have noticed I have a lot of security around me." Mercedes shook her head. "No, Boho's just going to have to be patient and understanding."

"Not his strong suit. He's a man of robust appetites, and you've got to do the deed on your wedding night. With your luck you'll get pregnant the first time you fuck, then none of this will be an issue," Cipriana concluded.

"I know we're supposed to outbreed the aliens, but there are five known alien races we've encountered. There's no way we can overcome the deficit."

"Paranoia's a bitch," Cipriana agreed. Then in quavering old lady tones she added, "There are more of them than us and even though we beat them they're wily and they're plotting and they have secret weapons and they'll win and take our women and produce monstrous half-breeds... Like that could ever happen," Cipriana said in her normal voice, then reverted to the trembling dowager's voice. "And... and... Oh God the sky is falling!" she concluded with a shout.

Mercedes was rolling on the bed, clutching her stomach and laughing. She finally sat up, wiped her eyes and said, "I'll worry about the coming alien apocalypse later. Right now I've got to deal with *that*." She pointed at the tumbled mass of material. "There isn't time to hand sew another one. Whatever you say about round-the-clock seamstresses."

"So get one printed."

Mercedes was appalled. "You know what all the gossiping, back-biting bitches will say."

"And what do you think they're going to say if you come down the aisle wearing *that* thing? Billions of people are going to watch the live feed. Over the Foldstream no one will be able to tell if the dress was hand stitched or not. They'll want to see their princess, the future ruler of the Solar League, marrying her handsome consort. It would be better if they're not giggling."

A wild thought intruded. "I wonder..." Mercedes began.

"What? You've got a look that I've learned to distrust."

"Tracy's father. He's a tailor. He's made suits for my father."

"Yeah, emphasis on *tailor*."

"Tracy told me his mother was also a seamstress. She might have left designs..."

Cipriana jumped to her feet. "You should not be doing this. You've stayed well away from him for the past two years. Which was very wise."

"He's still up on the station and I'm sure he couldn't afford to come home before graduation. And any money they had would go toward getting his father up the High Ground for the ceremony. It'll be fine," Mercedes said. "I can at least start there. And I never did get to meet his father."

"And you shouldn't be meeting him now," Cipriana argued.

"No, this could work, and be a great public relations coup. Vasilyev is known as the designer for the FFH. If I pick a little known commoner… well, we could make something out of this."

Cipriana pursed her lips, considered. "Now that's actually a good reason for this crazy idea." She hopped off the bed. "Come on, get dressed. I'll go with you."

2

WELL, THIS IS AWKWARD

"He's likely to become a puddle."

Those had been Tracy's words when she'd suggested he introduce her to his father. In another life. A time before she had effectively ended their friendship and put Tracy firmly in his place. Because of that final conversation she had never actually gotten to meet Alexander Belmanor. Now she had and indeed he had puddled. He stood in the front room of his tailor shop down in Pony Town, and gaped at her. His long, gnarled hands shook with nerves.

"Hi... hi... Highness, you do honor to my humble establishment, but I'm a tailor."

The room was circular, with mirrors on most walls, risers in front of those mirrors where fittings would take place. There was a small sofa against one wall, carpet underfoot, a chandelier that was a poor man's idea of elegance. Alexander himself was tall, but his hunched shoulders made him seem smaller. There were weary lines around his pale blue eyes and he had the same dishwater-blonde hair as his son, though Alexander's was liberally streaked with grey.

"I've had the honor of making for your noble father, but I've never fitted ladies, particularly ladies of quality."

"Your son once indicated that your wife was a notable seamstress. I thought perhaps she might have left some designs that I could examine, citizen."

"Of… of course, Highness, but so little time remains before—"

"Ample time for a dress to be printed."

Belmanor looked horrified. "Printed! Highness, that would be shocking."

She gave him a smile, trying to calm him. "Most people have their clothing printed. While the officers might treat themselves to handmade garments, those serving in the ranks wear printed uniforms."

A shadow flitted across Belmanor's angular face. She had touched a nerve though she wasn't sure what unpleasant memory she had evoked. "May I see your wife's designs?" Mercedes coaxed.

"Of course. Please, be seated, Highness. Bajit will bring you and your friend refreshment."

Belmanor vanished through a door set between mirrors. Cipriana leaned over. "You can see the family resemblance."

"Yes."

The door opened again and a Hajin minced in carrying a tray with two glasses and a bottle of champagne. The alien's wide eyes set on either side of the long face were netted by wrinkles, and the red mane running from the skull down his neck and disappearing beneath his shirt collar was touched by grey. He bowed, filled the glasses, left the tray, the bottle and a plate of baked dates wrapped in bacon on a small side table and skittered back through the door. Mercedes took a sip. The champagne was first rate, which surprised her. A moment's reflection and she realized that if the elder Belmanor catered to members of the FFH it wouldn't do to serve inferior drink.

The door opened again and this time it was Belmanor carrying a tap-pad. He offered it to Mercedes. "I loaded my wife's portfolio on this, Highness."

She set aside her glass and began to scroll through the drawings. "Will you be attending the graduation ceremony on the *cosmódromo*, Citizen Belmanor?"

"Most certainly, Highness." Pride brought a flare of color into his pale cheeks, and he added, "I am very proud of him."

"And so you should be. There were eight hundred and thirty-seven freshmen in our class. Only three hundred and three of us will graduate."

Winnowed away by the *prueba*, the vicious test of mettle designed to determine which cadets got to pass on after the first year and become midshipmen. It was a test she and a handful of other students, including Tracy and Cipriana, had avoided because they had thwarted a coup disguised as a terrorist assault. Everyone had tacitly agreed that putting them through a bogus emergency made little sense when they had proved they could handle a real one.

It sometimes worried her that she hadn't taken the test. What if she really wasn't competent and shouldn't have advanced? A lot of the tactical planning during those chaotic hours had been done by Tracy. At some point the lives of hundreds and perhaps thousands of soldiers would ride on her competence, and what if she didn't have Tracy or someone like Tracy at her side? She pushed away the thought and bent back over the pad.

Most of the designs were for day wear. Attractive but nothing terribly exciting. She nibbled on one of the dates. It had been stuffed with cheese and was quite delicious. "So, does Tra—your son ever mention… me?" she said in an oh-so-casual voice that displayed just how deliberate the question actually was. Cipriana's boot took her hard on the ankle and Mercedes winced. Belmanor looked confused.

"Um… not really, Your Highness. I mean, he wouldn't presume."

Mercedes nodded and went back to her perusal of the designs. She wasn't sure if the bubble of disappointment had more to do with Tracy never mentioning her or with the growing fear that she would have to appear in that grotesquery that Vasilyev had created. Just one more fear to add to all the others. Fears about her upcoming wedding night. Fears about her first posting. Fears about actually ruling.

Mercedes swallowed to ease the tightness in her throat and forced a smile. "These are all lovely, but is there anything a bit more formal?"

Belmont hesitated, then took back the pad, his fingers hovering over the screen. "This was something she did a few years after our son was born. When she was pregnant with another child. Our daughter. She wanted to design a wedding dress for her. Unfortunately she miscarried and we never… well…"

"I understand, Señor Belmanor." Mercedes dropped the formal honorific *Citizen* for the more personal *Señor*, and Belmanor noticed. He flushed from embarrassment this time. "No need to relive unpleasant memories. And if this dress represents something deeply personal and you'd rather not share it with me, I would quite under—"

"No, no." He smiled and like his son it was a transformative expression. "I think she would be honored to know her humble effort might grace the heir to the Solar League." He opened the file and Mercedes had a brief glimpse of a flash of crystals, a long sleeve on one arm, and only a shoulder strap on the other. "Let me send it to my ScoopRing so you can evaluate it fully."

A moment later and a three-dimensional hologram a meter tall of the dress appeared in the center of the room projected from his ring. It flowed across the body of the faceless female form that filled it. A swirl of crystals swept from the right hip across the bodice to the left shoulder like a spray of stars. The left sleeve ended in a V of material partway down the hand as if pointing toward the finger that would hold the wedding band. The right arm was bare. It was exquisite.

"You would look amazing in that, Mer," Cipriana breathed.

Belmanor flushed with pride then the worried expression was back. "A sleeve could be added to the right arm if you feel this is too déclassé for… for a royal wedding." He could barely enunciate the final words.

"Not on your life," Cipriana said. "Do you know how

hard she had to work for those biceps?" She laughed and glanced at Mercedes. "Why not show them off?"

Mercedes stood and held out her hand to the tailor. "Señor Belmanor. It would be my honor to wear this dress at my wedding. I see no reason why the body of the dress can't simply be printed, but the beadwork will require hand stitching, and obviously the crystals should be replaced with diamonds. Hire who you need, and bill me accordingly."

"Of course." He bowed. "Highness, if I might make a suggestion…"

"Please."

"You have a dramatic look, Majesty. Opals rather than diamonds would add to the impact."

Mercedes' hand traced the sweep of the crystals on the hologram. "The color in those opals would bring to mind the nebula," she said, referring to the most evident object that filled the night sky over Ouranos. "Could you accentuate the shape to make that even clearer?"

"Of course."

There was a clatter of boot heels; a light baritone voice called, "Hey, Dad, where are you?"

The door to the backroom was flung open and Tracy Belmanor entered. He was a bit taller than his father, and broad-shouldered after three years of physical training at the High Ground. The uniform displayed his physique in a very attractive way. He wasn't strictly handsome—his features were angular to the point of being harsh—but he had a good smile and he was smiling now. His best feature was his grey eyes, large and expressive. The scar on his left temple, a souvenir from his duel with Boho, tugged his eyebrow upward, giving him a faintly sardonic look. Right now his eyes were filled with excitement and pleasure. Both of which died when he saw her. He stared in shock at Mercedes. Blotchy red rose into his cheeks. She felt the heat rising in her face as well.

"Well, *this* is awkward," she heard Cipriana say.

His eyes fell on the holographic model of the wedding gown. Tracy's face carried every emotion—he would never be a card player—and she knew his features very well. She had studied his face hungrily over the past three years in moments when she wouldn't be observed. She read his rage and grief as surely as if he'd spoken. He swept a bow and then at the last minute turned it into a full court obeisance, which in this setting made it an insult.

Mercedes felt her lips tighten. "Such formality is unnecessary between classmates… *and friends*, Lieutenant."

If she thought to mollify him, the stressed *friend* just seemed to increase his anger. "Your pardon, Highness. One can't help but notice that with each passing day the gulf between us widens," he snapped. The air itself seemed to vibrate with tension. Tracy's father was looking at him in shock. Tracy's strange Cara'ot batBEM stood in the doorway, three of his four hands filled with a holdall and gaily wrapped gifts.

"I'm sorry you feel that way," Mercedes said. But she was hurt and decided to hit back. "Loyal officers are something I welcome and are not to be taken lightly." If he wasn't going to accept her friendship then she would put him back in the proper box.

"Oh, *thank you* for reminding me." The sarcasm barely covered the rage. Tracy braced and saluted.

Mercedes stared at him, confused. Her ScoopRing gave a subtle chime and she glanced down. A message had appeared, floating in the electronic gem. *Lieutenant J.G.* She looked around for the source of the message and met the batBEM's significant gaze. *Junior Grade?* Another insult directed at the man who had helped prevent a coup and who had graduated second in the class.

She resolved to speak to her father about it when she returned to the palace. But would it just make things worse if she intervened and drew more attention to Tracy? Then there was the long-simmering animosity between her fiancé and Tracy. Singling out the *intitulado*—she deliberately used the insulting term for a lower-class citizen of the League to make the point even more strongly to herself—would do Tracy no favors. No, it was time to end the visit and extricate herself from the situation.

"Then we are agreed, Señor Belmanor. I understand you will have expenses upfront. I'll arrange for the majordomo to contact you and for a draft to be sent to your bank."

He gave an impeccable bow, perfect in its depth and grace. "Thank you, Your Highness. We are honored."

Mercedes left the shop with Cipriana trailing after her. She imagined she could feel Tracy's gaze burning between her shoulder blades and she fought the impulse to hunch.

"Dad, you can't do this!" Tracy said after the front door had closed behind Mercedes and the echo of the bell was still hanging in the air. Inwardly he was kicking himself for entering through the back alley. If he'd come around to the front of the building he would have seen the flitters and security and known a member of the FFH was inside. He could have taken himself off for coffee to avoid them and would never have known it was her. Wouldn't have had to see her.

His father looked at him, a puzzled frown on his face. "Tracy, this is our chance—"

"And Granddad thought winning the claims lottery and getting that factory on Reichart's World after it was integrated was a chance too and look how that worked out. You lost the factory, racked up mountains of debt, mother died and it took how many years for you and Granddad to pay off what we owed? It's probably what killed him."

His father smiled, trying to lighten the mood. "I think that was more due to a build-up of bile and bitterness."

"And what caused that? The fucking FFH. The game is rigged against us. We need to accept that."

"Are you accusing our future ruler of bad faith? That we won't be paid? Is that what you are saying?" Alexander huffed.

"No, of course not—"

"Then we are not refusing the Infanta, Tracy. Period." His father brushed past Donnel and went into the workroom.

Tracy hesitated for a moment then ran out the front door hoping there was still time to catch Mercedes. There were four flitters just starting to lift off. Tracy got in front of the largest and most luxurious, and waved his arms over his head. There was a ratcheting sound as the armaments on the flitters carrying imperial security locked on him and Tracy's breath shortened. Unlike the weapons drills at the High Ground, these weapons carried live ammunition. The big flitter dropped back to the ground. The door lifted and Mercedes stepped out. Security was piling out of the other three. She waved them back.

"*Now* you want to talk to me? You couldn't talk to me in there. Instead you make a scene in the street? What do you want?" she said in an angry whisper. They were mere inches apart and her perfume washed over him, bringing back memories of holding her in his arms.

"Don't do this, Mercedes. I'm begging you." It was the first time he had used her name in two years. It didn't go unremarked.

"You forget yourself."

"No, I'm trying to reach you." His hands stretched out to her. "Remind you that once—" He bit off the words before he said something that couldn't be forgiven.

The stiffness leached from her shoulders and she looked more like the girl he had met on the beach on that long-ago evening. "I don't understand, Tracy. I thought you'd be pleased."

"Pleased? That you've come to Pony Town? Don't think the press won't notice that." He glanced around and sure enough there was a camerabot floating overhead. He suspected more would soon arrive. "We're going to be plastered all over the news feeds."

"Get in the flitter," she ordered.

He wasn't sure which was worse. Being recorded entering a vehicle with the heir to the Solar League or continuing to stand on the street remonstrating with her. He decided privacy was better and followed her into the plush interior. Cipriana looked from one to the other, sighed and nodded.

"I'll leave you two to it. Try not to get too bloody." She scrambled over their legs and left the vehicle.

Mercedes brought up the privacy screen shielding them from the driver and guard in the front seat and turned her ScoopRing to signal block. Once that was done she shifted to face Tracy and said accusingly, "You're just embarrassed."

"You're damn right, I am."

He gestured at a window indicating the run-down buildings, the tiny bodegas, the one-room restaurants with signs in the windows featuring cheap dinner specials, the payday loan shop on the corner, the Hajin hoof trimmer and mane salon, the Tiponi Flute water station and light salon, a garishly painted building that housed the Candy Box, which was the neighborhood's whorehouse, the shabbily dressed people and the large number of aliens.

"Everything isn't about you, Tracy. I didn't do this to remind people that you're an *intitulado*. I did it because my wedding gown is a horror—"

"Because everything really *is* about you."

"That is so unfair! I can't help who I am. I can't help that the whole League is going to be watching—"

"I bloody well won't be."

"Fine and I can't say I blame you, but that's not the point. I need a new dress so I picked…" her voice trailed away.

"Yeah, when you actually try to justify it, it doesn't make any sense, does it? There must be a hundred top designers who would leap at the chance to make your damn wedding gown. People who actually make wedding gowns." He paused and pressed the question. "So why did you really do it? Really?"

With her dark skin it was hard to tell that she was blushing, but he knew her so well that he could tell. That and the fact she couldn't meet his eyes. "I… I guess I wanted to feel close to you… one last time. I didn't think you would be here but I could pretend…"

"That life was different?" Mercedes nodded, seemingly unable to speak. "Well, it's not." It was hard to force the words past the aching pain in his throat. "We all have to play our parts." His hand moved, reaching for hers. He caught himself and drew it back quickly. "Please, Mercedes, don't do this."

"I want the dress, Tracy. It's beautiful. Don't you want your mother's design to be seen?"

"Not when you're wearing it and marrying *him*." Rage joined the grief. It was a toxic mix that threatened to choke him.

"That can't change. You know that. I understand I've hurt you so let me at least do something to ease your father's situation. He's going to become very fashionable."

"And that's the problem. He'll feel like he has to be worthy of the patronage. He'll move into a better part of town. Hire more people, and then when he ceases to be a one-day wonder the business will dry up and he'll be back in debt and back in Pony Town."

"I won't let that happen."

"And just how are you going to do that?"

"I'll instruct my staff. They'll make sure he has work."

Anger had him surging to his feet and he hit his head on the roof of the flitter, then dropped back onto the leather seat. "We don't want your charity!"

"What about my friendship and my patronage? Will you accept that? Or are you going to allow your anger to leave us with nothing?"

She had begun the sentence as the heir to the imperial throne. It had ended on a plaintive note that throbbed with unshed tears. It robbed him of rage and left him sad and empty. They stared at each other for a long moment. He longed to touch her cheek, feel her skin beneath his fingertips. Instead Tracy tried to commit each beloved feature to memory. He sighed and nodded.

"Yes. All right. I'll take that. But please, don't let my dad get hurt."

"I won't. I promise."

He climbed out of the flitter. As he had surmised and feared, the single camerabot had been joined by six others. He resisted the urge to give them the finger as he walked under the sign that proudly stated BELMANOR & SON. He paused and studied the sign. It would not be this son. Alexander had done everything in his power to get his only child out of the shop and into the imperial officer corps.

I'll do well, Dad, I promise. I'll win a title. Then you won't be sewing for anyone.

He ducked back into the shop. The scent of her perfume still lingered. He closed his eyes remembering—soft lips, a sigh slipped from between those lips like a song of joy, the tickle of hair against his ear—

I'll win a title and no one will doubt I have the right—

He shied away from what that right might be, fearing where the thought would take him and knowing it was mere delusion.

3

NOT MY DAUGHTER

The small anteroom just off the parade ground at the High Ground was not meant for four people, particularly when they included the obese Conde de Vargas, all the six-foot-five magnificence that was Boho, Mercedes' father who had developed an impressive belly over the past few years, and herself. Rohan Danilo Marcus Aubrey was the aristocratic patron of the High Ground and the Emperor's best friend. Right now his words weren't making the Emperor happy. Mercedes was equally flabbergasted over Rohan's proposal and Boho was wide-eyed with shock. For what Rohan was suggesting would shake society. He wanted the Rule of Service to apply to the daughters as well as the sons of the FFH.

"This is the time to make the announcement," Rohan was saying. "While the entire press is watching. The populace is feeling charitable toward the crown in general and the Infanta and her dashing consort in particular. Let's get the idea out there. Allow the public to become accustomed to it. And if we spring it on them like this the old guard won't have time to prepare their objections and bury the proposal in committee."

"We're taking a hell of a chance," the Emperor muttered. "This could backfire and blow up on us."

"Then why risk it?" Boho asked.

"Yes. Why *are* we risking it?" Mercedes echoed and stared at her father.

"There are reasons," he muttered, then added, "I'll tell you later."

Rohan rubbed plump hands together. "Then we're agreed—"

"Conde, most of the girls won't try," Mercedes warned. "They'll deliberately wash out at the end of the first year so you may end up causing an uproar for no reason."

Rohan turned to her, ran a hand through his thinning red hair. "Then you must be the example for them, Highness. Convince some of them that service to the League is a worthy pursuit."

"Their future husbands won't thank you if you do, Mer," Boho said with a laugh. "I expect a lady officer won't be the most compliant bride and wife."

Mercedes gave him a limpid look. "Well, you'll soon find out, won't you?" For an instant he looked startled, then he threw back his head and laughed again.

"So you approve of this plan?" her father asked Boho.

Her fiancé lifted Mercedes' gloved hand and dropped a kiss onto it. "I'd be foolish not to, wouldn't I?" He gave them all his patented sideways smile. "And if I may, sir, the conde is right about the timing. If you're really going to do this, this is the time. You've got the graduation and then the wedding. It puts everyone in a mellow mood. Oh, the conservatives will rage, but they'll look petty when everyone else in the League is celebrating our wedding."

"Your father has a great deal of power in the upper house," Rohan said. "Can you get him on our side?"

"He knows which side his bread is buttered on," the Emperor growled before Boho could answer. He made a testy gesture. "There's no way this station pod is large enough to contain an influx of girls. It will double at least the number of cadets."

Rohan shrugged. "So we build a station just to house the High Ground. With the recession we could use a new infrastructure project."

"That may be a solution for the FFH, but what do we do about the *hombres*? Recruiters are reporting a significant uptick in female *intitulados* trying to enlist. We have yet to give the recruiting stations guidance so it's a piecemeal affair with some recruiters allowing them to join and most not. And once the women reach basic only a handful are making it past the drill sergeants," the Emperor argued.

"Which is why we must do this, Fernán. It needs to be regularized." Her father was still frowning. "You had to know this was going to happen once you put forward Mercedes as your heir," Rohan said softly.

"Daddy… sir," she corrected herself. "You can't turn me into a unicorn. If you do no one will ever accept me as the commander-in-chief."

The Emperor paced, looked back over his shoulder at Mercedes. "You know that going forward this will have to be applied to your sisters."

That stopped her but after a moment of reflection she acknowledged the necessity. "Estella is already nineteen. It's too late for her to start, but…" Mercedes realized that her youngest full sister could start in the fall. Julieta had been betrothed to one of Mercedes' classmates and was supposed to marry him by the end of the year. Mercedes hated the match. Sanjay was known for his furious temper and his quickness to resort to his fists. If Julieta started at the High Ground it would postpone the marriage for at least three years. A lot could happen in three years. Mercedes decided she loved this plan.

"You really think this is necessary? You're shaking our society to its foundations," her father asked Rohan. The older men exchanged a very long look.

"We don't know, do we? Better not to be wasting half our populace if… well… Perhaps better to be…" Rohan's voice trailed away, but Mercedes thought she could guess the final word he hadn't spoken. *Prepared.* What did they know that they weren't telling?

The Emperor tugged at his upper lip then finally nodded. "All right. Do it. Add it into your speech."

"It was already in there," Rohan said and her father gave a sigh of exasperation.

"Someday you're going to guess wrong and I'll surprise you."

With a laugh in his voice Rohan said, "Maybe… but not today."

* * *

There was one place where rank and title couldn't dictate. The alphabet was the alphabet. Which meant Tracy was seated next to Mercedes while Boho was forced to sit fourteen chairs away. The parade ground was a stone garden where massive black stone colonnades stretched to the station's roof and slate tiles bruised the feet. In this place of stone Mercedes' gardenia and jasmine perfume was a memory of other gardens and softer times.

He glanced over at her. At the line of her cheek, the aggressive blade of her nose, the glint of a sapphire earring. She was knotting her hands, which caused the multi-carat teardrop diamond engagement ring to flash and sparkle. A sour taste filled his mouth and Tracy looked away. He longed to look over his shoulder and locate his father though he suspected the tailor had been seated in the very back row and couldn't be spotted. He just hoped his father would be able to see.

Alexander would certainly be able to see when Tracy walked across the tall stone rostrum directly in front of them. On stage there was a large throne in a sunburst pattern where the Emperor sat. On his right the Conde de Vargas, on his left Vertrant, Commandant of the High Ground. Also present was the academy's chaplain, Commander Father Lord Tanuwidjaja, and Musa del Campo, Duque Agua de Negra, cousin to the Emperor and at one time heir to the throne before Mercedes had been elevated to that position. He had a son graduating this day. Finally there was Lieutenant Marqués Ernesto Chapman-Owiti, the class valedictorian.

Tracy had come up a few points short of that honor,

but unlike the last time, when he'd been cheated out of the honor when he graduated from high school, he didn't resent Ernesto. The man was stone-cold brilliant.

Thinking about that other graduation led him inexorably to Hugo. The man who had replaced Tracy as the valedictorian despite inferior grades. All because his father got a title. Once Tracy had hated Hugo. Then Hugo had become Tracy's closest friend at the academy. The memories led inextricably to that ghastly moment when Hugo had died, literally cut in half by a broken cable, and Tracy would never stop feeling like it was his fault. If he hadn't rammed the docking bay doors the cable wouldn't have been weakened. He had proposed they spacewalk on the exterior of the station to try and retake the hub from terrorists...

Why couldn't it have been Boho who'd died? If Boho had been killed then Mercedes—Tracy cut off that line of thought. Even if Boho hadn't cowered in the computer center and had died instead of Hugo, Mercedes would still be marrying some other highborn jackass. Tracy's eyes shifted to his right where Lord Arturo Espadero del Campo sat. His father was the Emperor's cousin. It might have been Arturo marrying the Infanta. In no version of the future was it ever going to be the tailor's son from Pony Town.

There had at least been one salve to Tracy's bruised spirits. When the graduating class had formed up to march into the parade ground Tracy saw that Mark Wilson, the only other scholarship student and non-noble, had also been given the rank of lieutenant J.G. Tracy's resentment had been lessened, but only slightly. The weight of the Distinguished

Service Cross where it rested on his left breast seemed to mock him. He had won one of the highest military honors granted by the Solar League, done it in his first year at the academy, and even that hadn't been enough to raise him above his common birth in the eyes of the FFH.

Tanuwidjaja's reedy, diffident voice penetrated, and Tracy realized they were almost at the end of the invocation. He managed to join the rest of the assembled crowd in the *amen* and resolved to stop torturing himself with might-have-beens that were really could-never-bes. He took another quick glance around the assembly.

On the other side of the aisle were the faculty and seated among them was the High Ground's second-in-command. It was so typical of Vertrant that his second had been relegated to the audience along with family, friends and sweethearts. From where he sat Tracy could see Commander Marquis Chand Ganguly's profile. The muscles in his jaw were set and the dark brows drawn into a deep frown. He was starting at Vertrant. *No love lost there*, Tracy thought.

Rohan stood and approached the podium. The levimike spun down a few inches to compensate for Rohan being shorter than the priest. It hovered in front of the nobleman. He smiled at the assembly.

"Welcome, graduates. Yes, you made it! Get drunk later. I know I did." There was scattered laughter. Rohan continued, "I have never been prouder of this majestic institution. For over three hundred years the academy has sent graduates on to distinguished service in our armed forces, and at every step the High Ground has been willing to adapt and change.

This year is no exception. For the first time in its long and noble history this institution will graduate two young ladies whose strength, intelligence and bravery have shown that the weaker sex is anything but—as most of us husbands can attest!" There was more laughter.

"I am honored to be the patron of this school at this historic moment. And I feel so strongly that this is the right thing to do for our beloved League that I propose to introduce legislation during the parliamentary session to extend the Rule of Service to the young ladies of the FFH." There was a rising growl of shocked reaction from the assemblage. The students exchanged startled glances.

"No longer will our daughters remain behind while their brothers go out to safeguard the League. They will be taking their place, their *rightful* place, as defenders of our worlds, our homes, the children they will eventually bear, and indeed our very species." The reactions were getting louder. "Some will say this is a radical idea, a scrapping of our ideals and traditions. I say it is the very definition of conservatism and honoring those customs and traditions. Before we took our first steps into a wider universe, women served with honor and great distinction on old Earth. Do we argue that our daughters are less capable than their foremothers? I think not, nor would I insult my own daughters in this way."

The startled conversations were starting to resemble more the howl of the mob. The outrage echoed off the surrounding stone, threatening to drown out even the amplified voice of the conde. But he hadn't spent twenty-five years as a politician for nothing. Rohan held up his plump hands, palms out, and raised his voice almost to a shout to say, "And now it is my great pleasure to introduce the man who embodies our government, who has and continues to guard our League and our way of life—His Imperial Highness Fernán Marcus Severino Beltrán de Arango, our emperor."

The angry voices sputtered into silence. However offended they might be, no one would dare talk over the crown. Tracy found his own emotions were in turmoil. A deep-seated prejudice had been revealed. It had been easy to accept the presence of the women when it was Mercedes and her ladies, but this? Would he want his wife in harm's way? Or the daughters he might father by this mythical wife? Yet in a life-and-death crisis he had put Mercedes in a fighter and sent her up against a heavily armed ship. He could only conclude he was conflicted. Along with everybody else in the parade ground.

Tracy returned his attention to the rostrum. This was the first time in the twenty-six years of his reign that the Emperor had given the commencement speech at the High Ground. Tracy was living through momentous times. He should listen and try to set forever in memory the experience.

4

THE SATYR IN THE GARDEN

The air in the academy's gardens was heavy with moisture and the clashing scent of flowers. Boho's hand was at her waist and Mercedes discovered that it felt more confining than affectionate. She stepped away, using the cake-smeared mouth of her youngest half-sister as the excuse.

"Carisa, darling, don't you have a napkin?"

The youngest child of the Emperor had inherited her mother's nervous disposition and her lower lip began to immediately tremble. She was also well aware of the fishbowl-like existence of an imperial daughter. She eyed the surrounding camerabots with the air of a cornered rabbit.

"I... I must have dropped it," she whispered. "I'm sorry."

"No need to worry, sweet. Here." Mercedes knelt and offered her napkin.

As the nine-year-old mopped icing from her lips, Mercedes looked at her family. Estella, nineteen and as serene as always, stood with her fiancé Conde Alfred Brendahl. The widower was twenty-three years her senior and had five children from his first marriage, but he seemed kind and gentle and they shared many interests. His value to the throne was his powerful leadership position in parliament.

And if Rohan is going to pull this off we'll need him, Mercedes thought.

Her gaze found her youngest full sibling. Julieta stood with her fiancé and his family. Sanjay looked like a thundercloud, his wealthy banker father looked resigned. Julieta looked peevish. It had apparently begun to penetrate that there wouldn't be a wedding any time soon.

She ran her gaze down her half-sisters—Izzara and Tanis, Beatrisa, the twins—Delia and Dulcinea, Carisa. Her father stood with Carisa's mother, his fifth, current and probably final wife, Constanza. He was wearing his practiced public smile. Constanza radiated coolness and elegance. Suddenly a sharp frown furrowed her brows. Since Constanza was staring in her direction Mercedes wondered what she had done this time to provoke her stepmother's ire.

A soft voice from behind her called her name and memories came crashing back. Four years old, standing in the circle of her mother Maribel's arms. The ache in the chest, the trickle of tears down her cheeks.

Mercedes scrambled to her feet and whirled to meet her mother's gentle gaze. She hadn't been able to remember anything her mother had actually said on that long-ago day when Maribel had left the palace. Mercedes could only recall her confusion and fear, and her mother's strained smile.

When Mercedes asked about her mother's absence it had been soothingly explained how Maribel's new husband had a great responsibility assimilating a Hidden World, and how

Maribel had new babies to care for, and that's why she didn't come to Hissilek and the palace.

The last time Mercedes had seen Maribel had been at Mercedes' confirmation and the celebration of her tenth birthday. By then she had understood, at least in a vague way, about her father's desperate pursuit of a male heir and how that pursuit now had Mercedes dealing with yet another stepmother.

Now Mercedes knew Maribel hadn't come to visit because her father hadn't allowed it, nor had the parade of wives who'd come after her. Mercedes glanced back at Constanza. Clearly the presence of the first empress wasn't making the fifth empress very happy.

All this passed in a flash, and Mercedes found herself blurting out an absurdly childish greeting. "Mommy!" Her mother glided forward and enfolded her in an embrace, kissed her on both cheeks. "I didn't expect… What a surprise. I'm so pleased," Mercedes stammered.

Maribel glanced over at her current husband who was already deep in conversation with the Emperor. "Fernán felt it was only right I be present for your wedding. Since your graduation was so close to the wedding I suggested we come for both and he agreed. Also Hector needed to discuss some tax allocation issues with Fernán, and the children are at an age where I feel comfortable leaving them. That's really kept me close to home the past few years." She paused and added, "And Dullahan has proved to be a difficult world to pacify."

It was too much information and much of it unnecessary, presented, Mercedes realized, as justification and also a subtle apology for her eleven-year absence. Mercedes smiled and tucked her mother's arm beneath hers.

"I'm just glad you're here."

Maribel surveyed Mercedes' trousers, the jacket adorned with service ribbons and the medal, and shook her head. "You look shockingly attractive in your uniform."

"Or just shocking," Mercedes answered with a smile. "But people do seem to be becoming accustomed to the sight." She changed the subject. "So, tell me of my half-siblings." The minute the sentence was out Mercedes regretted it, for her mother cast her a guilty glance.

"It was my duty," she whispered.

"I know. It's all right. I hope someday to meet them."

"I'm sure you will. Julian will be here at the High Ground in three years. Martin two years after that."

"So... boys," Mercedes said.

"Yes." Maribel paused then added, "All six of them."

Mercedes threw a quick look at her father, then at her eight sisters. "Ah, yes, well... My..." she stammered.

"Probably *not* something we want to stress this week," her mother said softly and abruptly switched topics. "Please introduce me to your fiancé. He seems very dashing."

"Oh, he is. Boho, darling. I want you to meet my mother," Mercedes called, and he turned his thousand-kilowatt smile on both of them.

Tracy stared at the puff-pastry canapé stuffed with sour cherries and blue cheese that he held between thumb and forefinger, and reflected that every formal event surrounding the High Ground seemed to be an excuse to eat. It began in the very first year with the academy's patron, the Conde de Vargas's welcoming ball. Graduation even here on the station was proving to be no different.

After The Speech the three hundred and three graduates had trooped across the stage, accepted their diplomas, shaken hands with the Emperor, received his jovial congratulations, returned to their seats, and then in some bizarre custom dating back to old Earth had all thrown their hats into the air.

Now they were in the academy's garden where a band played appropriately martial music, alien waiters slipped through the crowd with trays of champagne, buffet tables groaned under a wide variety of delicacies, conversations bubbled in harmony with the fountain, and the gardenia bush near Tracy seemed to be trying to suffocate him with the sweet cloying scent of its flowers. Overhead the ceiling was a clear dome through which could be seen a trailing edge of the nebula and the bright glitter of stars. As Tracy watched, a space liner slipped into view, heading for the docks on the station's ring far above them.

"You planning on eating that thing or framing it?" a jovial voice asked. Tracy turned to see Davin Pulkkinen grinning at him over the rim of his champagne flute.

Tracy jammed the canapé into his mouth and mumbled around it, "Wool gathering."

"Personally I feel like I've been rooted. My legs are still aching, and there aren't enough chairs," Davin added as he surveyed the milling crowd. "I hate these mill-and-swills. You got your orders?" he asked in a sudden change of topic.

"Yeah, I've been assigned to the *Triunfo*."

"Ooh, big ship."

"Yes. Easier to get lost in the crowd," Tracy said.

"Like that would ever happen with you."

"Because I'm such an asshole?" Tracy grumbled.

"Yeah. And that's actually a compliment, you prickly bastard. You're too bright and too opinionated to keep a low profile."

"I have a feeling neither of those are real assets for a lowly lieutenant," Tracy said sourly. "How about you?"

"What I expected. Desk job on Nueva Terra." Davin glanced at his right arm and Tracy again had that flare of guilt. It might be covered by Davin's sleeve and glove, but Tracy knew what lay beneath. A very high tech and elegant prosthetic. Davin had lost his arm in the same accident that had killed Hugo and Tracy still felt responsible.

Davin correctly interpreted Tracy's frown. "Not your fault, *hombre*. How many times do I have to tell you that? And it's my fault I never managed to get proficient with my left hand."

"Why did you stay in, Davin?" Tracy asked, honestly curious. "You could have gone home after you were injured."

The customary crooked grin faded and the class joker looked surprisingly serious. "Don't laugh. I realized I'm actually pretty patriotic. And I wanted to serve. At least for a while." The merriment returned and he added, "I'm going to put in my five years, muster out and become an aristocratic parasite."

Tracy grinned. "And I expect you'll do it very well, my man."

"What about you?" Davin asked. "Are you gonna be a lifer?"

"Probably, since the parasite thing isn't really an option for me."

Davin clapped him on the shoulder with his artificial hand. It was a hard buffet made almost painful by the gel and metal that formed the hand. "Well, good luck and stay in touch, okay?"

"Sure." But Tracy suspected he wouldn't. He had never been good at optimizing his connections, as Mercedes had frequently told him.

His eyes drifted around the crowd. Mercedes stood with her two full sisters and a tall and graceful older woman. The three younger women were hugging her. They looked like a tableau of the Graces. To Tracy's eyes Boho, standing nearby and looking smug and contented, was the discordant note. The satyr in the garden.

He longed to talk with her. Tell her farewell. Ask about her posting. But he couldn't. An *intitulado* like himself could not walk brazenly over to the imperial party and speak to the heir to the throne, and if he did Boho would find a way to make him pay. Tracy found himself rubbing the scar at his temple.

He whirled, sickened by the sight. He looked for his father and found him in the center of a knot of women. Alexander was flushed and clearly torn between embarrassment and pleasure over all the attention. The word had gone out that he was making the Infanta's wedding gown, with predictable results. Women had flocked to the shop. The neighboring businesses were annoyed as hell over all the traffic. Fabric wholesalers were calling. Vasilyev's ire had exploded all over social networking, and Tracy feared that after his dad ceased to be a one-day wonder the fashionable designer would find a way to have his revenge.

It seemed both of the Belmanor men were walking a tightrope over a chasm filled with the flames of FFH resentment and disapproval.

He made his way through the crowd of graduates and families. Many of his classmates were in huddles comparing their orders. He once more felt that sense of isolation that had dogged him throughout his three years at the academy.

Almost the last person he ever wanted to speak to again laid a hand on his shoulder and brought him to a stop. Baron Jasper Talion was silver-haired, despite being only twenty-one, and his right cheek was laced with dueling scars. Talion had been cultivating Tracy since their first year. Talion wanted to have talent around him as he made (in his view) his inevitable rise to admiral, and he had assumed Tracy would service Talion's meteoric rise. It never seemed to occur to him that Tracy might have his own ambitions in that direction; Tracy had remained polite but tried to keep his distance because he knew Talion was a stone-cold psychopath. It was a very real concern what Talion might do if he ever decided Tracy was a threat. Or possibly merely inconvenient.

"Which ship?" Talion asked.

"*Triunfo*," Tracy replied shortly and tried to move on.

A bright smile touched Talion's lips. "Excellent. Me as well. Together we'll make an impression."

"I'm just planning on doing my duty," Tracy said and knew he sounded like a prig.

"What division?"

"Weapons."

Talion nodded sagely. "Appropriate given your math skills."

Tracy forced himself to ask, "And you?"

"*Infierno* pilot and I'll be gazetted to the *fusileros* if a ground action is required."

"Appropriate for you too." Talion wasn't stupid. He gave Tracy a sharp look, and Tracy once more wished he was better at hiding his emotions. "Well, I'll see you aboard," Tracy concluded lamely. Then added, "I need to catch up with my dad."

"Me as well." Talion frowned. "And they dragged along my fiancée." His tone was pure disgust.

"You're getting married?" It was a foolish question and Tracy mentally kicked himself.

"Yes. She's only sixteen. The plan was for us to marry next year, but now that's been tossed into the crapper with this nonsense out of de Vargas. Well, I haven't met her yet so I'd best go do that."

"Yes, that probably would be good."

"I want you to meet my father," Talion said and turned, assuming Tracy would follow.

Tracy had no desire to meet the elder Talion. It was Jasper's father who had bestowed those twisting scars to his face. Tracy sensed the psychopath fruit hadn't fallen very far from the sociopath tree. He was rescued by Ernesto, who grabbed him by the shoulder.

"Just the man I was looking for! Come on, I want you to meet my available sister." Ernesto gave a suggestive wink. "I'll bring him back to you later, okay, Jasper?" Ernesto finished.

For an instant a frown clouded Talion's face. It quickly cleared and he smiled. "Sure." He glanced at Tracy. "For someone in your situation the offer of an unmarried FFH sister should always be cultivated. Though I'm surprised you'd introduce him," Talion said to Ernesto.

They watched Talion stroll away. Once he was out of earshot Ernesto said, "He doesn't even realize he's insulted you. How do you stand it?"

Rather than answer and perhaps display how much it did rankle, Tracy said, "You don't have an unmarried sister."

"That's why I used the word *available*, as in available-to-be-met. How Talion chose to interpret that is not my problem."

"You should have been a lawyer rather than a biologist."

"It was my study of living creatures that told me you were an organism desperately seeking an escape from a dangerous situation."

"So you know," Tracy said softly.

"Like I said, I'm a biologist. Years of research has led me to the highly technical and very professional conclusion that *that*," he jerked his head toward Talion's retreating back, "is one sick monkey."

Tracy laughed. "Well, thanks for the rescue."

"Anytime."

"Where are you headed?"

"Post-grad work at SolTech. After I finish my doctorate

I expect I'll end up in an R&D lab somewhere, figuring out new and novel ways to kill aliens."

"Well, good luck. It was fun competing with you," Tracy said with a smile and held out his hand.

They shook. "And with you. Be safe out there," Ernesto added.

"Who knows, maybe I won't ever have to use any of those fancy new weapons you cook up."

"Here's hoping."

Tracy resumed his progress toward his father. Only to be stopped again. This time by Cipriana. She laid her fingertips on his forearm.

"Rumor has it you're going to be aboard the *Triunfo*."

"Rumor is correct."

"So am I." Her tongue wet her upper lip and she cast him a smoky glance from beneath her lashes and drew a finger across the back of his hand. Even through their gloves the touch was liquid fire.

"Uh... oh," he choked out while heat shot through his groin. It had been a long time since his last visit to the Candy Box, the pleasant brothel patronized by both the Belmanor men.

A smile danced in the back of her dark eyes. "I'm perfectly happy to be sloppy seconds."

"Wha... what?"

"I know how you feel about Mercedes, but you can't have her so why not—"

"For God's sake, Cipriana," Tracy hissed, grabbing her by the arm and giving a warning nod toward the camerabots hovering over the royal family, and ironically over his father. "Have a care," he warned.

"Worried Boho will hear and cut you again?" she asked, and traced the dueling scar. Her hand drifted away from his temple, down his cheek, and traced his lips.

"Worried about Mercedes' reputation, your reputation and my commission if we're caught—" he whispered.

"What? You don't think *hombres* fuck?" She stepped in close, her breasts brushing against his chest. Her arms twined around his neck. "Think of the money they'll save not having to roll into brothels once there are women aboard the ships." Her pelvis thrust against his groin.

"Sweet Jesus! Cipri, you are, you are—"

"Horny," she whispered in his ear then glanced down at his crotch. "Why look! Somebody's happy." Another sultry glance and she pushed away from him. "See you on board, Lieutenant."

Tracy dropped his hands to shield his raging erection and raced out of the garden. His father gave him a questioning, wistful look. By a jerk of his chin Tracy tried to indicate he'd be right back. He found the toilet and rushed into a stall.

The curve of her cheek, his hands crushing her dark curls, a mixture of aromas, vanilla and spice, jasmine and underlying it all the heady scent of woman. Her lips soft and welcoming, the tip of her tongue hesitantly touching his. Driving his tongue deep into her mouth tasting her, matching breaths and moans of pleasure. Her body pressed against his…

He rested his head against the stall wall, closed his eyes, tried to catch his breath. Shame gripped him followed by a soul-shaking sorrow. Mercedes would marry Boho, become empress, and he would never even speak to her again, much less touch her.

5

WHEN YOU NEED A WHORE

"You wanted to see me, Daddy?" Mercedes asked.

Her father stood, bouncing lightly on the soles of his feet, hands clasped behind his back. He was frowning down at an elaborate 3D holographic display that spread across the surface of his desk. It looked like an architect's rendering of towering office buildings and pedestrian market areas. With a wave he banished the images. He hugged her, then stepped behind the desk and keyed the office's security measures.

Her stomach clenched. Then this wasn't a "Daddy" moment. It was official. "Is something wrong, sir?"

"No, no. This is just a conversation that I don't want to go beyond this room." He gestured at the two high-backed leather chairs on either side of the now cold fireplace. Mercedes hesitantly perched on the edge of the seat.

Her father was frowning. He leaned forward, clasped his hands between his knees, and cleared his throat. "You know it's vitally important that you not get pregnant until after your first tour of duty. You must wait five years."

Hot blood rose into her cheeks. "I know that."

"So how are you planning on avoiding… that?"

"I… uh… I'm not sure. I know there's birth control, but it's technically illegal… I suppose we could argue that we are the law, but…"

"It's never a good idea to look like we're flouting it," her father said dryly.

"And then there's the church…"

"Which is already unhappy over your elevation. We don't need the Holy Father and the College of Cardinals to get their shorts in a twist."

Embarrassed, she focused her eyes on the carved mantel. "So, nobody can know if I use birth control."

"Correct." He paused and added, "Not even your husband."

Startled, Mercedes looked back at her father. "Don't you trust him?"

"I think it's good policy that a ruler play their cards close to their chest and not give *anyone* leverage over them."

Mercedes nodded. "That makes sense. So… do you have any suggestions?"

"Not really, my dear. My problem has never been trying to *prevent* pregnancies." He smiled but it was both grim and bitter.

Nine daughters from a man required to sire a son. It had to be a blow to his ego that he fired only girl bullets.

Mercedes stood and shook out her skirt. "I'll think of something."

Her father returned to his desk and deactivated the security screens. Mercedes paused at the door. "Daddy, I understand why you want Lady Poni and the Marquesa, and

Rohan's daughter and… well, I just wondered if I could have one of my friends in my wedding party."

"Who in particular?"

"Sumiko."

"She didn't come to your graduation."

"No, she's very pregnant. A shuttle flight wouldn't have been wise."

"Just as well, probably not the reminder we want to present since your lack of fecundity is undoubtedly going to become a topic of discussion a year or so on."

"I suppose so."

"Also her stepfather and husband aren't terribly useful to me."

"I understand," Mercedes said, but her voice sounded hollow even to her.

Condom? No, that would violate her father's desire that Boho not know. IUD? She'd have to find a doctor to insert the device and they might talk. Actually they would probably refuse. Her Lusitano stallion, Utopia, gave a sudden buck as if to say, *I know you're not paying attention and I'm going to take advantage.* Mercedes laughed, leaned forward and patted the glossy black neck. He was her favorite horse in the royal stable. She was going to miss her family, but Utopia was something else she would miss. During her schooling she had been able to return home for leave and holidays. During the five years of her tour such opportunities would be few and far between. Capital ships rarely returned to Ouranos so any leave she took would probably be on distant worlds.

She could hear the hoofbeats of her ubiquitous security riding in the trees to either side of her. Directly behind her rode Captain Lord Ian Rogers, who commanded her personal security. He was linked not only to the troops riding all around her, but to the camerabot floating overhead. For once it didn't belong to the press, but was being monitored by the chief of Servicio Protector Imperial, Agent Matthew Gutierrez. Presumably Ian and Gutierrez were talking. She wondered what they were saying. Were they talking about her?

She had grown up under constant surveillance. She was accustomed to it and normally didn't mind, but now the fish bowl was inconvenient when she was supposed to find access to birth control. Years ago both Cipriana and Mercedes' batBEM Tako had offered her a contraceptive patch. She probably should have accepted, though God knew it would probably have lost its potency by now. She probably should have used it back then. Slept with Tracy. She had ridden since childhood. Boho wouldn't know she wasn't a virgin. Well, it was too late now.

She cued the canter and Utopia went rocking off down the trail. Ironically at the High Ground she had been far freer than she was now, she reflected, as her body swayed in concert with the motion of the horse. She had been at a military academy aboard a space station. Also the batBEMs had been far more accommodating about outwitting High Ground security. Now there were literally thousands of people watching her, servants, cooks, chauffeurs, gardeners, guards both military and SPI, court functionaries and flunkies, petitioners, and family. Her every move was noticed and scrutinized. Resentment had her unconsciously tightening her legs and Utopia was now at a full hand gallop. Mercedes threw back her head and laughed. The frenzied gait matched her mad mood to the mad plan she had just concocted.

She needed birth control that wouldn't be recognized as birth control. She didn't dare ask her doctor—that would immediately be reported. She might trust Tako to go to the Cara'ot and purchase the patches, but the batBEM was probably being watched too, and even if the Hajin got it back undetected there was always the worry that a maid might discover the stash and rat her out. Not to mention that SEGU, the intelligence service, conducted routine sweeps of all the imperial palaces. She should have asked Cipriana for help and advice, but her friend had left immediately after the graduation to take up her post. Mercedes needed an experienced woman to advise her. What she needed, she had realized, was a whore.

There were brothels all over Hissilek, from the very elegant joy houses at the base of the Palacio Colina that catered to the males of FFH and initiated their sons into the mysteries of sex, to less exalted establishments that provided respite for horny tradesmen, and places where their less well born sons could shed their virginity. There were even brothels that serviced the various alien races. They were supposedly strictly off limits to humans, but there were whispers that some human males did sample the forbidden and illegal fruit. The very idea was revolting to her. She knew Boho had a reputation as a Don Juan, but she had to believe he had never stooped to *that*.

Mercedes sat deep in the saddle and brought Utopia down to a trot. The big stallion whinnied and tossed his head. He had been enjoying the gallop. She spent a moment trying to imagine how a human could possibly couple with a Tiponi Flute. Which of the many orifices on the aliens that looked like ambulatory bamboo would one use? She felt herself blush and gave an embarrassed little giggle.

She leaned forward and whispered into the horse's mobile ear. "Where can I go that I can slip the leash, my Iberian prince? Any suggestions?"

A sudden memory of that crowded street in Pony Town swam before her, the little shops, the payday lender, the Candy Box. "Oh shit," she murmured. "I don't think they're selling candy."

Another memory forced its way into her thoughts. Tracy seated with her in the flitter. *"I could pretend…"* she had started to say to him. He had stopped her from saying more. She stopped herself from even thinking it now. What was done was done.

She picked up the reins, and tapped Utopia with her leg. "Come on, I need to run an errand."

Once again her entourage was blocking the street outside the tailor shop. Mercedes turned to Captain Rogers.

"I'm just here for a fitting with Señor Belmanor. There's no need to overwhelm the poor man, and all of you crowded into the shop will make it difficult for me to change so please wait here."

Rogers turned to one of the *fusileros*. "Surround the building."

"Oh, please, Captain... Ian, just make a sweep of the area and then wait by the flitters. I seriously doubt there are assassins lurking among the garbage cans. And your behavior could be construed as insulting to the citizens who live here."

"I mean no disrespect, Highness, but there are a lot of aliens in this neighborhood," Rogers said.

"And I'm sure the revolution is about to be launched in Pony Town." He flushed at her sarcasm. "Please just wait. Señor Belmanor is tailor to my father and his son is one of my officers. Let us do him the courtesy of not treating him and his employees as if they were criminals."

She entered, the bell over the door ringing loudly. The older Belmanor shot out of the backroom.

"Hi... Highness," he stammered and bowed. He quickly keyed his ScoopRing. "Did we have an appointment today? I thought—"

"Mr. Belmanor. I need a favor."

"Of course, Highness. Anything."

"I need a veil, or something that will serve the purpose. And I need you to let me out the back door."

"Highness?"

"There's something I need to do and I really don't want my security detail to know. I won't be gone long." He looked terrified and trapped. "I know I'm asking a lot, but

I have always been able to trust your son and his service to me has been beyond exemplary. I know where he learned those habits of honor and loyalty. So I'm asking you to do the same."

Alexander Belmanor blushed just like his son, blotchy red patches that were painfully obvious on his pale skin, but the look of fear had been replaced with one of pride. His bow was deep and formal, a full court bow incongruous in the untidy room. "Come, Highness, I have just the thing."

"Perfect."

Mercedes followed him through the door into the backroom where the elderly Hajin and a female Isanjo with pale tawny fur were busy working at chattering sewing machines.

"You have seen nothing!" the tailor said, his tone severe.

The Hajin bowed his head. "Of course, sir."

Alexander led her to a small roll of dark blue material netted with tiny crystals. Grabbing up a pair of scissors he quickly cut off a length in a curving line that meant it would drape gracefully over her hair. The netting enabled her to see, but when she looked in the mirror her face was a mere suggestion, a shape and nothing more.

"Perfect."

She moved back into the front room and peeked out one of the bay windows. Her entire detail was back at the flitters, their sweep clearly concluded. The long gnarled fingers knotted nervously as Belmanor watched her.

"Okay."

Back through the workroom and Belmanor opened the backdoor and bowed her out. Mercedes noticed that he quickly closed it and she appreciated his consideration. He would not presume to watch where she went. She hurried down the odiferous alley past overflowing garbage cans. At the corner she pressed herself against the side of the building. The stucco was hot against her back. Just as she had been trained by Chief Begay, she took a quick three-second look. The nearest guard had his back to her. She darted down the side street and ran to the front door of the Candy Box.

As she suspected it was indeed a brothel. She knocked. The door was opened by a young woman with a toddler perched on her hip. The child's face was smeared with spaghetti sauce.

"Yes, Madama?"

Mercedes glanced back down the street toward the flitters and her waiting guards. "May I please come in?"

"Of course." The woman stepped back.

"I… uh… need advice. Could I speak to the person in charge of this… establishment?"

The young woman gave her a smile. "Of course. I will take you to her."

"Could I just wait?"

"We have several clients in reception right now. I wouldn't want you to be embarrassed when they go upstairs."

"Yes, that would be awkward."

Mercedes followed the girl down a hallway. Through an open doorway she spotted a large kitchen with a big wooden table in the center. A number of women were busy setting food in front of a group of preschool-age children. There was a woman nursing a newborn. It was not what she had expected in a whorehouse.

Her guide took her to a door at the end of the hall, tapped lightly and led her in. An older woman with beaded and cornrowed red hair looked up as they entered.

"This lady has questions for you, Margo."

The girl and the toddler left and Margo studied Mercedes. "Husband troubles, my dear? Can he not perform or is it something else?"

"Um… no, not that." Mercedes looked around the neat and professional office. "I'm not married. Well, not yet. I'm getting married in a few days and… and… I need to know how not to get pregnant. At least not yet." The words rushed out of her.

"Well of course that's not something we would ever do," Margo said, and Mercedes' heart sank. "Contraception isn't legal for League citizens."

Desperation formed a knot in Mercedes' chest. She had thought she was being so clever. The idea of trying to find a Cara'ot warehouse and a compliant alien ready to help her was daunting. "I… I understand. I just don't know what… where… but if you can't help…" She turned toward the door.

"Wait. I had to be sure. Sometimes the police send in plants to try and catch us breaking the law."

"Then—"

"Yes, we can help you. We keep a supply of patches—"

"No, I need something that won't be noticed."

"Well, we have a doctor on site who can implant either a contraceptive nano-needle or an IUD."

"Okay, those sound good." A concern intruded even as the madam was tapping her ScoopRing. "Wait, could either of those be detected during a physical exam?"

"Yes, but—"

"Then that won't work. I have to have one annually."

The woman gave her a puzzled look but didn't question. Mercedes supposed that was probably an asset for a madam. "What about a diaphragm?" Margo suggested.

Mercedes thought back to her biology class at the High Ground. Mostly they focused on alien physiology and how to efficiently kill them, but there had been no censorship of the textbooks, and she'd used the opportunity to fill in the obvious blanks left by her tutors when it came to human sexuality. She regretfully shook her head. "No, I need something that won't be seen for what it is. Not by anybody—maids, him... others," she added as she thought about the SEGU agents who would make regular sweeps through the small palace she and Boho had been given for their personal use.

"Real religious family, huh?" Mercedes made no answer.

Margo stood and walked over to a cabinet. Her back was to Mercedes. When she turned around she was holding a small sponge and bottle. "Sponge and spermicide. Really old-fashioned, but the Cara'ot make this spermicide and it's very effective. Soak the sponge with the spermicide and insert it before intercourse. He won't feel it unless he likes to pleasure you with his fingers." Mercedes felt herself blushing. "Put the spermicide in a pretty bottle among your creams and perfumes. Keep the sponge in your make-up drawer. No one will be the wiser."

Mercedes took the sponge and bottle and tucked them

into her skirt pocket. "Do you get women often?"

"Yes. And most of them are ladies of the FFH. I don't envy your lives."

"What do I owe you?"

"Fifty Reals."

Mercedes gave her one hundred. "I'm surprised there are children here given…" She gestured toward her pocket.

"My ladies have a baby because they want to have a baby."

"But this can't be a good environment for children."

Margo bridled. "They don't go in the public wing. I don't let diaper-sniper creeps in my place, and overall it's a pretty good life for a kid. They have playmates, there's always someone around to look after them. And having them gives me some padding for the lean times."

"I don't understand."

"We get the government subsidies just like anybody else."

"But the women are unmarried."

"Yeah, the church hates it, the government doesn't care. They just want kids. We're doing our part." A note of pride crept into her voice.

"So you think it's important—"

"Absolutely, there are more of *them*," disgust dripped off the word, "than there are of us. We're outnumbered in our own League. And those liberals in parliament better not keep pushing this full citizenship idea. The BEMs should be grateful they get to live and work among us."

Entering into a political discussion about work visas versus voting citizenship wasn't really what Mercedes had in mind. "Do the girls grow up and work for you?" she asked.

"Only if they show an interest and aptitude. Like all kids ours go to school, some even get to college if they're bright and can win a scholarship. They learn trades, they go out into the world. But we only have to worry about educating fewer than half of them. After a few years most of my girls get married, take their kids and go off with their new husbands."

"I had no idea."

"It would be different if there weren't subsidies. That would change the equation, but this works out for everyone."

"I should be going." Mercedes again touched her pocket. "Thank you for this."

"Good luck to you, milady. Come back whenever you need a refill."

Mercedes slipped back down the street. Alexander was waiting for her light knock. He quickly opened the door. "Thank you."

"My pleasure."

"You won't mention…"

"Mention what?"

"I think you're going to be very successful tailoring for the FFH, Señor Belmanor."

She started to hand him the veil. He pressed it back into her hands. "Keep it. You might need it again." She nodded her thanks, folded it and slipped it into a pocket. "As long as you're here we might as well have a fitting, Your Highness." His tone was diffident.

"Yes. You're right. We're running out of time, aren't we?" As soon as the words were uttered she regretted saying it since Belmanor tensed and began to stammer excuses. She cut him off: "I only meant that my life is about to change… again."

6

IS THIS ALL THERE IS?

It didn't look anything like the ones on the statues that had been rescued from old Earth. Those, enshrined in white marble, had seemed small, rather silly and even shy. Now she was faced with the reality of a live male member and it was daunting.

The ceremony was over, the banquet consumed, and now the couple had been whisked away to the jewel-like palace her father had given to them. Champagne was cooling in a *seau*. Candles had been lit. Mercedes had excused herself, gone into the bathroom, soaked the sponge and inserted it. She hoped she had done it right. What if it slipped out when they…

Mercedes stared again at Boho's rampant penis. An opening like a tiny mouth peered out from beneath a hood of flesh and it seemed to be questing toward her like a dousing rod. Mercedes clutched her dressing gown, a cloud of peach colored lace, close to her throat. Boho had already stripped completely. He ignored the silk dressing gown that his batBEM had thrown over the settee in their bedroom and advanced on Mercedes.

He reached down and stroked a hand along the length of his penis. "Yes, here it is. Already at attention, my love." Her expression and stunned silence finally penetrated. "Oh, sweetheart, you're scared, aren't you? Nothing to worry about." He gave her the grin. "I've done this more than a few times."

She found her voice. "Probably not the best idea to remind me of that," she managed to say.

He looked contrite. "I didn't mean it that way. Just trying to put you at ease." He pulled her hands away from her throat. She let them fall to her sides. Boho carefully untied the sash on her robe, and pushed it off her shoulders. "It's appropriate for a man to be experienced. That way we can make it memorable for our wives."

He took her hand and guided it to his penis. The skin felt like velvet and was hot in her palm.

The nightgown she wore was as lacy as her dressing gown. Only tiny ribbons tied into bows secured it at her shoulders. Boho tugged the loose end of one bow, gave her another grin.

"Like unwrapping a very nice present."

The second bow released and her gown fell to her waist. Only the swell of her hips kept it from slithering to the floor. He studied her breasts, grabbed them, one in each hand, and gave them a hard knead. Mercedes gasped as his thumbnails flicked across her nipples. It was painful and titillating all at the same time.

He leaned in and nibbled at her earlobe. She moaned and flung her arms around him. His lips moved down her neck and the nibbles became sharp bites. Sensation flared in her groin. He pulled her into an embrace, his mouth and teeth crushing against her lips. They had kissed before, but never with such urgency and violence. Tongues met, and a sensation like warm honey began to roil in Mercedes' belly. His lips left hers, and he bent to kiss her breasts, sucking and biting at the nipples. Once again there was pain but also pleasure.

Boho's hand swept the nightgown over her hips and the lace puddled at her feet. She shivered from the touch of cold air then gave a squeak and a gasp when his hand shot down. The squeak became a yelp as he thrust his fingers inside her. She remembered the madam's warning and tensed. The fingers were withdrawn, but he was grinning at her so her betrayal seemed to have remained undetected.

"You're very dry, my dear. We need to work on that," Boho breathed into her ear.

He surprised her by sweeping her up into his arms and carrying her to the large canopied bed. He spread her knees and thrust his face between her thighs. His tongue flicked across her clitoris. Mercedes gave a gasp and a moan as fire darted through her belly. His tongue darted inside her, sucking and licking. There was a sudden explosion of moisture and for an instant she feared the sponge had slipped.

Boho pulled back and grinned up at her from between her upturned knees. His mouth and lips were glistening. "You're not dry now." His voice was a husky rumble.

He pulled himself up the length of her naked body and she cried out in shock as he thrust into her. He was rocking, grunting. She tried to match his rhythm, but kept missing the timing. His cock felt huge inside her. She finally matched her hips to his, started to feel the wetness returning, fire rushing along every nerve ending.

Then he gave a shuddering cry; there was an explosion of warm liquid inside her. Boho collapsed onto her chest, breathing like a man who'd just run a marathon. He smelled of sweat and aftershave and this strange, musky, almost sweet scent. Fluid, viscous and sticky, was trickling down the inside of her thighs. There was a tight ball of tension deep in her chest, a feeling like a coiled spring in her groin.

"Lovely, lovely," he panted into her ear. His breathing slowed and she realized he'd fallen asleep. She was finding it hard to breathe beneath his weight.

"Boho." She shoved at him. "You're heavy. Get off."

He sleepily murmured something and rolled off her. A few moments later he began to snore. Mercedes lay still, gazing up at the ribbed vaulting and copper plating of the ceiling. Exhaustion dragged at her bones and her eyes were stinging. She slipped out of bed, went into the gilt and marble bathroom and began running a bath. She removed the sponge, washed it and placed it in a drawer. She walked down the steps into the sunken tub and washed herself.

The mirror-lined walls threw back her image, her skin dark against the white of the marble. Tumbled black curls falling below her shoulders. Lurid red blotches on her neck and breasts marked his bites.

Mercedes began to cry and she wasn't even sure why.

* * *

It was the first day of their brief honeymoon. Mercedes stood in the octagonal music room of the Phantasiestück Palace and watched the sun rise. The rays bounced in the diamond-shaped mullions in the windows that graced each plane, and darted across the sky-blue domed ceiling. The palace had been built by her great-great-great-grandfather Nicolai to house his lover Gerhardt, and they had both been avid musicians. Hence the jewel-box music room. Mercedes sang an experimental note and listened as the perfect acoustics of the room sent the sound shimmering to every corner. She wished she could hear Tracy sing in this room. He had a beautiful voice unlike her indifferent talent. It was not a good place for her thoughts to go, and whirling, she went striding out of the room trying to outrun the memories.

Feeling trapped she hurried to a door that was opened by a waiting Hajin footman who bowed her out. She headed up the hill toward the main palace. She wanted to talk to her mother.

It was June on Ouranos, and the location of the Phantasiestück Palace didn't offer any access to ocean breezes. It was set on the north side of the hill that held the royal residences and looked out across the rolling hills of the chaparral rather than the sprawling city that ran all along the coast and the ocean beyond. Sweat tickled her forehead and she was glad of the sleeveless dress.

Boho had awakened near dawn and wanted another round of sexual gymnastics. Mercedes had told him she needed to pee and gotten the sponge doused in spermicide and inserted. She really hoped they would settle into a pattern so she could plan for these encounters and have the sponge inserted without all this uncertainty. As for the sex, this second time had been easier, but she still felt this coiling tension, her hips and thighs ached, and she felt raw.

As she walked she reflected on the preferential treatment being shown to them. In addition to the time leading up to the wedding they had been granted five days after the ceremony to "become accustomed to one another". Added together it meant they were going to be arriving two and a half weeks late to the *Nuestra Señora de la Concepción* and would have to take the imperial yacht to catch up with the flagship.

The rest of their classmates had mustered the day after graduation. Well, that wasn't quite true. Lieutenant Lord Arturo Espadero del Campo had also been exempt, partly because he was one of Boho's groomsmen, but mostly because he was the youngest son of Cousin Musa. Mihalis, the eldest son, had been granted leave from his ship to attend the wedding. Mercedes was pretty sure they hadn't toasted the health and fecundity of the happy couple at the banquet last night. The del Campos would probably be thrilled if Mercedes didn't get pregnant.

What Boho didn't know and Mercedes wasn't going to tell him was that Cousin Musa had probably been party to the attack on the High Ground that was intended to discredit her. If Mercedes had fallen into the hands of the fake "terrorist", the attempt to place her on the throne would have failed and the succession returned to Musa. Of course there was no direct proof so everyone maintained the fiction of family harmony in public. She assumed her father was practicing the defensive strategy of keeping your enemies close.

A trickle of sweat coiled down her back and more sweat stung her eyes. She knew security was nearby, but here on the Palacio Colina it was less obvious. She could pretend she was alone. The imperial palace formed a marble and crystal crown on the brow of the hill. She pushed into a faster walk eager to ask her mother... what exactly?

It wasn't that she'd needed a sex talk per se. She had known in a general way what was going to happen. What she wanted to ask was if it was always this fast and... unsatisfying? There was really no one else for her to ask. Unlike Boho whose attendants had been his friends, her wedding party had consisted of women she barely knew. Cipriana was gone and Sumiko too ungainly in the eighth month of pregnancy to be a maid or even a matron of honor. So Mercedes had ended up with her sisters and women married to men whom her father wished to cultivate. Mercedes didn't know any of the women well enough to discuss sex with them. As for her sisters, all of them were virgins or babies so there was no help there. She had no one with whom to share a cup of cocoa and ask, *Is this all there is? If so, why all the fuss?*

So instead she was going to ask her mother. A woman she hadn't seen in years. Like that wasn't going to be awkward.

The sprinklers came on with a click and hiss. The soft ratcheting sound was soothing in the warm June air and formed a counterpoint to the squeak and neep from the tree frogs. Cool spray touched Mercedes' cheeks. She licked the drops of water off her lips. A few moments later she broke out of the trees and approached the back garden gate. It was a beautiful thing, formed of twining vines and leaves in crystal and silver. The *fusilero* on duty gave her a salute. She inclined her head rather than returning the salute because she was dressed in civilian clothes.

The fountains in the knot garden sang like bells and the herbs exhaled their aromas into the air. A riot of red bougainvillea tumbled over the walls creating the effect that the walls were bleeding. A palace cat was stalking one of the planet's Leporidae. For simplicity's sake the human settlers just called the creatures lapins. Despite their insect-like faceted eyes, they did sort of look like rabbits, though they had long filaments that brought in both sound and smell sprouting from all sides of their skulls. They also had long tails. This lapin's tail was twitching and the cat's tail was twitching in time with its prey's. Mercedes clapped her hands together and gave a yell. The lapin shot away. The cat gave her an accusing look and stalked off.

She slipped in the palace door. It was quite early so the halls were bustling with only servants. She headed to the guest wing, and the suite that housed Maribel and her husband. The door was open and a cadre of Hajin and Isanjo servants were stripping the bed and mopping the floor. Several tall Tiponi Flutes were polishing the crystals in the chandelier. They all paused and bowed as she stepped into the room.

"Lady Maribel—" Mercedes began.

"She and Lord Breganza have departed for the spaceport, Your Highness."

"Already? Why?" The Isanjo servant wisely made no

answer. The expression on the fur-covered face was impassive.

Mercedes spun and walked out of the suite. Who had been behind this? Her father not wishing the reminder of his first wife? Or Constanza, angered by the presence of her predecessor? It didn't really matter. Whoever it was they had succeeded in keeping her from her mother when she really needed her. Mercedes swallowed hard, trying to ease the tightness in her chest. She was the blissful bride. That was the face she needed to present to the world at large.

She leaned against a wall and tried to think. Cipriana would be perfect, but Cipri was light years away by now. Her thoughts turned to the other woman who had been with her at the High Ground for that first year. Sumiko with one child and a second on the way was clearly familiar with the sex act. Mercedes headed for the garage to get a flitter.

"Overall it went off pretty well. Most of the sisters behaved. The twins and Carisa were adorable as flower girls, and Carisa only threw up once. That child is so neurotic—but don't tell Constanza I said that. I think it's Constanza who makes her neurotic. Anyway, even Tanis managed not to say anything rude to anybody. This time it was Izzara who was in tears because she's put on this layer of puppy fat, and she's got pimples, unlike Tanis. Izzie is used to being the pretty sister, and Tanis was always the ugly duckling. Now Tanis is turning into a swan and Izzara looked like an overstuffed goose." Mercedes realized she was babbling, talking faster and faster in the face of Sumiko's obvious disinterest. She plowed on.

"Beatrisa squirmed and managed to get her bridesmaid dress smudged and torn. I have no idea how she did that. Julieta sulked and glared so everyone would be in *no* doubt that she was terribly, terribly upset about her wedding being postponed and having to go to the High Ground. Of course nobody noticed because who looks at a bridesmaid at a wedding? Which made her all the more angry. Thank God I had Estella. She remained calm throughout everything."

Silence. Mercedes shifted on the garden bench. Sumiko made no reply, just stood rubbing at the enormous mound of her belly. She seemed to be staring down at her eighteen-month-old daughter who squatted on her heels staring at a caterpillar that was inching through the grass, but Mercedes had a feeling she was looking at nothing.

"I'm really sorry you couldn't be in the wedding party," Mercedes added.

That finally roused Sumiko. She looked over at Mercedes. "Probably just as well. I would have had to leave the altar to pee. As it was I missed the exchange of vows because I'd gone to the bathroom."

"Yeah, a full wedding mass is really long," Mercedes said with forced brightness. There was again no response. More silence while Mercedes tried to figure out how to broach the subject that had brought her. Instead she found herself blurting out, "Are you happy?" She hadn't meant to be rude, but the words had flown and could not be recalled.

Sumiko waddled over to the garden bench and awkwardly lowered herself onto the cushions. Mercedes found it hard to pull her gaze from the massive belly and swollen breasts. The other woman sighed.

"Happy," she repeated as if tasting the word. "I'm resigned. Though it is diverting watching Edna." She looked over at the rapt child. "She's a lot more interesting now that she's ambulatory and becoming verbal." She rubbed her belly again. "I'll probably love this one too, but right now he's just making me uncomfortable."

"You got married so quickly after you left school."

"Yes, I settled. I realized after Hugo died that happiness is probably overrated and love is an illusion."

"That's a terrible thing to say."

"You disagree? You're not exactly the picture of a blissful bride."

"Boho is wonderful."

"But…?" Sumiko drew out the word into an interrogative and raised her eyebrows.

This was why Mercedes had come. She had been wrestling with how to broach the topic, but Sumiko had done it for her. Mercedes gulped, hesitated then plunged ahead. "Sex. Is it… I mean should it be… I mean I thought it would be… I mean it feels good… sort of, but well, should it be so… fast? And unsatisfying?"

"You're asking me? Frederick does his duty. I do mine. I'm obviously fertile so mission accomplished. What did you expect? We're all just doing our duties."

"I'm sorry to see you feel this way."

"I'm sorry too—for you." Sumiko's tone didn't match the words. She sounded spiteful. "You've never really had a choice. About anything. How do you stand it?"

"How do you?" Mercedes flared back. "You were the smartest of all of us. You could be doing something interesting rather than sitting here bloated and unhappy and trapped." If she'd been embarrassed by her earlier comment Mercedes was now mortified by her outburst. Her chagrin deepened when tears began to stream down her friend's puffy face. "Oh, Sumi, I'm sorry."

"No, no, you're right. I thought I was punishing the world. Instead I was just punishing myself. I was so stupid." The words emerged between snorting sobs. Edna, alarmed by her mother's distress, stood up and started to cry.

Mercedes joined Sumiko on the bench and put her arm around her shoulders. "What can I do? How can I help?"

"You can't. It's too late for me." She dashed away the tears, levered herself to her feet, and moved to her crying child. "Don't let it be too late for you, Mer," Sumiko said. "Promise me!"

"Okay, I don't exactly know what I'm promising—"

"Don't let them put you in a box." With a grunt she swung her daughter into her arms.

"Sumi, we're all in boxes—wife box, mother box, soldier box, princess box. Maybe the only place we get to be totally free is inside the confines of our own skulls."

"No, not even there. Eventually they wear you down until there's nothing of you left," Sumiko said hollowly.

"This is hormones talking. I remember how brooding my stepmothers got late in their pregnancies. Everything will look brighter once you're delivered," Mercedes said.

The other woman stared dully at her daughter. "They suck you dry too."

After that there didn't seem to be much more to say. Mercedes found an excuse and left. And realized she still didn't have any answers.

7

DEADENED TO THE PAIN

The troop transport carrying one thousand *estrella hombres* and officers deploying to new ships was due to come out of Fold in three minutes. Tracy stood in the observation pod eager for his first glimpse of the Isanjo system. Right now his only view was of the grey twisting reality of the Fold. Outside the port it looked like grey lint shot through with lances of prismatic colors as Foldstream messages raced past, leaving behind a scattering of chiming notes as if the encoded words had become music in the transition. How the sound manifested through the hull of a spaceship no one could explain. Nor could they explain why Foldstream messages physically manifested in the Fold. The average citizen just accepted that it worked and didn't worry too much about the why or the how. *Orden de la Estrella* was less sanguine; O-Trell scientists were constantly trying to decipher the mysteries of Foldspace.

Tracy found himself wondering about the content of those messages. Love letters from wives left waiting at home. Break-up letters. Orders from O-Trell Command. Business contracts. No one would know because the irony was that a ship in Fold could neither communicate nor receive communications. They could just wave at the messages as they flashed past. If there was a way to intercept them it would be a hell of an advantage to an enemy force. Hide in the Fold near a target world or battle group and snoop. It was why *Orden de la Estrella* scientists had been looking for answers for generations.

When a ship was traveling the vast distances between systems they rarely saw a message flash by. This close to a major League world and the shipyard in orbit above that planet, it looked like fireworks were going off beyond the view port.

"Thirty-second warning," a voice came over the intercom, interrupting his pondering. "All hands prepare for translation to normal space." Tracy gripped a handhold while navigation provided the countdown. "Three, two, one, translation."

For an instant Tracy had the sensation of being turned inside out and there was a sudden sharp pain in the back of his eyes. Then it was over. The view outside the port showed him Cuandru's distant sun; in the lower left corner was the edge of a gas giant banded in colors. It was the closest object in this part of the system. They were still too far out to see Cuandru itself or the Kawasaki shipyard where the *Triunfo* was being outfitted for its next patrol.

The intercom whistled and this time it was the voice of the captain echoing through the ship. "Attention—we are three hours out from the Kawasaki shipyard. Now that we have re-entered normal space we have access to the Foldcast of the royal wedding. All non-essential personnel gather in the galley for a replay."

Tracy stood and parsed the transport captain's words. He hadn't couched it as an invitation, which implied it was an order. But he hadn't actually ordered all hands to attend the Foldcast. Still if Tracy didn't show up it would be remarked upon, as there were only a handful of officers among the one thousand enlisted star men traveling on the transport. He reluctantly headed to the elevators.

Usually the passengers and the crew ate in shifts. With everyone present, apart from a skeleton crew on the bridge, the galley was packed with sweating male bodies and one lone woman. Tracy spotted Cipriana seated at a table closest to where the video was playing. She was surrounded by officers—including the transport's captain—all puffing and preening. Talion wasn't in the flirting circle. He was propping up a back wall looking bored and scrolling through his ScoopRing.

Cipriana laughed up at the adoring males and sipped a glass of champagne. Tracy noticed that while her hand might swoop toward one of the men she never actually touched them. That was not true of Lieutenant Vizconde Lucien Wessen. He was a transfer from the frigate *Eclipse* rotating to the *Triunfo*. A handsome man with red-gold hair, and a mustache that he constantly brushed with his index finger, he smirked more than smiled. His hand fell onto Cipriana's shoulder often and once even slipped beneath her braided hair and touched the skin on the back of her neck. Tracy didn't have a good enough view of Cipriana's face to tell how she felt about that.

There was muted conversation in the room overlaid by the sound of cheers and church bells from the download playing on the screen. Crowds lined the streets of Hissilek waving flags and tossing flowers at the royal carriages rolling past. The hoofbeats of the horses set a syncopation to the cathedral bells.

Every seat was taken. Tracy could have pulled rank and ordered an *hombre* to give up his chair, but he was just as happy to huddle among the men standing at the back of the room. BatBEMs were moving through the crowd handing out glasses of champagne. Donnel was carrying three trays and using his fourth hand to dispense glasses.

"Well, won't this be fun," he muttered out of the corner of his mouth. "Oh, and don't drink that," he said with a nod to the glass Tracy now held. "It's real cheap shit."

"Would it get me drunk?"

"If that's the goal I'll find you something better for later." Donnel moved on.

The carriage carrying the Emperor and his daughter reached the front of the Cathedral of the Holy Trinity. The white stone of the soaring building was blinding in the summer sun. The four matching palomino horses pulling the gilt-and-glass confection stamped and tossed their heads, setting their white manes flying. Guards lowered the steps and the Emperor stepped out, reached up his hand to Mercedes.

A stone lodged itself in Tracy's chest. He couldn't see her face through the veil, but the sleek lines of the dress accentuated her height and caressed her curves. The skin of her bare right shoulder was rich cocoa against the white of the gown. Another camera angle revealed the opals flashing in the sunlight. The other carriages were disgorging the sisters, the Empress, and the older woman who Tracy now knew was Mercedes' real mother. The three littlest princesses carried baskets filled with rose petals. The bridal party entered the church.

"They certainly know how to do a spectacle," Talion muttered into Tracy's right ear.

Tracy had been so focused on Mercedes he hadn't seen the other man approach. The pressure in his chest and the tightness in his throat made words impossible. Tracy gave a nod and managed a grunt.

Interior cameras took over. The nave of the church seemed dim after the brilliant sunlight outside, though the stained-glass windows wrapped ribbons of color around the guests. The great organ and a chamber orchestra played Handel as the wedding party arrived.

The Cardinal of Ouranos waited at the altar, impressive in his vestments. On the step below the prelate stood Boho in his dress uniform. He was surrounded by his groomsmen, among them one of Tracy's classmates—Lieutenant Lord Arturo Espadero del Campo. The inclusion of Arturo in the wedding party was interesting. He and Boho were good friends, but was it all that politic to have the youngest son of Musa del Campo, Duque Aqua de Negra in such public view?

Tracy knew that the del Campo family was not happy over the change in their status. Perhaps this was a way to signal peace between the families? Or maybe it was nothing more than friendship? Somehow Tracy doubted that. None of Boho's other compatriots were present. Like Cipriana they had been ordered to their postings. But not Arturo. No, this was political.

Tracy's mind continued to whirl, trying to think of anything other than the fact that Mercedes was about to marry Boho. He gave a mental head shake and corrected himself. No, she had been married to him for several days now. Tracy studied the faces of the guests as they came in range of the cameras following Mercedes and the Emperor's stately advance down the aisle to a classical trumpet voluntary. He tried not to look at Mercedes, beautiful Mercedes, but it didn't work.

The father and daughter climbed the steps to the altar. The delicate and understated train his father had designed flowed across the stone like snowfall. The music fell silent. There was a murmured exchange between the Emperor and the archbishop. Then the Emperor took Boho's hand and placed Mercedes' hand in his.

There was a sharp crack and Tracy reacted to the sudden pain and the flow of warmth across his fingers. He looked down at the snapped stem of his glass now coated with blood from his cut finger. Talion was staring at him.

"Must have been a flaw in the glass," Tracy muttered. "Be right back."

He ducked out of the galley and rushed to the bathroom. He started to pour the champagne down the sink then thought better and tossed it back. It was as terrible as Donnel had indicated, but the heat helped loosen the knot in his chest. He threw away the broken glass, washed his hands and wrapped the cut forefinger in his handkerchief. He stood with his hands braced on either side of the sink, reminding himself over and over that the wedding had already taken place. It shouldn't have this kind of power to affect him. Pretending he was convinced he headed back into the galley, and was relieved to discover he had missed the exchanging of the vows. The archbishop, hands upraised, was issuing the final benediction.

Talion held a second glass and offered it to Tracy. "Here. I was sure you would want this," he said quietly.

"Thanks."

"The only way to get through a wedding is to be deadened to the pain." Their eyes met for a long moment then Tracy nodded.

The captain of the transport stood, held up his glass. "God save the Infanta and her noble consort." The assembled crowd repeated the toast. Tracy remained silent. The second glass went down as fast as the first.

Cuandru was very green. Tracy didn't spot a single desert as he studied the world rotating beneath him. The polar ice caps were standard for a "Goldilocks" world, and oceans and rivers cut through the green that Tracy knew were immense forests. The transport moved into the night side of the planet and Tracy saw a tiny flare of fire out on one of the oceans. He had just seen a launch. To avoid disturbing the trees the Isanjo's launch facilities were on massive floating platforms on the equatorial band of various oceans. Most people reached the surface via the large space elevators that linked the planet to the massive shipyard stations orbiting overhead.

Since the trees hid most of the lights of Isanjo cities, Tracy brought up a new view on the screen of the massive shipyard toward which the transport was slowly maneuvering. Flares of light off welding torches lit the dark of space all around the skeleton of a ship that was tethered in a floating construction cage. Seven such cages were grouped on all sides and above and below the massive rotating ring of the Kawasaki shipyard. Each held a ship in various stages of construction.

All along the circumference of the ring, ships were nosed up against the *cosmódromo*. The large battle cruisers and flagships looked like nursing whale calves against the bulk of the station. Smaller ships were more like hummingbirds or mosquitoes suckling at the ring.

Tracy felt a pressure against the soles of his boots as the maneuvering rockets on the transport fired, altering their trajectory. The station drew closer, a wall of metal. Tracy was impressed. He had thought the *cosmódromo* that housed the High Ground was big. It was dwarfed by Kawasaki.

There was a bump that signaled they had docked. Tracy headed for the airlock where Donnel was waiting with his kit. The officers would be debarking first so there was a scrum of uniformed officers and their batBEMs at the doors. Cipriana was there with her batBEM, a pretty little white-furred Isanjo, which made her dark fur mask all the more startling. Cipriana joined Tracy while they waited for the egress ramp to lock and pressure to equalize.

"Well, this is it," she said.

"Yep."

"Nervous?"

Tracy analyzed his feelings. "I'm not sure. Yeah, a bit."

"Me too. The third-year cruise still felt like pretend. This is for real." Tracy nodded. "Do you know where we're headed?"

"Berth twenty-three. I downloaded a schematic."

"Duh, I should have done that. I was just relying on Kaat to get me there."

"Well, allow me to be your guide, Lieutenant Lady Delacroix." He offered his arm.

"With pleasure, Lieutenant Belmanor." She laid her fingers on his arm. Tracy noted with pleasure the stares and glares from the other officers.

The airlock cycled and the exodus began. It should have been senior officers first, but they all deferred to the lady, which meant Tracy and Cipriana were the first ones to enter the *cosmódromo*.

"Wow, what a shitho… letdown," Cipriana amended.

For the station couldn't have been more different than the *cosmódromo* that housed the High Ground. The latter was a station in orbit over the capital world of the League, catering to the rich and well connected, and was therefore lavishly appointed with shops, gourmet restaurants, hotels, even joy houses. Kawasaki was a military facility with all the charm or lack thereof that that implied. The flooring was a basic grey composite material. Instead of the scent of flowers from a park there was the tang of cleaning products, oil, and cheap food.

There was the sound of hurried footfalls and Talion

joined them, taking up a position on Cipriana's left. He twined her arm through his. "So here we are," he said.

Cipriana slipped her right arm through Tracy's. "Yes, here we are. Who knows what adventures await."

"I think when you're in the military you hope there won't be any adventures," Tracy said.

"Not if we want to advance. What was that old toast from the British Royal Navy?" Talion asked.

"To a bloody war or a sickly season," Tracy said.

"That was the one."

There was a call from behind them and again the sound of running footfalls. "Hoy, Cipri, wait." It was Wessen. Tracy watched Cipriana assemble a smile and turn to face the other lieutenant.

"Why, Lucien, how lovely."

"Allow me to escort you." He was a bit breathless, which implied the captain at Lucien's last posting had not been as rigorous about physical activity for his officers.

Cipriana lifted her arms wing-fashion, which perforce raised Tracy's and Talion's. "I'm afraid I'm all out of arms, but thank you."

A look of annoyance flashed across Wessen's face. "Well, then I shall see you aboard the *Triunfo*."

"I'm looking forward to it," Cipriana said, and began walking briskly away almost towing Tracy and Talion. The smile was wiped away.

"Want me to break some particularly vulnerable part of him?" Tracy asked.

"No." She flashed him a bright smile. "I can handle it."

"Don't hesitate to call upon us if you can't," Talion added.

As they walked around the hub there was the usual frenzied activity of *estrella hombres* and officers rushing about. They all looked very serious and focused, as if their various tasks were terribly important. After three years living in the military culture Tracy knew it was busywork bullshit that supposedly kept them prepared for when it might not be bullshit.

They could have taken a moving walkway or rented a cart but by tacit agreement the three comrades walked. It felt good to be moving after the confines of the transport ship. It was a long hike, but eventually they reached berth twenty-three. A pair of *fusileros* guarded the access ramp of the gangway. Tracy, Talion and Cipriana extended their rings to have their orders read. After a moment the *fusilero* on the left gave a nod, then both guards came to attention and snapped off salutes. Cipriana gave a giggle that she turned into a cough. The trio returned the salutes and started down the length of the gangway toward the airlock that was dogged open.

"So let's go make names for ourselves," Talion said. His eyes were bright with excitement.

"I'm just going to try to get through the next five years without screwing up," Cipriana said.

"I'm just going to try to get through the first day," Tracy said.

"You're a pessimist," Talion replied.

"I'm a realist. Some kind of shit will always happen."

* * *

"Welcome to the *Triunfo*, Lieutenant." Captain Marquis Dumas de Vilbiss looked to be in his mid-fifties. Slim without being fit, his spade beard was streaked with grey, and the grey at his temples added to his distinguished appearance. De Vilbiss had hazel eyes that held a wistful expression. He glanced back down at his tap-pad. "Your grades and performance reports are impressive."

"Thank you, sir."

"I also understand from Commander Baldinini that you have a beautiful singing voice."

"The commander is very kind."

"Jeffery said in his Foldmail that he gave you voice lessons for all three years at your academy. Jeffery doesn't do that unless the student is very talented."

Baldinini was the High Ground's choir director and bandleader. Tracy hadn't really wanted to add one more activity to his school schedule, but thought the training might prove useful if he washed out of the academy. Now it was back to haunt him.

"I was very fortunate to have the commander's attention."

De Vilbiss left his chair behind the desk and came closer to Tracy. He rested a hip on the desk. "I'm a great lover of music. One of my *hombres* is a particularly talented musician and he plays for me and my officers at dinner. I think it would be a very nice addition to have you sing while he plays."

"As the captain wishes," Tracy said.

"Let me introduce you." De Vilbiss keyed his ScoopRing. "Mr. Yamamoto, please report to my office."

De Vilbiss returned to his chair. "As for your more official duties, we'll clearly be utilizing your talents in Weapons, although I may have you take a turn on the bridge in Navigation as well."

"Yes, sir. Thank you, sir."

The door chime sounded. "Come in, Akihiko," de Vilbiss called.

A young man entered. He looked to be in his late twenties and he was a very handsome man with dark ivory skin, a classically straight nose, and thickly lashed black eyes. The affection in the captain's eyes was unmistakable. Tracy looked up at the bulkhead so he could pretend he hadn't seen. Fraternization was accepted between officers, but was frowned upon between officers and enlisted men. Clearly the rule was being ignored aboard the *Triunfo*.

"Akihiko, this is Lieutenant Thracius Belmanor. He's the singer that my friend Jeffery told me about. He's going to be joining you during the evening meals."

"Very good, sir." Yamamoto saluted Tracy who returned the salute. "I look forward to performing with you."

"Knowing Jeffery, you've had your head filled with the classical repertoire," de Vilbiss said with an indulgent smile. "Akihiko will get you up to speed on the music I enjoy."

"Very good, sir," Tracy said.

The captain looked down at a new message that had arrived on his tap-pad. Tracy and Yamamoto stood at attention. After a few moments de Vilbiss looked up.

"Oh, yes." He gave a casual wave. "You're dismissed."

Out in the corridor Tracy and Yamamoto evaluated each other. "Baritone?" the enlisted man asked.

"Yeah. What kind of music does he like?"

"Jazz. Swing. He's very big on the music of the thirties and forties. *Nineteen* thirties and forties," Akihiko added. "He finds it romantic."

"Well, at least he didn't want me to rap. Or do Hindu pop."

"Or Tiponi warble."

"Do Flutes sing? And how would you tell? Their language sounds like pipes," Tracy said. They shared a smile.

"I can't imagine there's a race that doesn't have music," Yamamoto said. "They must have something that's music and not just conversation."

"Can you get me some music?" Tracy asked.

"Yes, we should probably practice at least once before we have to perform."

"Sounds good. Let me get settled and report for duty."

They exchanged ping codes and Tracy went in search of Weapons. He didn't worry about getting settled in his quarters. Donnel would handle that. This having a personal servant was one perk of military life he really liked. He wasn't sure he felt the same about becoming the captain's personal *chanteur*.

8

SING FOR YOUR SUPPER

"Belmanor, eh?" Lieutenant-Commander Golden grunted as he read the transfer orders projected by his ScoopRing.

"Yes, sir."

The Weapons deck was quiet apart from the hum from the computers and the click of keys as techs calibrated and ran checks of the various weaponry that lurked in missile tubes or bristled on the skin of the big battle cruiser.

"Impressive grades."

"Thank you, sir."

"Not a compliment. That's classroom bullshit. Out here is what matters. It's gotta count when we use these weapons."

"Yes, sir. I understand, sir." If there was one thing three years at the academy had taught him it was that you always agreed, and in as few words as possible.

"I'm assigning you to Captain-Lieutenant Lord Westley's unit." Tracy remained silent. "You'll find him in the wardroom. Dismissed."

Tracy saluted and left. He hadn't been able to download a schematic of the *Triunfo*. It was a warship and details weren't just randomly placed on the net. He thought about asking some of the passing *hombres*, but realized they might not know the location of the officers' wardroom, and as an officer Tracy didn't like to seem lost or confused in front of enlisted personnel. He spotted a Hajin. The alien kept having to press himself against the wall of the corridor as humans passed, which gave Tracy time to catch up. The batBEM would certainly know the location of the officers' wardroom.

"You there." The Hajin rolled a terrified eye toward him. Tracy, acting more out of instinct than thought, held up a soothing hand. "Sorry, I didn't mean to startle you." Mentally Tracy kicked himself because the tepid apology had drawn startled looks from the passing human soldiers. Three years rubbing elbows with the FFH and he still didn't know how to act with proper hauteur toward alien servants.

The Hajin bowed. "My apologies, milord. Forgive this foolish one's behavior." The creature was clearly terrified.

"Really, it's fine. I just need some directions." Tracy smiled. The Hajin's frightened expression didn't ease.

"Of course, sir. Allow me to guide you, milord. Where did you wish to go?"

"The wardroom. And just tell me. I need to get my bearings."

"Oh, no, milord. My master would flay me if—"

"I'm not planning on telling him. And I don't know who he might be anyway. I just arrived."

The Hajin rolled a frightened eye at the passing humans. Tracy gave a mental sigh. Clearly the pony thought someone would rat him out to whatever officer he served. As if a human would care that much. "Fine. Take me."

The wardroom turned out to be one deck below. Apparently deck four was officers' territory, with the wardroom, captain's dining room, quarters for the officers and the officers' gym. The wardroom divided the cabins serving as a demarcation line, with lieutenants and lieutenant-commanders on one side and commanders' and captains' berths on the other. The cabins of the superior officers were closest to the elevators and manual ladders for quicker access to the bridge and weaponry.

Tracy had done his third-year tour aboard a small frigate. That wardroom had all the ambiance of a bus station restaurant. This wardroom looked more like a gentlemen's club, with deep armchairs, bolted down of course but still plush, a long polished wood dining table, china and crystal in a tall cabinet, a billiard table, and a large vid screen on one wall. A group of young officers were chatting. There was the thrum and crack of billiard balls rolling and colliding, taunts and jibes from the two players and the onlookers.

One of the group noticed Tracy hesitating just inside the door, hat turning nervously in his hands. The man broke away from the group and approached. Tracy quickly evaluated the rank device, tucked his hat beneath his left arm, and snapped off a salute.

It was lazily returned then the man thrust out a hand. "Lieutenant-Commander Marquis Xiang-Loredo."

"Lieutenant Belmanor."

"J.G.," someone from the crowd drawled. Tracy felt his jaw tighten painfully.

"I'm one of the wardroom XOs. We need to arrange for your dues to be deducted."

"Of course," Tracy said. They keyed their rings and the automatic withdrawal was set up. It was much higher than the frigate.

"Are you married?" Chen asked.

"No, sir."

"Then we won't have to be worrying about baby gifts for a while," Chen said with a smile.

"No, sir."

"What can we do for you?"

"I was told to report to Captain-Lieutenant Westley."

"Westley, get over here," Chen called. One of the spectators of the billiards game pushed away from the wall and sauntered over. He was an ordinary-looking man with brown hair, brown eyes, and brown skin, who looked to be in his late twenties. His bearing was anything but ordinary. He swaggered and the look he gave Tracy was reminiscent of a man inspecting a bug. "Here's your new transfer."

Wesley inspected Tracy's rank device and gave him a condescending smile. "Just finished OCS, *hombre*?"

Tracy was offended by the suggestion that he was an enlisted man who had been jumped up to officer. "No. I just graduated from the High Ground."

Westley's expression was that of a man who'd just discovered dog shit on his shoe. "Great, I get sent the reject who barely scraped through and couldn't even make full lieutenant."

Tracy told himself to let it pass. Take it. Nod and smile. Say *yes sir* and eat the shit and thank the pompous asshole for it. Instead he said, "I graduated second in the class. The demotion was so my competence wouldn't damage any fragile FFH egos."

"You are out of order, Belmanor! You will stand the middle watch until further notice. You are dismissed."

Tracy came to attention, snapped off a salute, spun on his heel and left. It was going to suck doing night after night of the midnight to four a.m. watch but it had been worth it to stuff it up the asshole's nose.

A scrabbling overhead had Tracy's head jerking up to see Donnel crawling across the ceiling just outside Tracy's assigned berth. Apparently he'd been roosting up there to stay out of the way of the foot traffic in the corridor. The three-legged alien's strange claw-like feet somehow gripped the metal as he made his way to the wall and walked down until he stood before Tracy.

"Well, congratulations. We haven't been aboard an hour and you've already established your bona fides as a stiff-necked prick and all-round asshole... sir."

"News travels fast," Tracy replied casually, though inwardly he was a bit shocked and dismayed at how quickly news of his confrontation with Westley had spread. He tried to comfort himself with the thought that the alien servants always seemed to know everything before their human masters. Maybe he still had a chance to make a good impression? "And if you're not happy you can quit," Tracy added as he stepped around the alien toward the door.

"Oh, no, sir. Life with you is just too entertaining. I should warn you that I couldn't get you a great bunk. The only one available was right next to the head."

"If there's one thing I've learned it's how to sleep anywhere, any time." Tracy touched the panel on the wall to bring up the names of his suite mates. *Gupta, Eklund, Bellard and Belmanor.* He was surprised to find his name already added, but the *Triunfo* did seem to be efficient. "Any of them in there?"

"Eklund."

Tracy entered.

A young man who appeared to be in his mid-twenties looked up. His rack had been folded out of the wall and he was kicked back reading. His ScoopRing projected the print and images in front of him. It appeared to be porn.

"Did no one teach you to knock?"

"You wouldn't hear it through composite steel," Tracy answered.

"Christ, literal much? There is a chime."

"And I don't normally ring to enter my own quarters."

"So you're Belmanor."

"Yes."

Eklund looked him up and down. Once again the gaze lingered on his J.G. insignia. "The *intitulado.*"

Tracy didn't dignify that with a response. He moved to the bunk panel nearest the head. He opened his wall locker to find his uniforms hung and his kit laid out. He opened the door to the bathroom. The tiny space held just a toilet.

"Where are the showers?" he asked Eklund. No response. He turned to find Eklund standing directly behind him.

"My father is the Duque de Crédit-Faber. You will refer to me as milord—"

"No."

"You're refusing an order from a superior officer?"

"I'm pointing out that the officer must be unfamiliar with O-Trell's regulations regarding honorifics. It would be a shame to point out this shocking deficit in that officer's understanding to his superior officer."

For a moment it hung in the balance then Eklund stepped back. "I won't forget this," he muttered as he returned to his bunk.

"Neither will I," Tracy said under his breath and stepped into the head to take a piss.

He returned to the room to change out of his day uniform and into his duty dress, which was a T-shirt worn beneath a multi-pocketed jacket, and cargo-style pants with a multiplicity of pockets. While in duty dress he was required to carry a sidearm so he hooked the webbed belt and holster around his waist, checked that the safety was on and thrust the pistol into the holster.

He had just finished when his ScoopRing pricked his finger to indicate a message. It was an invitation to a welcome dinner at the captain's table that evening. Dress uniform required. Perhaps life aboard the *Triunfo* wasn't going to be all disdain and condescension.

The argument began immediately after Donnel smoothed Tracy's jacket across his shoulders. The alien skittered around to face him. He was holding the box with the *Distinguido Servicio Cruzar* nestled in velvet.

"No."

"You're in full dress. Regulations say you wear your medals."

"I'll look like a conceited prat."

"Right now they think you're lowborn riffraff. This might help disabuse them of that idea."

"I think this is more for you and your standing among the other batBEMs," Tracy said with a chuckle.

Donnel's four eyes held a look that Tracy had never before seen and it shook him a bit. "I am a Cara'ot. I have no need for that. My status is assured," Donnel said.

"Wow. Superior much?"

Donnel didn't reply, just pinned the medal onto Tracy's coat.

Tracy met another of his roommates at the door. His name tag read *Gupta* and his eyes widened when he saw the *Cruzar* on Tracy's breast. The surprise was quickly shaken off and the normal FFH sneer was slapped firmly into place.

"Ah, you're the *intitula*—the J.G."

"Belmanor."

Gupta ignored Tracy's outstretched hand and pushed past him. "Don't let me keep you."

Well, at least there wasn't a verbal insult this time, Tracy thought. Perhaps that could be considered progress.

He made his way across the deck to the captain's private dining room. He touched the chime pad and the door slid open. He was bowed into the room by a white-coated human rather than an alien. That was a mark of either extreme discomfort about aliens by the captain or a signal of privilege that he could afford a human bat—Tracy broke off realizing the usual appellation didn't apply. *Batmen*, that's what they had been called when humans were confined to a single planet and had to subjugate each other rather than aliens.

Tracy removed his hat, braced and saluted the assembled men. His salute was returned languidly by the gaggle of high-ranking officers. Tracy noted that there was no one below the rank of lieutenant-commander present. It was a bit intimidating.

The dining room was even nicer than the officers' wardroom. In place of wood panels it had mirrors. Tracy assumed that shielding would slide over the glass when the ship was in combat. There were spaces between the mirrors where paintings were displayed. A magnificent chandelier hung over a table that was draped with a white tablecloth, glittering with crystal and groaning under the weight of silver and china. A large epergne formed of winged rearing horses adorned the center of the table. Tracy gave himself a mental pat on the back for remembering the name for that kind of centerpiece. He had learned it the one time he was a visitor at the Talion home on Hissilek.

He looked for Talion and found him near an art deco bar where another white-coated servant was serving drinks. Talion held a champagne flute and was talking with a heavy-set man who also sported a number of facial scars. They formed a white web against his ebony skin. The cheerful, almost jolly smile that curved his lips didn't seem to fit with the scars.

There was the soft sound of a guitar tuning. Yamamoto was seated on a small gilt chair. A pair of enameled screens formed an alcove so while he was present he wasn't a focal point. He was surrounded by a gaggle of chaplains. There were two Christian priests with crosses on their sleeves above their insignia. Tracy assumed one was a Catholic and the other a Protestant—or perhaps a Mormon. One was small and slender with blue-black hair and skin that was paler than Tracy's. The other was tall and balding. There was a Muslim officer with the crescent moon on his sleeves and collar. He had a neatly trimmed beard and rather terrifying bushy eyebrows. A rabbi with the Star of David rounded out the representatives of heaven. He leaned on a cane and Tracy noticed the sole of his left boot had been built up.

It seemed like a lot of holy in one place. At the High Ground there had only been Catholic services and every cadet was required to attend chapel regardless of personal faith. Since most of the students were part of the FFH, that wasn't controversial. The nobility all tended to be members of the state religion. Even when Tracy had done his senior tour it had been on a small frigate that had only a priest. Now this ecumenical gathering. On a ship that held six thousand and the majority of crew not members of the FFH, Tracy supposed that it made sense to have a multiplicity of faiths represented. He'd have to find out which one was the Catholic.

Tracy moved to the bar and accepted a glass. Unlike the champagne on the transport, this was first rate. Cipriana entered. Tracy noticed that she was wearing her medal so he didn't feel quite so conspicuous. Wessen was at her side, and Tracy's eyes narrowed as he watched Wessen lay a hand on her shoulder, and how Cipriana shied away. Captain de Vilbiss carried a glass of champagne over to Cipriana. She accepted it with a smile and a half-curtsy, which drew an indulgent chuckle from several of the men.

"Well, now that we are all assembled allow me to make introductions." De Vilbiss laid a hand on the shoulder of a slim man whose pencil mustache and slightly longer than regulation black hair gave him a piratical look. He was also older than the other men in the room. Arching brows over green eyes with slight epicanthic folds gave him a quizzical look. "My XO, Commander Anusanatha Sukarno." Tracy noted the lack of a title after the rank and took a closer look at the tawny-skinned man. The other thing that stood out was the lack of dueling scars, unlike every other officer in the room. Sukarno was becoming more and more interesting and Tracy resolved to try and overcome his innate shyness and actually talk to the man.

"Our chief medical officer, Commander Dr. Lord Trayvon Exeteur." That was the man with the net of scars. *Physician heal thyself*, Tracy thought and gave a mental head shake over O-Trell's officer class's love of the duel. "Lieutenant-Commander Baron Kyle Golden, head of Weapons division. Lieutenant-Commander Marquis Xiang-Loredo, head of Navigation. Commander Conde Gustav Eichenbrenner, who leads our contingent of *fusileros* and our *Infierno* fighter pilots, and finally, last but not least, our chaplains, Father Kenneth Russell," the captain laid a hand on the small man's shoulder, "Elder Joshua Brown, Rabbi Rabinowitz and Imam Christopher Sulieman."

De Vilbiss turned to them, elevated his glass and said, "To our new lieutenants. Welcome aboard." Murmurs of welcome and they all took sips of their champagne. Yamamoto began to softly play. Since it was background music it was classical and soothing.

Tracy stood dithering, trying to figure out how to approach Sukarno. Turned out he didn't have to, as Sukarno approached him.

"Lieutenant Belmanor."

"Sir."

"Very happy to have you aboard."

"Thank you, sir."

"You have an impressive record from the High Ground." The green eyes drifted down to the *Distinguido Servicio Cruzar*.

Tracy realized he probably wasn't impressing with his monosyllabic answers so he tried to elaborate. "Thank you, sir, but as Lieutenant-Commander Golden pointed out, the grades don't matter when the situation is real."

"Don't assume that everyone here has been under enemy fire. Most of them haven't, Lieutenant. We've had a long stretch without a shooting war. The aliens are fully pacified and we haven't found a new Hidden World for almost twenty-five years. It's hard to stay frosty when there's no one to fight."

"Uh, I suppose that's true, sir."

Sukarno reached out and lightly touched the medal with a forefinger. "The fact you and the young lady are both wearing *that* tells me more than your companion Talion's scars or letters of recommendation from previous captains.

I'd say you probably have more experience with real combat than Lieutenant-Commander Golden."

The flush rose up his neck and into his face. Tracy ducked his head and stared down at his toes. "Ummm, thank you?" He couldn't keep his voice from rising on the final word, making it an almost-question.

The XO clapped him on the shoulder and leaned in. "We have a lot in common, Lieutenant. I'm a 'Knife and Fork' officer."

The phrase was unfamiliar and Tracy overcame his shyness to meet Sukarno's gaze. "I'm sorry, sir, I don't know what that means."

"That I didn't go to the High Ground. I was an enlisted man, pulled out and sent to Officer Candidate School. The knife and fork thing refers to the fact I had to be taught how to behave. We're neither one of us members of the FFH, Lieutenant." The blunt fingers gave his shoulder one more squeeze and Sukarno moved on to talk with the others.

Tracy stood contemplating that for a few moments. He remembered the welcoming banquet at the High Ground when he'd been faced with an array of cutlery and no idea what to do with it all. He'd watched his table mates and imitated them. His father might have drilled him on proper etiquette and deportment from an early age, but that had been so he knew how to behave toward the FFH as a decorous servant. He had no idea of the proper cues between noble equals, nor was he likely to learn since none of them considered him their equal.

As was his wont he retreated to a wall to stand and

observe. It didn't last for long. Cipriana crossed to him and pulled him away to meet Dr. Exeteur, who despite the web of scars turned out to be friendly to the point of seeming jolly. He was delighted to see Tracy's scar and immediately invited him to join the fencing club.

Talion broke off from his conversation with Eichenbrenner to say, "He doesn't actually know how to fence. He knows how to get cut."

"Well, we should fix that," Exeteur said cheerfully.

Tracy stood frozen with indecision. His initial reaction was to refuse. The voice of Mercedes that seemed to be constantly in the back of his mind counseled him to accept. He had a sudden satisfying image of parrying and slapping the saber out of Boho's hand and then holding the point of his saber against Boho's throat.

"Excellent! We'll see you on Sunday after mass then." Exeteur winked broadly. "Give a little nod toward God then a little wink at the devil, eh?" Tracy received another buffet on the shoulder. As was so often the case in the military it seemed that Tracy had accepted without actually accepting.

Tracy had a brief conversation with Xiang-Loredo who told him, "I let Golden have the first crack at you since he seems to have a team of mathematical dunces down there, but I'll get you on the bridge in due course. Math skills shouldn't be wasted on weapons drills."

Tracy would have taken it as a compliment but for the fact Xiang-Loredo's eyes never actually looked at him, and Tracy had the decided impression that this was more about a power struggle between Golden and Xiang-

Loredo than it was about him and his skills.

The smell of aftershave, Cipriana's perfume and alcohol was replaced by the smell of roast meat, the yeasty warmth of freshly baked bread and ginger carrots. A bell was rung and Captain de Vilbiss clapped his hands together. "That's the call to supper."

Tracy moved to the foot of the table. Given his status as a Lieutenant J.G. and an *intitulado* he assumed he wasn't going to be seated near the captain. The chair to de Vilbiss's right was given to Cipriana. Eichenbrenner was on his left. Sukarno was seated several chairs down from the head of the table. Apparently rank could not trump low birth. Tracy stalled so all the titled officers could take their chairs then headed for the one remaining open chair. De Vilbiss looked startled when he started to sit down.

"Oh, Lieutenant Belmanor, I thought we were to be treated to your singing."

A knot comprised of ice and acid formed in the pit of Tracy's stomach. He couldn't even have one night before he became the captain's trained seal. He examined and discarded a dozen responses while the silence stretched between them. Cipriana was staring at her plate, clearly embarrassed for him. Heat washed through Tracy's body. It felt like everyone was staring at him.

Yamamoto set aside his guitar and moved to de Vilbiss's side. He bent down and whispered into the captain's ear. Two red spots bloomed on the captain's cheeks. "Oh, yes, quite, I see your point," he murmured. "Forgive me, Lieutenant. Of course you and Akihiko haven't had a chance to put your heads together about a repertoire. Blame it on my eagerness to hear you sing. Please, be seated. Of course you shouldn't have to sing for your supper."

Tracy, his appetite gone, sank down into his chair. Sukarno gave him a look that might have been sympathy. Everyone else studiously avoided looking at him. He passed the rest of the evening in silence.

9

GOODBYES AND GRIEVANCES

"This is *your* fault!" Julieta shrieked. A bottle smashed into the door next to Mercedes' ear. Perfume dripped down the wall and she was enveloped in a choking miasma of attar of roses.

"Well, the academy will certainly improve your aim," Mercedes said calmly.

"I *hate* you!" Julieta screamed.

"Really? You avoid me completely after the wedding and this is how we're going to say goodbye? And I didn't do anything. You want to pitch a fit and fling things? Fine, then throw things at Daddy or at Rohan. They're the ones sending you to the High Ground."

"I love Sanjay and now it's going to be *three whole years* before we can get married," Julieta wailed. "Maybe more! What if he meets someone else?" The words emerged in little hiccups interspersed with sobs.

Irritation ripped through Mercedes. "Oh don't be an idiot. No one's fool enough to walk away from a royal marriage."

"You make it sound like he doesn't love me," Julieta sniveled.

"He doesn't." Mercedes wasn't fool enough to add *and you don't love him, not really.* Her sister's sobs filled the room. Mercedes softened her tone, and added, "I mean really, how could he? He doesn't know you."

"And now we'll never have the chance. We're going to be separated for *years* and *years* and *years.*"

Mercedes found herself remembering her own heart burning when she'd cried herself to sleep over Riccardo when she was sixteen. He was a hazy memory now, but at the time she'd thought her heart would break. Pity replaced irritation. Mercedes crossed to her youngest sister.

"Julieta, you're just seventeen. There's so much more world for you to explore. You don't want to be like Sumiko, do you? And as for Sanjay, it might be only ambition now, but once you two have a chance to spend time together he will fall in love with you." She gave the smaller woman a hug. "How could he not? You're wonderful and beautiful." Mercedes hesitated then added, "And, sweetheart, don't discount the idea that your feelings might change. You might meet somebody else."

"*Never!* And even if I did the marriage has been announced, Daddy would never let—"

"Daddy isn't the only factor here. I'm the Infanta. I'm going to have some say in what happens to my sisters."

Julieta stared up at her, lips parted in an "ooo" of amazement. "You'd argue with Daddy?"

"I've done it a few times," Mercedes said. *And lost every time*, her inner, honest voice added. *But we're talking several years. I'll be much more grown up then. He'll listen. I hope.*

* * *

There was going to be a farewell dinner, but Mercedes wanted a chance to see her sisters in a less formal setting. The long table, the army of servants, and the presence of parents rather discouraged private moments. Mercedes found Tanis and Izzara in Tanis's room and locked in one of their ferocious and all too frequent fights. A pink and gold dress hung between them, each of them clutching at the material.

"It's *my* dress! You had no right to take it!" Izzara screamed.

"It suits me better. With your hair you'll look like a carrot wearing cotton candy," Tanis yelled back.

Their Hajin maids were flapping their hands and making miserable noises as they stood shoulder to shoulder. Unlike their mistresses they were united in their distress.

"It makes your skin look like suet. In fact you're too fat to wear it now anyway," Tanis gleefully threw out the most horrible taunt a woman can give.

Izzara let out a shriek and slapped Tanis. The dress, forgotten, fell to the floor between them. Before the slap fight could really get underway Mercedes intervened. Interposing herself between the younger girls she used her capoeira training to take Tanis to the floor with a leg sweep. Leaping to her feet Mercedes grabbed Izzara by the wrist. A quick twist had her sister screaming in pain. Izzara dropped to her knees in front of Mercedes. Mercedes sensed Tanis coming up behind her. She lashed out with her free hand, and bopped Tanis in the nose. Her shrieks blended with her sister's.

"That's better. Now you're both singing the same tune."

"You *punta!*" Tanis spat. Mercedes glanced over her shoulder. Blood was gushing from Tanis's nose, spattering on the abused and now forgotten dress.

"I was going to say you're an emperor's daughters not fish wives screaming in the market, but clearly I was wrong." Mercedes released Izzara who nursed her abused wrist. Her screams subsided into sniffles. "I came here to tell you goodbye." Mercedes pulled a handkerchief out of her skirt pocket and thrust it into Tanis's hands. "I'm going to be gone for a long time, years, and I hope to hell when I come home I'll find you better behaved."

"Am I going to learn... that?" Izzara made a vague gesture. "When I go to the High Ground?"

"You'll study unarmed combat, yes." Mercedes didn't like the speculative look Izzara gave her younger sister. She turned to the maids. "Please get rid of this dress. It's quite ruined now."

The aliens exchanged quick glances. The one with the buckskin-colored mane darted forward and snatched up the abused dress. Mercedes had a feeling it wouldn't end up in the trash but instead be cleaned and then sold second-hand to some *intitulado* woman down in Pony Town.

Mercedes opened her arms to her half-sisters. "Well, tell me goodbye."

"I hope you get killed out there," Tanis said nasally from behind the handkerchief pressed tightly against her nose. She stormed out of the room.

Izzara reacted to Mercedes' expression. "She didn't mean it. She's just mad. She says things when she's mad."

"Well, she better learn not to the first time she backtalks a drill instructor."

"Will they beat her up?" Izzara asked hopefully. Mercedes sighed.

She moved on to the twins' room and found more chaos. Only a year separated Delia and Dulcinea from Carisa so all three girls often played together and today was no exception. Unfortunately Mercedes walked in when the twins were being roundly scolded by Constanza.

"How dare you bring that ragged stray into the palace! Carisa is *highly* allergic."

"Mummy please, I like the kitten," Carisa whimpered. As usual she was a neurotic mess, shaking and crying.

Delia, clutching the unprepossessing kitten to her chest, looked defiant. Her twin was giving her worried, warning glances. The kitten, yellow eyes locked on Constanza, was emitting a low warning growl that occasionally crescendoed into a yowl.

"It's our cat and our rooms. You can't take him away," Delia yelled.

"Fine, then Carisa will no longer be playing with you."

"Mummy, noooo!"

"Carisa, come along!"

Dulcinea darted forward and clutched at Constanza's skirt. "No, please don't. We'll... we'll do what you want."

"No we won't!" Delia shouted and gave her twin a betrayed look.

"Constanza, wait," Mercedes said. She stepped in close to her stepmother. "There are treatments that can deal with cat allergies."

"For most ordinary people, but Carisa is highly sensitive."

Mercedes, her patience all but gone, snapped back, "Because you've made her that way."

Constanza glared at her. "When you're a mother you can give me advice. Otherwise, young lady, you can keep your opinions to yourself."

It was rather rich coming from a woman a mere six years older than herself, but Mercedes let it pass. Constanza gripped Carisa's hand harder and tugged.

"At least let me say goodbye to my sister," Mercedes said. She bent and hugged the nine-year-old and kissed Carisa on the cheek. "Bye, bye, sweetheart." To her consternation Carisa cried harder. "Cari, what's wrong?"

"You're going to die! Tanis says so."

"Tanis says a lot of silly things. Don't pay any attention."

Constanza swept them both out of the room. Dulcinea rounded on her sister. "Now you've done it. We'll never get to play with Carisa again."

"I don't care," Delia shot back and she kissed the kitten's ripped ear.

"Yes you do," Mercedes interrupted. "I'll talk to Daddy. We'll figure something out."

Delia frowned toward the door where Constanza had just exited. "Constanza hates spiders. I'm gonna put a whole bunch of them in her bed."

"You'll do no such thing," Mercedes said, trying to

sound stern. "Not if you want to keep this kitten. And are you taking lessons from Tanis on how to be naughty?"

"Tanis uses words," Dulcinea said. "I think that's worse."

It showed a level of understanding and sophistication that Mercedes hadn't expected. "It can be," Mercedes said. "But putting spiders in Constanza's bed would be pretty bad too."

The twins shared a look and giggled. "But fun," they said almost in unison.

"She never lets Cari have any fun," Dulcinea said sadly.

"We'll see what we can do about that too. I'm going to miss you," Mercedes added.

"Us too," came the duet.

"Now give me a hug, but put that wild cat down first. I don't think he likes me very much."

"He likes you. It's Constanza he hates," Delia said, but she did set the cat on her bed where he began to wash himself with that sublimely superior feline attitude.

As the girls hugged her, Mercedes reflected that they would be twelve by the time she returned. The thought left her with an ache in her heart.

If she had been looking for a calm and safe haven, Estella's bedroom turned out not to be the place. Mercedes found her usually placid sister crying over the body of Belle, her pet aria bird.

"Dinnea didn't latch the door tight after she cleaned her cage. Belle got out and she got scared when Dinnea tried to catch her and she flew into the window and broke her neck." The story emerged in explosive bursts interspersed with sobs.

Mercedes took the sad limp little body of the aria out of her sister's hands and gave the feathers a brush with her forefinger. In life the creature had been almost iridescent. Now the feathers were dull, the colors muted.

"I'm sorry, sweetie."

"I'm going to kill that pony!" Estella burst out. "Or at least make her buy me a new aria."

Mercedes considered the cost of one of the local song birds. It probably wouldn't set the Hajin maid back too much, maybe half a month's salary, but it wouldn't look good for a servant to be buying something for the very wealthy imperial daughter. Mercedes decided to find Dinnea and give her the money to replace the aria.

"You wash your face and take a lie down. I'll take care of Belle."

Estella nodded, gulped. "Okay."

Mercedes brushed back her sister's hair. "It's my last night home for a long time. I just want to be with my sisters."

Estella had found a pretty metal mesh box decorated with enamel flowers and twining leaves as a casket for the late lamented Belle. Mercedes had slipped money to Dinnea, and now was walking through the park looking for a place to bury the dead bird. A place where the ground was soft enough for her to dig with a stick. After the afternoon spent dealing with emotional outbursts, Mercedes' mood had soured and she was considering just chucking the corpse into a bush for the scavengers. But she knew Estella would probably ask about the avian funeral at dinner and they knew each other too well for Mercedes to successfully pull off a lie.

She realized she had been gone from the Phantasiestück Palace for hours, and wondered if Boho would be angry. She hoped he wasn't. She had wanted to see her sisters and a day spent not in bed with Boho had seemed attractive. Now that she had the sponge and spermicide she could be sanguine about his constant desire for sex, but it was becoming boring and she still didn't know what all the fuss was about. She shook her head trying to dislodge the thoughts and stepped off the path and into the trees looking for a stick and a burial site. There was a rustle in the bushes and she tensed. Her sister Beatrisa peeked out through the leaves.

"There you are. I wanted to say goodbye, but you weren't in your rooms," Mercedes said.

Beatrisa stepped from behind the screening bushes. She was dressed in too-big slacks that were tightly belted at the waist with the cuffs rolled up. Her half-sister rightly interpreted her expression and a defensive frown wrinkled her brow.

"What? You wear pants."

"Only when I'm in uniform," Mercedes said.

"Well if I'm going to be going to the High Ground I may as well get in practice."

Mercedes relaxed and gave a laugh. "Well, you've got a point."

Fourteen now, Beatrisa was tall and likely to get taller. Her black hair fell in tight curls to her shoulders and her pale golden-brown eyes set in her dark face reminded Mercedes of a cat. Beatrisa had always been a tomboy and apparently hadn't outgrown the tendency.

"I have a feeling you're the only one of my sisters who is happy about this."

"You'd be right," Beatrisa said. She sighed. "I hate that I have to wait four more years."

"Make use of them. Get your tutors to push math and the sciences. I had a terrible time trying to catch up on the STEM courses."

Beatrisa made a face, but then nodded. "Yeah, that's probably good advice. I'll do that. Whatcha got?" she asked with a nod toward the box.

"Estella's pet aria. It got loose and broke its neck. She wanted me to bury it."

"I'll help."

"Okay." They walked along in a companionable silence. Mercedes found an appropriate stick for grave digging and Beatrisa led her to a small pond where the surrounding soil was softer.

A hole was dug. Beatrisa dropped to her knees and used her hands to shove the dirt over the box.

"Do you play hooky often?" Mercedes asked.

"Yeah. As long as I'm there for lessons with my tutor nobody notices what I do."

"Now that can't be true. You're a royal daughter."

"Yeah, one of many useless royal daughters. Too young to get married. Too old to be cute." Bitterness laced the words. "Not that I want to get married."

"You might change your mind. I know it's hard to believe, but boys stop being yucky at a certain point."

"So you say. How's your boy?"

"Pretty wonderful."

Beatrice gave her a shrewd look. "So why do you sound like you're convincing yourself?"

"And when did you get to be such a smart aleck?"

"Like… forever."

Mercedes gave her a hug. "I love you, Bea, you're the only person who hasn't cried at me today."

Her younger sister made a rude noise.

10

THE MONSTERS IN THE DARK

"Where have you been?" Boho tried to make it sound casual, but Mercedes heard the small thread of annoyance.

He was seated in the bay window of the morning room with its view of the treble-clef-shaped fountain outside. He set aside his tap-pad. Mercedes had a quick glimpse of the marauder game before the screen went dark.

"Hoping for some private, quality time with the sisters. Didn't exactly work out as planned." She shook her head and sighed… "I can't believe we leave tomorrow."

"Yeah, me neither."

"You seem upset," Mercedes said.

"Not upset. Worried."

"About?" She joined him on the window seat.

"That maybe we shouldn't have indulged quite so often. I'd—"

"And whose fault was that?" Mercedes demanded.

"Oh, mine. I accept all the blame." He gave her his roguish smile. "I just couldn't help myself because you are beautiful and sexy and generally magnificent and you drive me mad." He punctuated each compliment with a kiss and Mercedes giggled. "Anyway, I would hate for us to get out to the ship and discover..." His voice trailed away. "I was thinking maybe we should make sure you're not pregnant before we leave. The surgeon general does recommend that pregnant women avoid the Fold as much as possible."

He gave her a smile that their arms instructor Chief Begay would have described as shit-eating, reached into his pocket and pulled out a home pregnancy test kit. Mercedes felt a twist of guilt. There was no chance she was pregnant, but he couldn't know that. She took the box and smiled at him.

"Good thinking. Be right back."

"I'll come with you. This is going to be... well, a special moment." She obediently followed the instructions on the box while Boho looked on. "It's really going to be hard to leave you tomorrow," he continued. "I'll miss you so much. I don't know how I'll stand it."

Their heads were together, bent over the stick. Boho had a look of smug anticipation. A red minus sign appeared on the stick. The smug expression vanished and Boho leaned back with a huff that was part surprise and part annoyance. Mercedes noted that Boho wasn't nearly as handsome when he was frowning.

"Looks like you won't have to find out, darling," she said.

As family dinners went this one was a ten on the horrible scale, though Mercedes did notice that the meal had been all of her favorite foods, beginning with lobster bisque, a delicate caprese salad, crab legs, creamed spinach, crispy shoestring potatoes, and concluding with a chocolate lava cake. Judging by the glares Constanza was sending her way, it hadn't been her stepmother who had set the menu. As for the rest of the family: Tanis's nose was swollen from Mercedes' blow; Julieta had transferred her glares from Mercedes to the Emperor; Estella was looking forlorn; Delia was glaring at Constanza; Carisa was sniveling; Dulcinea was darting glances all around the table and then would go back to staring at her plate and playing with her food. And Boho was sulking. Mercedes assumed it was because she wasn't pregnant. Only Beatrisa seemed impervious to all the emotional turmoil around her. She ate with happy abandon.

Her father was pretending to be completely unaware of all the tension, or maybe he really was unaware. He kept up a constant flow of conversation, and didn't seem to mind it was a monologue. As the servants cleared the cake plates and brought out the port and cheese the Emperor leaned back in his chair, beamed at them all and said, "Well, this was lovely dining *en familia*. We need to do it more often." He placed his hands on the arms of his chair and a Hajin footman rushed forward to pull out the chair. The Emperor stood. He smiled down at Mercedes. "I can't believe you leave tomorrow. Perhaps I should talk to the joint chiefs about making it a two-year tour rather than five."

"Remember, Daddy, no unicorns," Mercedes said, her voice catching on a laugh.

"All right. I won't pull rank just to get my girl home sooner."

"Oh, Daddy, won't you come and play Lego Heroes with us," Delia wheedled.

He tousled her hair. "I'd love to, sweetheart, but I've got some work to finish. Mercedes, Boho, will you join me?"

Another footman had her chair pulled out almost before Mercedes had processed the request. Boho stood up, wiped his mouth and tossed the napkin onto the table.

They followed him from the family wing to his office. Once inside the Emperor began activating security measures. Shutters fell across the windows, a low buzz showed that electronic countermeasures were in place. Mercedes and Boho exchanged glances. The readout over his desk projected several pages of a complex tax return. One side held Arabic numerals, the other the strange symbols that the Tiponi Flutes used.

"Have the Flutes emptied the treasury, we're broke and you don't want the citizens to know?" Boho quipped.

"Oh, this." With a sweep of the hand her father closed the file. "Just some tax figures from Xinoxex. I know the Flutes are supposed to be master mathematicians, but trying to make head or tail…" He shook his head. "Sorry. Unimportant."

The Emperor sighed, ran a hand through his hair and settled into his desk chair. "This is highly classified," he said.

"I sort of got that idea, Daddy," Mercedes said.

"You had asked why Rohan and I forced female service in the armed forces." He tapped his ScoopRing and a hologram appeared in the air over his desk. It showed a section of the Milky Way far out on the reaches of the galaxy. Next to it was a list of ships—nine of them—a crew roster, and next to each entry was the terse appellation—*lost.*

"Sector 470," her father said. "The first ship lost was a scientific survey vessel doing research on dark matter. It was actually going to leave the galaxy to run experiments. We sent a scout to search for them thinking it was a Foldstream communication failure. The scout vanished. The next three were small, fast and armed *exploradors*. Again all lost without getting out a message or distress beacon. We followed up with a frigate. Same result."

"Why did you keep sending in one lone ship after another? Why not a fleet or at least a squadron?" Mercedes asked, hoping it didn't come across as too accusatory.

"We did after we lost the *Nasiriyeh*. We sent a three-ship squadron. They were lost as well."

Mercedes' finger brushed through the name, *Nasiriyeh.* "Commander Zeng was assigned to that ship."

"Yes."

"That's what you meant when you said he'd been sent on a dangerous mission. You knew he'd most likely die or at least vanish."

"Yes."

Boho's head was swinging back and forth between them. "What? Wait, I thought Zeng was promoted. That's why he left the High Ground."

"Oh, he was promoted. Right to heaven," Mercedes said dully.

"He was part of the plot against you. Wow." Boho shook his head then looked approvingly at his father-in-law. "Well done, sir. The actual facts stay hidden, but the message was sent and received for any others who might be thinking about making a move against the throne."

The two men in front of her suddenly morphed into one and Mercedes wasn't sure she liked either of them. "There were one hundred and twenty-four other men on that ship," Mercedes whispered through stiff lips.

"Yes. I regretted that," the Emperor said.

"You could have just executed Zeng," Mercedes countered.

"No, he couldn't," Boho interrupted. "I just explained that to you." There was a sudden sharp pain. Mercedes uncoiled her clenched fingers. Her nails had left imprints in the skin of her palms. "If he had it would reveal the true nature of the plot against you."

"The military could not be implicated—" her father said.

"Even though they were!"

"This was cleaner."

"Your father's right. If there had been a trial who knows what Zeng or the others might have said."

"It's still murder," Mercedes whispered.

The men's eyes met. "Don't worry, sir," Boho said. "I'll help her."

That snapped Mercedes' control. "I don't need to be *handled*! I understand I have to be a military leader and that in war there are casualties. This was different and if the two of you can't see that… well, that disturbs me."

"Once you're in my position you'll understand. There's not a lot of room for idealism. Now can we get back to this?" Her father brushed a hand through the image. "Bottom line we don't know what's out there. So we're preparing for any eventuality."

"By not figuring out what's out there?" Mercedes snapped.

"We can't lose any more ships. It became increasingly difficult to hide the losses from the press, the rest of O-Trell and the crewmen's families."

"Have we tried drones?" Mercedes asked.

"Same result. They never report back."

A hard knot formed in the pit of her stomach. There was something in the darkness that killed ships. And she was about to serve on a ship. "So we're pursuing a defensive strategy."

"For now."

"Smart," Boho said. "Build up our forces with women."

"You think it's an unknown alien race?" Mercedes asked.

"That or some unknown and deadly space phenomenon. Neither makes me very happy." The Emperor paused, frowning off into space. "And of course the third option— that it's the Cara'ot. They were the last of the aliens to be subdued and the most technologically advanced. They could be building a massive weapon out there."

"I assume SEGU has been watching for Cara'ot activity on the edges of that sector?" Mercedes asked.

"Yes, to no effect," her father answered.

"The last great battle between us and the Cara'ot was almost two hundred years ago. If they had a weapon that could destroy a ship before it can even issue a mayday don't you think they'd have used it by now?" Boho asked.

"I think they're aliens and therefore, ultimately, inexplicable to us."

"So we've closed the closet door and we're not looking under the bed. That's our strategy?" Mercedes asked.

"For now. There are plenty of other areas where we can advance. For now Sector 470 and all adjacent sectors are off limits." He gave her a level look. "Unless we find ourselves in need of it again."

"Yes, I suppose it is a convenient place to hide the bodies," Mercedes said, her tone waspish.

"It's one of the consequences of rule—there will always be bodies." The Emperor ran a hand across his face, and shut down the holo. "Perhaps it would be better if there had been a real hot war in the past hundred years. I fear we have become complacent."

The security shutters whined back into their slots and sunlight danced off dust motes, echoes of the stars from the holo. The buzz of the electronic countermeasures ceased, to be replaced by birdsong. Mercedes shivered.

An alarm was blaring through the corridors of the battle cruiser *Triunfo* and the robotic voice of the computer was intoning, *"Hull breach. Hull breach."* Tracy came out of his bunk as if he'd been catapulted. He had once again fallen into bed at 4:10 a.m., exhausted from having been on duty from midnight until four. He had been doing this for twelve days despite the rule that he should have been rotated off the middle watch. It was a flagrant violation of the rules by his immediate superior, Captain-Lieutenant Lord Karl Westley, but no one higher in the food chain had noticed so Tracy continued to be on duty in Weapons night after night after night.

The three men he bunked with also made certain he snatched only a few hours of sleep. Lieutenants Gupta, Eklund and Bellard continually rousted him out of bed for breakfast despite the fact he'd had not quite three hours of sleep. Because they outranked him he had no choice but to comply. Three nights ago he'd gotten no sleep because he'd returned to his quarters to find all his toiletries broken and strewn onto the floor of their bathroom. He had been ordered to personally clean up the mess rather than turning to his batBEM before he hit the rack. It was stupid, juvenile behavior not even worthy of high-school bullying, but lodging a complaint was not an option.

If it had just been Gupta and Eklund, an uneasy balance might have been achieved, but Bellard had thrown in with Eklund. Cold shoulders and contempt were nothing new to Tracy. He could have ignored that and gone on, but Eklund and Bellard escalated and Gupta went along. An easier choice than defending the *intitulado*.

His bunkmates were throwing on battle dress, lacing up their boots. It was a bit past five a.m. Tracy turned to his wardrobe to discover his utility uniform wasn't hung there. *"Report to battle stations,"* the robot voice continued.

Eklund smirked at him as he headed for the door. "I had my BEM fold it and put it in your footlocker." Tracy, sick with anger and exhaustion, leaped to his locker and yanked up the lid. He tossed underwear, socks and T-shirts onto the floor scrabbling for his clothes. His utility dress was at the very bottom.

Gupta loudly cleared his throat and looked pointedly at

the chronometer woven into the sleeve of his uniform. "Out of time, J.G. Hop to it!" He left.

Tracy had no choice but to gallop into the corridor dressed only in his underpants. The emergency equipment locker was just outside their quarters. His three bunkmates were already pulling on their rebreathers. Tracy pushed past them. The fourth mask was not inside.

"Where is it? What did you do with it?" Tracy yelled.

"Watch your tone, J.G.," Bellard snapped. "I guess the *hombre* servicing this locker thought there were only three officers in this block."

"He'd be right," Gupta sniggered. "There are only three *actual* officers."

Their laughter was muffled behind their masks. Slapping each other on the shoulders they headed off to their respective posts. Tracy was going to arrive at Weapons without his proper kit and dressed in his briefs and nothing else. Or he could dress, be late and not have his proper kit. It was going to be a shit storm either way. He was damned if he was going to face it dressed only in his shorts. He returned to his room to dress.

Frowning, the drill inspector marked down *belated response and insufficient kit* as Tracy entered Weapons. The captain-lieutenant on the morning watch took a look at Tracy's bare face, and said tightly, "You're dead. Get out of here." The words were muffled by his emergency breather.

The dismissal meant Tracy wasn't even able to offset

those failures by performing well. It also meant the entire fire team was operating a man down so their performance wasn't going to be stellar either. There were more than a few mutters and glares directed at Tracy as he left the Weapons deck.

Tracy headed back to his quarters. His clothing was strewn across the floor and that was going to earn him another reprimand if he didn't get it cleaned up. On his way his ScoopRing pricked his finger. He keyed the message and received the news that he would be receiving a letter of admonition that would go into his permanent file. Another message arrived informing him he would pull extra duty as punishment. As if the admonition wasn't punishment enough.

The door slid open and Tracy was met with a barrage of sound. He recognized Caratolian, but despite the lilting quality of the language it was clear Donnel was cursing. The batBEM was already hard at work folding the clothes and repacking Tracy's footlocker.

"Interesting how even in Caratolian a person can recognize cussing," Tracy said. He pinched the bridge of his nose and tried to push back the bone-deep exhaustion. Tracy sat wearily on the edge of his bunk.

"Yeah. A beautiful and complex language. Far beyond the ability of humans to grasp, much less master," Donnel shot back.

When Tracy didn't rise to the barb Donnel said gently, "You should grab some sleep."

"Can't. Extra duty. I get to inventory every emergency locker on the ship."

"Pricks!" the batBEM snarled. "This is *not* going to

happen again. And I'm going to see to it you have something better than those piece-of-shit rebreathers."

"And if I'm wearing something other than standard issue I'll get busted for that too. So please, don't be helpful."

"Oh not for these pissant drills. No, I mean when it really counts. When… if this ship ever comes under attack. Those ass wipes can choke."

Tracy rocketed to his feet, and slapped the Cara'ot hard across the face and kicked two of the three legs out from under him. Donnel fell over. "*Never* speak of a human that way again. Especially not a human officer in the *Orden de la Estrella*." Tracy had to control himself not to kick the crumpled alien again.

Donnel regained his feet. The absurdly round head drooped, and the four eyes swiveled to the floor. "Your pardon, sir. I was out of line. It was merely my concern for my master that led to my intemperate words."

Tracy didn't dignify the overly obsequious words with a reply. He left to fulfill his extra duty. With luck his anger-fueled energy would sustain him through the day. And there was always O-Trell's notoriously horrible coffee.

11

AGAINST INFINITY

I'm a glorified telephone operator, Mercedes thought as she sat on the hushed but still bustling bridge of the *Nuestra Señora de la Concepción*. Admiral Mustafa Kartirci, Duque de Monsarat, was seated in his command chair. He was silver-haired, his face a net of wrinkles. He was also a legend in the fleet and an inspiration to his crew. That was about all he did—inspire.

Most of the actual work of commanding the enormous flagship fell to his flag captain, Lord Carl Vink, a thin, intense man with eerie yellowish-brown eyes set in a round face. It was an odd juxtaposition on a man so spare. He was also bald as an egg. Vink was known to be tough and not particularly fair. He did not approve of Mercedes, so despite her evident skills in the *Infierno* she had been assigned to Communications. On the bridge she routed messages to the command podium and scanned the welter of messages arriving at the ship and flying between the decks and the crew. Every other week she cycled down to the *Infierno* bay where she directed traffic and stayed in touch with the men flying the fighters. None of whom were as good as her.

She was bored, angry and jealous of her spouse who was getting to fly.

Vink directed an order to the lieutenant at Navigation. "Prepare for translation."

"Preparing for translation, aye, sir," the lieutenant repeated.

The warning was echoed through the massive ship. Mercedes checked her couch restraints. The dirty grey wool outside the view screen vanished, there was the inside-out feeling and they were in normal space, which actually wasn't all that normal. For the system they'd just entered was clearly a young system being riven by violent forces.

They were on the edges of a protoplanetary disk. Formation was far enough along that a lot of the gas and dust were gone and three gas giants had managed to form. They were striving for primacy as they tried to negotiate their orbits. The rest of the material had begun to coalesce into rocky planetesimals though there was still a lot of material occluding the visual view. At this distance the system's star was a white-hot ember.

One gas giant was misshapen as if a bite had been taken out of its side. Another showed jagged red lines where impact forces had released some of its molten core. The hydrogen in the atmosphere was starting to burn. It appeared there had been a recent (in terms of system formation time) collision between two of the planets. The third, smaller giant had been left unscathed for now. There was a welter of moonlets being tugged to and fro by the gravitational forces of the three massive worlds.

Now that they were out of Fold, Mercedes had a flurry of messages to comb through, finding the ones that needed to be sent to Monsarat or Vink right away. As she prioritized messages and sent them over she listened to the chatter from various decks and the discussions on the bridge. Scans were being run, readings taken, planets charted to see if there was anything useful or of interest on or around any of the fifteen proto-planets orbiting this white-hot star. What was clear was that there was no Goldilocks world. Any planet that wasn't a gaseous ball was a slowly accreting ball of rock.

"Radiation off these giants is playing hell with our sensors. Not to mention the gravitational forces and magnetic fields," she heard Vink tell the admiral.

"I doubt there is any danger, Carl, apart from the vagaries of this system. We'll take our measurements and move on."

Unless an officer was on a private channel, Mercedes got to hear and monitor all communications to and from the bridge so she heard when Commander Lord Lewis requested permission to send out the *Infierno* pilots for a drill.

"Dangerous with these tricky conditions," the admiral said.

"It'll be good for them," Vink countered. "Most of the time they may as well be delivering mail."

"Exactly," Lewis said. "Let's shake them up a bit."

"You're not going to risk them all," Kartirci warned.

"No, sir. We'll send them out in two groups."

"Very well then," Kartirci said. The order to the pilots went out to report to their fighters.

Mercedes' relief arrived as she was sending a handful of

messages down to the autocrat who ruled engineering. Gelb had been two years ahead of her at the High Ground. His father was a mere caballero so Gelb wasn't getting a lot of attention. Two years on and he was still a lieutenant. They both felt stymied, which had created a sense of camaraderie. Mercedes stood, they saluted each other and she handed over the headphone.

"Anything pressing?" Gelb asked.

"No, just the usual."

"What are you up to?"

"I should go to the gym, but I think I'll go watch the fun from the launch deck," Mercedes replied.

"Torture yourself, you mean," Gelb said with a smile. The downward-curving dueling scar on his chin set an odd counterpoint to his upturned lips as if he wore a comedy/ tragedy mask.

"A little of that."

Gelb took her chair and she moved to the command podium to salute the admiral and flag captain. "Lieutenant Princess Arango requesting permission to leave the bridge."

"Granted." Kartirci gave her an indulgent, grandfatherly smile. Vink gave her a tight nod, his lips set in a thin line.

Various *hombres* and officers got on and off the lift as it moved through the decks. It still felt strange to receive a salute. She was used to giving crisp salutes and getting back rather dilatory salutes from superior officers. To have ordinary star men snapping to attention was almost embarrassing. Especially since she was a mere lieutenant. Though to be fair she was also the heir to the Solar League so that was probably part of the reason for all the spit and polish.

Eventually all the other officers were gone as they descended to the bowels of the ship. The two young *hombres* and a *fusilero* pressed themselves against the walls of the lift. There were surreptitious glances, elbows dug into sides, head ducking when she would manage to catch an eye, and outright blushes when she smiled.

"So, crazy solar system, huh?" she said, trying to put them at ease.

It didn't work. They all snapped to attention again, saluted and said, "Yes, ma'am." One of them slipped and said "sir" which earned him a fist slug on the shoulder and a glare from his companion.

Woman and princess aboard a ship of war. No matter what I do I'm a unicorn. Will that change when women become more commonplace?

"Be at ease," she said to them all, and then said to the blushing S-1 who had called her sir, "It's okay. I know this is confusing." That made him blush all the harder.

The *hombres* bolted when they reached their deck, and Mercedes was left with only the *fusilero* who, emboldened by her deigning to speak to them, explained how he was heading to the armory because the targeting system on his rifle was on the fritz and he needed to get it either fixed or replaced.

She made sympathetic noises and then they arrived at the lowest deck. The *fusilero* went left toward the armory and the virtual range and Mercedes turned right toward the *Infierno* launch deck. As she was walking there was a lurch and Mercedes found herself heavy enough to make her ankles ache for a second or two, followed by a flash of weightlessness.

"Whoa!" She grabbed for a handhold. Vink's voice came over the intercom. *"Personnel be advised that the gravitational forces have briefly affected our artificial gravity systems."*

"Well duh," Mercedes muttered.

"Engineering is recalibrating to account for these forces and there should be no more fluctuations, but be alert and exercise caution."

Exercising due caution Mercedes slipped through the doors of the launch deck. Pilots were donning their battle armor. Commander Lewis was talking with Captain-Lieutenant Lord Novek who commanded first squadron. Mercedes scanned the crowd for Boho and found him checking the seals on his battle armor, in particular the pressure webbing that would keep blood from pooling in his legs when pulling high gees. Her husband didn't look happy.

He was standing with the third-year ensign Caballero Jace Turner, who was doing his fleet rotation aboard the *Concepción*. He should have done his rotation with the rest of their class the past fall, but a drug-resistant case of Markham's disease had sent him first to the hospital and then home to recuperate after the Isanjo virus had run its course. It wasn't common for a human to catch an alien bug, but Jace had been unlucky. Which was sort of his M.O. If some outlandish accident was going to happen it would happen to Jace. Right now his cheeks were as red as his hair and he looked both excited and scared.

Commander Lord Lewis broke off talking with Novek, walked over to Boho and Turner. Mercedes arrived just as he said, "I'm pairing you with Turner, Lieutenant. Ride shotgun with him and keep him safe."

"Yes, sir," Boho said. "Begging the Commander's indulgence... perhaps this is a bit too tricky for a third year."

"Begging the Consort's indulgence, but that's why I'm pairing him with you. You're one of our best."

Not true, Mercedes thought, *I am*, but of course she didn't say it. Lewis moved away, Jace went to his fighter, and Mercedes went to her husband. She went on tiptoes and kissed his cheek. The frown didn't ease.

"This is nuts," Boho grumbled.

"I think it looks like fun."

"Oh yeah, just tons of fun. Fuck up and fall into the gravity well of one of these giants, get crushed into paste. Real fun."

"So don't fuck up," she said lightly.

"Wow, that's helpful!" he replied.

Mercedes took a step back, both hurt and angry. "I was just teasing."

"Well don't!"

"You're really worried."

"Yeah, I am."

"You're a terrific pilot."

"With an anvil tied to my ankle," he said with a jerk of his chin toward Jace. "And it won't matter how good I am if the magnetic fields fry our electronics. We become just another piece of detritus to get sucked in by one of the planets."

"That won't happen. The shielding on the fighters is too good. And as for Jace, you're good enough for the both of you," she said soothingly.

He forced a smile. "I'm sorry. I didn't mean to snap at you. Jack me in?"

"With pleasure."

They moved to his fighter and climbed the sloping sides of the saucer. Boho dropped down into the cockpit and closed his helmet. Mercedes laid down on the skin of the craft and plugged his helmet into the fighter's control panel. The gimbaled couch molded to Boho's body ready to read even minute muscle movement. She patted the top of his helmet and slithered down off the *Infierno*.

The ground crew, Lewis, and Mercedes retreated from the launch deck. Lewis turned to her. "I know you're off duty, but would you like to run on ops for this drill?"

"Yes, sir."

They entered the control room. Lewis tapped one of the controllers on the shoulder and indicated for him to move. Mercedes took the chair, slipped on her headphone and eyepiece that would enable her to shift between cameras both in the pilots' helmets and in the cockpits of the different *Infiernos*. It was a pale semblance of flying, but it was something.

On the launch deck the giant bay doors finished their ponderous slide. The view outside showed a quarter of one planet, the bands of color like a mad artist's palette. Beyond it to the left was the burning world. The wounded planet was out of view on the other side of the *Concepción*. Mercedes pulled up a hologram so she could see all three worlds, their eighty-plus tiny moons that they traded back and forth like square dancers in an elaborate do-si-do. The fighters showed as tiny sparks, lightning bugs against infinity.

She brought up an overlay of gravitational fields. The path for the fighters was a narrow one. She next added a layer for the magnetic fields. She was starting to be glad she wasn't flying this particular drill. A final layer detailed the rocks they had managed to locate using the ship's sensors. There was no way they had tracked all of them.

The holo was a kaleidoscope of intersecting and twisting lines and colors. Her fingers flew across the keyboard calculating safe routes for the fighters. She adjusted the colors so the flight paths were a heavy red line. A hand squeezed her shoulder, startling her. She had been concentrating so deeply she hadn't heard Lewis's approach.

"Good work, Lieutenant Princess. Send it."

"Yes, sir." Mercedes sent the image and her calculations to the fighters.

"Well… fuck." Novek's voice coming in over the radio.

Like most disasters it came suddenly and without warning. A large rock struck Lieutenant Milán's *Infierno*. He overcompensated and threw the fighter into a tumble. Mercedes heard Jace yell excitedly, "I'll get him."

Boho's frantic order, "No! Wait!"

"I can nudge him," the ensign replied.

"Let him try," Novek ordered.

Mercedes switched to monitor Jace's helmet. "Jace, you're coming in too hot!" she said. "Give Milán a chance to right himself."

But her warning came too late. Milán did manage to regain control, which Jace had not expected. His fighter skidded across the edge of the other *Infierno*, which sent Jace caroming off in an unexpected direction and directly into the pull of the battered giant. He was burning his engines in a desperate attempt to escape but it wasn't working.

Lewis grabbed up a headphone. "Cullen, get in there. With both engines you can pull him out."

"It won't work. We don't have enough thrust," Boho yelled.

Lewis glanced over at Mercedes who was running frantic calculations. "He's right."

"Very well—" Lewis began, but Mercedes interrupted.

"There is a way. If they fire their slugs in concert and at the right moment it will add enough thrust to break them free. But it would take both fighters."

"And if you're wrong we lose two ships and two pilots," Lewis said.

"I'm not comfortable with this," Boho said. Mercedes had a sudden uncomfortable memory of Tracy saying something hateful when he received the news that she would marry Boho. *He's a coward.*

"It's all right." Jace sounded young and frightened, but determined. "My mistake. I'm the only one who should have to pay for it."

"You're a brave man, Jace," Boho said, and there was something about the remark that just infuriated Mercedes.

She stood and ripped off the headphone. Lewis misinterpreted her action. "Yes, Princess, you shouldn't have to see this." Condescending, sympathetic. Mercedes wanted to slap him.

She left the control room, went to her locker and donned her battle armor. She was trying to go fast so of course it made her clumsy. It seemed to be taking forever even though only a few minutes had elapsed. Once armored and helmeted she raced onto the launch deck and climbed into a fighter. The pilots of second squadron stared at her. The lieutenant assigned to the *Infierno* she'd commandeered gaped at her.

"Well, don't stand there. Jack me in!"

"Ma'am, I don't think—"

"I am the Infanta. That is one of *my* subjects out there and a fellow officer. *Do it!*"

He did. "Clear the deck and launch," she ordered the others.

They clattered off the deck and the bay doors began to open. Lewis had been too involved with the unfolding crisis to notice. Until now. "Who authorized a launch?" he howled.

"I did, sir," Mercedes replied and she launched even though the doors weren't fully open.

12

HEROICS AND HYSTERICS

"Lieutenant Princess, I order you—"

She tipped the *Infierno* so it was flying edge-on and shot through the door. She locked in on Jace's signal and opened up the throttle. She was pulling close to eight gees, and for a moment her vision greyed out. She reversed thrust to slow down her speed and began running calculations.

"Jace, I'm going to link with you using the hooks on the tops of our fighters."

"Hi… Highness?"

"Mercedes, what the *hell* are you doing!" Boho's voice was practically a howl.

What you should be! But that wasn't what she said. She tempered it. "What has to be done."

She was now in the grasp of the planet. She glanced between her readouts. They only had bare minutes to link, burn engines and time the firing of the slugs to catapult them out of the gravity well. She flipped the *Infierno*. She had long ago lost all sensitivity to vertigo and nausea. She lined up with the other fighter and dropped onto it. It took two tries before she managed to hook one of the lift hooks on her fighter with the hook on the other craft. Their canopies were kissing. Jace looked up, his face twisted with fear and hope behind the faceplate of his helmet. She gave him what she hoped was an encouraging smile.

"Okay, Jace, I'm sending over the calculation for firing the slugs. Program it in. You'll probably lose consciousness because we need full burn."

"O… okay."

"Ready?"

"Yes."

"In four, three, two, one…" A giant hand pressed down on her chest. Her vision narrowed to a mere tunnel, the lights on the control panel seemed very far away. She faintly heard Commander Lewis bellow, "What the fuck is that?"

An alarm was screaming though it sounded muffled. Her neck seemed to have turned to iron, and her head weighed a thousand pounds. She managed to move it slightly though she felt something pop. She shifted her eyes side to side. A mass of lights and shadow loomed below them. It was a ship. A massive ship.

Captain Vink is going to be so *pissed that we missed this*, she thought.

A sharp vibration passed through her fighter and then they were being pulled into a dark cave. Mercedes passed out.

When consciousness returned she realized her neck was a column of pain and her head was throbbing. She was lying on a foam couch inside a translucent envo-pod, her helmet next to her. Another bubble held Jace, who was still unconscious. Outside enormous shadowy forms seemed to swim or fly through thick green-tinted atmosphere.

One of the shadows drew close and resolved into a creature with a ten-foot wingspan. There were six-fingered hands at the tip of the wings and hands where there should be feet. It had a long proboscis instead of a nose and huge oval eyes. The monstrosity was smiling. Mercedes tried to sit up.

"Be at peace. You are well and safe. You are aboard the *Wealth Maker*."

"You're Cara'ot."

"Yes, Princess."

"You know who I am?"

"Of course. Cara watch the news too. Cara have programmed this deck for gravity appropriate for your bodies and placed you in pods with an oxygen/nitrogen mix. Your ship has been informed that Cara have you."

That's right, Mercedes thought. *They don't use pronouns or possessives since both gender and form are so mutable with the aliens.*

"What are you doing here?" she asked.

"Harvesting. It's often easier in these proto-systems."

Mercedes lay back down. "Thank you."

"Cara pleasure."

She had to ask. "Would we have made it?"

"Probably. Your plan was a good one, but Cara feared a random element might have upset the balance so Cara," the mouth stretched into an even wider smile, "thought Cara would give you a lift."

"Thank you. Our craft?"

"Undamaged. Once your companion regains consciousness you will be able to fly triumphantly back to your ship and receive their congratulations."

"Yeah, that's probably not how it's going to go," Mercedes said wryly.

The creature's long wings gave a lazy flap. "This ship also carries trade goods. We would be happy to arrange a showing of our products to your crew."

"Thank you, I'll pass that on." She could only imagine how well that would go over. On the other hand it might distract the brass from her transgression.

Mercedes stood at attention while a torrent of words washed over her. Lewis and Vink were taking turns delivering the tongue lashing. A word or phrase would occasionally pop out but overall it was just an angry drone that made her pounding headache even worse. *Outrageous! Insubordinate! Willfully disobedient! Anyone but you… cashiered!*

"On the other hand," Lewis said, and Mercedes decided she better start paying attention. "Anyone who can fly like that needs to be… well, flying." Mercedes risked a glance at Vink. He looked like a man who'd bitten into a rotten lemon. "The admiral agrees. You're in command of second squadron."

Mercedes staggered a bit. Just getting to fly would have been enough. She started to smile, but another look at Vink made her decide against it. She braced even harder and snapped off a salute. "Thank you, sir. I'll try to live up to your confidence in me."

Vink gave a snort of disgust. "Don't think it's all perks, Lieutenant Princess. You've still earned an admonition for this."

"I understand, sir."

"And I want you to report to medical for a full exam," Vink ordered.

"I'm fine, sir, really. Just a high-gee headache."

"You were unconscious on that ship. God knows what those devils might have done to you," Vink said.

"I'm not sure I understand, sir."

"They corrupt nature at its most basic level. They could have done something to you that might affect your offspring. Do it!"

"Yes, sir," Mercedes said, but she was talking to his back as he left.

Lewis sagged. "Whew. Thought he'd never leave."

Emboldened by the informality of the statement Mercedes said, "Love how he was so concerned about my unborn children, but he wasn't terribly concerned about me."

"He lost family in the last battle."

"That was almost two hundred years ago."

"Some people can hold a grudge."

Mercedes remembered her history classes: Lord Trent Crispin's lecture on the American Civil War and how it hadn't really ended in the hearts and minds of some people until humans made contact with aliens. At that point superficial racial differences had suddenly seemed unimportant.

"You get on to medical," Lewis said. "And after... well...

I'd find your husband." His look was significant.

"Uh… right. I will." She paused at the door. "Oh, one more thing. The Cara'ot said that while they're mostly a harvesting vessel they are carrying some goods. If we wanted to shop."

Lewis pressed a hand against his forehead. "I'm *really* glad you didn't say that in front of Captain Vink. His head would have exploded. I'll tell Communications to quietly and politely decline."

"I can do it."

"No you can't. You're no longer a comm officer."

"Oh right." And Mercedes knew she had a foolish grin.

"I didn't do it to show you up!"

"Then why did you do it?" Boho demanded. He had a thunderous frown and he seemed to loom over her.

"So Jace wouldn't die!"

They were in their quarters. Quarters that had once belonged to Commander Riley, the requisition officer now forced to share quarters with Commander Lord Le Blanque who led the *fusileros*. Neither of the officers were very happy, but the princess and her consort were to take precedence even though they were lowly lieutenants.

"Sometimes sacrifices have to be made."

"Just as long as *you're* not the one making it!" Mercedes flared. Something flickered deep in those green eyes and Mercedes was seized by guilt. "I'm sorry. I didn't mean… I just wish you'd let me talk you through the maneuver. You could have easily done it. And it turned out to be moot anyway. The Cara'ot ship was there."

"Which has Vink's shorts in a bunch, let me tell you," Boho grunted. "He's been roaring through the ship calling snap inspections and drills on sensors and weapons. Said we should have spotted that Cara'ot ship."

"Yeah, he made me go to medical for a full physical. That's why I didn't come to you right away."

He clutched her close. "Physical? You're all right, aren't you?"

"I'm fine. Paranoia on the part of Vink. Dr. Donato practically took out my teeth so he could inspect them."

That won a small smile. Mercedes studied his face. The overt anger was gone, but there was a tension in his jaw, the set of his shoulders. She ran her fingers down his cheek.

Keeping her tone light and flirtatious she slipped her hand inside the jacket of his utility uniform and said, "I think we just had our first fight." She glanced up at him from beneath her lashes. "What do you say to a little make-up sex? I hear it can be wonderful."

He clasped her hands tightly and leered down at her. "I'd love to find out."

Mercedes retreated to the tiny head, doused the sponge with spermicide and inserted it. She touched the extra bottles she had obtained from the Candy Box just before she left. She thought she had enough to last through her tour. If not there were always whorehouses on frontier worlds. They would probably have what she needed. Mercedes felt terribly manipulative, but maybe that was what wives had to do to keep the peace? She figured she would wait until after they made love to tell Boho that not only was she going to be flying, but she was now a squadron leader.

After sex they were hot and sweaty, but showering together was not an option in the tiny bathroom. Boho let Mercedes go first while he scrolled through his tap-pad. She glanced back at him as he sprawled on the narrow bunk shamelessly naked, one knee up.

Cleaned up and dressed they emerged to discover that the admiral had overruled Lewis and the Cara'ot had come aboard with a selection of goods. They joined the parade of officers heading down to the shuttle deck. No enlisted personnel were among them, which wasn't surprising. The Cara'ot specialized in the rare and exotic and would have nothing that an *hombre* could afford.

Mercedes had been in an envo-pod on the Cara'ot ship. Here the aliens were encased in much larger ones, like floating snow globes filled with poisonous air and shadowy forms partially obscured by the viscous green atmosphere. Tables of clear Lucite had been set up between the boxy shuttle craft. Black velvet cloth, artistically rumpled to create fabric frames, displayed the wares. Mercedes noticed that the tables weren't cluttered with goods for sale. Instead they held only a few items arranged for maximum impact. Jewelry designed to grace a human woman's neck or arms or ears glittered on the first table. Another held enamel and gold Tiponi Flute icons and Sidone spider weavings. Another offered perfumes in graceful twisting glass bottles, creams and unguents, and rare liquors. The bottles alone were works of art. The final table held weapons. Mercedes saw the boot knife that Tracy had given her two years ago at Christmas. There were dueling rapiers and sabers with exquisite filigreed grips. Boho headed straight for them.

The admiral was talking with a Cara'ot inside one of the pods. He was chuckling, nodding. The chief engineer was in conversation with another alien. He was leaning in so close that he almost had his face pressed up against the side of the pod. Mercedes was sure he wanted to know how the Cara'ot ship could maneuver so easily in this gravitation vortex.

Mercedes moved to a table and examined the jewelry, thinking she could find Christmas gifts for her sisters among the shimmering display. She made her selections and pressed her ring against the reader. Reals were transferred and her purchases whisked away to be boxed and wrapped.

"If Highness will permit, this pin would suit her." A waldo hand folded off the pod. It was holding what appeared to be tiny stars caught in a net of silver threads.

She couldn't control it, Mercedes gasped. "What are they?"

"Phantasm gems."

"I've never seen clear ones before."

"They are very rare. Only one in ten thousand Scalewings produce the clear ones."

Mercedes studied the number of glittering gems and did a rough calculation of how many flying lizards had given up their gizzards to create this pin. "I don't even want to ask how much it is," she murmured.

"Cara would work with you on the price. At least try it on."

"Well, all right."

Another hand joined the first waldo, and stretched out to her. While nimble, the hands were a bit clumsy and before the pin was safely clasped the tip pierced her uniform and pricked the skin above her left breast. "Cara begs pardon for Cara clumsiness."

"It's all right." A mirror was picked up and held so she could see the effect. It was breathtaking. She pictured wearing it on the shoulder of a raven-wing black dress that hung in her closet back home. "I have to have it." The creature told her the price and she blanched, but then indicated the discount. It was still outrageously expensive, but not hideously so. And it wasn't like they had household expenses right now. They were being fed, housed and shod by the imperial fleet.

"Would you wish to wear it?"

"No. Personal jewelry apart from wedding rings aren't allowed while in uniform. Box it for me. I'll send my batBEM to collect my purchases."

"Very good, Highness." The undulations of the winged body made her suspect the creature was bowing.

Scanning the room she spotted Boho making a payment. She went to see what he had bought, but before she reached him an alien pod traveling on its cushion of air swept up to her. "You fly very well, Imperial Highness," the occupant said.

"Thank you."

"It would be interesting to match skills with you."

"I'm not sure that would be a fair contest. You've been adapted for high-gravity environments. And one hopes we're not going to start shooting at one another again."

"Of course not, Highness. Just a bit of friendly competition."

"I would look forward to it." She nodded and walked away. Added under her breath, *"Not!"*

She finally reached Boho's side. He was running a hand gently down the blade of a rapier. The hilt was almost abstract in its shape and simplicity and made from an opalescent material. "Fits my hand like it was made for it. I'm going to wear it at our coronation."

"I hope you're going to enjoy it before then," Mercedes said somewhat dryly. "Because that's going to be a long wait."

He laughed. "Oh, I intend to. Clark needs a lesson on just who is the better duelist."

She shook her head. "Men. You're so cute."

The Cara'ot were packing up. Elaborate farewells were exchanged between the admiral and the creature everyone assumed was the Cara'ot captain. The humans retreated off the shuttle deck and the aliens launched. The moment the doors cycled closed behind them the admiral became grim-faced. He touched his ring. Vink's image appeared in the air in front of him.

"Vink, plot a course for Hellfire. I want to talk to the joint chiefs."

Hellfire: the planet that housed central command, and the largest military installation in the League. Mercedes and Boho exchanged glances as the admiral walked away with his top commanders around him.

"Well, clearly they're seeing something we're not," Boho said.

* * *

Hellfire was in a double star system which meant the planet had an eccentric orbit that part of the year had it freezing, in another frying, and in between it was just lovely. All of which meant it wasn't an appropriate choice for colonization, but perfect for the sadists who commanded the ground forces of the Solar League. The navy, of course, floated above it all and made use of the three large orbital dockyards. None of them were as big as the facility at Cuandru, but it was still impressive.

While Kartirci and Vink went down to Norfolk, the largest base on the planet and the one devoted to the *Orden de la Estrella*, the rest of the crew of the *Concepción* inventoried supplies, made up any deficits and rotated in new crew.

Lewis had the squadrons flying elaborate drills designed to show off to his counterpart and rival from the *Reina del Cielo* that his pilots were better than Commander Caballero Utrecht's. It was working, but that didn't matter to Mercedes. What mattered was how outright disdain and amused condescension had turned into first grudging respect and finally outright compliments as she out-flew both her shipmates and the pilots from the *del Cielo*. She was beginning to think... hope that by the time she ascended to the throne her bona fides as a military leader would be secure.

At first Boho had been sulky about her promotion, but as her successes grew he began to puff and preen, taking pride in her accomplishments. When she learned he'd implied and once had outright said that he coached her she was inclined to be angry and wanted to confront him. A few moments of consideration and she decided that if the little fib helped him salve his ego she was alright with it. It certainly did make things better between them.

It was Saturday and since she'd missed confession the past two weeks she thought she'd better go; her annoyance with her husband was certainly on her conscience. The confessional box aboard the *Concepción* was elaborate, very much in keeping with the chapel itself, which had a French rococo feel with shades of gold and blue with gold stars spangled across the ceiling. All of which was appropriate for a ship named for the Virgin.

Mercedes slid into the box, pulled out her rosary and kissed the crucifix. "Bless me, father, for I have sinned. It has been two weeks since my last confession."

"What rests on your conscience, my daughter?"

Mercedes reared back from the screen, for the voice was not that of old Captain Father Antonelli, but a voice she knew very well for she'd grown up with him.

"Jose? What are you doing here?"

Since Mercedes knew that Musa del Campo had been up to his nutsack in the plot that had nearly derailed her military careers it probably wasn't a coincidence that his son the priest was now aboard the *Concepción*. Who had arranged that? Could she trust him to keep the seal of the confessional or would everything she said go back to his father? She decided paranoia was vindicated. Confessing her irritation and resentments with her husband and her fears to the son of an enemy wasn't the wisest course.

Mercedes found herself wishing that her father had allowed SEGU to actually unearth evidence that Musa was plotting against them, but her father feared an airing of a schism between branches of the royal family could potentially lead to civil war. So they all pretended nothing had happened and watched each other. And now here was Jose... watching.

"You were making a confession, my child. We should focus on that. We can talk after." The paternal scolding had her wanting to reach through the carved wood and smack him, since only a year separated them in age.

"I fear my success as an *Infierno* pilot has quite gone to my head. I find myself taking great pleasure in the compliments of the other pilots." Even in her own ears she sounded like a simpering fool.

"That's all?" Jose said when she finished.

She thought he sounded disappointed. "That's it," she answered.

"Remember, Mercedes, that pride can be one of the mortal sins. Though in this case I think you are still in venial territory." The humorous conclusion had her remembering her childhood playmate and wishing she didn't have to be so suspicious. "I think ten Hail Marys will be sufficient."

"Thank you, Father," she said meekly and left the box at the same time as Jose.

He was a very attractive young man with pale brown eyes, and hair like burnished mahogany, though she did notice it was starting to recede. Mercedes wondered if the *Celestial Novias de Cristo* nuns would want him siring their children once he went bald. Stupid thoughts when she was faced with a more immediate problem.

Being direct seemed the best approach. "So why are you

here? Really? Was it your father or Mihalis who put you up to this?"

He feigned outrage. "What an odd notion. Both my brothers are serving. It seemed like I should also do my duty."

"Yeah, I call bullshit because you don't have to serve. Priests, ministers, imams, you're all exempt unless you choose otherwise." He seemed taken aback by her grilling. He opened and closed his mouth several times searching for an answer. "Jose, here's some friendly advice. Don't let politics replace your vocation. That won't turn out well for you, your family or the church. Now, if you'll excuse me I need to make my penance."

Kneeling on the steps at the foot of the altar she began to pray the Rosary. The rubies that formed the beads rang because her hands were shaking, and her mind wasn't on her devotions. Instead she was thinking about the message she would be sending to her father via diplomatic pouch. This wasn't something she could put in a Foldstream message, but he needed to know that Cousin Musa was once more dabbling in intrigue.

13

THE WORLD AS IT IS

Seven months. Seven months of casual insults, pointed insults, pranks, demerits, and feeling like the organ-grinder's monkey every evening as he performed at the captain's mess. He had yet to make a friend. Tracy sighed; he would almost have been willing to socialize with Talion, but they seldom saw each other apart from the Sunday fencing club. At least he had learned this archaic and pointless skill so there was one less area where they could mock him.

The grey twisting wool of the Fold beyond the port was as dull as his mood. He sank down on one of the benches that lined the wall of the observation lounge. He had thought that perhaps the *hombres* might accept him if the officers wouldn't, but that hadn't worked out either. They seemed suspicious or resentful.

Even Akihiko the musician was withdrawn and cautious around Tracy. The *hombres* treated Tracy as if he were one of the FFH. The FFH treated him with utter contempt; worse than they would have treated Tracy had he been an enlisted man. Tracy's sin was that he'd gotten above himself. He didn't have a place in either world.

He saw Cipriana at the dinners, but they never got a chance to talk since she was a guest and he was entertainment. He had noticed that the conversation around the woman sometimes passed the bounds of propriety, and as he moved through the ship he had heard rough remarks from the enlisted men and officers alike. He was worried about Cipri's safety. While it was comforting to have a familiar face among the thousands on this ship, he wished that Cipriana had been assigned to Mercedes' ship where they could have looked out for each other. It looked like Cipriana was feeling the tension too. She had always been slim but she was now a rack of bones and her dark eyes flicked nervously as if expecting a blow. He needed to force the issue and find out if anything was wrong.

A touch on Tracy's shoulder pulled him out of his bitter reverie. He whirled. "What?" His tone was sharp and angry.

Akihiko took a step back. "Sorry to disturb, sir, but it's time," Akihiko said.

Tracy forced the frown away. "Sorry. I should apologize to you. There's no reason for you to endure my bad mood—"

"You owe me no explanations, sir."

"Akihiko, call me Tracy. It's not like anybody else treats me like an officer."

"That is their shame then, sir. To show respect is only proper."

"Yeah, well, that's not going to happen. It's been months and nothing's changed. I'm just the organ-grinder's monkey. Oh, shit, I've done it again," Tracy rushed to add as he watched Akihiko's face stiffen. Tracy glanced at the guitar case the other man carried. "You're a brilliant musician. I'm just icing... or something." He paused. "I'm making it worse, aren't I?"

The enlisted man surprised him by laying a hand on his arm. "It is wrong and I'm sorry it happened. Perhaps you could request a transfer?" he suggested.

"Never a good move. If you ask to transfer during your first tour they assume you're the problem."

"Ah, yes. I suppose I can see that."

"I can tough it out. And it's not like I'd be in the captain's private dining room if I weren't performing."

"Others are. The young lady—"

"Cipriana is ornamental and I think the captain's sweet on her." That earned Tracy an odd look. "Hey, if we don't get going neither one of us will be providing background muzak, and that won't be good." Tracy forced a smile.

They set off walking from the observation lounge toward the elevator that would take them to the officers' deck.

"Why do you go to observation? We're in Fold. There's nothing to see. Just grey fog," Akihiko said.

"Because there generally aren't any people there when we're in Fold."

"Ah... I see. Why don't we use the access conduit?"

"In the mood for ladders?" Tracy asked.

"They are generally empty except during drills."

"Okay," Tracy said slowly. They turned away from the doors of the elevator and entered the long passageway that linked the decks. There were pressure doors at each deck, all standing open now. It was a dizzying view up the length of the ship.

They climbed up several decks. The very air seemed to quiver with suppressed emotion. Tracy stopped, hooked an elbow over a ladder run and looked down into the *hombre*'s face. "Okay, Akihiko, what's eating you?"

"How did you—"

"I could cut the tension. You want to say something then say it."

They had rarely discussed anything beyond what to perform each evening. From the expression on the *hombre*'s face Tracy had a feeling this wasn't about deciding between a Gershwin, a Rodgers and Hart ballad or a swing piece by Duke Ellington.

Akihiko glanced up at Tracy then stared down at the toes of his mirror-bright boots where they rested on a metal rung. "The captain is going to make a suggestion to you tonight. I want to prepare you so you can prepare your answer ahead of time and not react without thought."

"I take it I'm not going to like this *suggestion*?"

"No. You are very much a heterosexual male."

Tracy couldn't help it. He leaned back and felt his foot slip. "Oh God, you mean…?"

"Yes. I have been in his bed since I came aboard—"

"Wait! Akihiko. This is a violation of the military code of justice. Fraternization between officers and enlisted men is forbidden."

Akihiko shrugged. "Only honored when it's convenient. When command or the crown decide they want to ruin an officer they bring the charge. Otherwise they wink at it."

Tracy gave a bitter half-laugh. "No different back home. Humans aren't supposed to fuck aliens, but the alien brothels on Hissilek do a rousing business, and it isn't just aliens skulking through those doors."

"Exactly."

"I thought you were married," Tracy said.

"I am."

"Are you...?"

"No."

"Then why... Look, we can put a stop to this. I'll go to—"

"No!" The word was sharp, almost angry. "Don't *help*. He's promised to set me up with my own music store after I muster out. Be our patron. I don't need you fucking that up."

"I don't like this. I'm supposed to report violations of the code. Why did you tell me if you don't want my help?" Tracy was feeling aggrieved.

The *hombre* took a deep breath. "Because he'd like a threesome." The words emerged in a rush. Tracy almost lost his grip on the ladder. "He loves artists and his tastes are eclectic, so..." Akihiko's voice trailed away and he gave a shrug.

"Shit," was all Tracy could think to say.

"He won't make it an order. He's not that kind of man. But I wanted you to be forewarned so you could make your refusal a polite one."

"Can you head him off? Say that you felt me out—so to speak—and it's clear I'd refuse."

"I'll try. Sometimes people hear only what they want to hear, and if he doesn't hear it from you he might not believe me. I just wanted to warn you because you have a hasty temper and your feelings frequently show."

"Yeah, it's why I don't play poker. We better get going. We're going to be late as it is. And, Akihiko, thanks for telling me. And if you change your mind—"

"No, I accept the world as it is."

It had gone just as Akihiko predicted. De Vilbiss had asked Tracy and Akihiko to stay behind after dinner and made his proposal. Tracy had politely declined and talked about his girl in the most euphoric terms possible while Mercedes' image danced in the forefront of his mind. After Tracy finished his paean to love the captain got a sad, regretful little smile, then sighed and nodded. Tracy saluted and left, leaving Akihiko to assure his future by prostituting his present.

Today Tracy had been given another pointless and time-consuming assignment by his third bunkmate Bellard. There was no question it was an abuse of the minuscule difference in their ranks and done only to harass and goad but Tracy knew better than to complain. A couple of times Tracy had snapped and struck back verbally at the trio. That's how he'd earned those extra admonitions. Thus far he'd managed to keep it just verbal and not resort to his fists because he knew if he crossed that line his career would be over.

So now he was down on the cavernous supply deck doing a visual count of the crates of powdered milk even though a computer would do a far better job of tracking the supplies. In an hour he had to report to Navigation. Duty rotation had at least gotten him away from Westley and the middle watch.

Shelving, tethered both to the floor of the deck and to the ceiling, loomed around him. The upper shelves were in shadow in the enormous room. For Tracy walking the corridors between the shelving was like exploring an ancient temple if you didn't look at the prosaic labels on the crates strapped onto the shelves. Gigantic cherry-picker robots slumped, weary monsters in the shadows. Eventually he was going to have to fire up one of the behemoths and use the bucket to reach the highest shelves. His footsteps echoed off the metal walls and he shivered. Due to the perishable nature of some of the stores the room was kept very cold. Easy to do in vacuum.

A sound like the low cry of a dove reached him. Tracy froze. Listened. It came again and resolved into a woman's voice, crying. There was only one woman on the *Triunfo*.

Tracy ran toward the sound. "Cipriana! Where are you?"

"No. Go away. I'm all right." Her voice was thick with tears.

"Yeah, of course you are," he muttered to himself and followed the sound of her voice.

He found her on the floor in a narrow space between the wall and the final shelf. Even in the shadows the split and swollen lips, the blood from her nose congealed on her upper lip, the torn utility uniform told the tale.

"Oh God," Tracy whispered and dropped to his knees beside her.

She was naked from the waist down, her trousers an

inside-out ball next to her. Her panties shredded lace. There was blood on the inside of her thighs. A few beads from her beautiful cornrows had been torn loose and lay like scattered pearls around her. The remaining beads rang as she gave her head a violent shake. She grabbed for her wadded trousers and tried to cover herself. Pity and rage warred in his heart. Tracy started to reach out to her then thought better.

"Who did this?" he demanded. She flinched and he realized his tone was loud and harsh. "I'm sorry. I'm not angry. Not with you," he said, softening his tone. "My first question should have been... how badly are you hurt?"

"I don't think anything is broken. I think he sprained my wrist, and..." She gestured at her battered face.

"You fought."

"He won." She looked away. When she resumed talking her voice was flat and unnaturally level. That in itself was alarming. "They teach us, do the best they can, but in the end you'll always be stronger, have a longer reach. Be able to take more punishment."

"We need to get you to sick bay."

"And say what? I can't report this. You know that."

"But what if you're..." He made a vague gesture too uncomfortable to say the word.

"Pregnant? You're so cute. I've been on birth control since I was sixteen. Shhh, don't tell the chaplain." She gave him a wink then winced as it pulled the skin around her bruised eye.

She sounded like her normal insouciant self while tears leaked from the corners of her eyes and her body was shaken with shudders. The juxtaposition told him she was in real trouble. He didn't know what to do. Bodily carry her to sick bay? Run for a first aid kit and patch her up? Shake her until she told him who had done this? Rage and punch the wall?

"Who was it?"

"You're a smart guy, Tracy. You can figure it out."

"Wessen."

"Give the man a prize!"

"I'll handle him."

"No, you won't. You can't any more than I can. Turn your back." He did and heard her groan. "That nothing's broken thing? I was wrong." A few moments later she said, "You can turn around now."

She was dressed, trying to lace up her utility boots. "Let me," Tracy said. He knelt at her feet and laced and tied her boots. He stood and backed away until his shoulders rested against the shelving. She was pressed up against the wall. "You have to get off this ship. Request a transfer."

"No. You know how that looks. I have to stay for Mer's sake. Sumi never graduated. Dani's dead. If I'm perceived to have failed then everyone will say she's being carried because of who she is. That can't hap—"

"For God's sake, Cipriana. This isn't the time for political calculation! You can't stay on a ship with the man who raped you."

"I wouldn't be the first woman who had to stay in a job or a marriage with a man who… who…" She began to shake.

"Cipri." He stepped toward her then froze. "May I touch you?"

"Please do," she sobbed.

He took her in his arms. She clung to him and wailed, her tears dampening his shoulder. Eventually the storm passed. He offered her a handkerchief. She gingerly wiped her bruised face, blew her nose. "Ow," she said. "Add the nose to the broken ribs."

"You have to get medical attention."

"We need a story."

Tracy looked around. His eye fell on one of the loaders. "You were down here helping me with the inventory. I fucked up and left a loader in gear and you got injured."

"No, it's not fair for you to take the blame. I'm the one who got my… myself… in this mess."

"I've already got so many admonitions on my record one more won't—"

"No! I'm not adding that guilt to everything else I'm feeling."

"Okay."

She began limping toward the doors. Tracy walked beside her. She stopped before the sensor could read their presence and open the doors. "Promise me you won't do anything about Wessen. It won't work and it will just hurt both of us. It's just how things are. I won't be stupid again. And I don't think he'll try again. I'm sure it wasn't all that fun. I did get in one or two good hits." She gave him a brave but sad little smile.

"I don't know if I can do—"

"Please, Tracy. Promise me."

"All right. I promise."

* * *

Commander Dr. Exeteur stepped out of the examination room. Tracy stood up. He had reported the accident to the bridge and Sukarno had excused him from duty, telling him to "see to the young lady".

"Interesting story the two of you spun. Unfortunately for you two I wasn't born yesterday, and I did go to medical school so she stopped lying, but she won't permit me to report the rape or tell me who assaulted her. Do you know?"

"The lieutenant asked me to keep her confidence," Tracy said stiffly.

"And if I order you?"

"I gave the lady my word."

"You took an oath."

"And you took two. Medical privacy versus good order and discipline. Which one are you going to obey?"

"And an armchair lawyer too. Damn you, boy. You can escort her back to her quarters." He started to turn away.

"Sir, she thinks he won't try again," Tracy blurted. "I'm not sure that's true. She won't transfer, and well, I wondered if you had any advice?"

"That she shouldn't be here at all, but that ship has sailed." Exeteur sighed. "I can make a suggestion to the captain that she not wander out of officers' territory."

"You're assuming it's an *hombre*." Blood was pounding in Tracy's temples.

"That would be easier."

"For who?"

"Good order and discipline," Exeteur said with a significant look. "But in the highly unlikely and very hypothetical chance it *was* an officer then a man's name might help."

"Sir?"

"Husband, Lieutenant. Husband. A man is hesitant to touch another man's property."

"She shouldn't be forced to marry just to stay safe."

"An engagement might do as well," the doctor mused.

"I could do that."

"You?" Incredulity dripped off the word.

Given the doctor's reaction Tracy hastened to add, "Of course I wouldn't hold her to it."

"Good God, boy, no one would believe it. She's the daughter of the Duque de Nico-Hathaway. The idea she would affiance herself to someone like you…" He must have read something in Tracy's face for he added, "It was kind of you to offer, but… no." He shook his head. "Also, think what it would do to your reputation. You'd be viewed as an encroaching *intitulado* looking to use marriage to better himself."

"Yes, God forbid any of us ever try to better ourselves." Acid laced the words.

"Don't fire up, boy. I didn't mean to insult you." *Which you did, you pompous prick*, but Tracy managed not to say it aloud. "You'd best shove off. I'll discuss options with the young lady. Perhaps I can convince her to go home."

Tracy saluted, whirled on his heel and headed for the door of Medical. "Don't count on it," he muttered under his breath.

* * *

The priest was a shadow behind the wood grating. Tracy rested his head against the wood, cleared his throat and said, "Forgive me, Father, for I have sinned. It's been seven months since my last confession."

"I had noticed that I hadn't seen you beyond dinners at the captain's table and at mass." He paused then added gently, "Would I be right in assuming your presence on Sunday is only because the captain insists, Lieutenant Belmanor?"

"Yes, that would be correct."

"Have you lost your faith, my son?"

"I don't know, Father. There just doesn't seem to be any justice anywhere."

"*If God exists and really loves us why does he permit bad things to happen?*"

"You're making fun of me."

"No. I struggle with doubt every day. You went through the catechism, right?" the priest asked.

"Yes."

"Then you know the answers the church—"

"Free will, trust, greater good, blah blah blah," Tracy recited. His bitterness showed.

"Why don't you tell me what's happened that has you so bleak."

"There's a man aboard, a fellow officer who assaulted a woman, and I can't do anything to him."

"What do you want to do?"

"Beat him to a bloody pulp."

"Thus compounding the evil."

"Not if he got the message and never touched her again."

"Ah." The shadow shifted and Tracy had a brief glimpse of the priest's profile, the jawline already beset by a dense five o'clock shadow.

"So you know?"

"I was called to minister to the young lady. She was quite concerned about *you*. That you not do anything foolish and endanger your career."

"Is a career worth my honor?"

"But it's not just your honor. You have to consider her wishes and reputation. Her honor." Tracy slumped back against the wall of the confessional. "What else is bothering you?"

"My bunkmates. I hate them. They never let up on me, reminding me that I'm just lowborn scum. Nothing I do, nothing I accomplish is ever going to erase my background. I'm smarter than any of them! I work harder! I'm not asking them to respect me, just leave me the fuck alone! Sorry, Father."

"I have heard strong language before." There was a chuckle in the light tenor voice. "As to your bunkmates, you understand they're scared of you, right?"

"Huh?"

"They've been raised to believe their titles and the circumstance of their births prove they're superior in all respects. Then you come along and threaten that comforting world view."

"So you're an *intitulado* too."

"Oh no, I was the Duke of Bedford; my full name is Kenneth Robin Herbrand Francis Russell. But you can call me Father Ken." The humor and the warmth in the priest's voice removed any embarrassment.

"I don't know that title and my father made sure I memorized them *all*."

"It's an old Earth title dating from the seventeenth century, not one of the new League titles. I'm quite the black sheep of my family. Wanting to be a priest, renouncing my title. Fortunately I have a younger brother, and he's managing perfectly well. Though heating Woburn Abbey is a struggle with the North Atlantic Drift shutdown. Anyway, I do hope you'll forgive me for being a member of the FFH, and I'm sorry for maundering when I should be listening to you. I do understand your dilemma. You're between worlds and as a result you can't feel comfortable anywhere. I can't promise you that it will get better, but I think you have the strength to endure and come through this difficult period. You won't always be the junior lieutenant. I want you to reflect on the fact that you are a worthy man, and that people care enough about you to put aside their own pain to protect you. I also want you to say the Rosary and promise not to maim or murder any of your fellow officers. And I want you back here next week to tell me how it's going."

"I don't—"

"Please."

"All right."

I may have just made a friend.

14

DECISION POINT

Cipriana didn't go home. She also didn't go to the captain's table for dinners any longer. Tracy missed seeing her there because he could at least judge how she was doing from her expression. She had been assigned to Medical even though nothing in her training supported that posting. As near as Tracy could determine she had become a glorified secretary to Dr. Exeteur.

He tried to follow Father Ken's advice, but it seemed like his entire world was filled with entitled assholes who demanded he kiss those noble asses each and every day. Rage was a foul taste on the back of his tongue and his gut hurt. He wondered if he was developing an ulcer. Mostly he wondered if he could face one more day. He kept his word to the priest and went each Saturday to confession even though there was a monotonous theme to all of them. Most began with "I want to kill—fill in the blank." Anger and pride, those were his sins. He struggled, tried to find peace because he didn't want to disappoint the gentle little priest, but neither prayers, confession nor violent exercise seemed to help.

* * *

The first year of Tracy's tour had come and gone, and now the *Triunfo* was in orbit around the particularly undistinguished colony world of Wasua. Shuttles had been busy delivering a rotating group of crewmen to enjoy some leave, while the *fusileros* were going to play war games. It was either wisdom or sadism on the part of their commanders that the soldiers were going to be permitted to get shit-faced and laid before they had to play pretend war.

The main city looked like it had been thrown up in a day and would disappear just as quickly. It was a place where colonists stopped to outfit their vehicles, pick up their homesteading permits and headed out to break sod on a new world. It had a lot of cheap wheeled vehicles and trailers for sale, stores selling overpriced portable shelters, tractors, seed, fertilizer, frozen livestock embryos and the livestock to carry them. And bars. It had a lot of bars.

Tracy had found one well away from the spaceport. In this dank, dark space smelling of cheap beer, rancid grease and lost dreams he was unlikely to run into anyone from the ship. A soccer game played on a screen over the bar with the sound turned down to a low growl. There was no conversation among the surly customers who all seemed to seek the shadows. The only other sounds were the dull clunk of glass on glass as the bartender filled orders and the click of hooves as the Hajin waitress delivered them. She had a long, tangled red mane and her top barely covered her sagging teats.

He wasn't sure why he'd picked a place on the edge of

the city. Maybe a sense that he could run. It was easy to get a homesteading permit. He could ask Donnel about putting him in touch with a Cara'ot surgeon. Change his face. Take off, start over.

As a farmer? He didn't have the first idea about farming. He had been raised in the biggest city on Ouranos. He'd be bankrupt in a season. He gestured to the bartender to fill his glass again. It was cheap whisky and it went down harshly, etching pain down his throat to land like a smoldering coal in his already roiling gut. He thought about finding a brothel—he'd been celibate for over a year—but that would require effort and he was too depressed to muster up the energy—for either the search or the activity. He motioned at his glass.

The bartender, a big man with tattoos on his arms and a dirty apron that strained across his gut, tipped in another shot. The harsh fumes made Tracy's eyes water. "You've been hammering those down, son." Tracy looked up to meet his surprisingly kind brown-eyed gaze. "Sure you're going to be able to find your way back to your ship?"

"Don't care."

"Yeah you do. They hang deserters in the League."

"They wouldn't even look for me. I'm the embarrassment. The *intitulado*. They'd be glad I'm gone."

"Pretty thin thread to hang your life on. Look, son, I can see you've got troubles."

"Wow, you always this perceptive?" Tracy snarled.

"Don't piss off the bartender. I might cut you off. Look, you want to hear a real tale of woe… go talk to *that* guy." The bartender jerked a thumb at a fat, sweating man sprawled in a chair and staring morosely into his empty glass. "It's a load of bullshit, but it's entertaining as hell and after you hear it your troubles won't seem so big."

Tracy took another look at the man. Even with his dark skin the broken veins in his nose were visible and the sclera around the dark eyes was bloodshot. The tight curls of his luxuriant hair were streaked with grey. The bartender moved away to place full glasses on the Hajin's tray. Tracy dithered; finally he grabbed up his glass and walked over to the man. It wasn't like he had anything better to do.

He sat down at an empty chair. "He," Tracy said with a jerk of his thumb toward the bartender, "says you have a story that will put everything in perspective for me. Amaze me." A quivering ran along his nerves. He really hoped the man would object. Jump up and take a swing at him. Tracy longed for a fight, a chance to pound on somebody. He'd been stopped from dealing with Wessen by Cipriana and Father Ken and he couldn't start a fight on the ship. He'd either end up cashiered or in another stupid duel. He absently rubbed the scar at his temple. Unfortunately the man didn't object. He leaned forward over the bulge of his gut and blinked owlishly at Tracy.

"Loren doesn't believe me. But it's all true." Even slurred by alcohol Tracy recognized the round vowels and clipped consonants of a member of the FFH. God knew he was familiar with it after three years at the High Ground and now aboard the *Triunfo*. He was afraid he had begun to acquire the aristocratic accent.

"Okay, I'll bite. What's all true?"

The tip of the man's tongue wet his lips. "I could tell the tale better if my throat weren't so dry."

Tracy almost left, but something made him decide to play along. He went to the bar and bought a bottle of bourbon. He slammed it down in the middle of the table. Filled his glass and filled the man's.

"Okay. Talk."

The man drained his glass in one long swallow. Tracy refilled it. The man tried to straighten, swayed a bit in his chair and gripped the edge of the table with a pudgy hand to brace himself. "I am much, much more than I seem."

"Okay."

The man looked around nervously, leaned in and whispered, "I have to be very careful. They're everywhere." He looked around again, and gulped down his second drink. "If they knew I was talking to an officer…" He made a throat-cutting gesture. He started to reach for the bottle. Tracy pulled it away from him.

"Uh uh, not until you sing your song."

The man laid a finger against his lips and leaned in close to Tracy. His breath was a nauseating mix of booze and halitosis. "What I'm about to tell you could shake the very foundations of the League. It will put you in grave danger. But perhaps you are the man I've been waiting for."

"If we keep waiting long enough another man might come along."

The drunk gave him an aggrieved look. "I hope you intend to take this seriously." Tracy grabbed the bottle and started to stand, but then words tumbled from the man's mouth like spilled marbles. "It all began with a bachelor party. Did I mention I was a very prominent individual? I had staff and one of my young aides was getting married."

Tracy sank back into the chair. The man continued. "His friends had arranged for a night out at one of Hissilek's more elegant strip clubs. I shouldn't have gone. It was beneath my dignity and while one hopes to be on good terms with your assistants one can't make friends of them." The man frowned, which gave him the look of a petulant baby. "If only I hadn't, but the lads pleaded and the atmosphere at home hadn't been precisely warm." Another frown. "My wife's current lover was the age of our nineteen-year-old daughter." He gave an irritated gesture. "Whatever. Suffice it to say I agreed."

Intrigued despite himself Tracy refilled the man's glass.

"The club was very exclusive, catering to only the very best of the FFH. All human waitstaff. Oh, I presume that BEMs toiled behind the scene, but in the club proper only our kind. Beautiful naked women posed on rotating platforms suspended from the ceiling. The platforms were shaped like galaxies and made of faux diamonds. You could see the gems dimpling their bare buttocks. On the stage a constant parade of dancers writhed and undulated." Once again the tongue touched his lips and the man's hand disappeared beneath the table. Tracy had a feeling it was exploring the man's crotch.

"What I didn't know was that in addition to the normal human dancers they had a few to appeal to those with... exotic tastes."

"You mean aliens."

"Yes."

Tracy sneered. "I can't imagine being aroused by a Hajin or Isanjo. Much less a Flute or a Sidone—I mean, spiders?"

"Good God, man, no. I'm not a pervert."

Ah, Tracy thought.

"No, this was a Cara'ot. You know they can change their forms and this one was most alluring. Most alluring indeed." The puffy lids closed over the bloodshot eyes and the man smiled, clearly viewing a pleasant memory. "She arrived to a drum roll, the clash of cymbals and a single spotlight in the darkness. Leaping to center stage like a gazelle. She wore an elaborate mask and headdress and unlike the others she was cloaked and veiled. She began to dance and she was quicksilver and starlight. None of the harsh gyrations of the other girls. This was a song in motion. There were light-emitting diodes set into her claws. Streaks of multi-colored light wove about her." His voice had taken on a singsong quality.

"Bit by bit the concealing layers fell away until a tail, streaked and ringed with red and white fur, began to undulate with her. Another layer of veiling fell, and the fur that banded her crotch like a bikini and rose to a point between her perfect breasts was revealed. My young aides were disgusted. I was mesmerized. I gripped the table begging her to remove the mask. To show me all that she was.

"Unlike the other women she wouldn't allow us to grope and stroke her. If you held a credit spike she would dance close enough for you to insert it into the credit belt she wore, but if you touched her body those claws would rake you."

Tracy had a sudden vision of aroused and sweating

human males, their credit spikes outstretched like pecuniary stand-ins for dicks. It was a reminder of his own horny state. Tracy gulped down his drink.

"She gave a final breathtaking leap and she posed center stage and removed the mask and headdress. She had this small upturned nose, tiny fur-covered ears thrust up from the red and cream curls that fell to her shoulders and her eyes... ah those eyes. Deep green and slitted like a cat's. I was lost." The man hung his head. "You see, I had a taste for the exotic. I frequented an Isanjo massage parlor in Pony Town. They knew that. That's how they got me."

"The government?" Tracy asked.

"No, them."

"Who—?"

"I will get to that. Needless to say I made her my lover. And believe me it wasn't easy. She mocked me, but I persevered and eventually she relented."

"And did she fuck as well as she stripped?" Tracy asked.

"Please. Don't be crude about Samarith. My beautiful Sammy." His voice was as mournful as a debt-ridden Flute singing of woe. "I called her Sammy and she called me Han and we pretended the world wasn't as it was; that our love could be accepted. For you see it wasn't all sex. She was the companion of my heart, the keeper of my soul. Some nights we would just sit and talk, the tips of her ears tickling my chin as I held her in my arms. I poured out everything to her. My hopes and dreams, regrets and fears. My secret shames and my deepest desires. She was interested in everything about me: my economic theories; my old fencing master when I had been a boy; the furnishing in our house on Grenadine. I showered her with expensive gifts. She was like a drug. I began to shirk my duties so I could spend more hours in her company."

"Might have been cheaper to just hire a therapist instead of a mistress. They'll listen to you talk too," Tracy said.

"You don't understand. It was all part of the plan." Han slammed the flat of his hand on the table. The glasses jumped and liquor spilled. The drunk looked horrified as he stared at the puddle of bourbon.

Tracy put that together with the earlier statement about the mysterious *theys*. His lip curled. "Ah, so there's a secret cabal and shadowy plots to this story too."

"You mock, but it's true. Once they had what they wanted they put their plan into effect."·

The man waved his glass at Tracy. Tracy filled it. Filled his own. Han gulped down his drink and snatched the bottle before Tracy could prevent him. Filled his glass yet again. Tracy grabbed the neck of the bottle and there was a brief tug of war. Han finally released it and pouted.

"I'm not sure I want to talk to you any longer," the fat man huffed. Tracy sloshed the liquid in the bottle. Tongue again touched lips and Han nodded. "Anyway, they put the plan into effect the night of the first grand ball of the season. I wanted to be with Sammy but had to escort my wife and daughter to the Palanis' house. My wife and I had a fight. She had learned about my alien lover and there was a scene. I left and ran to my kitten girl. Told her what had happened, told her I didn't care. I would cast away everything for her. She took me back to her apartment and drugged me.

"I remember waking once. I was naked and cold, lying on metal. She told me she was sorry." His brow wrinkled. "Well, I think she did. Then blackness. When I awoke I was laying on the metal bed frame. Everything was gone, mattress, linens. I staggered through the apartment. It had been stripped bare. My ScoopRing, signet ring, everything was gone."

"So she was just a thieving whore," Tracy suggested.

"No, no. This was far more. I finally went into the bathroom to relieve myself and get a drink and a stranger was looking out of the mirror at me. *They had altered my appearance.* All my life I had skin almost as pale as yours and red hair. But suddenly…" He gestured at his dark hair and skin. "And I was fatter so my clothes barely fit. I managed to get decent enough to go outside and discovered that months had passed. I had gone to the ball in early fall. It was now high summer."

"I went to the police and reported that I had been robbed and violated. My very appearance changed. Told them who I was. They didn't believe me. I went to my office and the young men who'd taken me to that bachelor party all those long months before ejected me from the building. I went to my home and forced myself past the butler and up the stairs searching for my wife."

Han's delivery had become rushed, the words staccato punctuated by panting breaths. Tracy began to fear the man would have a coronary right in front of him.

"I found her in the bedroom being enthusiastically rogered by a man with pale skin and red hair. Juliana screamed. The man looked around. *And it was me.*"

"The authorities arrived and took me away. I tried to make them understand that the Cara'ot had placed an agent at the very heart of the government. Replaced me with an alien who could stand at the Emperor's right hand."

"Let me guess. Nobody believed you."

Han nodded. "Then I began to fear that the aliens might decide that silencing me was the safer course. Once I was released from the sanitarium I fled Ouranos. Made my way to distant worlds trying to stay ahead of my hunters. I tell my tale to people like you. To people who might listen."

"And who'll buy you a drink," Tracy snapped.

Han staggered to his feet and stood swaying as he intoned, "I am Rohan Danilo Marcus Aubrey, Conde de Vargas, and I adjure you to act! Inform your superiors! Alert them to the danger." Exhausted the drunk collapsed back into his chair, his chin resting on his chest.

Disgusted by his gullibility and the waste of his money, Tracy kicked back his chair and stood. "Nice. Sweet scam you've got going. You and your buddy Loren." Tracy jerked his chin toward the bartender.

"Wha…?"

"I've met the Conde de Vargas. Been a guest in his home. Done a service for him. Saw him at my graduation. Peddle your bullshit somewhere else!"

Tracy started for the door. "Wait!" The desperate cry stopped him. Han was hugging the almost empty bottle to his chest. "Your duties take you throughout League space. If you see her tell her… tell her…" His voice was thick with tears. "I never saw Sammy again and I need to… I need to… I love her so much."

Broken words from a shattered man. Pity stirred and Tracy brutally quashed the feeling. Applauding slowly he said, "Nice touch."

He walked out into the darkness and found his swaying steps carrying him back toward the spaceport. If he deserted he would end up like that pathetic drunk. Skipping from world to world, hunted (though in his case it would be true), broke, searching for an easy mark. And what tale would he spin? *That once I knew the Infanta. That we shared a secret love.*

Was that any more fantastic than the tale he'd been told?

What if there *was* a plot against the humans? Aliens were integrated into every facet of their lives. Second class, overlooked, taken for granted. Would the human masters even notice? Tracy shook his head. The motion sent him staggering and nausea washed through his gut. He was drunker than he'd realized. That was fueling these paranoid thoughts.

He looked toward the port. A ship was lifting on a pillar of fire. His heart lifted with it. He would return to the *Triunfo*. He would win glory and acclaim. He would change the equation.

Commander Sukarno was waiting for him when he got off the shuttle. Tracy snapped to attention and saluted. The vigorous gesture sent him tottering sideways. The executive officer grabbed his shoulder and steadied him.

"You came back, Belmanor," he said.

"Yes, sir."

"I wasn't sure you would."

"Wasn't gonna let the assholes beat me... sir," he added when he realized several heartbeats had passed without the honorific.

Sukarno gave his pirate's grin. "I thought you were tough enough, but you never can tell."

"Glad I met your expectations," Tracy said dully.

"I'm not sure you will, but I'm going to find out. Get sober and report to my office. You're my new adjutant."

The room seemed to be ballooning and Sukarno looked like he was standing at the end of a very long, very bright tunnel. "S... sir?"

"If your batBEM is anything like mine he'll have a remedy that will put you back on your feet. Well, snap to it!"

15

BY LUCKY CHANCE

"Pilots to your ships," Lewis's voice boomed over the intercom. *What the hell?* Mercedes wondered as she jogged toward an elevator. Tension snapped at her nerve endings. They didn't usually deploy fighters when they entered a new system.

Boho had beaten her to the flight deck and had almost finished donning his armor. He assisted her, and before they locked their helmets they exchanged a quick kiss. His lips were dry and cold.

"Must be something out there," he muttered.

"Probably just Vink being paranoid," she soothed. She closed her helmet, took a running start, climbed up the side of her *Infierno* and slid into the couch. An *hombre*, belly down on the skin of the fighter, jacked her in, and patted the top of her helmet. As he slid off she closed the canopy.

The warning light strobed. The warning siren was muffled. *Hombres* streamed toward the doors that slid shut behind them. The bay doors began to cycle open. She gave a gentle boost of her trim jets and her fighter lifted a few inches off the deck. She glanced to either side. The rest of second squadron were following her example. The year they had spent flying together had given them all a good sense of each other so that she rarely needed to give mundane commands.

Lewis's voice rang in her helmet. "*Infiernos* launch."

First squadron led off with their leader, Captain-Lieutenant Lord Novek snapping out multiple orders as the fighters went spinning off the deck. Mercedes gave a mental sigh and once they were clear she said only, "Second squadron, launch." The edges of the bay flashed by briefly in her peripheral vision and then they were out.

As always, for a fleeting moment the backdrop of eternity held wonder, then she was back to work. After the experience in the proto-system, Navigation had decided to bring them out of Fold closer to this new system's star in the hope they would avoid gas giants and debris fields. The ships were outfitted with highly sensitive scanners so if they were about to appear in the path of something large they would automatically shift back into the Fold. That was not a happy occurrence because during those abrupt translations was when ships got lost. The advantage they had was that space was *big*. The chance of actually running into something was vanishingly small.

Mercedes checked her instrument panel. There was an object at a Lagrange point, a place where gravitational forces allowed an object to remain stationary, and it was hot, emitting signals that were being beamed to the icy planet below. Novek had noticed it at the same moment. "Arango, take Turner and Fellon and investigate."

"Aye, aye, sir."

Mercedes sent her fighter looping toward the object. Turner and Fellon orbited her in an intricate dance in case unfriendlies decided to toss something their way. The object resolved into a long cigar-shaped asteroid. Solar panels flared on all sides. At one end there was the corroded nozzle of a thruster. It was a ship, a long view ship built from a hollowed out asteroid. The three fighters explored the length and breadth of the ship sending back pictures to the flagship.

"Clearly human," Admiral Kartirci said. She realized he was probably talking to Vink.

Gelb's voice came into her helmet. "Picking up signals. The ship is beaming to the planet."

Curious, Mercedes dipped into the stream. It was a series of numbers. She was still puzzling it out when Gelb provided the answer.

"It's sending our coordinates and our physical specs down to the planet."

"There's going to be some soiled underwear down there," Vink remarked. "Novek, Arango, take the squadrons into near orbit. Scan for population centers. We'll hold at perigee."

"Aye, sir," they said in chorus and gave the order to their squads.

It was going to take a while to close on the planet. Mercedes allowed herself to sink into the couch and tried to ignore the catheter. She was beginning to wonder if a diaper might be a better choice. Boho sent her a private message.

"There may be defensive platforms in orbit."

"Even if there are I don't think they'll offer much of a threat to us. That ship was pretty low tech."

"Poor suckers," Boho said with a hint of a laugh in his voice. "They probably headed out just a few years before we discovered the Fold technology. While they were crawling through the galaxy we were lapping them several times over."

"I doubt they're going to find that as funny as you, but I'm sure they'll be glad to see us," Mercedes replied.

Hours passed. Mercedes sipped at the nutrient mix built into her helmet. Eventually the planet began to loom. It wasn't a very welcoming sight. High mountains, clouds whipped by high winds, ice and snow over much of the surface. Only at the equator was bare ground visible.

"Doesn't look very hospitable." Jace's voice over the radio.

"Judging from the corrosion on the nozzle my guess is they had limped as far as they could go," Mercedes answered.

"Can you imagine? Hundreds of years inside that ball of rock," another pilot offered.

"No," Boho answered.

There were a few crude satellites in various orbits around the planet. Mercedes dipped into the signals from them. Cell phone conversations, women's voices.

"…pick up the children…"

"…have to go…?"

"…Where's Gabbi?"

There were other messages that had been encrypted. Undoubtedly from whatever government agencies ruled the planet. She boosted them back to the *Concepción*. She figured the computers and SEGU officers on board would make short work of the code.

The two squadrons swept around the planet, and on the night side they spotted the lights of several small cities sprinkled around the equator.

Vink radioed to her and Novek. "Send down recon drones. We need to estimate the population so we know how to proceed. Then return to the *Concepción*."

It was done and the *Infiernos* turned for home. Mercedes was glad. This was the longest she had been in the armor and she was desperate to be free of the catheter and take a shower.

The top officers of the *Triunfo* were gathered at the table in the captain's conference room. Tracy sat behind Sukarno and slightly to his left. His counterpart, Captain-Lieutenant Conde Tyler Vebrant, sat behind de Vilbiss, also taking notes on the meeting. Occasionally Tracy reached up and touched the first lieutenant bars on his collar. It had taken almost a year, but Sukarno had finally succeeded in getting Tracy promoted. As an added bonus Tracy also wore the ribbon signifying he was a captain-lieutenant. The bunkmates had not been pleased, but the overt harassment had stopped because at this point Tracy technically outranked them.

"We've received a call from Admiral Kartirci on the *Nuestra Señora de la Concepción* requesting support," Captain de Vilbiss said.

A thrill of excitement swept through Tracy. Mercedes was aboard the *Concepción*. Perhaps he would have a chance to see her, perhaps even speak to her. *You're not getting within two feet of her, you fool.* The voice of his *intitulado* self tried to remind him that he was and would always be "lowborn scum". He could almost hear Boho's hated voice. Uncomfortable thoughts. Tracy pushed them aside.

"They've found a Hidden World," de Vilbiss continued. "Based on surveillance it's a rather small population so they feel two ships will be sufficient to effect annexation and incorporation."

Eichenbrenner said, "You'll have need of the *fusileros*."

"One hopes not," de Vilbiss countered. "According to the admiral the planet is hardly a garden spot. We can help with terraforming. Also their technology is primitive; we can improve their lives. The capital is sending a team of diplomats to undertake the negotiations."

"We're just there to back up their statecraft," Sukarno said dryly and a chuckle swept through the room.

"Hopefully they won't be as tough as those bastards on Reichart's World," de Vilbiss said, and a few of the older officers nodded in agreement.

Reichart's World. There had been two worlds found relatively recently—Dullahan and Reichart's World. Reichart's had a particularly unpleasant resonance for Tracy. It had been opened for League citizens to immigrate a year after its discovery and Tracy's family had been among the émigrés. His father and grandfather had taken the family's savings, borrowed heavily and bought into the lottery to obtain a business on Reichart's World. They had succeeded, winning ownership of a textile mill, and moved to the planet when Tracy was four.

But the new life and the riches that were supposed to

follow had proved to be a chimera. A member of the FFH had wanted the Belmanors' mill and suddenly they were beset with unanticipated expenses and lawsuits. Tracy's mother had died, and Tracy knew his father believed that the stress was what had ultimately killed Viola. How he had managed to keep working for the members of the FFH Tracy had never understood, but his father had never lost his esteem for and deference to the FFH.

Forced into bankruptcy they sold the mill to the nobleman. Broke and deeply in debt the two men and the boy returned to the tailor shop in Hissilek and spent the next seven years working to pay off their debts. Tracy's grandfather, a bitter and angry old man who had never recovered from his daughter's death, died just as they succeeded.

"Well, we know what we have to do." De Vilbiss stood and all the officers followed suit. He turned to Xiang-Loredo. "Set a course for..." The captain turned to his adjutant. "What do the locals call the damn place?"

"Sinope. The *Concepción* grabbed a few city names too— Pygela, Latoreria and Amastris."

They all headed toward the door. Sukarno glanced over at Tracy. "Research those names. See if they give us any idea what ax these folks were grinding when they left Earth."

It was a good question because most of the people who were willing to risk their lives in long view ships tended to be nuts who wanted to try bizarre social experiments. Since the *Triunfo* would be three days in Fold there would be plenty of time for Tracy to find the answer.

"Yes, sir."

* * *

Sukarno waved him into a seat. Tracy unbraced and sat down. Sukarno's office contained not a single personal item. Tracy had wondered if that was due to a secretive nature on the part of the XO or just an *intitulado*'s sense that anything could be taken away without a moment's notice so you didn't want to have a lot to pack.

"Uh… Commander, are those diplomats already on their way? Because if they're not the government might want to include at least one woman," Tracy said.

"They are and they are all men. Apart from a few human secretaries there are no women who are… well you know, real secretaries as in secretaries of state."

"Did the folks on the flagship report if they intercepted any men talking?"

"No."

"We should ask about that when we arrive."

"Why?"

"Because Sinope, Pygela, Latoreria and Amastris are all names associated with the Amazons." Sukarno frowned and Tracy hastened to add, "Not the FFH family, sir. The myth. A society of women warriors."

"*Wald il qahbaa.*" Tracy could recognize swearing even if he didn't understand the language. "Well, let's hope when we arrive we find out the men were all out preparing their defenses." Sukarno waved his hands over his head. "Forget that. The last thing we want is a pitched battle. It always makes the initial annexation that much harder."

"By sheer luck we will have in orbit the two ships with women aboard and one of them is the Infanta," Tracy offered. "Having her on the negotiating team might make this go more smoothly. Assuming it is what I fear."

"Good thought, Belmanor. Send Lieutenant Delacroix up to see me. I'll notify the captain that we need a conference."

Tracy saluted and left.

The admiral and Vink were greeting the *Triunfo*'s captain. Behind the admiral and the flag captain were a gaggle of lower-ranked officers. The *Concepción*'s gaggle had already been in place on the flight deck when the shuttle from the battle cruiser arrived. The prerogative of Admiral Duque Kartirci dictated that the captain of the *Triunfo* come to them.

Captain Marquis de Vilbiss's group was dribbling down the gangway of their shuttle. Cipriana was among them and Mercedes wanted to squeal and bounce like a schoolgirl when she saw her. As to why Cipriana was among the *Triunfo*'s delegation she couldn't say. Then her breath stopped in her throat, for Tracy was with them. Standing next to a rather piratical-looking older man whose insignia indicated he was a commander. Boho, standing next to her, stiffened when he noticed the tailor's son. Tracy glanced up. His eyes met hers and then he looked down at his tap-pad and didn't look up again.

The captain and the admiral completed their greetings then the pirate and Tracy joined them. There was more hurried conversation. Boho leaned down and grumbled, "Why is that jumped-up *intitulado* included in *that* conversation?" It was clearly rhetorical so Mercedes didn't bother answering.

Vink turned and locked eyes with Mercedes. "Captain-Lieutenant Princess, if you will please join us in the admiral's conference room." He raked the rest of the welcoming party with a look. "The rest of you are dismissed."

"What? Wait. Shouldn't I be there?" Boho asked.

Vink glanced over at the admiral. "He is the consort."

"Yes, yes, I suppose he should be present," Kartirci said.

To Mercedes' surprise Tracy and Cipriana were part of the group that moved off toward the elevators. Mercedes managed to fall into step with Cipriana. She gave a cautious glance at the three top officers, but they were deep in conversation. She leaned in and whispered, "I'm *so* glad to see you."

"Me too." Cipriana's tone was flat and a shadow lay deep in her eyes. Mercedes frowned and studied her friend. Cipriana had lost that impish sparkle that had, even more than her astounding beauty, been her most defining feature.

"Is everything all right?" Mercedes whispered. Cipriana just shook her head, though whether it was an answer or an indication she didn't want to say Mercedes couldn't tell.

The top brass took the first elevator, which left Cipriana, Mercedes, Boho, the commander and Tracy riding together in the second car. Boho and Tracy were on opposite sides of the elevator trying to put as much distance between each other as possible. Tension fluttered in Mercedes' chest. Cipriana glanced from one man to the other then leaned in and whispered in tones more like her old self, "Awkward."

It was unbearable. Mercedes decided to take command.

She held out her hand to the commander. "I don't believe we've met."

He bowed over her hand. "Commander Anusanatha Sukarno." He indicated Tracy. "My adjutant, Captain-Lieutenant Thracius Belmanor."

Boho reacted at the rank. Mercedes could read his mind. He was still just a first lieutenant. She studied the white scar at Tracy's left temple. She thanked God the two men weren't on the same ship. If they had been there was no doubt her husband would try to give Tracy another.

"The captain-lieutenant and I are already acquainted. We were classmates at the High Ground."

Tracy snapped to attention, then gave her a court bow. "Highness." When he straightened she could see the anger and betrayal in those amazing grey eyes.

He hates me.

He has cause.

"We're going to send two girls to negotiate?" Vink's tones of incredulity had Mercedes digging her nails into her palms. "And one of them the heir to the throne," he added rather belatedly. "Forgive me, Admiral, but this is madness." Mercedes thought it was to Captain de Vilbiss's credit that he maintained his cool smile in the face of Vink's disdain. "And do we have any proof that this mad—" Vink gestured at the history entries that hung in the air over the center of the table "—theory is even correct?"

They were all gathered in the admiral's conference

room. Kartirci's Hajin batBEM brought in an assortment of finger sandwiches and pastries, served tea and coffee, bowed and withdrew.

"Have you heard a single male voice?" the *Triunfo's* XO asked. Sukarno was frowning at Vink with an expression that was rather more dismissive than was proper from a commander toward a flag captain.

"Whether this theory is in fact the truth is beside the point. I don't think it's proper for my wife to take this kind of risk," Boho said.

He's just reduced me to merely his wife, Mercedes thought and once again her nails bit into her palms. *Or perhaps he's not trying to diminish me, but is honestly worried.*

Tracy gave voice to her troubled thoughts. "She's not just your wife, Cullen. She's the heir to the Solar League. And if this is a society of women, what better person to make the appeal that they join the League than its future *female* ruler?" It was all very logical but Mercedes suspected his full-throated defense had more to do with Tracy's animus toward Boho than realpolitik.

"Not that it's going to be so much of an appeal as a politely phrased demand," Captain de Vilbiss murmured. "But I see your point, Captain-Lieutenant."

Admiral Kartirci's gaze flicked from person to person. He looked faintly bewildered, and once again Mercedes had the uncomfortable feeling that perhaps the old man was no longer totally in control and abdicating far too much of his authority to his flag captain. She glanced over at Cipriana who had remained silent through all of the discussions even though any plan would involve her as well. Cipriana gave her a tiny nod. Encouragement or merely acknowledgment? Mercedes assumed it was the former.

She decided it was well past time they let her speak. "I don't wish to be presumptuous, but I fill dual roles. There is my rank as a military officer but I'm also the representative for the crown and by extension my father. I think the preponderance of the evidence does support the theory that this is a female-centric society." She glanced around the table. "It hasn't gone unnoticed that many of the worlds we've annexed have contained societies that are... are..." She paused, looking for a polite way to phrase it.

Sukarno stepped in, saying dryly, "Riding particular hobby horses?"

"Both political and societal," Mercedes agreed.

"Trying to create nostalgic visions of societies that never really existed," de Vilbiss added.

"Well then there'll be a lot of new women to be wives and mothers," Kartirci said archly, and bit into a sandwich. As an attempt at humor it failed. Everyone else at the table looked grim or worried.

"If they have perfected parthenogenesis that puts them in violation of League laws regarding genetic engineering," Tracy said.

"Disgusting," Vink muttered.

"The Minister of Justice will have to handle that," Mercedes said. "But the people... women on the planet can't be held responsible for violating a law they didn't know existed. They'll just have to obey it going forward."

"It's a harsh world, barely acceptable for colonization. We can make their lives a good deal easier," Captain de Vilbiss said.

"We should do them the courtesy of sending a delegation of top officers," Admiral Kartirci said. "Captain de Vilbiss, I presume your XO is as competent as Vink here. I suggest that you and I accompany the ladies."

"With respect, sir, I should be there as well," Boho said.

"No." The vehemence of the word startled Mercedes even as she uttered it, and her teacup rattled in its saucer. She softened her tone and said, "If you're there and introduced as my husband it undercuts my authority and they need to think I'm their equal and... unattached."

She heard Tracy at the same time say under his breath, "Unencumbered."

"I think we should have Belmanor as well," de Vilbiss said. "After all he's the one who's done all the research. Save someone else having to learn all this."

"What about the padres?" Kartirci asked. "They're going to want to go."

Mercedes knew the admiral's faith was deep and real, but there was something in the request that niggled at her. She also really didn't want Jose in the party watching her, making her self-conscious, and prepared to report everything back to his father.

De Vilbiss spoke up. "We don't know their religious beliefs. We could offend without meaning to. This discussion is going to be rough enough without adding theological debates." Mercedes nodded with approval. Her estimation of the *Triunfo*'s captain was rising by the minute.

"To back up these… discussions there should be a squad of *fusileros* from both ships. Not enough to seem threatening but enough to make the point," Vink said. He turned to Mercedes. "The transports will arrive in four days. You just need to keep them talking for that long, Princess."

16

GOOD NEWS! THE LEAGUE IS HERE

Radio contact had been formally made. The flagship had made the hail in *Español* and got back a response in *Inglés*. It was a widely used language favored in business and law, and most League citizens spoke both. They settled on *Inglés* as the default. The women on the planet were still a bit hard to understand. The accents were strange with long drawling vowels and mushy consonants. Tracy wondered how long ago they had left Earth. There had clearly been a lot of language drift on the part of the League. Linguists were going to have a field day studying a language that hadn't changed significantly for almost five hundred years. Tracy had a sudden sharp childhood memory of arriving on Reichart's World. He didn't recall the language seeming strange to him.

The three shuttles were instructed to land at an airbase near the city of Amastris. One shuttle contained Mercedes, Cipriana, Captain de Vilbiss, the admiral, the two adjutants to the top officers, and Tracy. The other larger shuttles, one from each ship, carried the *fusileros*. Tracy studied Mercedes.

She was biting at the corner of her lower lip and staring off into space. It meant she was nervous and thinking hard. Tracy smiled, remembering. She began to spin the elaborate wedding set on her left ring finger and his pleasure at seeing her evaporated. She drew in a quick breath and pulled off the ring and tucked it into a pocket.

They entered the atmosphere. A nimbus of fire surrounded the shuttle. The pilot used both drag and the rockets to slow their descent. Mercedes looked up and shot the pilot a sharp glance. Once again Tracy smiled. He knew what she was thinking—that she could have flown the shuttle better. Her eyes briefly met his and she beckoned to him. Startled he moved to her side.

"This is my private scoop number," she said softly and touched her ring. "Just in case we should get separated. In an emergency you know you could... should use it."

"Thank you. I won't abuse the privilege." They touched their rings together and he returned to his seat.

The sharp peaks of ice and snow-covered mountains rose up around them. The shuttle was buffeted by wild and erratic winds. Snow blew across the canopy and withdrew as if massive white shutters were being opened and closed. Fortunately the pilot had locked onto a homing beacon and was making an instrument landing. There were a few more wild tips and swoops and then they were flying down the length of a deep valley, the mountains to either side like grey and white fortress walls.

They had a brief glimpse of dwellings dug into the canyon walls. Beneath them were clear domes where crops were growing. The blinking orange lights of the airfield beckoned them. The shuttle hovered, dancing on blazing jets, and slowly dropped in to land. The other two shuttles settled in moments later.

The engines whined into silence. Tracy listened to the wind's mournful wail outside and the pock of snow against the canopy.

"I'm betting they've perfected the sauna," Cipriana said, breaking the silence and the tension. Chuckles ran through the cabin.

They stood and pulled on the winter parkas that the quartermaster had provided for them. "Remember," Mercedes said. "Let Cipriana and me do the talking until we get a feel for the society."

They waited for the call from the commander of the *fusileros* before they allowed the door to cycle open. The ramp extended and Tracy saw that the *fusileros* were in place to either side of the ramp. As Mercedes appeared at the top of the ramp they smacked the butts of their rifles against the ground, and took up parade rest positions. The League officers walked down to greet the three women who waited for them.

One was very young. To Tracy's eye she looked to be in her late teens and she was a bit plump. Next to her stood a woman in her forties, heavyset and solid. Tracy could feel the reason for a bit of padding. He was shivering despite the parka and the windblown snow stung his cheeks.

The final woman was very elderly. Tendrils of white hair blew across her face, pulled loose from a bun coiled at the nape of her neck. The trio were also flanked by soldiers but theirs were all women. They carried old-style pulse rifles plugged into a power deck at their waist. The League had abandoned the rifles almost three hundred years ago. The power packs were prone to overheat and shut down the gun's ability to fire. In worst case the packs sometimes exploded, taking out a soldier's hip or gut.

Tracy noted that the women forming the welcoming committee looked only at Mercedes and Cipriana. The only women eyeing the men were the soldiers and they didn't look friendly, though in the case of the younger ones there was also evident curiosity.

The old woman spoke. "Welcome to Sinope."

She extended both hands toward Mercedes and Cipriana.

Mercedes stepped forward and offered her hands. "Thank you. We are happy to have found you."

"I am Melodia Kristin Olmsdahl's Datter."

"Lieutenant Princess Mercedes Adalina Saturnina Inez de Arango, the Infanta."

The three Sinopians exchanged glances. "A monarchy," the matronly woman said. "How quaint." Everyone on the League side stiffened.

"It's a constitutional monarchy with a parliament," Cipriana said. To Tracy's ears it sounded defensive.

Once again glances were exchanged, and the old lady gave a discreet cough. She indicated the middle-aged woman. "Virginia Lily Nielsen's Datter and Amelia Christina Mamaroni's Datter. We are the governing authority for the colony."

"My associate, Lieutenant Lady Cipriana Delacroix."

Mercedes then went on to introduce the officers, stressing their titles. When she got to Tracy and his lack of a title he found three pairs of eyes suddenly focused on him. He bowed to the three women and they exchanged glances.

"Let us get you out of the cold," the youngest woman said and with a graceful sweep of the arm she indicated the cliff behind her. There was a door set into the rock, and windows had been carved out. The light from the windows was butter-gold and warm against the blowing white snow.

The entire crowd shuffled into motion and headed inside. Tracy hurried forward and fell into step with Mercedes. "This appears to be a political entity based on a neo-pagan concept of a triple goddess," he said softly in Mercedes' ear. "Maiden, mother and crone."

"A hobby horse indeed." She shook her head then added, "Who holds the most authority?"

"Damned if I know... Your Highness," he belatedly added.

"Make a guess," she whispered back as they stepped out of the wind.

"The old lady, I guess. With age comes wisdom?"

They found themselves in a large anteroom with curving chairs made of white plastic. On the far side of the room were large doors that judging from the placement led deeper into the cliff.

"The males can wait here guarded by our troops," the middle-aged woman said.

"That is unacceptable." Mercedes had drawn herself up to her full, impressive height. "In the League there are no second-class citizens. I will not treat my shipmates and fellow officers with such contempt solely because of their gender." *What an empress she will be*, Tracy thought and the gulf between them widened even further. "I will leave my soldiers with your troops, but my fellow officers will join us."

The three women went into a huddle. The old woman said, "We agree, but tell your males to be respectful. Our daughters have never dealt with their sex."

There were murmurs from the League troops, which earned them flat, almost hostile stares from the female soldiers. The next room was warmer and more sumptuously furnished in that the chairs had padding and the walls were hung with heavy woven tapestries. The scenes depicted in colored thread were beautiful and seemed to detail the story of the ravaged Earth and the colony's flight. The conference table in the center of the room was stone.

Not a lot of usable wood on this planet, Tracy thought as he settled into one of the chairs set against the wall. He found himself between Captain de Vilbiss and the admiral. Mercedes glanced back at him.

"I would like Captain-Lieutenant Belmanor to join me. It was he who did the research that indicated you were a matriarchal society."

Tracy didn't wait for permission. He took the chair to Mercedes' left. Cipriana, seated to her right, leaned back and gave him a speaking glance. He was pretty sure he understood because sitting this close to Mercedes he could see the subtle trembling in her fingers, and beneath her perfume was the musky scent of sweat. He was sweating too. So much could go wrong in the next few moments or the next few days. On a very personal level Mercedes had been given an enormous amount of authority while under the eye of a fleet admiral. Reports on her performance would undoubtedly be sent back to the capital and whispered through the fleet.

Mercedes dropped her hands into her lap. A moment later and he felt her hand reaching for his. He caught it and gave a reassuring squeeze. He wanted to hold fast, but she pulled away and leaned across the table.

"Shall we begin? We're very eager to tell you about the League and outline the benefits of membership."

"We are interested in hearing about human history after our departure," Lily Nielsen's Datter said.

"But we see no reason to join with you," Kristin Olmsdahl's Datter said. Her voice might be an aged quaver, but it was implacable.

"How about the fact you've settled on a barely marginal planet," Cipriana said.

"And that there are alien races that I'm assuming you've yet to meet," Mercedes added.

That caused a reaction. "Aliens?" the youngest woman asked.

"Oh yes. Aliens that we defeated, but you might want our protection. Space is big. Who knows what else is out there?" Mercedes said. There was something in her tone that led Tracy to think that wasn't just hyperbole.

Sector 470—could she know? Probably, and she probably knew more than he did. Years ago Rohan had tasked Tracy with investigating that sector. What he found had been disturbing. Given her access to intelligence service reports, Mercedes probably knew a lot more than he did about the missing ships.

His attention snapped back to the meeting when the two older women began laughing. "Aliens? You expect us to believe that? Decades of listening without any evidence of non-terrestrial life beyond algae and microbes," Virginia, the middle-aged woman said. "I'm outraged you would try such an obvious ploy. We don't frighten."

Mercedes was rendered speechless by the reaction. She and Cipriana exchanged flummoxed glances.

Tracy leaned in and whispered, "Perhaps an object lesson? I've got a Cara'ot batBEM. There are Hajin and Isanjo on both ships."

Cipriana leaned into the huddle and added, "Buys us some time too."

Mercedes nodded. She leaned in at the ruling triumvirate. "Shall we take a break while I prove to you I'm not lying?" She jerked her hand back over her shoulder.

Tracy left the table, hurried to the waiting officers and filled them in. From their positions at the far end of the room they hadn't been able to hear much. Admiral Kartirci nodded. "Good call, Belmanor. Use the shuttle radio to contact the ship. Bring them in once they land."

"Aye, sir."

De Vilbiss caught his elbow before he could move away. "Don't waste time sending up one of the shuttles. Burn the fuel and bring down another." His fingers tightened on Tracy's arm, and his gaze was intense.

"Should I add those items you forgot, sir?"

"Yes. Do that."

Four of the female troops surrounded him and made it clear he was not going to go anywhere unattended. Tracy quickly added four of the League troops to the mix and they moved out of the building. The snow crunched and squeaked beneath his boots and Tracy felt like an idiot in the midst of this heavily armed scrum. What the hell did the women think he was going to do in the forty seconds it would take to cross to the shuttles? Find some woman and ravish her? Cipriana's bruised and bloody face seemed to float before his eyes and guilt slammed down. That was probably exactly what they feared.

The women soldiers accepted that they were not going to be allowed inside the shuttle. Once the hatch dogged closed Tracy moved to the radio and sent a coded message to the *Triunfo* requesting the batBEMs, but also another squad of *fusileros* with the order that the extra troops remain onboard the shuttle and maintain radio silence.

Tracy settled down to wait. Orbital mechanics had the battle cruiser on the far side of the planet. He tried to use the opportunity to sleep, but there was a fluttering deep in his gut. There was a superiority and disdain on the part of the colonists that didn't bode well for the coming annexation. Tracy hoped the revelation of the aliens would quell those attitudes, but it was only a hope. He drank coffee, ate a protein bar, paced. Eventually the other shuttle settled onto a snowy runway nearby. Tracy pulled on his parka and hurried over followed by his escort. The big side door didn't open. Instead he slipped in through the pilot's hatch.

The sergeant braced and saluted. "What's the plan, sir?"

"Stay here. Maintain radio silence, but monitor all communications. We may need you."

"Aye, aye, sir."

"Sorry about the cramped conditions."

A brief smile flickered across his lips. "We've had worse. This is like a room at the Ritz."

Tracy moved to where Donnel waited with an Isanjo and a nervous Hajin. "So this is how humans do diplomacy. A little bit of charm, a whole lot of deceit and overwhelming firepower," the Cara'ot said.

"I'm hoping you three are going to render the firepower unnecessary," Tracy said.

"What do you need us to do, sir?" the Isanjo asked.

"Look scary."

A grin made the fur-covered gamin face even more gamin. The Isanjo unsheathed his four-inch claws. "Will this do?"

"Excellent."

The Hajin looked even more distressed. "I don't really do... scary."

Tracy glanced up into the long face. Like most of the males of his species, the Hajin topped out at a bit over seven feet. "Loom. Glower. These are all females on this world."

"Oh, your precious League is gonna get their panties in a twist over that," Donnel said. "And what's my role?"

"You're horrifying without doing a goddamn thing," Tracy responded.

Donnel smiled. "I'll scuttle up the wall and hang off the ceiling. And do tell 'em about the Sidones. Humans hate spiders."

The reaction was everything Mercedes could have hoped for. During the wait refreshments had been served and Mercedes and Cipriana had chatted with Virginia and Melodia. Amelia hesitantly approached the male officers, studying them with fascination. The admiral's adjutant, a handsome young lieutenant, bowed and kissed her hand to her evident confusion and some delight. They began to talk until Melodia noticed, and summoned Amelia back with a sharp word.

Mercedes had just lifted the teacup to her lips when there was a babble of confusion and alarm from beyond the double doors. Melodia strode over and threw them open as Tracy led his group of aliens through the soldiers waiting in the antechamber. The female soldiers were recoiling in alarm, and the male troops from the League ships reacted with amusement. Mercedes noted the exposed claws and Tracy's batBEM scuttling across the ceiling and she hid a smile.

"Oh Goddess preserve us," Virginia whispered.

"We don't lie," Mercedes said. "This," she thrust a finger at the aliens, "is why you need us." She checked the data deck set into her sleeve. "I think you've got quite a lot to think about. Shall we resume in the morning?"

"Yes. Yes." Melodia suddenly sounded old. "We've arranged accommodations for you and your males."

Glances were exchanged. "Thank you for your

hospitality, but I need to consult with my officers before I can accept." Mercedes moved to Admiral Kartirci. "What do you want us to do?" she asked quietly.

"I'm quite certain Carl Vink will want us to return to the *Concepción*."

Mercedes considered. The advantage was that it would eat up more hours, leaving the planet, resting, returning. It would also be rude and the clearest indication of their distrust of the women of Sinope. "I think we have to stay, sir."

"I don't disagree."

Mercedes returned to the triumvirate. "Thank you. We accept."

17

DUTY

They were taken deeper into the cliff, and down various corridors to a suite of rooms. Mercedes was very aware of the female troops who surrounded her people, but comforted herself with the knowledge that the League soldiers were better armed and probably better trained.

They were led to a large metal door that wouldn't have been out of place in a prison. Mercedes' pace slowed but she forced herself to step through. Inside was far less intimidating. There were cushions and rugs on the stone floor, a few of the plastic chairs and couches piled with pillows. There were more of the wall hangings separated by numerous doors. She opened one to find four bunk beds. Another door inside the bedroom probably led to a lavatory. They appeared to be in some sort of barracks.

The adjutants began to get the *fusileros* arranged. Tracy set his tap-pad and ScoopRing to privacy settings and de Vilbiss, Kartirci, the admiral's adjutant, Cipriana, and Mercedes went into a huddle within that protective buzz of cyber and audio security.

"This room is undoubtedly bugged," de Vilbiss said.

"And they're advanced enough to know we're jamming them," Kartirci said.

"Makes us look just the tiniest bit suspicious, don't you think?" Cipriana offered.

"They're just as suspicious of us. I don't think they'll think it's strange," Tracy said.

"I wish we'd gotten a bit more information. How long they've been here? How many people were aboard that long view ship?" Mercedes shook her head, frustrated. Tracy cleared his throat. "Yes, Captain-Lieutenant?"

"While I was waiting for the batBEMs to arrive I communicated with Flag Captain Lord Vink. Fortunately he's…"

"Paranoid as all hell?" the admiral offered with a smile.

Tracy smiled back. "Cautious. He sent a team aboard the colony's abandoned long view ship. Based on the equipment they estimate they started with only about forty thousand individuals. Most of the cryo units were for animal embryos and seed banks."

Diego, the admiral's adjutant, spoke up. "As for how long they've been here… I only had a few minutes to talk with Amelia, but she indicated it had been about a hundred and fifty years."

"Population can't be that big. Not all forty thousand would have been of childbearing age," Cipriana said.

"Or had viable ova," de Vilbiss said. "Remember they're not doing this the old-fashioned way."

"If they've got artificial wombs they could have rapidly expanded the population," Mercedes said.

The men looked shocked, then Tracy shook his head. "Unlikely. Even if they'd developed that tech they wouldn't have increased the population by that much. It's a marginal world. They're growing food in domes." He did some fast calculations on his pad. "Best guess, and it is a guess, but I think there can't be more than three or four hundred thousand people."

Kartirci grunted. "That's a relief. Reichart's World had four million. That was a bitch to coordinate. We were digging people out of rat holes three years on."

"Given the harshness of the environment they won't be able to run," Tracy said.

"This is going to be a lousy provincial governorship," de Vilbiss said.

"Well, the Emperor can use it as one of those rewards that's its own punishment," Kartirci said. The laughter rippled through the group.

"We need to wrap this up." Mercedes interrupted the merriment. "So, tomorrow… what's my play?"

"History, lots of history," Cipriana suggested. "Bore them insensible."

"And ask them questions," Tracy added. "Everybody loves to talk about themselves. And, Your Majesty, there's another fire team aboard the fourth shuttle. Should things go pear-shaped."

"Well, let us hope for harmony and comity until the transports arrive," Mercedes said.

Tracy shut down the isolation protocols and moved away. But he kept glancing back at her.

"You can't." Cipriana's voice was soft, her breath puffing against Mercedes' ear.

"Are you sleeping with him, Cipri?" Mercedes was startled at how harsh her voice sounded.

"No. We're just friends." Cipriana bowed her head and stared down at the carpet that covered the stone floor.

Mercedes gripped her friend's wrist. "Cipri, I need your advice. About sex."

"I've sworn off men," she replied with forced lightness.

"Since when?"

"Since I got raped."

The flat tone and level delivery left her breathless, but also didn't fool Mercedes. She pulled Cipriana into the bedroom and ordered that they not be disturbed.

Cipriana's voice was emotionless, which made the tears running down her face all the more heartbreaking. Mercedes wrapped her arms around her friend's shoulders and hugged her tightly as the story ran down to its conclusion.

"So now I work for Exeteur in Medical keeping his files. It's make-work since I have no training to be of any actual help to him. The only bright point is Tracy. He stops by when his duties permit and checks on me."

"I assume the man has been dealt with," Mercedes said.

Cipriana shook her head. "Exeteur kept quiet—medical privilege, and I made Tracy promise. He's kept his word. The captain doesn't know. No one knows except Tracy, Exeteur and me. Well, and Wessen of course."

"Tracy didn't take care of the fellow?" Mercedes felt disappointed.

Cipriana drew back, pushed Mercedes away and gave her an incredulous look. "Don't be absurd, Mer! This isn't some *novela romántica*. The man's FFH and Tracy's not an idiot. What did you expect him to do? Challenge him to a duel? Beat him up in some secluded corner of the ship? Kill him? One false move and he's drummed out. Same goes for me."

Mercedes felt both guilty and hurt. "You getting raped is not making a false move. You're the victim here. You should have contacted me. We would have seen to it this man was removed and punished."

"Are you really that clueless?" Cipriana bestowed a sharp rap to the side of Mercedes' head. "You know how the world works. *I* would be the one to get the blame. And then it would spread to your father. The debate would begin all over again about the wisdom of having women in the military. Then where would you be? I have to endure until there are more of us to give you cover."

"I never demanded that of you."

"You didn't have to. It was expected and you and your father never doubted that. We all do our duty to you and the crown, and do our best to survive while we're doing it."

"And you think that doesn't apply to me too?" Mercedes cried. "I went to the academy, graduated, married Boho—" she broke off.

The look Cipriana gave her was disconcertingly astute, but she stayed mercifully silent. She sighed, stroked a hand down Mercedes' arm and gave her hand a squeeze. "Maybe that's all any of us, princess or commoner, can hope for."

The metal door whispered closed behind her. Mercedes sat on the bed and bleakly contemplated duties that lay ahead.

Tracy was restless, unable to sleep and the dinner that had been brought to their suite lay heavy in his stomach. Finally he got up, dressed and went out into the central room. He paced, lit one of the herbal sticks the Tiponis liked to smoke. Its effect on humans was minimal, but it smelled good and tasted pleasant. It also gave him something to do with his hands, a way to burn off nervous energy. The blank door of Mercedes' room both beckoned and repelled. She was mere feet away. Only a single door separated them. His earlier joy at being assigned to assist her had given way to despair. She seemed to be looking through him. She was polite enough, but he felt diminished. Perhaps she had fallen in love with Boho. Perhaps if he heard that directly from her the longing would pass.

He stubbed out the stick, contemplated the blank face of the door, willed himself to sense her. Read her mind. Know her heart. He walked to the door. Stopped. Not only were their hosts watching, the *fusilero* squad leaders had set peeps to watch the bedroom doors. Mercedes wasn't really alone.

In one moment he could ruin not only himself and her, but these delicate negotiations. He walked away.

Mercedes listened to the retreating footsteps. Every muscle in her body had tensed, her lungs seemed to be repelling the air. She knew it had been him. She waited but Tracy didn't return and the knock never came. She sat up, the covers falling to her waist, hugged her knees and tried to ignore the twinge of sorrow and focus on being relieved.

Anxiety formed a sick churn in her stomach. She got up and went into the small bathroom for a drink of water. It was numbingly cold as if it came directly off the glaciers that hung like white curtains on the canyon walls. She returned to bed and pulled up the covers, shivered.

She should be thinking about the coming day. Prepare her talking points, make sure she didn't give away too much, but her mind kept darting between Cipriana and Tracy. She felt guilty over her disappointment. Was ambition enough of a reason not to act, not to have found a way to punish Cipriana's attacker?"

And should he have found a way into your room tonight?

Evil little voice. Mercedes tossed aside the covers and went to the door. Leaned against it for a moment, pressing her cheek against the cold metal. What would the watchers make of her disquiet? Would they know it had more to do with a pair of grey eyes and less to do with the fact she had to keep a shooting war from breaking out for another forty-eight hours?

She went back to bed, but sleep continued to elude her.

"Glad to see you grew a brain." The words whispered into his ear caused Tracy to jump and a yell rose in his throat. Donnel clapped one of his hands over Tracy's mouth so he wouldn't disturb the sleepers in the room. The alien was clinging to the wall next to the door halfway between floor and ceiling.

Tracy pulled away the six-fingered hand and whispered angrily, "I'm not a fool. Why are you up? Are you spying on me?"

"It's my duty to serve. You get up—I get up."

Tracy glanced at the bunks. Shattering snores from the sleeping men filled the room. He backed out and returned to the common room. Donnel followed.

"I do have a question," the alien said. "What do you want us bug-eyed monsters to do? Wait here, go back to the *Triunfo*?"

Tracy keyed his ring to privacy and leaned in close. "We want to keep all four shuttles close to hand, but you've served your purpose. Go back to one of the shuttles and wait. It's only another two days."

Donnel made a face. "Oh goody, two days of K-rations."

"You'll survive."

"You should focus on that too," the alien said.

"You think they'll be trouble?"

"You're all humans. Of course there will be trouble."

18

LIES AND DAMN LIES

Tracy looked like he'd had as little sleep as her. Mercedes also noticed that he took the chair next to Cipriana rather than the one at her side. It felt as if she had a stone lodged beneath her breastbone. What if he had tapped on her door last night? Would she have... She pushed the thought away and smiled at their hosts.

"Thank you for your hospitality last night," she said to Melodia.

"Our pleasure. Was breakfast acceptable?"

"Yes, it didn't taste like any oatmeal I've ever eaten," Mercedes said.

"It's an heirloom grain that we took from the vaults in Svalbard." Melodia's wrinkled lips quirked in a smile at their evident confusion. "Svalbard was a seed bank in Norway," she explained. "It was located above the Arctic Circle. It was meant for a doomsday scenario, but doomsday came creeping up on us. By the time we left they were trying to put the bank in orbit since temperatures on Earth had risen enough that they were having to run air conditioning during the summer months to keep things frozen."

Mercedes seized on the remark as the perfect opening. "So climate change was the reason you left?"

"One of the reasons, but wars were breaking out all across the globe," Virginia said. She paused and considered then added, "Primarily over water, so I suppose the climate crisis was the proximate cause of most of the Earth's problems."

"That and men," Melodia said. Her eyes beneath the withered lids were reptile-cold.

"Well, you'll be pleased to know that the League is taking steps to reverse the effects of climate change on Earth. The Rothschilds have made it their personal cause," Mercedes said.

"Just as we're doing on Earth, we have the technology to help turn Sinope into a more livable world," Cipriana added. "As you probably know better than we do, humans are really good at heating up planets. Which this one definitely needs."

"That might be of interest to us," Virginia said.

"So tell us of your journey," Mercedes asked. "How you picked candidates for your LV ship."

The youngest member of the triumvirate enthusiastically began the story. "The world was beset with wars, famine, drought and vast poverty. All of these ills fell most heavily on women and their children, and so our founder, Selene Dukmajian, said *enough*…"

The story played out. Amelia's delivery had the feeling of myth or dogma rather than a dry recitation of history. Engineering both mechanical and genetic was discussed, how the final selections were made for the *Argand*, their ship. Tracy ran the word through his tap-pad and inclined it so

Mercedes could read—*Language Armenian, meaning womb.* She nodded and went back to listening.

"Selene attempted to find men worthy of inclusion, but they always failed to overcome their biology." There was a subtle reaction from the listening men that was quickly quelled at a look from the admiral.

"Please explain that," Mercedes interrupted.

"Women are collegial. We know how to set aside competition. How to work together in harmony," Virginia said.

Cipriana let out a snort. "Oh please. I went to an all girls' school. Talk about a bunch of backbiting bitches. Don't tell me you've never met a mean girl."

"There are disputes," Melodia admitted. "But we can resolve our differences without resorting to violence."

"So your troops are just decorative?" Tracy asked and got a glare for his trouble.

"Testosterone is poison," Melodia said firmly. That brought another reaction from the men.

"I think it would be more accurate to say that we're humans and humans are flawed," Mercedes said.

The story wound down to the women's eventual arrival at Sinope. Virginia sighed. "It was a less than ideal planet, but the cryo units were beginning to fail, and seed has to occasionally be planted. It can only last so long in storage. The soil on the *Argand* was played out. So we made the best of what we had found. Here in the deep canyons we are sheltered from the worst of the storms and can safely settle."

"And now it's our turn to hear your story," Melodia said. "I assume you've perfected faster than light-speed travel."

"Yes. The Fold technology. It was approved for general use in 2117."

The glances this time were dismayed. "That's only thirteen years after we left," Amelia said.

"I'm sorry," Mercedes said. "It must be very hard to hear."

"It's done and we're building the kind of society we want." Melodia's voice was firm and uncompromising. Mercedes looked down at the table, worried what her eyes might reveal.

"So tell us about the League," Amelia said.

"Yes, why the whole aristocracy thing?" Virginia's tone was amused.

That had her stumped. Mercedes had grown up in the heart of her society. Accepted it as normal. She looked to Cipri who gave a baffled shrug.

"Perhaps we could hear from the one person who merited an introduction, but didn't spray around their title and family tree." Virginia looked pointedly at Tracy. He looked to Mercedes and raised his eyebrows, a clear interrogative.

"By all means. Do answer the lady's question, Captain-Lieutenant." Mercedes leaned back, feigning a relaxation she so didn't feel. Tracy's resentment of the FFH was well known to her. It was anybody's guess what he might say. She had to trust his loyalty to her station if not to her, the League and the service.

"Our history professor at the academy pointed to the shock of discovering that aliens existed as one major reason," Tracy began. "Take your own reactions. All through human history there had been a sense that humans were unique,

God's most perfect creation. Suddenly we were just one among many. There was fear and we found ourselves in combat with the more advanced races. Notably the Isanjo, the Sidones and the Cara'ot. We beat them, but I think there was a need to underscore our superiority. Titles were given to powerful corporate and military leaders. The FFH was born."

Virginia frowned. "When we left Earth those initials stood for the Fortune Five Hundred."

"They still do, but in a hereditary sense now," Mercedes said.

"So it's still all about money and war," Melodia sniffed.

"And we should probably add sex," Cipriana said.

Stifling a giggle and pleased to see a flash of Cipri's old insouciance, Mercedes added, "Though never with aliens. That is strictly forbidden."

"How do you feel about same sex coupling?" Virginia's tone was challenging.

"It's accepted though we insist that homosexual couples bank their sperm, and we encourage lesbians to have children using some of that sperm. Male couples frequently adopt children from—" She broke off abruptly, then went on. "We also sanction three-party marriages. Though those are less common in my class," Mercedes added.

The three women stiffened. "Polygamy leads to the subjugation of women," Amelia said.

"Don't assume it's just multiple women. Polyandry is also allowed," Tracy said.

Melodia pinned him with a look. "How do you feel about this?"

"Well, I couldn't afford even one wife right now, but I'd be open to being kept," Tracy said lightly.

Her hand brushed the air as if shooing flies. "No, no, about not having a title?"

Mercedes held her breath. "The League rewards intelligence and competence," Tracy said. "I was given a full scholarship to the High Ground. My father could never have afforded to give me that kind of education so I'm grateful." The tone was level, unemotional, which Mercedes knew indicated how much was roiling just below the surface. Tracy was nothing if not passionate, but these women didn't know that. Didn't know his actual meaning.

"And what do you give up for that education?" Amelia asked.

"I have to serve five years in the *Orden de la Estrella*. After that I'm free to do something else."

"And will you?" Mercedes blurted out.

"No. I'll probably stay in the service. That's the only way I'm likely to win a title."

"And that's important to you?" Virginia asked.

Tracy shrugged. "It's one way of keeping score." He turned his gaze on Mercedes and it was almost physical in its intensity.

To break the tension that gripped her Mercedes abruptly asked, "So, what sort of industry have you developed on Sinope, and what resources could this planet offer to the League?" It was an inelegant transition at best, rude at worst, but Mercedes wanted to turn the discussion back to the women.

"We have yet to decide if we want to offer anything to your League," Melodia said dryly.

"Oh, of course," Mercedes hastened to say. "I didn't mean to imply otherwise."

They had gotten through the rest of the day discussing industry, mining interests, the government structure, but by the time they returned to their quarters Mercedes' exhaustion could be read in every line of her body. Tracy knew how his muscles ached from tension. He could only imagine how much worse it was for Mercedes. Tracy longed to shake out her braid and give her a neck rub. Instead he had returned to a shuttle to send a tight beam to the ships and learn the status of the transports. Best guess they were fifteen hours out.

The evening meal was eaten in near silence. "They never offer to dine with us," Cipriana remarked.

"Maybe it's better that way," Mercedes muttered.

People had retired to bed early and this night Tracy managed to sleep. Now they were once again assembled in the conference room.

He glanced at the chronometer inset in the sleeve of his uniform. *Three hours. Give or take.*

"So how do you produce only daughters?" Mercedes took the discussion right to what was going to be the flashpoint once the League came in.

"I sense some criticism," Melodia said.

"No." To Tracy it was apparent Mercedes was lying, but he knew her very well so perhaps it would fool the women.

"It is different though and not something we would ever do."

"You don't do IVF?" Virginia asked. Her surprise was evident.

"We do that. As we said yesterday, gay men are required to donate sperm," Cipriana spoke up. "To be childless is a great tragedy in our culture."

"We just don't manipulate the genetic… well, you know," Mercedes stumbled into silence.

Admiral Kartirci was unable to contain himself. "To select for sex would be, well, criminal."

Mercedes looked over her shoulder. "Let's not be judgmental, Admiral. Different culture, different norms."

"Your pardon, Majesty."

"Might we see one of these labs?" Mercedes asked.

There was a discussion between the trio. "We have no objection," Melodia said.

"But you must leave all these troops behind. It's delicate work; we don't need a crowd tromping through," Virginia added.

"Her Majesty should not be denied her security," de Vilbiss said.

Melodia gave him a look that was both amused and contemptuous. "Do you find us so frightening, Captain, and aren't you up to the task of protecting Ms. Arango's person? More to the point, do you feel she and Ms. Delacroix are unable to defend themselves?"

"Umm, no of course not, but… but…"

"She is our ruler," Tracy said smoothly. "I presume that's why the three of you have a security detail."

"And going back to an earlier discussion. If women

are so nurturing and collegial why do you have police and soldiers?" Cipriana asked.

"Possibly because of the intrusion of people like you," Virginia snapped.

Tension crackled through the room. Tracy found himself literally holding his breath and wondering how quickly he could call in that extra fire team.

Mercedes patted the air placatingly. "Please, none of this is necessary. Of course any society needs police forces. None of us are angels." She smiled at the three women. "We'll leave behind our troops, but may the admiral and Captain-Lieutenant Belmanor accompany us?"

Smart, Tracy thought. *Leave behind the captain of the* Triunfo *to coordinate with the* fusileros *and Flag Captain Vink should that become necessary.*

After another consultation Melodia nodded. "That's agreeable."

This time they left the cliff dwelling, and took an enclosed snowmobile farther up the canyon and into the opposite cliff wall. They passed women who were using extendable brushes to remove snow from the top of the domes. Through the transparent walls they could see more women working among the trees and rows of food. In one dome sheep and goats were grazing.

"It seems a fragile ecosystem," Kartirci said softly.

"We have two other settlements and a distributed population so we can cover for each other if any one system has a failure."

"And what if you have multiple failures?" Mercedes asked.

"Sometimes you just have to have faith," Amelia said softly.

They pulled up in front of another entrance and moved quickly out of the wind and into the hollowed-out cliff. Tracy noted that their driver accompanied them and that the woman was armed. Inside there was the sound of power tools being utilized. Clearly this section of Amastris was given over to industry.

They reached a doorway that led into an antechamber where they were instructed to put on clean room coveralls complete with gloves, booties, hoods and masks. They were then led into the IVF laboratory.

Five women garbed in the same fashion were working with pipettes, test tubes and petri dishes. Tracy recognized a number of powerful inverted microscopes that had the light source at the top rather than the bottom, and the lenses beneath the stage rather than above it.

Melodia spoke softly to one woman who moved aside from her microscope allowing the visitors to look. Tracy was the last to look and he saw an ovum floating in solution. He stepped back and listened as the woman doctor described the ICSI—intracytoplasmic sperm injection—needles that were used.

"Though in our case they aren't sperm injectors, instead we're injecting the genetic material of one ovum into another to give us the necessary number of chromosomes to create our new daughter, so I guess they'd be ICOI needles."

Tracy wondered if his face held as shocked an expression as the others. He had a feeling it did. "So no families or pair bondings?" Cipriana asked.

"No, we form families, but they may involve multiple women," another technician said.

"The advantage to this method is that we're able to detect and weed out any genetic abnormalities before a fertilized egg is implanted. We can do our genetic testing before a woman gets pregnant."

It seemed the reaction of the League guests had finally penetrated. "You do do genetic testing, right?" Amelia asked.

Mercedes hedged and dodged. "Well, not really. I mean we could, and sometimes we do but…"

She really needs to get much better at lying if she's going to rule, Tracy thought.

Unfortunately the women weren't fooled. "So what you're really saying is that fetal abnormalities aren't detected, corrected, or aborted." Virginia's tone was disgusted.

And then Kartirci stepped in it. Tracy had been too busy watching Mercedes to notice the older man's growing anger and revulsion. "No, because genetic engineering is against the law."

"That's just… crazy." Amelia wasn't looking at them with the same enthusiasm she'd shown up until this point.

Hoping to salvage things Tracy rushed to say, "You saw my batBEM. He's a Cara'ot, but that's not the physical norm for that race. No one knows what's normal. The Cara'ot traded in genetic material. They've been altering themselves for eons."

Cipriana picked up the tale. "They were our toughest adversaries when we stepped beyond our solar system. We realized we couldn't be sure they wouldn't alter our

DNA, change what makes us essentially human, conquer us from within."

The three women exchanged glances. "That seems quite… paranoid," Melodia said.

"You didn't fight the bastards," Kartirci said grimly. "My grandfather fought them and told me stories."

"We have to make sure that humans stay human," Cipriana added, her voice pleading for understanding. Based on the hostile looks it wasn't working.

"Is genetic engineering outlawed in your League?" Melodia stared coldly at Mercedes. Tracy watched his love struggle, trying to find a way to dodge the blunt, implacable question. Seconds passed. "I'll take your silence as a yes."

A space seemed to have magically developed between the women of Sinope and the four League officers. Tracy's eyes met the eye of a technician. She took another step back as if his mere gaze was dangerous.

"I think it's time you left," Virginia said. Her tone was flat, implacable. "There is clearly no point in continuing these talks."

"We're not that different. We're both trying to keep our societies pure," Mercedes said. "Please, we're all humans."

Amelia's communicator chimed. She stepped aside, listened. Tracy was trying to watch everyone and listen to the argument that was going on between Mercedes and Virginia. The blood drained out of Amelia's face. Tracy tensed.

"Ginny! Melodia! Seven more ships have arrived in orbit. Security says they're huge!"

Virginia lunged for Mercedes. "What are you up to?"

Mercedes grabbed the older woman's wrist, spun away and dumped her onto the floor.

Amelia scrambled away clutching at her phone. Melodia looked like an ancient raptor as she stared at the four of them. "She is their princess." The final word was an epithet. "We hold her. They'll think twice before they move against us."

Tracy tapped his ring. "Chief, we need you," he said at the same time he sent an emergency signal to the orbiting ships.

"Your troops are confined and under guard," Virginia said with bitter pleasure. She was rubbing her wrist.

"Well, not all of them," Tracy replied.

They began to hear gunfire in the distance.

19

THE WORST KIND OF WOMAN

Five technicians, the triumvirate and driver/security guard. Versus the four of us, assuming the admiral is up to a fight. Perhaps he and Melodia can cancel each other out. The thoughts flashed through Mercedes' head as the driver and Virginia advanced on her. She danced back from them and evaluated the room for possible weapons. There were a lot of choices. She had the Cara'ot knife in her boot sheath, a Christmas gift from Tracy years ago, but with the sterile coveralls she couldn't reach it.

A massive crash followed by screams of dismay briefly drew her attention. Kartirci had dumped over one of the tables holding dishes of fertilized ova. It was certainly distracting, but Mercedes had a feeling it was just going to make their foes that much angrier.

Cipriana braced her hands on the top of a steel table and vaulted over. Her momentum sent her barreling into the driver/guard who was attempting to unzip her coveralls. Presumably she was going for a weapon. With her forearm Mercedes blocked a blow from a technician. Sharp pain followed by a dull ache, but she'd endured a lot worse in her hand-to-hand combat classes. She grabbed the woman, yanked her in close while at the same time spinning so she could bring her elbow into contact with the woman's face.

There was a crack as the cartilage in her nose broke. The woman screamed, hands flying to cover her face. The white material of both her suit and Mercedes' were spattered with blood. Mercedes shoved her into Virginia and they both went down. With a moment of breathing space Mercedes could evaluate the situation. What was abundantly clear was that Tracy and Kartirci were fighting defensively not offensively.

The words of her first hand-to-hand instructor floated up. *"There are going to be women on the other side. I lost a friend when he underestimated an Isanjo bitch. She was holding a cub, sweet little mother. She disemboweled him."* Chief Deal bellowing at a male cadet to overcome his programming and actually hit one of the woman cadets.

She yelled at Tracy. "For the love of God! Hit them!" Surprise followed by a setting of his jaw. Tracy whirled, grabbed a beaker off a table, and smashed it into the side of a technician's head. He followed it up with a hard punch to her jaw. She went down.

Cipriana rolled across the floor struggling with the guard. Their hands were clasped around the pistol, which was pressed against their breasts. Mercedes' breath went short, but she couldn't interfere. If she tried the weapon might discharge and it was even odds who it would hit. Instead she grabbed up one of the tall stools by the legs and swung it into another technician. It took her in the midriff and the woman bent over retching. Tracy came up swiftly behind her and chopped her hard across the back of the neck, sending her to the floor.

Amelia was running for the door. Virginia had regained her feet and was struggling with Kartirci. She was bigger and broader than the older man and he was still trying to just hold her at bay. Melodia was yelling into an intercom. The sounds of gunfire were getting closer. Even though Cipriana and the guard were lying face to face like bizarre lovers Cipriana still managed to kick the guard in the face. A testament to those years of ballet—she was still very flexible. The shock and pain loosened the guard's grip on the pistol and Cipriana wrenched it away and leaped to her feet.

Cipriana's eyes flicked about the room evaluating the situation and then she shot Virginia who was on the verge of strangling Kartirci. That knocked all the fight out of the remaining techs. The three of them backed away, hands raised.

Tracy ran across the room, grabbed Melodia and yanked her away from the intercom. She stumbled and fell against a table, then slid slowly down onto the floor clutching her ribs.

Mercedes raced for Amelia and grabbed the back of her suit. For an instant she had her, then the material tore and the young woman was out the door. Mercedes lunged after her only to be brought up short when Tracy yelled, "Mercedes! No! We can defend here. Wait for the fire teams."

Mercedes took a last glance down the corridor and at the fleeing Amelia, and the doorways lining the walls. She stepped back into the lab. "Right, they could get behind us, do a wolf pack."

Kartirci was leaning against a table, hand to his throat. He looked rocky. Cipriana continued to hold down on the women, the barrel of the gun flicking between Virginia, Melodia, the guard, and the techs.

Tracy knelt at Virginia's side, pulled off his glove and laid two fingers against her throat. "She's still alive, but we should probably try to stop the bleeding."

"Why?" Cipriana asked.

"Because that way we won't have killed anybody," Tracy replied.

"You don't think the *fusileros* haven't tangoed down a few of them by now?" Cipriana snorted.

"This is one of their leaders. Let's try not to kill her," Tracy said as he folded a towel and pressed it on the wound in the woman's back.

"You've got the only weapon, Cipri. Go guard the door," Mercedes ordered.

Stripping off the clean suit Mercedes pulled out her knife. The three techs whimpered. Mercedes cut off lengths of electrical wire and bound the women and the guard. Melodia lay on the floor glaring up at her.

"You're the worst kind of woman. The kind who betrays her own sex."

"And you're a terrible human. The kind who rejects half the population," Mercedes retorted.

"What happens now, *Princess*?"

"You join the League."

* * *

The backup squad reached them some fifteen minutes later. Amelia was with them, each arm held firmly by a *fusilero*. Tendrils of hair had escaped from her braid and were plastered on her tear-stained face.

"Colder than a witch's tit out there, sir," the sergeant said as he saluted Tracy. He then noticed Mercedes and fell into incoherence. "Sir! Ma'am! Highness! Beg pardon."

Tracy was glad to see Mercedes give the man a kind smile. "No problem, Chief. Was it hot work out there?"

"Not really. Their military forces don't seem to have much experience with actual… fighting."

Tracy's ScoopRing pricked his finger. De Vilbiss's face appeared shimmering in the air above Tracy's hand. "Ah, Belmanor." The captain of the *Triunfo* was flushed and looked like he was enjoying himself. "Tell Her Highness we're inbound on a shuttle, landing momentarily. What's your situation?"

"Under control, sir. We have all three of the leaders but one's been shot. We'll need a medic."

"Damn, that's what we forgot."

"Any casualties on our side?" Tracy asked.

"A few. Nothing life-threatening. Landing now. We'll be there shortly."

A few minutes later de Vilbiss strode in. "Ah, Highness!" He saluted. "Quite bracing isn't it? Sir!" Another salute to Kartirci. He glanced around the devastated lab. "It seems you've had a bit of a dance as well."

"What's the situation, Captain?" Kartirci's voice was hoarse from the near strangling.

"We have two shuttles outside. Two flying to make sure no support comes in from the other cities."

"You didn't have any trouble dealing with your guards?" Tracy asked.

"No, we relieved them of their weaponry, used it to reach the shuttles, rearmed and headed out. They fought bravely, just not well. I suggest we return to the flag ship. We can more forcibly make our demands from there."

They made a makeshift gurney out of a table and lifted Virginia onto it. Melodia was bound, as was Amelia. They left the techs and guard bound, and started down the hallway. There were a few attempts to interfere. Doors popping open and women taking a pot shot, but the armored squads formed a cover for the unprotected, and the merciless return fire that the attackers received discouraged more such attempts.

Tracy was still concerned. Sometimes people got lucky and he didn't want Mercedes on the receiving end of a lucky bullet. He cupped his hands around his mouth and yelled down the hall. "We have your leaders. Keep shooting and you're likely to kill one of them." After that the sniping stopped.

They reached the shuttles and climbed aboard. The pilot boosted for space. They were all flung sideways as an air-to-ground missile hit them. Tracy got an arm around Mercedes and grabbed the back of an acceleration couch with his free hand. She was pressed against his chest. She smelled of sweat, cordite, perfume and woman. Her breath was warm against his neck and the hair that had come loose from her braid caught in his chapped lips.

There was a cracking sound and one port formed a spiderweb of cracks. One of the pilots jumped out of his couch as if he'd been catapulted, moved to a storage locker, pulled out sealant film and began covering the window as they blasted for orbit.

"Need some computation up here," the other pilot yelled.

Mercedes stepped back, placed a hand against Tracy's chest and pushed him toward the cockpit. "You're up, Captain-Lieutenant."

Tracy joined him. "I can do it. I'd like to be airtight before we reach vacuum."

"Yeah, no shit," the pilot muttered.

Tracy calculated the fastest route for them to intercept the *Concepción*. By then the secondary pilot had completed his patch job and returned to the cockpit. Tracy vacated his couch and returned to the body of the shuttle. The air smelled of blood, sweat and gunpowder. Virginia was moaning. Kartirci was muttering to de Vilbiss. Amelia was still crying.

Mercedes looked up at him, and inclined her head toward the seat next to her. He took it, waited. It seemed like minutes passed before she said, "You've been... most helpful, Captain-Lieutenant."

The formality of the words turned his heart to stone. He stared down at his clasped hands. "The honor is mine, Highness."

Silence again. "I think I messed this up, Tracy," she whispered.

He turned to face her. "Why in heaven would you think that?" he whispered back.

"It all turned so ugly. I should have... Maybe if I'd..."

She shook her head helplessly.

"It was always going to be bad. It's an annexation. I'm trying to remember but wasn't there only one time in our history class when a Lost World was eager to join?"

"Paradise. Ironic name when the soil, water and pollens were literally killing them. There were only twenty thousand of them left when we found them."

"And they renamed it Paradise Lost," Tracy said.

Mercedes sighed, a sad little sound. Tracy's arm jerked as he went to put it around her shoulders and then yanked it back. "This is going to be a bad one."

"Yes, because they've set up an unnatural society," Tracy said.

She had now turned to face him. Her breath puffed softly across his face. They were inches apart. He remembered the kiss she had given him after she'd taken out the fighter threatening the space station.

"You're right. We've got to get these children… these girls away from here before they're completely warped. Really it's for the best. It's going to take years and a lot of effort to bring this planet to a truly habitable state. In fact it might not be worth the expense, but we'll have to wait and see what the terragineers think." She was babbling.

"Mercedes." He took the risk and used her name, laid a finger on her lips. "It's way above our pay grade now. We get to just be lieutenants again."

She managed to smile, laid a hand briefly on his forearm. "Thank God." The thick lashes fluttered down, brushed her cheekbones. She glanced up. "It was good working with you again. I hope, as time goes on, that you'll always be… an advisor to me."

The ache in his chest intensified, but he bowed his head and said, "I'll always be there."

They didn't speak again. Tracy was very conscious of de Vilbiss's gaze. Discomfort drove him to move to a seat further away from Mercedes. A few hours later their shuttle settled into the dock on the *Concepción*.

A welcoming party was waiting. Flag Captain Vink of course and Boho. Mercedes didn't even make it down the ramp before her husband ran forward and gathered her in an embrace. Watching them kiss was a punch to the gut. Tracy stepped backwards trying to escape the sight and trod on someone's foot.

"Your pardon," he muttered savagely. A hand closed hard on his shoulder.

"Restrain yourself, Lieutenant," de Vilbiss whispered softly in his ear. "Try for a little of that noble composure."

"My darling, I was so worried." Boho's voice. To Tracy's ears it sounded unctuous and self-serving. "Let me look at you." Tracy stepped out onto the ramp to see Boho holding Mercedes at arm's length and appraising her.

"She's not a prize fish," Tracy muttered under his breath.

"I'm fine, Boho, really."

"But there was fighting—"

"Which we won," Mercedes replied. She smiled at him and trailed her fingers across his cheek. "But thank you for being so concerned, my dear."

Boho spotted Tracy. He lifted Mercedes' hand and

pressed a kiss into her palm. "My love," he said, but his eyes were on Tracy and there was a smirk on that handsome face. Boho slipped an arm around Mercedes' waist and they left the docking bay.

"I thought you were exaggerating your lady's charms, Captain-Lieutenant, but I now see you were moderate in your praise," de Vilbiss said.

"Captain, I meant no disresp... I don't... I'm not..." Tracy choked out.

De Vilbiss went on as if Tracy hadn't spoken. "I do hope you'll recall that hearts heal and new loves can arrive when you least expect it." Tracy couldn't face the pity in his captain's face. He looked away, struggling for calm. "We should return to the *Triunfo*, Captain-Lieutenant. Things are going to get very busy now."

"Really, it's an easy decision. We're in orbit with two warships and thousands of troops. If you don't order your people to surrender, the first thing that's going to happen is we drop your former spaceship onto one of your cities. Even hollowed out it's got sufficient tonnage to reduce Amastris to rubble. Oh, and thank you for leaving it so conveniently close to hand. If that fails to convince you we'll find a few more big rocks and pound the rest of your cities into dust. Or you can accept the reality."

Vink was taking far too much pleasure in delivering the ultimatum, Mercedes thought as she sat at the conference table next to Kartirci. The three erstwhile leaders of Sinope with guards to either side stood at the end of the table facing the military officers. Virginia, pale and swaying a bit, looked confused; probably an effect of the painkillers. Her injury had been treated, but she probably shouldn't have been out of sick bay. Melodia's look was one of naked loathing. Amelia was devastated. Her hands were shaking and she was ashen.

"We are a representative government. We have to discuss this with the mayors and counselors of the cities," Melodia said.

"Your politics are of no interest to us, and what in my statement suggested there was anything to negotiate?" Vink countered. "We'll have your surrender or rocks start to fall. Now are you going to order them to surrender or have a ringside seat to the destruction?"

"What if they don't agree?" Mercedes whispered to Kartirci.

"They will." He was unperturbed. "No society is mad enough to choose death over annexation. And they'd be monsters if they allowed their children to die."

Mercedes made sure that Vink and Melodia were still arguing. She lowered her voice even further and said, "But they're going to lose their children."

"They don't know that yet."

Vink turned and looked at Kartirci. "Should we give them an object lesson? Maybe the smallest city?"

"No!" Mercedes blurted. "Sir. We'd look like monsters." She turned to the women. "We're just trying to bring you home. Help you join the broader society. Please, please, work with us."

"They'll know we agreed to this under duress." Amelia

finally spoke. "They know we're your prisoners."

"It gives them a fig leaf," Mercedes said. "You can tell them we've been negotiating."

"The League's version of a *negotiation*," Virginia grated.

"We need your answer," Kartirci said gently. "Please consider the wellbeing of your people. There are many benefits that will accrue once you're citizens."

The three women exchanged glances. Spoke softly among themselves. In the end they agreed. What choice did they have?

The order to surrender was broadcast. The warships sent all but a handful of their ground troops who disarmed the local militia, and then set about building citizenship-processing centers outside of the three cities. If there was one thing the military could do it was put up camps in short order. Between 3D printers and the materials carried aboard the warships, they soon had two fenced compounds outside of the smaller cities and three outside of Amastris. Because of the building frenzy there had been a steady flight of shuttles coming and going from the planet's surface ferrying down personnel from the transport ships, and materials from the warships. It made the constant flights seem normal, which was good in light of what was about to happen.

It took three weeks, but everything was now in place. After much discussion it was decided that Mercedes would record the announcement that would be sent out over the cities' emergency broadcast networks. Even though she was technically one of the enemy, this occupying force, at least it would be a woman issuing the order and not a man.

"Citizens, League processing centers have been completed and we are ready to welcome you into the galactic family. Trade will soon be flowing, bringing with it microbes from distant worlds. In an effort to protect you everyone is required to be immunized. At this time you will also be issued your League IDs, which entitle you to medical care, housing and a basic income. Also government subsidies for families with children. Therefore all citizens will report to the nearest processing center beginning at 0800 on Thursday morning. Transport will be provided for those who lack the means and for any individuals needing assistance. We're so happy to be welcoming you into our galactic family."

She finished the recording and it was sent to the troops who now controlled all means of communication on the planet.

Boho had been listening and he gave her a hug after she set aside the headphone. "Beautifully done, my love."

"I know we have to trick them, but I wish we didn't." She sighed. "This is one group of people who aren't going to love their empress."

20

CONFISCATION

Mercedes wanted a briefing on how the seizure would take place. Boho accompanied her when they returned to the planet since she no longer needed to hide the fact she was married. Mercedes had seen Amastris and wanted to see more of the planet so they chose a processing center near the smaller city of Pygela. It was also closer to the planet's single ocean.

The couple were met by Placement Administrator Marquez who oversaw the doctors, nurses, psychologists and female childcare experts who had arrived with the transport ships. He was an officious bureaucrat with a tap-pad under one arm, and despite the early hour—it was still pre-dawn—his grey suit was perfectly pressed.

"Highness." His bow was elegantly executed. "Consort." A less deep bow to Boho, but still appropriately obsequious. "We are ready."

"Please take me through the process, administrator," Mercedes asked.

He bustled to a desk with an elaborate computer array manned by two data-entry techs. A pair of guards flanked the large desk. "The colonists will stop here first. Have their names, ages, sexes—well I guess that's not actually necessary in this case, is it?" He tittered. "Really, whoever heard of anything so unnatural? Almost as bad as the Cara'ot. Anyway their information will be recorded and after that they'll be issued ScoopRings, but they'll only be able to download not upload. We want them to be able to dip into the web, entice the teenagers, but we don't want the adults to be able to whine and complain."

"Our citizens know the assimilation policy," Mercedes said.

"True, but there's a power to seeing a weeping woman talking about her stolen child. Makes policy seem very real. No sense upsetting our populace with sob stories."

"The sausage theory," Boho offered.

"Beg pardon, my lord?"

"People like sausage, but they wouldn't want to see it made."

"Oh yes." Marquez laughed. "Quite so. Very droll."

"Could we continue?" Mercedes broke in.

"Uh, yes, of course. Women without children or who have children over the age of ten will be directed to the right where they'll receive their immunizations and be chipped." He bustled over and touched the door as if they might not understand left and right. "After that they will be held for an orientation so there won't be an opportunity to witness the confiscation."

"And how will that take place?" Mercedes asked.

"Women with children aged ten and under will be

directed to the left." He minced to the other side of the room and touched that door. "They will also be immunized and chipped, but also administered a sedative to render both parties unconscious. The children will be transferred to the care of a nanny, taken to a shuttle and brought to a transport. The women will be kept unconscious until all the children have been removed."

"Won't there be violence when they wake up and realize what's happened?" Boho asked.

"Oh yes, but that's why we have the troops on hand and the children beyond their reach. There are always, regrettably, some deaths during a confiscation."

"Of just the adults, correct?" Mercedes asked. Her stomach felt a bit hollow and she was suddenly that five-year-old with her mommy telling her goodbye. What would it have been like if she hadn't been able to have that moment? Would it have been better or worse?

"Occasionally we lose a child, but that's why we have such comprehensive teams in place to prevent just such a tragedy. These children are precious and we take our duties very seriously."

"I'm sure you do, Citizen Marquez. How long before the operation will be complete?"

"Based on our initial census we hope to have this completed in nine hours."

"Long time to be held for an orientation," Boho remarked.

"There's a lot of history for them to be shown, not to mention cultural and social mores. We'll keep them busy, well fed and lightly drugged."

"Thank you, Administrator. You seem to have this nicely in hand," Mercedes said formally. "My husband and I are going to take a hike and look at the surrounding area. I expect sunrise will be quite beautiful."

"It is indeed, Highness. The way the light shatters into colors on the glaciers is quite spectacular."

Wrapped in a parka Mercedes stood on a snow-covered hill and surveyed the landscape. It was both bleak and breathtaking. In three directions jagged snow and glacier-covered peaks stretched to the cloud-streaked sky. A grey-green ocean seemed to be trying to tear away the rocky beach with a massive boom and splash followed by a sibilant hiss as the water withdrew, grumbling in frustration. The waves formed foam-capped peaks rising like liquid mountains. Any walk there would be treacherous given the ice-rimed stones. In the far distance Mercedes could make out the shape of an iceberg on a majestic journey to nowhere. The cold air bit at the membranes of her nostrils and carried the scent of brine.

Boho walked down to join her. He had climbed higher on a glacier to have a better view of the processing center. "Women and kiddies are starting to gather. Staff are going up and down the line with hot drinks and donuts. The construction team did a good job. No way they're going to be able to see the kids being taken out the back." He beat his gloved hands together and blew on them. "Brrrr, what a frozen hell. I have no idea how the League will monetize this place."

"Ski resorts?" Mercedes suggested.

Boho studied the distant mountains. "Extreme mountain climbing? And maybe the scans will reveal something worth Reals." He slipped a gloved hand around her waist and pulled her close. "I know Kartirci called you in for a private meeting. What was that about?"

"He counseled me not to come down for this. Said it would only upset me."

"Why would he think that?"

"Maybe because he knows my mother was sent away when I was really young. But I think it's because I'm a woman and he believes anything that involves crying babies will upset me."

"So you did it to prove you won't be bothered?"

"No, I did it because in a way this is being done on my authority since I'm my father's heir. I should witness the process at least once."

"We know how it turns out. We get loyal League citizens."

"And leave behind how many resentful people?"

"Not enough to matter in the grand scheme of things. Settlers will arrive and some of these crazy women are going to decide that maybe a little man meat wouldn't be so bad." Boho waggled his eyebrows and leered.

Mercedes chuckled and punched him lightly on the shoulder. "You men all love your baloney ponies, don't you?"

"Señora Cullen! I am shocked! Shocked that you would say such a thing!"

"Would you prefer tallywhacker? Cock rocket? Trouser snake? Giggle stick?" She had been struggling to hold back laughter and finally succumbed.

Boho was also laughing. He grabbed her in a tight embrace. "Giggle stick? There isn't a man alive who'd use that phrase."

"Not everything's about you males," Mercedes said demurely and lowered her lashes.

"God, I love you." His lips were cold but his mouth warm. After the kiss he looked down toward the lines of shuttles. "Shall we go back up?"

"We're going to be in a tin can for months after this. Let's take a hike, spend a little more time with ground beneath our feet and sky overhead," Mercedes said.

"I like this plan."

The glacier made for smooth if slick walking. Boho spotted tracks in the snow off to the side and went to investigate. Mercedes followed. It was definitely a paw print, but it seemed to have multiple toes that were abnormally long and based on the track it had six legs.

"Wonder what the rest of the critter looks like?" Boho mused.

"It's probably white given this planet and evolutionary biology," Mercedes said.

"Might be something interesting to hunt." Boho started following the prints. "It looks like it was casting around. Suggests it's a predator."

They climbed higher. Mercedes' breath was a white banner before her face, but exertion had her sweating. She opened her parka halfway. Boho was ahead of her and she enjoyed the sight of the muscles in his butt bunching beneath his trousers. He stopped so abruptly that she ran into him.

"Wha—"

He pressed a finger against his lips and pointed at a particularly large snowdrift at the base of a black basalt cliff. Mercedes studied the area. The animal prints crossed and recrossed the area then moved away farther up the mountain. Then she saw it. A small pipe poking up out of the snow. It was barely visible. Boho snapped open the holster guard and drew his service pistol. Mercedes followed suit. Despite the cold there were trickles of sweat in his sideburns. With hand gestures he sent her off to the left, and he went right.

Mercedes cautiously climbed the large drift and as she breasted the top she realized that a trail had been dug between the cliff wall and the drift. She moved slowly to the pipe and held her hand over it. Warm air was flowing from it. She tried to walk down the other side, but ended up dislodging snow and sliding down. Boho was still climbing down the drift when she hit the bottom. She slid into the rock, and threw up her free hand. The rough stone cut through the material of her glove and scraped her palm. She bit back a cry of pain.

A sound from behind her had her scrambling to her feet and trying to turn. A sudden weight slammed into her back and sent Mercedes back into the cliff. This time with her face. Training took over and she got her shoulder under her attacker's arm and flung her off. She attempted a spinning kick, but discovered that snow underfoot and heavy boots made capoeira anything but easy. As she managed a glancing blow to the woman's knee Mercedes resolved to find some way to make her training sessions more challenging.

Boho was halfway down the drift; his gun was shifting as he tried to get a bead on the woman. "Don't shoot!" Mercedes screamed. *You might hit me* was the rest of that sentence, but she didn't say it. Mercifully Boho holstered his gun, slid down the hill and wrapped his arms around the woman to hold her still. Mercedes grabbed up her pistol from where she had dropped it, and pressed the barrel against the woman's forehead. All the fight went out of her.

Panting, Mercedes looked and spotted the small makeshift door set into the snow bank. She yanked it open as the captive gave a low moan of despair. Mercedes bent down and peered inside, where a younger woman huddled in a nest of blankets. She clutched a toddler against her. The little girl—who looked to be about two—was crying. Her white-blonde hair was a flyaway halo, and she wore a little romper suit with kittens embroidered on it. As Mercedes' face appeared in the doorway the quiet whimpers became sobbing screams.

Mercedes crawled inside. It was tall enough that she was able to stand up once she was through the door. The small space smelled of sweat, food, stale milk and feces emanating from a bucket set on the far side of the room. A space heater powered by a generator warmed the igloo. A pot was simmering on a two-burner hot plate.

Mercedes held out a hand. "It's all right, we're not going to hurt you. But what are you doing here?" she called over the wails of the child.

"Waiting for you to be gone!" the young woman spat.

"That's not going to happen," Boho called from

the doorway. "You're a League world now. Colonial administrators have arrived. A governor is on his way." Boho forced his captive inside. His nose wrinkled at the mélange of smells. "You were supposed to report for processing."

"We get an order from a bunch of fascists to report to *processing* centers and bring our children. How stupid do you think we are?" The older woman's eyes were burning with hate. "I know my history. The last time that happened people were loaded onto trains, sent to concentration camps and *gassed*."

Mercedes tried to figure out what in heaven's name the woman was talking about. She had a vague memory of some sort of mass deportation of people from her history class but couldn't recall any details. "We're not like that. You're not going to be moved off world. This is your home. We understand that, but you can't stay up here. It isn't safe."

"Will you guarantee our safety?" the younger woman quavered.

Mercedes stared at the toddler whose sobs had subsided and who was now sucking on her thumb. She was a pretty little thing, and with her unusual coloring Mercedes suspected she would be fostered with a family very quickly. Blondes were rare in the League.

"You won't be hurt," she said.

Boho released the older woman, who ran to her partner and their daughter and enfolded them in her arms. Boho jerked his head toward the door. Mercedes followed him outside. He leaned in close and whispered, "We can't take them back. From up here they'll be able to see everything that's happening and by now some of these kids will be getting carried to the shuttles."

"We could just leave them," Mercedes said feeling queasy.

"And when they come down and find out they're the only couple left with a young kid? Their friends and neighbors will hate and resent them, and once it's discovered by colonial services the kid will be grabbed, potentially leading to a riot."

"There's going to be a riot when those women down there wake up," Mercedes argued.

"And think how much worse the next one will be when they're defending this little girl. The last young child on the planet."

"So what do you suggest?"

"Restrain the women. Take the kid. Send troops up to free the women after the operation is complete."

"Restrain them with what?"

"There are blankets in there. Tear them, tie them up."

"They're not just going to stand there while we do that."

"We've got guns."

"I'm not going to shoot them."

"They don't know that."

Her back was to the door so the only warning she had was Boho's eyes widening with alarm. He grabbed her around the waist and flung them both to the side. There was the roar of gunfire that echoed off the mountainside and the wind of a bullet passing perilously close to them as they tumbled to the ground. Boho rolled off her, drawing his pistol as he did, and fired at the older woman. From their position on the ground the bullet went up through her chin and the top of her head erupted in a spray of blood and brains. She collapsed, the rifle falling from her hands. The younger woman knelt in the doorway screaming.

Boho scrambled to his feet, grabbed the young woman by the hair, and pulled her outside. He punched her hard in the face. She tried to ward him off, crying out in pain and fear, but he kept punching her. Her nose broke, blood streaking her face. Boho's expression was murderous. Mercedes grabbed his arm before another blow could fall.

"Boho! Stop! That's enough!" The woman was laying partially across her lover's body, the older woman's blood caking her hair.

"We're fucked now," Boho said. "They would have heard those gunshots down at the base."

"We'll think of something. I have to get the child."

Mercedes went back inside the cave. The toddler was standing on the makeshift bed. She clutched a teddy bear and she was knuckling her eyes. Her upper lip was covered with snot.

"Hey, sweetie," Mercedes said softly. Using a blanket she wiped the child's upper lip, and dried her eyes. "What's Teddy's name?"

"Pumpkin." Between the accent and the baby lisp it took her a moment to figure out what the little girl had said.

"Would you and Pumpkin like some hot chocolate?" The child looked confused and Mercedes realized that chocolate probably wasn't one of the crops grown on this subsistence world. "A cookie," she quickly amended.

The little girl nodded. Mercedes picked her up. "What's your name? My name's Mercedes."

"Dino... mak... e." That was how it sounded to Mercedes.

"What a pretty name," she said even as she thought, *What a terrible name for a child.* "Dino. Do you like dinosaurs?" she asked as she pulled the child's face down against her shoulder. It was tough getting through the low door while still keeping the child's eyes covered, but she managed.

"Go," Boho said. "I'll catch up."

Mercedes switched to *Español.* "Don't leave the mother out here. She'll freeze."

"Serve the bitch right."

"They were trying to protect their family. You'd do the same if someone tried to take our child..." Her voice trailed away.

For an instant she was gripped with doubt. She shook it off. Early on the League had tried assimilations without taking the children, but had found that the practice had led to generation after generation learning hate at their parents' knee. By removing the youngest children and overwhelming the local population with League settlers they'd managed to wipe out resistance within two generations. It was sound, if painful, policy, Mercedes thought as she headed down the mountain toward the processing center.

She could see that the bureaucrats handing out treats had been replaced by soldiers. Clearly there had been some sort of altercation. She could see bodies on the snow, but mercifully no blood that she could see. The soldiers were keeping the now restive line in place and under control. *Well,* she thought, *with luck this will be the only center where there was trouble.* Of course it would be the center where she had chosen to go. She was certain that information would somehow get back to Cousin Musa to be used as one more example of her unsuitability to rule.

The little girl wriggled in her arms. "I want my mommy," she said.

So did I, Mercedes thought.

21

THE CHILDREN'S HOUR

"Boho is returning to active duty."

Estella, seated on the floor, looked up from where she was helping her eldest daughter decide whether the ballerina or the fairy princess outfit was the better choice for her doll. When Mercedes had left for her tour of duty, Estella hadn't been married. Now seven years later she had a six-year-old daughter and the newest edition to the Brendahl family, Estella's three-week-old son, Benjamin. Mercedes, sitting on a small sofa, was holding the baby. He was solid and warm and smelled of talc and milk and baby. His eyes were screwed shut as if he was concentrating on the act of sleeping. Mercedes ran a finger across one fat cheek marveling at the softness of his skin.

They were gathered in the ladies' salon on the upper floor of the mansion. It was the winter rainy season and the downpour beat a tattoo on the roof, and raindrops ran weeping down the windows. The overcast had darkened the room so a soft-footed Isanjo had entered and lit several small table lamps, giving warmth to the room and deepening the jewel-like colors in the Sidone rug that covered the wood floor.

Estella gave Mercedes a sharp look then told her daughter, "Jacinta, take Tammy doll and give her a bath before you dress her."

The little girl, precocious for a six-year-old, gave them a sharp look. "You and Tiá Mercedes want to talk about Tió Boho, don't you?"

"Yes, we do," Mercedes said. Her voice caught on a laugh.

"Nurse says he's been naughty."

"Boys are often naughty."

"Will Benjie be naughty?" the little girl asked, peering at her little brother.

"Go!" Estella ordered. Hugging her doll, Jacinta left the room with the air of an offended dowager.

"She's going to be a handful," Mercedes remarked.

"She already is. And I'm surprised you can laugh about Boho."

"So I don't cry. Or kill him."

"It's Donatella isn't it?" Estella asked as she stood up off the floor and joined Mercedes on the sofa.

Mercedes sighed and shifted the baby. He gave a mew of protest then a bubble appeared from between the lips of his bud-like pink mouth. Mercedes wiped it away. "Yes. She made a frightful scene at the Ponis' ball. Fainted in the midst of a dance. Now the entire FFH is buzzing that she's pregnant with the consort's bastard—"

"Is she?" Estella asked.

It almost choked her to say it. "Yes. SEGU verified. Which

means there is yet another opportunity to talk about how the Infanta has been home from active duty for two whole years and still hasn't produced an heir."

"Do you think it's because you used those... products?" Estella asked.

"I consulted a gynecologist. She says I'm fine. There's no reason I shouldn't get pregnant."

"Maybe it's Boho. Of course suggesting to a man that his sperm is defective is—"

"I did. I think that's why the record number of *chillas* over the past year."

"I'd call them *putas* even if they do have noble titles," Estella sniffed.

Mercedes slipped an arm from beneath Benjamin and hugged her sister. "I love you."

"I love you too."

Mercedes sighed. "Now Boho can strut and preen because Donatella's pregnancy proves it's not his fault. Of course we're going to smear her, imply she had other lovers and the child isn't Boho's but no one will believe it. It's just plausible deniability." She sighed again and realized that her burning anger had morphed into weariness and sadness. "I know men have affairs, but I guess I never thought it would happen to me. It hurts and makes me feel terrible about myself. What didn't I give him that he's in some other woman's arms? Then I get mad. If he won't consider my feelings then he should at least think about his position. God, he's the consort. He should know better. And know better than to get some girl knocked up."

Estella paused and pleated the material of her dress for a moment. "You don't seem very happy with your husband."

"Well, yeah."

"I didn't mean it quite the way it sounded. Of course you're upset about the mistresses but is there something more?"

"We grew up together. Have been married almost eight years. We know each other. Maybe too well. And I've started to realize that... maybe what we had wasn't... love. He was handsome and dashing. I think I was infatuated more than in love."

"Do you think he loved you?"

"I think he was blinded by the lure of the crown. *What* I was more than *who* I was. There's only been one man who's seemed to see *me*."

"You were in love with him. This other man."

"I don't know. I don't know what love is any more, if I ever knew. I couldn't have had him anyway. No, Boho was the perfect tool for the task at hand."

"Marriage shouldn't be a task, Mer, it should be a partnership."

"But it can't be. I'll be empress. He'll be the consort. He'll always be less than me."

Mercedes handed Benjie off to Estella, stood and paced. The swish of her skirt around her ankles felt strange even after two years at home. Often she returned to her trousers within the walls of the palaces. Five years of freedom aboard ship made it hard to go back to dresses. "I've got to get pregnant, Stel."

Her sister looked around as if worried that eavesdroppers

might be hidden behind the curtains. "There's always the Cara'ot," she said softly.

Mercedes gave an emphatic head shake. "Not a chance. Cousin Musa's got eyes on me constantly. With every passing barren year I can see him licking his chops."

"Daddy could always designate another of us. Julieta would be next in line—"

"No, you would be."

"Oh, no, no, no. I'd be a terrible empress."

"So would Jules."

"True."

"She made damn sure she washed out of the High Ground at the end of the first year *and* got Izzie and Tanis to do the same thing so *she* didn't look so bad. She might have considered how it makes Father look."

Estella joined her, tucked her arm beneath Mercedes and turned her nervous pacing into a more decorous stroll around the sitting room. The baby gave a belch and the sisters laughed.

"Typical boy." Estella shook her head. "Well, there's Beatrisa. She did Daddy and you proud."

Mercedes smiled fondly. "I get these enthusiastic messages from her every few days. She loves being on a ship and apparently her captain is very pleased with her. I knew she would take to military life like a duck to water." Mercedes shook her head regretfully. "But there's not a chance in hell the parliament would approve it and if Daddy tried, Musa probably *would* start a civil war. He wouldn't stand for getting passed over a second time. No, the only solution is that I have to get pregnant."

"Wish I could do it for you," Estella said.

"Or Sumiko. God can she pop them out. Another one last year."

"How many is she up to… seven, eight?" Estella asked.

"Eight, but that's if you count the little girl from Sinope they're fostering. She's only had seven."

"Are they broke and need the child subsidies?" Estella asked.

Mercedes sighed. "I don't know. Maybe Sumiko does it so she won't have to think about what she doesn't have. I better get back home, pretend I'm sorry Boho is leaving."

Estella kissed her cheek. "Maybe a break is what you both need."

"Are you coming to this banquet?"

"Not a chance." She hugged her son close and kissed the top of his head. His eyes opened, he yawned and his wandering eyes found his mother's face. He gave a little toothless smile and Mercedes felt her heart squeeze. "I have the perfect excuse. New baby, jealous six-year-old. Though that second part's not true, Jacinta loves him, but I'll embellish like mad if I can avoid Cousin Musa."

"Did I say I love you? Actually I hate you," Mercedes teased. Estella laughed and they hugged one last time.

Her security detail was waiting outside the Brendahl mansion. As she came down the steps Ian raised the door and she stepped in. The captain climbed in after her and took up a position on the seat facing her. Mercedes' flitter was surrounded by five identical flitters and they flew an intricate pattern so no one could get an easy fix on which vehicle held the Infanta. While she had been serving aboard the *Concepción* there had been no worry that she might be assassinated or kidnapped. Such an attempt on a warship would have been suicide, and there hadn't been any attempts during the two years she had been home. Perhaps her five years of service had proved to the old guard that she could rule, she thought, but she also touched the knife Tracy had given her, which she still carried strapped to her leg, and the pistol in her pocket. Not that either of them would do much against an air-to-ground missile. Still, their presence made her feel better. The chances that someone could launch six missiles to take out all the flitters was remote, and if they could only fire one she had a Russian roulette player's odds that it wouldn't hit her.

She wondered why she was having such paranoid thoughts. Probably because she had to face Musa, his eldest son Mihalis and Jose. The priest had left military service when Mercedes' tour ended, proving beyond any doubt that he'd joined just so he could keep tabs on her and hear her confessions. Which she had limited to the most venial of transgressions, to his evident frustration. Jose was now secretary to the archbishop of Hissilek, and seemed destined to become a prince of the church.

Sometimes she wished she'd continued to resist her father's wishes. Refused to go to the High Ground or washed out like her younger sisters and then married either Mihalis or Arturo. If she had, Musa wouldn't be a seething mass of resentment, and perhaps she might have conceived with one of the del Campo sons. She'd be home with her children and not worried about being assassinated. Right now a worse fate awaited her—she had to face her disgruntled husband.

Ian gave a soft cough. She looked up at him. "Yes, Captain?"

"You seem… sa… distracted," the officer amended.

"A bit." She studied his features. He was an attractive man though his ears stuck out a bit. Chestnut hair, golden-brown eyes and skin like pale tea. She realized his eyes were devouring her face.

Oh dear. Don't fall in love with me. I should have replaced you with a gay man when I returned, she thought. But if she had it would have been seen as a black mark on his record. She couldn't do that to him. So she lied.

"Just thinking how sad I'll be to see Boho leave. I'm going to miss him very much."

Rogers nodded and the glow faded from his eyes. He leaned back in his seat. "I'm sure you will, Highness," he said formally.

Message received, Mercedes thought and felt a momentary flare of regret.

It was a short hop onto the Palacio Colina, the large hill that housed the palace at the top with the homes of the aristocratic families clustered like gilded mushrooms just below. For a wild moment as they were heading in to land Mercedes almost instructed them to go to Sumiko's house. She could visit with Christina, the little girl she had rescued from Sinope. She had felt a sense of obligation to the child and seen to it she was fostered in a home on Ouranos so she could keep an eye on her. At nine the child seemed well adjusted and happy and didn't seem to miss or even remember her other mothers.

Mercedes knew the impulse was driven by cowardice, a desire not to face her husband, so she bit back the words and let them land. She found Boho in their bedroom kicked back on a settee smoking a Tiponi herb stick and directing his long-suffering batBEM in packing his kit. The Isanjo scurried about adding clothes to the large garment trunk.

"Good lord, you really think you're going to need that many clothes?" Mercedes blurted.

Boho's satisfied expression curdled. "I'm a captain with my own ship now. I have to set an example."

"And set the hearts of provincial noblemen's daughters palpitating with your splendor," Mercedes shot back. She was immediately chagrined at her waspish tone. "I'm sorry. I shouldn't have…" *Why in the hell am I apologizing to him?*

They stared at each other for a long moment. "Get out!" Boho snapped the order to Ivoga, who left like his tail was on fire. He stubbed out the stick, stood and walked toward her. "What happened to us, Mer? How did we get here?"

"You slept with a string of debutantes."

"I needed to know… prove I was still a man. You can't imagine the pressure I've been under. From your father, my father, Rohan, the parliament."

"And you don't think I haven't felt it? Maybe we're just not compatible. Maybe I ought to try a string of lovers and see if I'm fertile with any of them."

"You would humiliate me like that?" She had hoped for

anger so they could fight, but Boho just sounded hurt.

"Sauce for the gander, Boho." Her own anger ebbed, leaving in its place a melancholy exhaustion. Mercedes turned away shaking her head. "No. I wouldn't do that to you."

"I'm sorry, Mer." His arms went around her and he leaned in over her shoulder to press his cheek against hers.

"I need to bathe and change before dinner," she said.

"Will you forgive me?" Boho asked.

"Probably. Someday."

It was a lot of family to be wedged into a sitting room. In addition to Cousin Musa and his wife, a mousy little woman who rarely said much, there were two of his three sons, and the eldest of the three unmarried daughters. The girl Sofia, and Izzie who also had yet to be affianced, had their heads together as they gossiped. The lack of a fiancé was something Izzie whined about constantly. Mercedes made a note to ask her father why he hadn't used her as collateral in the never-ending game of governance. Perhaps he was punishing Izzara for washing out of the High Ground. Tanis had taken vows and become a Celestial Novias de Cristo, and had already borne a child sired by Jose.

Constanza sat on a gilded chair and looked aloof. Now that Mercedes was approaching thirty the six years that separated them didn't seem like much. Not for the first time Mercedes wished she and her stepmother were closer.

Delia and Dulcinea were spending Christmas with their mother, Inez, on Kronos. Once they started at the High

Ground next year there would be little opportunity for them to visit. Julieta was home on Kronos with Sanjay and Beatrisa was off happily soldiering. Mercedes hoped Julieta was safe and happy. They hadn't really been close since Mercedes had made less than tactful comments about Sanjay, and been very critical of Julieta's failure at the High Ground.

Mercedes' gaze went to her youngest sister. Carisa was sixteen now. Delicate, with perfect features, she surpassed all the other eight daughters when it came to sheer beauty. In two years she would enter the High Ground. Mercedes feared how that would go. Carisa had been coddled nearly to death by her mother.

The rest of the room was filled with shirttail relatives whom Mercedes barely knew. She privately congratulated her father for thinking to include the gaggle of cousins. It would force Musa to be on his best behavior. Good manners were de rigueur for the FFH.

Mihalis stood next to Carisa leaning over her like an enfolding shadow. As Mercedes watched she saw Carisa reach up and give her earring three tugs. It had been a signal created by Mercedes, Estella and Julieta when they were trapped and needed rescuing. Someone had obviously clued Carisa in about the gesture. Mercedes crossed the room.

"Sorry to interrupt, cousin. Carisa, your mother wants you."

Carisa curtsied to Mihalis and gave him one of her secretive smiles. The long lashes brushed at her cheeks as she looked down and then peeped up at him. "Lovely talking with you, Mils," Carisa said.

She slipped her arm through her half-sister's and they

moved toward Constanza. "Thank you. I wasn't sure you'd get the message," Carisa said.

"Fortunately I was looking your way. Does he bother you often?"

"Oh yes. I think he's quite desperate to marry me," Carisa said.

"You don't sound excited at the prospect."

"I'm not. I think he only wants me because my mother is still empress, the last wife standing as it were, and they think that makes me more important."

"And because you're beautiful, sweets."

"Aren't all royal daughters beautiful?" Carisa murmured.

"When did you become such a cynic?" Mercedes asked, startled at the rare display of teeth from this timid girl.

"How could I avoid it in this family?"

Mercedes steered them into a quiet corner behind the large grand piano. One of the distant cousins was pounding out, quite badly, a recent hit tune. The music would help cover their conversation and there wasn't room in the corner for more than just the two women.

"I don't think I know you very well, and I'm sorry about that," Mercedes said bluntly.

"Mother had something to do with that; maybe we can make use of the time we have before I leave for the High Ground."

"I'd like that. And I won't have a husband to coddle so I'll have more time."

"No, just an empire to learn to rule," Carisa said with a smile.

Mercedes lowered her voice. "Are you worried about the academy?"

"No, I'm actually looking forward to it."

Surprised yet again, Mercedes pulled back to get a better look at her youngest sister. "Really?"

"Don't act so astonished. I can't wait to get away from Mother and the latest doctor who's taken her fancy. This one will probably last. He agrees with her assessment that I'm at death's door and then compliments her on being so brave and holding up so well under the stress of a sick child."

"Ouch. So, I take it you're not planning on following Julieta, Tanis and Izzara's example."

"*No.* I'm going to make it and then spend five blissful years somewhere far away from here."

Mercedes hugged her. *What a sight we must make,* she thought. *Me a giantess and this tiny fairy princess.* "I'll just be a shuttle hop away and you can call me anytime for advice or encouragement."

"Believe me, I will."

They parted and Mercedes moved through the crowd to join Boho. It was their last night. She ought to be at his side for part of it. She had already decided they would make love tonight. Perhaps it would work like sympathetic magic. She was ovulating so perhaps this time she would get pregnant. Boho was busy charming a circle of women ranging in age from the teens to grandmothers. Mercedes paused to appreciate his skill. Cousin Musa appeared at her elbow.

"Mercedes."

"Cousin."

Musa was Great-Aunt Patricia's son and he was a bit older than the Emperor. Where her father tended to pack flesh on his tall frame, Musa was equally as tall, but very spare. He had a fringe of grey hair just above his ears, and the light from the chandelier made his bald pate shine. The only real resemblance between the men was the shape of their eyes and their arching eyebrows.

"You must be bereft losing your dashing husband."

"We all do our duty, cousin."

"True… as best we can."

"Good of you to be concerned, cousin, but completely unnecessary. I'm quite certain we won't have to disrupt the course of either yours or Mihalis's life with the tedium of the throne," Mercedes snapped.

Musa tsked. "I'm quite shocked. The military give you that sharp tongue, Mercedes? That can drive a husband away."

"No, I was being polite. If I were to use military speak, cousin, I'd have said… *fuck off*."

Her heart was pounding and there was an aching knot in her stomach as she walked away. She was angry with him, angry with herself for becoming angry. The only consolation was that they were within the walls of the palace so the exchange wasn't going to end up on the news. Once she reached the other side of the room she put her back to the wall, surveyed the crowd and realized she had not a single friend or confidant present. It was a lowering thought.

22

THE MONSTERS AMONG US

He knew better than to read the latest postings out of O-Trell, but Tracy couldn't help himself. He'd already endured the news that both Mercedes and Boho had been promoted to captain two years before. Today he learned that Cullen had been given command of a state-of-the-art frigate, the S.L.S.S. *Lord Nelson*, while Tracy still languished as a captain-lieutenant. After his initial tour aboard the *Triunfo* he had been posted to the S.L.S.S. *Preble*. The ship was an aged attack transport ferrying *fusileros* to lend aid during natural disasters and occasionally apply the boot to strikers and malcontents. Once in a great while there might be a riot or a half-hearted rebellion from disgruntled Hidden World colonists or alien workers but mostly it was dull work.

I clearly hitched my wagon to the wrong horse, Tracy thought as he left his small cabin heading for the bridge. Sukarno had been a terrific teacher and role model, but as another untitled, former scholarship student he didn't have the pull to get Tracy promoted. De Vilbiss would probably have gotten around to exerting some influence on Tracy's behalf, but an untimely heart attack had taken him out of active service.

I probably should have slept with him. The bitter thought didn't bring much comfort and he couldn't maintain the anger toward his former captain, because after two years serving under Captain Caballero Carl Reginald Carson, Tracy was missing de Vilbiss. The man might have violated regulations by forcing an enlisted man into a sexual liaison but he had been extremely competent.

Carson was a lazy bastard who treated O-Trell like a hammock. As the sixth son of a baronet he was one of those noble parasites that Tracy especially despised. It sometimes seemed the lower the title or placement in a family the more that individual brayed and sprayed around their family connections. Carson didn't condescend to Tracy the way many had. Instead he let him do all the work aboard the ship while he stayed drunk in his cabin with whatever joy girl he'd picked up at their last port of call. The arrival of the *Preble* meant an all-expenses-paid trip for some whore to a different planet.

The XO and the lieutenant-commander were clearly just marking time. One until his retirement and the other until his next rotation would move him to a new ship. Tracy had briefly proposed that they report Carson to the Admiralty and gotten incredulous looks and very quick refusals. Apparently a way *not* to advance in O-Trell was to make waves or enemies.

As for Tracy, he was getting a lot of time down various gravity wells. Carson's slackness had affected the *fusileros* as well. Most of the competent officers had managed to get transferred or resign along with their competent sergeants. They were understaffed and the sergeants they did have were shiftless and surly. The result being that Tracy often found himself leading a squad on planetary missions.

They were now en route to a planet whose recently appointed governor had sent out an urgent call for troops. Alien issues apparently, and some kind of rebellion among the few humans on the planet as well. The world, renamed Dragonfly because of the elliptical rings that surrounded it, had been a Cara'ot supply base, but some sort of bureaucratic screw-up within the Department of Planetary Affairs had left the alien world without proper human authority.

Until now. And now that authority was screaming his ass off for help five weeks after he'd taken up his post.

Tracy had been on the computer trying to figure out what kind of problems could have possibly arisen on an unprepossessing planet with little to recommend it apart from the pretty rings and its location. As for the provincial governor—Caballero Royce Epps had been a parliament backbencher of low title whose one flash of fame had been his attempt to offer legislation that would have banned aliens from owning businesses. An attempt which resoundingly failed, but had made Epps the darling of the most conservative press outlets and leader of the Human First movement. Which made his appointment to govern a Cara'ot world seem a blunder on the part of the Planetary Governance Department. Since Dragonfly had belonged to the Cara'ot, Tracy had asked Donnel to see what he could discover.

His batBEM caught him before he could climb the ladder

to the bridge. Over the years Tracy had learned to read the nuanced expressions on Donnel's round, four-eyed face. "What?" he asked, his heart sinking.

"You should call for a flagship," Donnel said.

"Why? There's a bunch of Cara'ot traders and a handful of humans."

"You need an admiral. Preferably one with a direct line to the palace."

"What the fuck is going on?"

"I can't say more."

"But you know something."

"Be careful, sir," the alien said. Tracy reacted. His mouthy batBEM didn't often call him "sir". Donnel went skittering off so quickly that his three legs were almost a blur. He suddenly stopped and spun like a grotesque top to face Tracy. "I think I know you."

"After ten years you better," Tracy growled.

"Just... just be the human I think you are."

Donnel vanished around a corner. Tracy shook his head and climbed up the ladder to the bridge.

"Go, go, go!" Orders from the shuttle pilot who was hovering some fifteen feet off the ground.

Tracy hugged his rifle and jumped, letting his knees and the servo mechanisms in his battle armor take the shock of his landing. He felt the concussion through the soles of his feet as the nine other men in his squad joined him. Three shuttles had been sent to the governor's residence, where rioters were assailing the gates held off by a small number of *fusileros*. Tracy's shuttle had been deploying troops in a warehouse district, dropping off the other three squads. Tracy was reminded of the Greek myth of dragon's teeth and how if planted they would grow into armed warriors.

The night sky was cut with the fire of tracer rounds. His helmet dampened the sound of gunfire and of screams. Off to his left a couple of buildings were engulfed in flames.

He could hear reports over his helmet radio. *"Coming under heavy fire from an apartment building." "Snipers on the roof." "Barricade on the street."* Major Lord William Hu, commander of the *fusileros*, snapped back orders. "Fire at will. Take out all resistance. If they won't surrender drop the building!"

Tracy checked his heads-up display. Their target was a warehouse near the edge of the city. He raised his hand and made a fist. "Let's go, double time."

He led his men down a street. Gunfire erupted from behind a barricade formed from crashed flitters and furniture. The squad scattered and returned fire. One of the *fusileros* fired a grenade into the barricade. It tore apart, sending pieces of flitter, broken chairs and bodies flying. Tracy was startled to see how many women had been manning the barrier, as well as men and a number of aliens. Judging by the variety of disturbing shapes they were Cara'ot.

"Shit, is the war starting again?" one of the soldiers muttered.

"Let's hope not," Tracy replied. "Let's go."

He led them at a jog down the street. Their boots crunched over the remains of the barricade. Around him he heard sobs and screams, cries of pain. He blinked to turn off night vision and thermal for a clear look. A woman held her belly. Glistening viscera were spilling from the wound and her hands were red with blood. Tracy hesitated. There was a medic in his squad, but his own men might need his services. He set his jaw and went past the suffering woman. Maybe she would live until this was over and they could render aid.

They reached their target, a large warehouse with no windows. Tracy sent a tiny drone flitting over the roof. It sent back images of eight skylights, but they weren't clear glass. He didn't want to burn through the doors until he had some idea what was inside so he directed the drone toward a ventilation shaft. It dropped about three feet then hit an obstruction of wadded packing material and steel wool. The people inside weren't fools. Tracy pulled the drone back and turned to his comms man.

"Plant an MoR on the wall. See what it can show us."

The corporal saluted, crouched and duckwalked up to the wall. His communications array bounced lightly on his back. He slapped a sensor on the wall and sent the data back to Tracy's helmet. The device was incredibly sensitive. It registered not only movement, but breathing and even heartbeats. Particularly when the hearts were beating this fast.

"Shit, there are eighty-three people in there," Tracy muttered. He considered the nine other men in his squad.

His sergeant looked over. "Wait for reinforcements?"

Tracy considered. He could already imagine Major Hu screaming, calling him a pussy. "Use the lance on the wall. Once we've got a hole, lob in some stun grenades. That should help them calm down."

"Yes, sir."

It didn't take long to execute. The thermite lances had a limited lifespan, burning through their fuel relatively quickly, but they were easily able to cut through the metal and concrete that formed the building. Anybody who was too close when the lances cut through was going to have a bad day, but he couldn't worry about that. They needed to neutralize the structure.

Metal slumped and concrete cracked and they had their opening. They tossed in grenades. Their battle armor damped the sound and flash. Tracy gave the *go* signal and the squad rushed through the opening.

Despite the skylights it was dim in the interior. Shelves and crates had been piled in front of the doors. More boxes had been arranged to form a sort of fort. The defenders had been clever about surveillance drones but had never considered that their attackers might eschew the doors. He and his men charged the fort scattering boxes. There were a few muzzle flashes; his *fusileros* returned fire just as Tracy realized what he was seeing.

Children. The majority of the people inside the makeshift fort were little kids. He was no expert, but they looked to be between three and six. They were also not human. They all had luxurious curling multi-colored hair, tufted ears pricked up through the curls, and they had furry tails in the same mix of colors as their hair. The faces were elfin with sharply pointed chins and high cheekbones. The children stared at them, terror writ large in big eyes with slits like a cat's and jewel-like colors—green, gold and blue.

"Hold your fire! Hold your fire!" he bellowed at his troops.

There were a handful of human adults who were mostly women. There was one Cara'ot among them. The Cara'ot was roughly bipedal in shape with a head in the right place. He… she… it had taken a bullet to said head and was dead. One of the men was bleeding from a wound to the chest.

"Weapons down!" he ordered the defenders. Most of the guns clattered to the floor. A man and one of the women hesitated.

"Are you going to kill us?" the man asked.

"Yeah, if you don't drop your guns," Tracy answered.

"Are you going to kill our kids?" the woman asked.

"What?" Tracy tried to process that. "No."

"You're not the governor's troops?" the man asked.

"No, we're off the *Preble*." The couple exchanged glances, hands convulsing on the stocks of their rifles. "You're running out of time," Tracy warned. They disarmed. Tracy gestured toward the man with the sucking chest wound. "Take care of that," he ordered his medic.

Guth didn't bother to salute. Just unlimbered his med kit and knelt at the man's side.

Tracy grabbed another of the men, who winced as his armored hand exerted too much pressure on his arm. "Now tell me what's going on. These kids are Cara'ot, right?"

"No," the woman said. "Well, sort of. They're human and Cara'ot."

"Oh… shit." He paced a tight circle. "You've been

breaking the genetic laws." The couple just exchanged glances. Suddenly Tracy could see it all. "You fucking morons thought you were off the beaten track enough to get away with it. Then the League assigns a governor who finds out what you've been up to." He wanted to rub his suddenly aching temples but the helmet kept him from applying that small relief.

"And he ordered the children killed." The woman's voice was harsh with both grief and rage.

The research Tracy had done before their arrival gave him the rest of the horrible picture. Maybe Governor Epps hadn't just been garnering points with the conservative press with his legislative initiative. Maybe he actually was a true believer in the intrinsic superiority of humans and the vileness of aliens.

What Tracy *did* know was this was a problem way above his pay grade. He chinned his radio to call to Captain Carson, then hesitated. He'd have to report to his superior officer, but relying on Carson to do jack or shit was another matter.

He made the call and delivered his report. There was a long pause that had nothing to do with the time lag between the planet and the ship in orbit. "Well," Carson finally said. "That's going to be a shit storm. I need to think on this."

"Captain, might I respectfully suggest that you get down to the residence. Declare martial law. Take control of the planet," Tracy said. He hoped he sounded respectful.

"That's a rather extreme reaction, Lieutenant, don't you think?"

"At least have the governor call back his security forces.

Otherwise there's going to be a confrontation."

"Let me see what I can do."

The connection broke. Tracy considered. A bearded older man hesitantly approached. "Sir, can we tend to the children? They have very sensitive hearing and I'm worried about the effect the grenades might have had."

"Yes, of course. Guth," Tracy called to his medic. "When you're done there render whatever aid is needed." The man hesitated briefly then nodded.

Tracy sent five of his team to guard the hole in the wall. The other three he put on the barricaded front door. He then moved on to the children. A number of them had blood staining the hair at the base of their ears. One little girl with a riot of black, red and gold curls toddled to him, stopped and stared up into his face then wrapped her arms around his armored leg and pressed her cheek against his thigh. Conflicting emotions twitched through him. *Disgust. Fascination. Confusion.* For a brief second he felt the muscles in his leg tighten as he prepared to kick her loose. He fought it down and let her cling to him.

He wished they hadn't killed the Cara'ot. The creature would have been able to tell Tracy if his theory about the kids was correct. A human woman walked past and he caught her arm. "So whose idea was it to go with kittens?"

"Saw that did you?"

"I'd have to be fucking blind not to," Tracy replied.

"It was a joint decision." She reached down and stroked the little girl's curls. "We considered having them be indistinguishable from humans without a genetic test, but we wanted to foster the idea of sharing and compatibility."

She shrugged. "So we went with something we thought would be appealing and non-threatening." Her face twisted and she fought back tears. "Guess that didn't work out."

The child clinging to his leg looked up. Her eyes were gold, swimming with green flecks. "I'm hungry," she lisped.

He dug a ration bar out of a pocket on his armor. That caused a stir among the conscious children. "Distribute your rations," he called to his squad. "We need to get these kids fed."

Helmeted heads cocked and turned. Tracy could read the reactions.

"We're going to need rations if we're down here for long," one of the *fusileros* said.

"I think we can manage to miss a meal or two, *hombre*," Tracy snapped back.

Sergeant Greene came to his side and went to a private channel. "Sir, what if we get the same order as the governor's guards? Gonna make it harder for us if we've… if we see them as…" He gave a vague arm wave at the children.

"Human?" Tracy looked down at the child gnawing at the dense bar. She still had one arm wrapped around his leg. "I don't think killing children is what the League stands for, Sergeant. It's certainly not what I stand for, and I won't allow it."

"It might not be up to you, sir."

"What happens in this building is up to me."

"Yes, sir. I'll make that clear to the men." He moved away.

By breaking the bars into pieces they managed to get food into all the children. There was a working bathroom in the warehouse so water wasn't a problem. He stood and watched the handful of humans interacting with the children, leading them in games, dispensing hugs. The Cara'ot half-breeds seemed just like normal children.

Except they're abominations.

Who didn't ask to be born. They're victims of their creators' hubris. Their punishment shouldn't be death. A final look at the half-breed and Tracy keyed his radio for a Foldstream transmission and radioed Sukarno aboard the *Triunfo*.

"Belmont. How's life among the *hombres*?"

"Right now not so great. I've got a problem and—"

"In the best military tradition you're kicking it upstairs."

"That's exactly right, sir."

"So why me and not your captain?"

"I tried that and I think he's relying on another fine old tradition—stall until the problem solves itself. Only in this case it's going to be dead kids."

There was silence for a long moment. "Okay. Talk," Sukarno ordered so Tracy did.

"I'll send word to the capital, and talk to my captain. Assuming he and headquarters agree we can't reach you for at least three days."

"Understood. Your new captain. He's highborn, right? Has he got enough status to lean on this governor?"

"Maybe. Problem is this is a clear violation of our laws and the treaty. The fucking Cara'ot should have known better."

"It wasn't like they kidnapped and forcibly impregnated these humans. They were willing participants."

"So some folks are going to jail... or worse," Sukarno concluded glumly and ended the communication.

23

PLEASE THINK WE'RE NICE

Hours passed without word from the *Preble*, then Tracy's motion sensor lit up. A group of about twenty was approaching, presumably local government troops. "Get the civilians in cover," he ordered his sergeant.

Tracy moved to the hole in the wall, slipped outside, and ran down the length of the building until he reached the front. He took up a position blocking the main doors. Tracy noted the way the approaching men's hands nervously clenched and released on the stocks of their rifles, the set of their shoulders. These were men hyped up on adrenalin and fear.

The man in command swaggered forward. Tracy held up a hand when he was still ten feet away. "That's close enough. State your intention."

"Just a little soldier boy, aren't you?" the officer in charge scoffed. "Our *intention* is to kill those monsters in there. We got intel on where they were hiding so don't try and snow me and say they're not there."

Tracy went for a sense of camaraderie. "Look, these are decisions that should be made way above our pay grade.

How about we wait for instructions from Ouranos?"

"Come on. You can't be that raw. Forgiveness rather than permission, *hombre*."

"You're not killing these kids... *hombre*."

"They're not *kids*. They're fucking horrors. Now get the fuck out of the way." Tracy raised his rifle and allowed the laser sight to caress the man's exposed face. "Fuck!" The man's visor snapped down.

"I will shoot the first man who takes one step closer."

"I don't believe you."

"Try me."

The troops behind their commander shifted nervously. The platoon leader seemed to realize he was on the verge of losing authority. He raised his rifle and advanced. Tracy fired a shot just over the platoon leader's head, close enough to scrape the top of the helmet. The man's head jerked back and he went staggering.

"Son of a bitch!"

Tracy threw himself to the side, running for the corner of the building. Gunfire sprayed the doors where he'd been standing. A couple of rounds hit Tracy's shoulder, staggering him, but were sucked up by the armor. It still hurt and he knew he'd have a bruise. Then gunfire chattered from overhead right at the feet of the security forces. Bullets sent chips of pavement ricocheting against the security team's armor. They fell back, firing wildly at the sky. Tracy had a feeling some of those rounds were going to come back down on the men who'd fired them. He glanced up to see an armored figure on the roof that gave him a clenched fist gesture. Tracy responded with a salute and ran back to the burned hole in the building.

He took cover and waited. It took a few minutes, but the leader of the governor's forces managed to get his troops reassembled and they headed down the side of the building. Tracy evaluated their armor. It was standard planet issue, not as hardened or as tough as what space-based troops wore. He also knew from lectures by his firearms instructor that the design had weaknesses at certain joints—the upper thigh, beneath the arm. The downside of both was that there was a real risk he'd kill any man he shot, but clearly he was going to have to make the point.

He sucked in a deep breath, held it, then swung back around the wall and targeted the commander. Sniping had always been his specialty and this shot went true. It took the man in the joint where the thigh piece tied into the body of the suit. Screaming the man went down. A few of his men again fired wildly at the building, but the bullets missed him by a mile. From the roof gunfire again rained down. That broke the will of the governor's troops. They grabbed their groaning leader and pulled back in confusion. Whoever was on the roof, Tracy wanted to kiss him.

He moved deeper into the building and was intercepted by his sergeant. "Sir, some of us don't want any part of this."

"You gonna shoot those kids?" Tracy growled.

"No, sir, but we don't want to shoot fellow soldiers. We want to just leave."

"How many of you?"

"Six of us."

"Okay. Go. Send me the three who are sticking."

"Yes, sir." Greene stepped back and snapped off a perfect salute. "I don't agree with your actions, sir, but you're a real ballsy bastard. Can't help admiring you… but only a little bit."

A few minutes later the three remaining *fusileros* joined him. The medic was among them. When Tracy looked surprised he gave a rueful smile. "I just finished treating those little guys. Not real keen on having all my work undone with bullets."

The other two consisted of a short, slim man who was younger than Tracy and a hard-bitten trooper whose face was a net of wrinkles.

"It'll take them a few minutes to radio back to the residence for instructions," Tracy said. "Then they'll dither. Maybe try to encircle us."

"I'll get back on the roof," the young soldier said.

"So you were my guardian angel."

The young man shrugged. "It was easy to get up there, and I figure we might want a vantage point." He patted his grenade launcher. "I can drop a few stun grenades in the middle of them if you want, sir."

"Go," Tracy ordered.

The older man shifted a wad of gum to the other side of his jaw and blew a large bubble. "Once *el chico* drops his surprise I'll pop out the front and shoot 'em up."

"Let's try not to kill anybody," Tracy said.

"Nah, just shake 'em up, scare 'em, keep 'em off balance."

Tracy caught the man by the arm as he turned away. "Thanks." He was embarrassed to realize he didn't know the man's name. Worse was the knowledge that he had been treating them like disposable cogs. Carson's sloppy leadership was apparently catching. He tried to excuse himself with the dodge that he never knew which men he might lead and he wasn't meant to be a *fusilero* commander. He checked the man's dog tag. *Mogdahtar Bahir A.* "Thanks for this, Mogdahtar."

"I know I oughta hate 'em, but the little critters are kinda cute. Remind me of kittens."

So the Cara'ot weren't completely off base, Tracy thought and had a momentary flare of admiration for the aliens. Maybe it hadn't worked on everyone, but it had worked on a grizzled vet.

Tracy radioed up to the youngster on the roof. "Let me know when you're in position and if anyone is pulling security."

"I doubt it with these clowns," the *hombre* responded.

"If you're right I'm going to add to the general excitement."

Tracy slipped back out through the hole in the wall, and took a fast look. There was no one in evidence along the side of the building. He pressed his back to the wall and slid toward the front of the building.

The radio in his helmet came to life. "They're all gathered in a circle arguing about what to do. That guy you shot is lying in the middle and bleeding all over the pavement."

"They don't have a medic?" Tracy asked.

"Guess not. And nobody's keeping watch."

"I'll radio you when I'm at the corner of the building."

"Roger that."

Tracy covered the final thirty feet. "I'm in position."

"Ready at the front," Mogdahtar responded.

The sensors in his helmet allowed him to hear the *whump* as the launcher fired, then immediately dampened the sound as the stun grenade detonated. Tracy swung around the corner. The main door raised four feet, Mogdahtar rolled under and came up firing. Tracy fired at the men left standing. This time he aimed for heavily armored areas. He'd hoped they'd retreat and his hope was realized when almost half the men took off running, leaving the wounded man and the stunned lying on the ground.

Tracy slung his rifle and ran to the wounded man. He heaved him over his shoulder in a fireman's carry. Mogdahtar rolled back under the door and raised it high enough for Tracy, bearing his load, to run in. The man was big and when the armor was added it was a significant load. Tracy staggered toward the box fort that defended the children. Behind him he heard the door whine down, and the barricade boxes being pushed back into place.

The medic looked up from the wounded human. "Just curious but how many more are you planning on delivering to me?"

"With luck this is it." Tracy turned to leave then looked back. "Keep him alive."

The medic nodded and cracked the suit. "He's lost a lot of blood, Lieutenant. He needs to be in a hospital. Like my other patient."

"Do what you can. This can't go on too much longer." Tracy turned away and added under his breath, "I hope."

Eighty pairs of eyes tracked him. The man who'd waved a gun at Tracy came cringing up to him. "We heard a lot of shooting," he said. He had to force the words past chattering teeth.

Tracy felt the weight of children's gazes as he weighed his words. "Mostly for show. Just buying us time."

A woman joined them. "Can you get us to your shuttles? Get us off planet?"

"I can't effectively guard this many people in open ground with only four of us. I think we're better off staying here."

"What if they send in shuttles? Bomb us?"

"That would be bad," Tracy agreed. "But I don't think they'll go that far. Not with O-Trell soldiers inside the kill zone."

Realizing his capacity for happy talk had reached its limit, Tracy went to join his corporal on the roof. Some of the stunned government troops were starting to stir. The soldier had one foot on the parapet and was staring down at them through his rifle sights.

"What's your name, soldier?"

"Brinkerhoff, sir. Hans."

"Drop a few puke grenades on them," Tracy ordered. Unlike the space armor, the helmets of the security forces weren't hermetically sealed, and O-Trell had developed a substance that played hell on the vagus nerve and caused uncontrollable vomiting. It was an effective and non-lethal form of crowd control.

The younger man laughed. "Man, these guys are having a really shitty day."

"I'd say we are too," Tracy replied as the young soldier fired two grenades.

His radio sprang to life with a call from the *Preble* and the helmet quickly adjusted for volume since the captain was bellowing. "Belmanor, what the fuck is going on down there?! We're there to assist the civilian authorities in restoring order and instead I've got the governor crawling up my ass. He says my troops are firing on his men. Then Hu reports that half your squad has turned up and they say you've lost your fucking mind."

"I would dispute that characterization, sir. As for the governor's forces—they're operating under an illegal order. It was my duty to resist that order."

"Don't play armchair lawyer with me, Lieutenant."

"I'm playing a sworn officer in His Majesty's armed forces. Which means *I don't kill children*."

"Fuck you, Belmanor! You self-righteous prick."

The connection was broken and Tracy realized he was the one who had done it. Probably not the best career move he'd ever made. He paced the roof weaving between skylights and vents. The corporal watched him. From below the sounds of retching, then retreating footsteps, were picked up by his sensors.

"Sir, are you okay?"

"Corporal, this isn't likely to end well for me. I can't ask you to risk your career. You, Guth and Mogdahtar should go."

Brinkerhoff chuckled. "Sir, I don't have a career. I had a way out of the swamps in the Netherlands back on Earth. A chance not to live on basic subsidy and get to see the stars. I'd rather be on your side in this."

"You okay with aliens then?"

The boy shrugged. "Why not? They seem nice enough. And I suppose to them *we're* aliens. I'd rather have them thinking I'm nice too."

Tracy clapped a hand on Brinkerhoff's shoulder. "You just said some wise shit there, Corporal."

"Just wish we knew the cavalry was coming."

"It is, but it's three days out. Unless…"

"Sir?"

"Foldstream's faster than a ship," Tracy muttered.

He retreated to the far end of the roof, removed his glove and keyed his ring.

"Tracy?" Mercedes said.

As his girth had increased, her father's gait had become more rolling, but the pace he was setting had Mercedes struggling to keep up. When she had come to him with Tracy's information he had heaved up from behind his desk with a curse and yelled to his long-suffering assistant, "Emmett! Get the Cara'ot ambassador over here now."

"Sir, what if he has other—"

"Get him here!"

"Very good, Highness."

Now they were on their way to a conference room deep in the official side of the palace. "Private meeting rather than in the throne room?" Mercedes asked.

"I can't keep the vultures in the press out of official venues. If what you're telling me is true, that the Cara'ot have broken the genetic laws, we do not want this out in the news."

"What about these children? And we've got an officer in trouble."

"Put on your uniform and put the fear of God in Epps. If you hadn't given this man private access we could have remained serenely unaware," the Emperor added and his tone was petulant.

Shocked, Mercedes stumbled to a halt. "Father, these are children being killed."

"We make tough decisions about children all the time. You were there for the relocation of the children from Sinope."

"That's different. We weren't *killing* them. We're giving them a better life."

"And what kind of life are these illegal half-breeds going to have? But it's too late now. We have to act. Go!"

Mercedes called her maid and had her dress uniform rushed to the palace. She changed in her old bedroom and tried to remember the eighteen-year-old who had thrown a hairbrush at the dresser mirror in her fury over being required to attend the High Ground. From the vantage of almost thirty Mercedes wished she could go back and give that younger self a hard shake.

Once dressed and with her medal conspicuously on display, she moved to the communication center and ordered them to contact Epps. The Foldstream call went through and the screen came to life.

Epps was a portly man with thinning hair and heavy pouches beneath his eyes. Those eyes held a wild light. Mercedes had the feeling the man was on a hair trigger. She drew herself up and assumed her haughtiest expression.

"Oh thank God," Epps began.

"Governor Epps, my father is currently in talks with the Cara'ot ambassador. By your actions you have threatened a two-hundred-year-old peace." There was a short delay as her words reached him. She knew when they had because he gaped at her.

It turned to a glare and he made a wild gesture that swept the air. "They're the ones who risked the peace, not me!"

"You should have informed the crown when you discovered this violation, not taken matters into your own hands. You will pull back your troops and order them to stand down. The battle cruiser *Triunfo* is inbound and will take control of the situation. Your presence is required on Ouranos. My father wishes to speak to you."

Epps visibly shrunk into his chair, outrage melting into fear and chagrin. He ran both hands through his hair, leaving wisps sticking up like feathers on a maddened hen. "I was just trying to do the right thing," he whined. "I'd only been here a few weeks when I discovered this horror." He raised bloodshot eyes to the camera. "They thought they could get away with it. That here on the edges of the League they could avoid notice until they were ready to unleash these monsters. I was protecting us."

"By killing children. Very heroic. Issue the order."

"All right."

"Now. I want to hear it given."

Epps shot her a brief hate-filled glance then brought up another screen, which showed an armored figure. "Major, new orders from the capital. They're ordering us to stand down. Return to the residence."

"By whose authority, Governor?" the soldier asked. His tone was dismissive.

"Mine! Captain Princess Mercedes Adalina Saturnina Inez de Arango, the Infanta. Will that do?"

The man came to attention and snapped off a salute. "Highness! At once."

The second screen vanished. "Epps, we expect you to make all haste."

"I'll have to make arrangements."

A wild notion intruded. "I'll instruct the *Preble* to bring you to Ouranos." She gestured and the communications officer broke the connection. "Get me the captain of the *Preble*." She issued her order. One last call remained. She debated whether to make it on official channels or use her ring. She decided to put it beyond the reach of a Freedom of Information request. She left the communications center and returned to her old quarters. The rings lacked the power and range to give her a visual, but she could at least hear his voice.

Tracy answered immediately. "Well?"

"They're standing down."

"Oh thank God." His voice was hoarse with fatigue.

"I've instructed Epps to return to Hissilek aboard the *Preble*. You'll get to see your father," she concluded awkwardly.

"Any chance—"

"That probably wouldn't be wise. This is going to have to be handled… delicately."

"Yeah, because God forbid the murder of children discomforts anyone."

That stung. "You're tired. I'm going to pretend I didn't hear that."

After a long moment his voice came back. "I'm sorry. You help me and I act like an asshole."

"Take care, Tracy."

"Back at you."

And he was gone.

24

HEROES AND POLITICS

The troops that had been gathering around the warehouse abruptly withdrew. Traffic began moving in the streets outside. Guth called to a local hospital and rode with his patients in the ambulance. Tracy, Mogdahtar and Brinkerhoff stood together studying the children.

"What do we do with all of them?" Mogdahtar asked.

"No idea," Tracy said. He beckoned to the two adult humans he'd spoken to earlier. "Do these kids have parents? Homes they can go back to?"

"We had group homes since we all volunteered to have our DNA blended with Cara'ot volunteers," the bearded man explained.

"We thought of the children as belonging to all of us," the woman added.

"Can you go back there? Presumably you have food, beds, clothing for the kids."

"I don't know. There are probably bodies there," the woman said.

"We had a warning from another crèche that the

governor's troops had broken in and were killing the children. The Cara'ot at our location held the doors while we gathered up the kids and got out the back," another man explained. "I think it's safe to assume they've been killed." The couple exchanged a glance. "We wouldn't want the children to see that and be traumatized."

Like they haven't already been traumatized by the gunfight, the dead Cara'ot and the bleeding guys here? Tracy managed not to say it.

"This was supposed to be a safe rendezvous point," the older man continued. "But someone must have given away the location."

The sunlight streaming through the hole in the wall was briefly blocked. Tracy swung his rifle to his shoulder and whirled round. Coming through the door were three enormously tall and broad figures. They were cloaked and hoods concealed their features.

"Hold it right there!" Tracy yelled.

They ignored him and continued to glide deeper into the building. The man gave a cry of joy and ran toward one of them. A long arm and a hand that ended in twelve tentacles came out from beneath the cloak and held him off. "Saa'bet, what's wrong?"

He too was ignored and Tracy realized the aliens were ignoring the children, the humans and the three soldiers and moving toward the body of the dead Cara'ot where it lay sprawled among fallen crates.

Tracy followed them. "Look, I'm sorry. We didn't understand the situation. We thought we were facing armed rebels." No response. Another of the figures produced a shimmering cloth that seemed woven from an aurora and reverently wrapped the body. They then carried it away, two on each side, the third supporting the head. They vanished back out the opening in the wall.

"They don't want anything to do with us now," the woman said, her tone mournful. "We've proved we're monsters."

Mercedes hurried back to the conference room, eager to see how her father would handle the Cara'ot ambassador. The advantage to being home and not posted to a ship was she could take a masterclass in governance and politics from the best purveyor in the League.

The conversation was well underway when she slipped into the room, the security screens causing her teeth to buzz as she passed through them. There were two aliens facing her father. One was amazingly tall and thin, with skeletal head and face. No hair adorned the bald head but rather seven floating fronds like the tendrils on a Tiponi Flute waved like seaweed in a tidal pool. The other Cara'ot was tiny, sitting in the crook of the tall one's arm. It reminded Mercedes of an Isanjo but with disturbing differences, in that the limbs had multiple joints as if a Sidone spider had been added into the genetic mix. Neither of them had taken a chair. They stood, quivering with rage, in front of her father. Violence hung in the air. Mercedes tensed, prepared to leap to her father's defense.

Fortunately her entrance broke the tension. The sense of

threat diminished, but not the rage. The Cara'ot ambassadors regarded her. That's when she realized there were tiny eyes set in the palms of the Isanjo-like creature's hands. She couldn't control the shudder. They turned their attention back to her father.

"Why should we not call this an act of war?" the smaller alien piped.

A cold knot settled in Mercedes' belly. The war with the Cara'ot had killed hundreds of thousands on both sides. How much worse would a new war be? Tracy and Boho were on active duty. Serving on ships that would be swept up in that bloody wave.

"Because it was a tragic misunderstanding. May I present to you my daughter, Mercedes Arango. Mercedes, these are Juniae." He indicated the tiny Cara'ot. "And Puukal." Mercedes exchanged a formal nod with the aliens. Her father continued. "You can't hold the entire League responsible for the actions of one frightened man," he said.

"A man cannot become such a monster unless he swims in an atmosphere of hate and fear and violence," the tall Cara'ot said.

"Do all League humans hate us so?" Juniae added.

"No, of course not. This man is not representative of all humans."

"Then you are saying he is mentally ill and will of course be removed from office," Puukal said.

Her father coughed. Mercedes moved to a credenza where snacks and drinks had been arranged. She poured him a glass of water and carried it to the table.

"He will be dealt with, but carefully. For the sake of both our species I think this needs to be kept quiet. My people would be alarmed if they found out about these... offspring."

Mercedes winced. Never before had she seen her father be so inartful. The small alien pounced, and given his physical stance Mercedes was surprised it wasn't a literal pounce.

"So you admit that your kind fear and despise us. These are lovely, appealing *children*." Juniae's voice was a mournful bell.

"We have communicated with our people on Dragonfly. Three thousand children were born. Nearly two thousand were killed," Puukal said.

Her father gaped. Exhaustion pulled at his jowls. Mercedes stepped in. "It's difficult to remove such deep-seated prejudices and it wasn't all that long ago our species were at war. For the sake of your people and for these children, my father is right. It's best if this is kept from the general public. I can promise you that Governor Epps will not prosper." The Emperor nodded in agreement.

"So will you take custody of the... children?" her father asked.

"They were born by their human mothers with admixtures of DNA from human fathers. To break such a bond of birth seems cruel," Puukal said.

The Emperor opened his mouth, then closed it. He exchanged a long glance with Mercedes. "We'll save that for later discussions," Mercedes said. "For now I think it best if both sides focus on how to keep these events from becoming broadly known among our respective peoples."

"What of the men who pulled the triggers and killed those children?" Juniae asked.

"They will no longer have such comfortable postings guarding governors' mansions and embassies," the Emperor said. His silvering brows drew together in a tight frown. Mercedes had a sudden vision of the galactic map and the enigmatic and ever useful Sector 470—the place where inconvenient people were sent to disappear.

"Very well, we will speak to the individuals who were part of the parentage unit," Puukal said.

He gathered Juniae back into the crook of his arm and turned to leave, then paused. "We have heard there was a young soldier who defended one group of children. We would like to commend this individual."

"That would be Captain-Lieutenant Belmanor," Mercedes said, feeling a certain proprietary pride. "He'll be on his way back to Ouranos shortly."

"Excellent. Please inform us when he arrives."

They left. Mercedes sank down into a chair, realizing that her muscles ached from the tension she'd been holding in her body. "Well, I think that went as well as it could."

Her father gave a snort. "As in it wasn't a total disaster. This Belmanor. He needs to understand the play. Keep him away from the Cara'ot and make it clear he has to keep his mouth shut."

"I'll see to it. So… Epps."

"Nothing is going to happen to Epps. After a discussion that will put the fear of God into him he'll return to Dragonfly and resume his duties."

"But I indicated—"

"Doesn't matter. I'm not going to make an enemy of the darling of the conservatives just to placate a group of BEMs who broke the law. They're lucky we're letting these abominations live, and not putting to death every human and Cara'ot who took part in this." Her father grunted as he pushed back from the table and stood.

Mercedes watched him leave and tried to picture the upcoming talk with Tracy. The *intitulado* had a rigid sense of right and wrong and what was fair. It was not going to be a pleasant conversation.

As Tracy debarked from the shuttle with the fulminating former governor of Dragonfly in tow the *fusileros* waiting on the flight deck muttered among themselves and cast both dark and puzzled glances his way. Tracy was glad he had Mogdahtar and Brinkerhoff with him. He glanced up and saw Donnel clinging to the roof of the bay. The alien was glaring at Epps. Tracy frowned at the batBEM and jerked his head toward the door. The alien skittered away across the ceiling and vanished into a corridor.

The trio escorted Epps to the bridge and turned him over to Captain Carson. Brinkerhoff and Mogdahtar rushed to get out of navy territory. Tracy saluted and also prepared to leave when Carson grabbed his arm and hissed, "You seem to have friends in high places, Lieutenant." There was no good answer to be made so Tracy kept silent. "And you brought *so* much attention to me and my ship."

"Happy to oblige."

Carson leaned in so close that his spittle hit Tracy's ear. "You arrogant, self-righteous prick! I won't forget this, *intitulado*." He released Tracy's arm with a violent shove. "Get off my bridge. You're relieved of duty until we reach Ouranos."

Tracy saluted, bowed and left. He stopped on the Weapons deck and stripped out of the battle armor. His body was slick with sweat and even to himself he reeked. Around him other *fusileros* were also stripping out of their armor and heading for the showers. He had hoped to grab a shower too, but given the glares from the *hombres* and remembering how he had gotten attacked in the showers back at the High Ground in his first year, Tracy decided to dress and let Donnel launder the uniform.

"I'm filthy," Tracy said as he entered his closet-sized cabin. "I'll be going to the officers' lav."

"Very good, sir," Donnel said as he unbuttoned Tracy's coat and eased it off his shoulders. The small button nose wrinkled as the stink hit him. "Not sure we shouldn't just burn this uniform."

"Yeah, fuck you too." Tracy then whirled and grabbed the alien by the neck. It wasn't easy because Donnel's overly round head rested almost directly on his shoulders. "You knew, didn't you? You knew what was down there and you didn't warn me. You let me go in blind, you bastard!"

"I didn't know the particulars," Donnel whined. "I was told there was some dangerous shit going down and I was instructed not to say anything. I may be a black sheep to my people, but there are some lines I won't cross. Not even for you."

Tracy released the alien and sank down onto his bunk. "They were killing kids down there."

Donnel knelt at his feet, unlaced and eased off his boots. "But you didn't. You saved them. You were a—"

"*No!* Don't make me out to be some kind of a hero. I shot a fellow soldier, I disobeyed orders."

"You were a hero to those children," Donnel said softly.

Tracy covered his face with his hands and muttered, "Why couldn't you people just obey the laws?"

"Why couldn't you people? It takes at least two to make a genetic soup."

Allowing his hands to fall into his lap Tracy gave a small laugh. "How many normally go into your soups?"

"Oh lots." Donnel stood and indicated Tracy should do the same. He helped Tracy out of his shirt and trousers, then handed him a bathrobe. "Seriously, sir. It's an honor to serve you," he said.

25

SUCH AN EASY THING TO GIVE

It still felt strange to come home to his father's flat. Alexander no longer lived over his shop. Instead the flat was a few blocks away from the new shop in the MidVale neighborhood. It had functioning air conditioning, three more rooms than their old digs, and even a security door into the lobby. Tracy had teased Alexander that a few more years of good sales and he'd be moving into a building with an actual doorman. His father's cheeks had reddened but Tracy knew he had been pleased. Tracy hoped the shop's success helped ameliorate his dad's disappointment over his son's slow advancement. They were in the elevator when Tracy's ring tapped his finger. He checked the ID of the caller.

"Dad, I need to take this, privately."

"Of course. Duty calling?"

"Something like that," Tracy muttered as he punched the next floor up so the elevator would stop. He stepped out, waited for the doors to close and answered. Mercedes' image appeared. "Wait until I get someplace more private." He reduced the image and went into the stairwell. Brought her back up. "Okay, all good now."

"I need to see you. We have to discuss…" she hesitated and he broke in.

"Dragonfly?"

"Yes."

"You look worried. Is there some problem?"

"No, but we need to make sure it doesn't become one. Please come to Conde de Vargas's office at the Exchequer. One hour."

Her tone made it clear this was the heir to the Solar League speaking to a loyal officer. He altered his tone to one of clipped efficiency and said, "Ma'am." He gave a salute. Mercedes broke the connection. Tracy took the stairs the rest of the way up to the apartment.

"Donnel!" he bellowed as he came through the door. "I need my dress blues."

The alien emerged from the kitchen with an onion in one hand and a knife in the other. "You want dinner or you want help?"

"Both," Tracy said. Donnel gave a long-suffering and exasperated sigh. Tracy headed on to the bedroom that was filled with his childhood memorabilia and in which he'd only spent a scant few days. He didn't have the heart to tell Alexander that he really didn't need those posters of the actress Riena Valdez that had served as the inspiration for a number of teenage fantasies.

He was pulling off his boots when the batBEM entered. Excitement gleamed in the alien's four eyes and the round face was flushed. "The palace or the admiralty? Will it be another *Distinguido Servicio Cruzar*? That would stuff it up the bastards' noses if you won another one of those."

"Calm down. It's not official."

"Then why am I fucking in here? And why the dress uniform?"

"The Infanta wants to see me."

"Oh."

"But privately." The Cara'ot's frown brought Tracy up short. "What?"

"Call me paranoid but meetings between the heir to the throne and a guy who should be getting hailed as a fucking big hero doesn't bode well to me."

"Yeah, you're paranoid. Come on, I'm running out of time." Tracy ran a hand across his chin. "I should probably shave again."

"Anticipating a kiss?" the alien asked.

Tracy thrust a finger at the closet. "Hop to it."

The expression would have been enough but now Tracy spoke and made his feelings abundantly clear.

"You're not serious? You're not actually going to allow this asshat to continue to govern a planet. A planet previously controlled by the Cara'ot. A planet where this man ordered the murder of their *children*."

Mercedes glanced back at Rohan. He sat, fingers laced over his paunch, an expressionless Buddha. The Chancellor had offered his office for the meeting. It was away from the palace and journalists tended to avoid the Exchequer. By their lights, finance was dull. Mercedes looked back to Tracy. It had been years since they'd last met. She had been shocked to see that he still wore only a lieutenant's insignia. Well, that would be seen to once this current crisis was resolved. She noted the fine lines forming around those incredible eyes, the gouges at the sides of his mouth, the wrinkle between his brows. She had a feeling he frowned more than he smiled and that made her sad. He was certainly frowning now.

"I don't like it either—"

"Then why the fuck are you doing it? Highness," he belatedly added.

"Lieutenant, I fear at this point I have to object," Rohan said. "This is your ruler."

"Then she needs to act like it." Tracy gave Mercedes a brooding glare. "And look out for *all* her subjects."

Mercedes sighed and sat on the corner of Rohan's desk. "Conde, I think it best if you leave us. The lieutenant and I are old friends. I know he can be a stiff-necked, self-righteous prig." *He is also the kind of man who would risk everything to prevent a genocide*, she thought. "But I think we can reach an understanding if we're not constrained by protocol."

"As you wish, Highness." Rohan stood with a grunt and waddled to the office door. The formal mask broke and he gave them a brief smile. "Don't kill each other."

There was a soft click as the door closed behind him. "So tell me what you really think," Tracy snapped.

"You *are* a stiff-necked, self-righteous prig. And in a more just world you'd be a hero, *but* if we go public there will be a backlash, maybe even violence. Humans against Cara'ot.

Maybe Cara'ot against humans, which could endanger the peace. It's better for both species if we keep this quiet. You were in the middle of the situation. I need to know we can count on you." He opened his mouth and she rushed on to forestall the objections. "So who have you told?"

"Just my father, but aren't you missing a critical point? These kids, at least what's left of them, exist. Are you going to sweep them under the rug too? Just how *inconvenient* are they?"

Furious, she came to her feet and closed the gap between them. "Don't you dare imply that I would let any harm come to these children, they're blameless." Only inches separated them. The scent of his aftershave swept over her. Conflicting emotions—love and anger—tore through Mercedes over their situation, what he was and what she feared she was becoming. "We weren't able to get a commitment from the Cara'ot to take them so we've come up with a plan in case the Cara'ot continue to shirk their responsibilities. Resettlement."

"Habitable planets aren't all that common."

"We've got one we can use. Sinope. We haven't had a lot of luck getting League citizens to settle there, given the harsh environment and the hostility of the women. The surviving children, the humans and the Cara'ot who violated the law by taking part in this debacle will be sent there." Mercedes shrugged. "It will beat prison."

"What about the settlers on Sinope? How are they going to feel about this?"

"We took their children six years ago. Since then there have been very few births. A handful out of secret fertility labs—those children we seize and shut down the labs—and a handful from normal relationships. You would think they would start to accept a more normal society by now." She was surprised by her querulous tone and the deflection. She forced herself back to the matter at hand. "Be that as it may, they need population. I expect these children will be welcome along with their parents. Then they can all commiserate about how awful we are, but that's all they'll be able to do."

Tracy paced away. "I don't know. What you're asking feels… wrong. Against our oath. Against our faith. Has the church been consulted?"

"No. We want to limit the number of people who know."

"There were a shit load of soldiers taking part in that operation."

"They've been ordered to keep quiet. We're relying on their training, good order and discipline."

"It was their training, good order and discipline that had them shooting kids, Mercedes. And why don't you just order me?"

"Because you're the only officer to disobey. Why should I think you'd obey this order?"

"I don't know if that's a compliment or if you're slamming me."

"I'm not sure either." She smiled at him, but didn't get a response. His expression was thunderous. She sighed. "Rohan thought it might come to this. He says he knows your mettle."

She moved to the desk and picked up the paper she had left there, held it out to him. He hesitantly took the heavy parchment, studied the seal and ribbon.

"The Emperor is very cognizant of your exemplary service, Captain-Lieutenant," Mercedes said formally. "He instructed me to tell you that in recognition of that service you are to be immediately promoted to commander and made the executive officer aboard the *Estrellas del Cielo*."

"That's a fire lance frigate," Tracy said slowly.

"Yes," Mercedes said. "The first in the fleet."

"I'd skip a rank."

"Yes."

Time seemed to slow down and it was as if he was looking at Mercedes from a great distance. He looked back down at the paper. "So instead of ordering me you're bribing me," he said slowly.

The hurt in those deep brown eyes stabbed him. He tore his gaze away and stared down at the elaborate pattern on the Sidone rug. She was only asking for his silence. Such an easy thing to give.

"Just... just be the human I think you are." Donnel's anguished words before he'd deployed to the surface of Dragonfly came rushing back to haunt him.

His mind skipped wildly, unable to process the request, shying from the decision he faced. He studied his surroundings—the thick carpet under foot, bookcases lining the walls with actual paper and leather-bound books on the shelves, the heavy purple drapes sweeping gracefully over the mullioned windows, a marble-topped wet bar set off to the side. Tracy supposed the office of the man who controlled the funds of an empire would be opulent. He remembered the favors he'd done for Rohan. Acquiesce to this request and he would have the favor of the Emperor and his heir. This world of power and opulence might open to him.

"We can't openly acknowledge your actions, but this is a way for us to honor your heroism," Mercedes continued.

"…don't make me out to be some kind of a hero."

"You were a hero to those children."

"Am I now betraying them?" Tracy murmured.

"What?"

"Nothing. Doesn't silence make me complicit, Mercedes? Dear God, we studied these kinds of events at the academy— My Lai, Abu Ghraib, Nairobi, Shanghai."

"The stakes are higher on this. We risk a war of civilizations." She gripped his arm. "I don't have the luxury of high-minded and, frankly, naive principles. The consequences are just too dire."

"And what about the consequences of a cover-up? Have you considered those?"

She pressed her palms against her eyes. "I don't know. I don't know. I can't foresee all outcomes. The Emperor and I can only do what we think is best."

"And that's all I can do." The paper fell from his hand and fluttered to the carpet. A dead dream. "I'm sorry. I can't do it. Epps needs to pay. The men who pulled the triggers need to face justice."

"We'll have to stop you," she called as he walked to the door.

"You can try."

26

MOSTLY WE MAKE SHIT UP

"That's one hell of a story," said the enormously obese human seated behind the desk. His triple chin quivered as he talked.

"A fucking *great* story," added the Isanjo perched on the desk.

Tracy sat in front of the desk of the owners and editors-in-chief of The Straight Dope. Randolph Culpepper was the human owner of the bottom-feeding news outlet. Tangret, the Isanjo, was lean and fit and his claws were out, adding to the scars they had previously left on the desk. His jet-black fur with gold highlights gleamed under the lights.

It was unlike every other reaction Tracy had gotten through the day. He had started at the venerable and respected LBC, the League Broadcasting Company. Tracy had met with a slim polished man with videogenic good looks whose response had been a blunt—

"There's no evidence of what you're claiming, and the palace says it isn't true."

Tracy stared at the reporter. "Is Spanish not your first

language? I'm the evidence. I was fucking there. I and a few of my squad protected the half-breeds. I was on the ship that escorted Epps back to Ouranos."

"The governor is on Dragonfly."

"No, he's not."

"I checked with the palace. Look, Lieutenant, I can't take just your unsubstantiated word on a story like this. You're alleging murder and corruption and a cover-up at the highest levels of government."

"My battle armor. It uploads data and pictures to the servers on the *Preble*. It keeps a record. Also there were three *estrella hombres* who supported me and helped me protect the children."

"Fine. Then bring me the suit and those men."

"And then will you do something?"

"If the evidence supports your claims."

Tracy left the soaring glass building that housed LBC. He had only a short time to find someone willing to run with the story. The *Preble* was due to leave dock in three days. He had requested leave, which had been denied. He had also requested a transfer to another ship. He had a feeling continued service on the *Preble* wasn't going to be a comfortable experience. That request was still pending.

He had called Donnel and ordered him to return to the ship and bring his armor. Calls had been placed to Mogdahtar, Brinkerhoff and Guth. A pleasant female voice informed him that those individuals were no longer listed as having scoop service. A bit of research revealed that the three *hombres* were no longer serving aboard the *Preble* and there was no indication where they had been transferred. As quickly as he had moved the crown had moved faster. Tracy's only hope was that they had overlooked the recording in his armor, but he knew it to be a very faint hope. SEGU was notoriously efficient.

Instead of waiting for Donnel to come back with the information that his suit was missing or the files wiped he went out to another news service in the hope they would take the story. News Corp refused to even meet with him. Planetary News suggested he write a tell-all book but maybe make it fiction, and did he know they had a publishing division? With each stop the buildings were becoming less elegant, the neighborhoods more seedy.

Donnel called him with the news Tracy had been dreading but expecting. His suit was gone, replaced by another. By this point it was mid-afternoon and the air seemed to waver from the heat. Tracy pulled off his uniform coat even though it would reveal the sweat stains beneath his arms and down his back. He was on the border between Stick Town and Furryville when he entered the offices of The Straight Dope.

"I'm sorry I don't have any proof beyond my word. The cover-up has been very efficient," Tracy said.

"Hell, we usually don't have *any* evidence. In fact we mostly make shit up," Culpepper said.

"This'll be a nice change for us," Tangret added with a chuckle.

"The crown will try to stop publication," Tracy warned.

"Hell, we're a boil on the ass of society. I doubt the crown even knows we exist," Culpepper grunted.

"Our readership isn't exactly the cream of society," the Isanjo said. "But the ordinary folk will know what you did."

"No, please, this isn't about me. Or it shouldn't be. It's about holding those responsible accountable."

"Nah, kid, we gotta have a face for the hero and that's *you*."

Now that the story was set to go live Tracy told his father about the meeting with Mercedes, and his subsequent efforts to get the truth out into the League.

The shock etched even deeper lines into his father's face. "The story is hitting the Foldstream today so get ready to be mobbed by reporters, Dad." If anything his father's expression became even more horrified. "Hey, no such thing as bad publicity, right?" Tracy said, trying to lighten the moment. "Bet you get even more business."

"I can't believe you did this. You turned down a request from the *crown*."

"I turned down a *bribe*."

Alexander waved that away. "Not the promotion. Not that it wouldn't have been nice. No, you violated your oath to the Emperor. You shirked your duty."

"I *did* my duty. It was an illegal order."

"Yes, yes, on the planet that was one thing, but now... now you've disobeyed the explicit wishes of the Infanta and the Emperor. How could you, Tracy? I raised you better than this."

It wasn't like Tracy had forgotten his father's fawning,

almost slavish dedication to the FFH and the throne. He just hadn't thought it would lead to this.

"Jesus Christ! I never thought your boot-licking these parasites in the FFH would lead you to take their side over me."

The blood that rushed into his father's face showed the remark had stung. "I'm trying to protect you. And if you hated them this much why did you stay in the *Orden de la Estrella* after your five years were up? My guess is you were hoping to win a title."

That was also a truth that stung and Tracy felt his own face flush. "Well, it's done now. Nothing to be done. The story goes live in…" He checked the watch set into the sleeve of his uniform. Donnel had helped him don his dress blues. He was anticipating a lot of press once the story hit. "Twenty minutes."

Except it didn't. Tracy waited almost forty-five minutes in the hope it had been a technical glitch, but he finally had to accept that somehow the crown had spiked the story. He tried calling the office only to be told the number was no longer in service. He then brought up a street view of the neighborhood on his tap-pad. Donnel hovered and peered over his shoulder. Not only was there no activity around the building… there was no building. It had been demolished and salvage crews were busy removing the debris.

"Wonder if they let the staff get out before they brought it down," the alien said.

"They wouldn't just murder people."

"You hope," the Cara'ot grunted.

Fear clenched his gut. He swallowed, trying to moisten a suddenly very dry mouth. He sent a message to Mercedes'

private account. *Don't hurt my father. He's not part of this.*
There was no response, and in that moment he knew he
stood alone and naked against the power of the crown. The
doorbell rang. A murmur of male voices. His father appeared
in the door of the bedroom.

"Tracy." His voice quavered. "There are *fusileros* here."

Tracy stood, picked up his hat, settled it perfectly, and
squared his shoulders. He touched the *Distinguido Servicio
Cruzar*, then on sudden impulse he removed the medal from
his coat and thrust it into one of Donnel's hands. "Keep this
for me." He also tore off his ScoopRing and handed it over.
"Mercedes' private number is on this. I don't want them to
find that."

"Still worrying about the bitch," Donnel growled.

Tracy's fist clenched and Donnel braced for the expected
blow, but Tracy let it go. Maybe the alien wasn't wrong. She
had shafted him. Tracy walked into the living room. The
officer in command of the four troopers didn't bother with
a salute.

"Lieutenant Thracius Ransom Belmanor, you are under
arrest for violations of article 123 of the Uniform Code of
Military Justice for the unauthorized sale and disposal of
property belonging to the *Orden de la Estrella*. You shall be
brought before a general court-martial. You have—"

"Yes, yes, I know the code. I demand my right to counsel."

"Tracy," his father quavered.

"It'll be all right, Dad. Just the crown sending me a
message." Tracy turned back to the young officer. "Shall we?"

"You need to be secured." He gestured and one of the

men stepped forward with force bracelets.

"Do I look like I'm resisting?"

The officer had the grace to look embarrassed. "I'm sorry, sir, we have our orders."

"I see. So how much press is there out on the street?" Tracy didn't get an answer as they clasped the cuffs on his wrists.

He glanced back once as they went out the door. His father seemed to have aged twenty years in an instant. One hand gripped the back of the sofa. A man needing support. And no one to provide it.

The military policeman in the cage was impassive as Tracy set his credit spike, a handkerchief, a tube of lip balm and his ear piece on the counter. Each was carefully logged in. The man's eyes flicked across the combat ribbons on his jacket, and he said quietly, "You might want to leave those too." Tracy nodded and broke the static seal that held them in place. Combat ribbons weren't all that common and would probably bring a pretty price at one of the military memorabilia stores.

He had hoped to be held at O-Trell Point Magu. The base was on the other continent, but at least reasonably accessible to his father. Instead he had been brought to the O-Trell Orbital Base Montero. A shuttle trip would put a severe strain on the family budget, leaving his father with the choice of never visiting his son or going bankrupt.

From processing Tracy was taken, still in security cuffs, to a room where he was told to strip. A humiliating search followed and he was given the electric-green jumpsuit that marked him as a prisoner. The reaction set in as he watched them bag his uniform and carry it away. A hollow appeared where his stomach once resided. He had never thought it would go this far. For an instant regret washed over him. If he had just bowed the head and gone along. But he hadn't and it was way too late for second thoughts. He was escorted to a cell.

The caged men he passed stared at him with either empty or hungry eyes. Were there any like him? Men destroyed because they had challenged authority? But wasn't that the very definition of dereliction of duty? He knew from his previous postings the kind of offenses that got a man court-martialed: acts of violence against fellow soldiers or civilians, insubordination. It also fell exclusively on the enlisted men. Officers were by and large members of the FFH. Their transgressions were either ignored or they were quietly removed to a different posting and then allowed to muster out early. No, there weren't likely to be any other political prisoners at Montero. Which meant he would need to watch his back. How convenient it would be for the crown if he died in prison and they never had to hold his court-martial.

Tracy was used to close quarters. His cribs on the ships had been small, but you were only in them to sleep; the days were filled with duties, mess time, and workouts. Inside the prison the only breaks from the monotony were the meals and the one hour of exercise time. Pacing in the cell put a strain on his knees because it was three steps and turn. He took to doing sit-ups and stretching exercises on the cold metal floor. He tried to remember every book he'd ever read, song he'd learned. Each night at bed check he'd ask the guards when he was going to see his advocate. They never gave him an answer. He inquired about a library and was told that until his arraignment those privileges were off limits for him.

As the day lighting came up on the twentieth day a guard stopped by his cell. "Get dressed, Belmanor, your lawyer's here."

He scrambled into his jumpsuit, pulled on the soft shoes and allowed the guard to clasp cuffs on his wrist. They took an elevator ride up five floors and he was led into a small room with a table with a large metal hook in the middle and two chairs. Fisheye lenses from cameras were in the corners. A JAG officer was waiting in one of the chairs. He looked younger than Tracy and terribly nervous. He shot out of the chair, banging his knee on the edge of the table, and grimacing he thrust out his hand. "Lieutenant Edmund Clancy, Judge Advocate General's office." The man seemed confused when Tracy thrust both his hands out, then he registered the cuffs. "Oh."

The guard laid a hand on Tracy's shoulder and guided him to the chair, forced him to sit down and cuffed him to the ring. He left. Tracy nodded toward the cameras. "What about attorney-client privilege?"

"Oh, they don't listen—"

"So they say."

"No really, they just watch. To make sure you don't do something."

Tracy rattled the cuffs against the ring. "Not likely." The cold metal of the seat cut right through the thin material of his jumpsuit and chilled his buttocks. His balls tried to retreat into his abdomen.

The young officer pulled out a tap-pad and turned it on. "Okay, well the charges against you are quite serious and they have a lot of proof—"

"I'm exercising my right to civilian co-counsel," Tracy interrupted.

The young lawyer gaped at him. "Huh? Wha—"

"I have that right. Check the Code of Military Justice."

"Who's going to pay?"

"O-Trell."

"What if they say no?"

"Then you make a big deal about that." Tracy sighed at the kid's confusion. "In the press."

"I don't think that's a good idea."

"Are you my lawyer or are you working for O-Trell?" Tracy asked sweetly though it was a struggle not to snarl the words.

"Yours, of course."

"I wasn't sure."

"Do you have someone in mind?"

And there was the rub. He really didn't. Tracy ran a hand through his hair, his thoughts whirling like startled birds. The red, round face of an older man swam into focus. "Sir Malcomb Devris. Call him. Tell him I need a criminal defense lawyer."

"The Flitter King?"

"Yes."

The lawyer's nose wrinkled. "He's terribly low class."

"Yeah, well so am I. I know him. Went to school with his son. He'll help."

"Being associated with him might not be the best thing for your reputation. He's been quite public over his dislike of the FFH."

"Which is why I know he'll help." Tracy reached as far as his shackles would permit and grabbed Clancy's wrist. "Please, contact him." He looked up into the young lawyer's face. "And for the record, I didn't do it. Any of it."

"All right. I'll call him. He can certainly afford to pay if O-Trell should refuse."

"Thanks."

"I'll be back once I have co-counsel."

"The jumped-up little *intitulado* never understood how the world works. Really O-Trell is better off without him."

Mercedes studied Boho's face on the screen. The words and the movement of his mouth weren't quite in sync and the Foldstream transmission flattened his features so he looked like an eerie puppet.

She was in her office in the public wing of the palace. It had felt strange when she had first been given an official place inside the government, but in the past year she had found she used it more and more, which had required that she get staff. What had started out as only one young bureaucrat cutting his teeth by acting as her personal assistant had now grown to a team of four. As Mercedes glanced around the room she realized that bit by bit and piece by piece it had become her space rather than a space devoid of personality that oozed bureaucratic competence and nothing more. The top of a credenza was covered with family holograms, all of the nine sisters together when Mercedes had been seventeen and Carisa just five. It was time travel as her eyes moved across the images. Wedding pictures. Estella with her husband and children. Julieta with her growing family. Tanis and Izzara dressed for a ball. Tanis in her nun's habit. Beatrisa in her uniform. The twins in their cadet uniforms. Carisa no longer a big-eyed waif but a young woman in riding clothes. Mercedes wondered how long it had taken the girl to get Constanza to agree to her learning to ride.

As she contemplated the images she thought about all the nieces and nephews her sisters were producing, and found herself thinking about them not as children and relations but as potential problems. Multiple people with potential claims to the throne. Would any of her sisters challenge her because of her childless state? Push forward their own offspring? Turn against each other in a battle for the throne?

Her gaze drifted to the Sidone tapestry she had bought years ago when she was at the academy. Tracy had bought a tiny piece as well. They had then gone on to have a picnic together with grass underfoot and stars just outside the observation glass. She realized Boho had been talking and she had missed most of what he said.

"I know you never liked him, but he was very competent," Mercedes broke in. "I just worry when O-Trell loses competent officers. We might need them some day."

"You shouldn't let your father's nerves over Sector 470

affect you, sweetling. There's nothing to indicate there's a real threat out there."

"Except seven lost ships. And if you're so sanguine about it why don't you take the *Intrepid* there and take a look."

He laughed and it seemed forced. "Oh, sweetheart, always teasing. I've got plenty to occupy me here without chasing after boogiemen. You know Belmanor's going to try to bring up all that unpleasantness on Dragonfly rather than address the charges."

"Daddy and I have already spoken to the judge. He knows to exclude any testimony that touches on Dragonfly."

"As he should. This is about theft of government property. I wish you had shown me the list you created before you sent it to the JAG office though. Some of those items may be problematic. The generator for example, but the rest of them are perfect. Spare electronics, medical supplies, rations. I should have known you wouldn't have missed a trick. Though I still think you should have added providing arms to the enemy."

"Except we're not technically at war with any of the alien races right now, and it's harder to fake discrepancies in weapons inventories. We do take that very seriously. Also given his class it's more likely he would have been stealing supplies that could be sold on the open market."

"True. I'm glad to see you're being so hard-nosed about this, my dear. I know you had a certain fondness for him."

"Don't condescend to me, Boho. I let Dani go to her death. I'll break Tracy before I let this turn into a crisis with the Cara'ot."

"I know, love. I was just concerned for you. I'm glad to know I don't have to worry. I just wish I was there to give you at least moral support, dear heart."

"I'm fine, Boho. Enjoy your ship."

"It is a sweet machine. Until next time, my sweet."

Mercedes broke the connection and pressed the heels of her hands against her eyes. *Seven fawning endearments in a single conversation. Oh yes, he's got a mistress stashed in his cabin.* She sighed and clicked on the intercom. "Jaakon, bring me those mining reports from Nephilim."

His voice floated out of the intercom. "Right away, ma'am."

27

WOULD YOU DO IT ALL AGAIN?

Another week passed before Tracy was pulled out of his cell at a non-scheduled time. He expected to be brought back to the interview room. Instead he was brought to the visiting area. On the other side of the glass partition were his father and Malcomb Devris. Tears pricked the back of his eyelids and his throat ached. The guard secured him in the chair and stepped away. Tracy pulled the headset off the wall and fumbled to get it into place. The handcuffs made him clumsy.

Alexander was seated; Devris loomed up behind him, one shovel-sized hand on the slender tailor's shoulder. Tears swam in his father's faded blue eyes. "Tracy, Tracy. How are you, son?"

"I'm okay, Dad. Hanging in there."

"Caballero Malcomb offered me a ride up on his shuttle. He's been more than gracious."

Devris's hand tightened on Alexander's shoulder and the smaller man winced. Even through the soundproof glass Tracy could hear the rumble of the Flitter King's voice even if he couldn't make out the words. "He says it's the least he could do," Alexander passed on.

"Tell him thank you. It means so much to get to see you."

Alexander repeated the words and Devris beamed. "I brought you some of that spicy Isanjo food you like. Once they search it they say you can have it."

"Thanks. Food is pretty basic and bland up here."

"What else do you need?" Alexander asked.

"Something to read. Maybe some candy. How's Bajit? And the shop?"

"Bajit's fine. Said to tell you hello. Don't worry about me, son. You're the only concern right now." Based on the response, Tracy assumed that the business was probably tanking. One more calamity to add to the others he'd already chalked up. "Now, Caballero Malcomb has some things to tell you."

The men traded places, Devris wedging his prodigious belly into the space between chair and wall. "So how are you really?" the businessman asked.

"Getting fucked. Uh, not literally. But the crown is sure making it clear that I'm going to prison."

"We'll see about that. I've retained Caballero Waseem Gurion. He's the top criminal lawyer in Hissilek. He's already contacted that clueless kid they assigned to you."

The tension he had been holding in his shoulder lifted and exhaustion took its place. Tracy slumped in his chair. "Thank you, Caballero Devris—"

"Just plain 'mister' is good enough for me, lad. I took the stinking title because I thought it would improve my business opportunities. Instead it ruined my life. But I keep the damn thing 'cause it gives me more leverage with these assholes."

"I understand, sir. Anyway, thank you and I will pay you back."

A meaty hand was waved. "Don't give it a thought. You were my Hugo's friend. O-Trell's got its claws into my other boys and two of my girls because I took that damn knighthood. I welcome the chance to put a spoke in their wheel. I'll give you back to your dad now."

Alexander squeezed past the massive businessman and slid into the chair. After the bulky Devris his father seemed shrunken and frail. "We're going to weather this."

"I know, Dad."

"You'll be reinstated in no time."

"I'm not sure I really want that." And yet when he remembered removing the uniform, the pang of loss returned. That uniform had defined him for the past eleven years of his life.

"Well, we'll worry about that once it's all over."

The cuff bit into his wrist as Tracy stretched so he could press his palm against the glass. "You know I didn't do this. I didn't steal anything."

"I know."

"I was just trying to get justice for those children."

"I know. But forgive me, son, but I have to say this. Maybe a little of it was ego. Trying to show you were better than these sons of privilege?"

"What? No! I did the right thing even if you think I did it for the wrong reasons."

"I'm sorry. I just don't want you to make more trouble for yourself. I made you too proud."

"Hardly. You did everything to convince me I was less than they were." His father reacted as if he'd been struck. Remorse swept through Tracy. "I'm… I'm sorry, Dad. I didn't mean it. It's just… the situation."

"I understand. Well, things are going to be better now. Don't you worry anymore."

The guard returned and touched his shoulder. "Time's up."

Once again the glass was cold against his palm. His father mirrored the gesture. The guard unhooked the cuffs and pulled Tracy out of the chair. Back in his cell Tracy rubbed at the bruises on his wrist and tried to forget his last glimpse of his father's anguished face.

"You must have antagonized someone pretty damn important to have them go to this much effort to fuck you."

Tracy gaped, then gave a rueful smile and nodded. "How did you know?"

Waseem Gurion was as old as the JAG officer was young. Tracy figured he was pushing one hundred. His flyaway white hair formed a halo around his head and the dark eyes were bright in a nest of wrinkles. He laid a blue-veined hand on the tap-pad. "When I see this much evidence so perfectly assembled I'm pretty damn sure it's a setup. Actual crime is messy and most criminals stupid. I've checked you out. You're not stupid and you're not careless. So who'd you piss off?"

"The crown."

Gurion leaned back and gave a small whistle. "Well,

now I know why Malcomb told me I could charge whatever I wanted. What did you do?"

Tracy told him. He expected the tale to rock the lawyer back in his chair again, but instead the old man leaned forward, clasped his hands on the table and stared intently at Tracy. "I'll try to bring this up, but the judge won't allow it to come in. I may be able to get in a few hints and suggestions, enough to maybe get some intrepid journalist interested, but we can't use it. It's irrelevant to the charges being brought against you."

"So I'm fucked."

"Pretty much. You know they're planning to bury you deep?"

"What does that mean?"

"Prison."

A cold stone replaced his stomach. Tracy leaned forward, fighting nausea, and rested his forehead on the metal table. The cold helped, but he still felt like puking when he did straighten. Unable to sit still he stood and paced the small interview room. Thanks to Gurion he wasn't cuffed to the table. "So what are my odds?"

"Well, you've got me so…" He pondered. "Sixty/forty."

"For acquittal?"

"Oh hell no, that's to keep you out of jail. An acquittal— more like ninety/ten. So, who have you got to speak on your behalf?"

A month ago he would have said Mercedes. Tracy mentally reviewed his friends and realized it was a short, sad list. "Come on, there must be someone? You can't be that much of an asshole."

"Commander Anusanatha Sukarno, I was his adjutant. He was the XO aboard the *Triunfo*. Lady Cipriana Delacroix, I served with her. Maybe Marqués Ernesto Chapman-Owiti. I went to school with him." He correctly interpreted the lawyer's expression. "Look, I don't fit in any world. The FFH never accepted me because I'm low-born scum, and because I went to the academy on a scholarship and became an officer I'm not trusted by the enlisted men either. Also, if I pull in some *hombre* it's just going to get a raft of shit rained down on his head."

The quizzical look gave way to one of dawning understanding and then sympathy. Gurion stood and held out a hand. "I'll do my best, son, and my best is pretty damn good. Keep your chin up. You're going to be arraigned on Monday. I'll see you then."

The arraignment had the quality of a nightmare. People seemed distant, their words muffled and faint as the charges were read out. The list of items he had supposedly stolen included a Delphi generator, medical supplies, rations, fuel cells and electronics. Tracy almost hadn't recognized his own voice as he said, "Not guilty." After that there had been a back and forth between the military judge, a rear admiral with a lot of cabbage on his coat, and Gurion. The young lawyer remained silent. Tracy wondered if that was deference to the older attorney or if Clancy would have remained this quiet had he been Tracy's only defender. He suspected the latter.

His father had been in the room looking small as he

huddled in his best jacket. Malcomb, brows knitted into a fierce frown, had glared at the prosecutors. Then it was onto an elevator and back to detention on the space station. Gurion had been whispering urgently in Tracy's ear as he had been escorted away.

"I pushed for a speedy trial, but the judge is balking. They're going to drag their feet on creating a panel. You're just going to have to hang in there for a while." Tracy had been too numb to answer.

That had been five months ago. Malcomb had been beyond generous. He allowed Alexander the use of his shuttle to visit twice a month. Each time Tracy saw his father the man seemed older and smaller. Alexander was melting away before Tracy's eyes. His fellow prisoners changed. They faced their court-martials and were sent on to military prison. Perhaps a few of them were even exonerated and returned to duty. Tracy remained in judicial limbo. He had seen Gurion only twice. Once to be told that Sukarno would testify, and de Vilbiss also, but he'd gotten no response from Ernesto. It was better than an outright refusal, but it still hurt. The next visit had brought a list of those testifying against him. It was an impressive list and included Mark Wilson, Gupta, Eklund and Bellard, Captain Carson, also a few names of *hombres* and *fusileros* that he didn't recognize. When questioned about them by Gurion Tracy could only shrug helplessly. He had no idea who they were, much less what they might say.

"Not that it matters anyway," he muttered at the ceiling. He was spending too much time lying in his bunk and a mere hour of exercise wasn't offsetting the starch-heavy meals that were served in the prison mess. He slid onto the floor and started doing sit-ups. A guard came by.

"You have a visitor, Belmanor."

"My lawyer?"

"Nah, some priest."

He almost refused, but boredom and a desperate desire to get out of his cell overrode that first impulse. He stood, ran a comb through his hair and allowed himself to be cuffed and escorted down the walkway to the visitors' room. He wondered who would be waiting on the other side of the glass. But he wasn't taken there. Instead he was brought to the small room where a priest celebrated mass each Sunday. A bare metal table bolted to the floor served as an altar, a crucifix bolted to the wall behind it. The scent of extinguished candles hung in the room, a miasma of lost hopes. Five rows of metal chairs.

Waiting in one of the chairs was Father Kenneth Russell. Tracy hadn't seen the man since his transfer off the *Triunfo*. The intervening years had left little trace of their passing on the still-youthful face. Russell stood and addressed the guard.

"Neither your presence nor those," the priest indicated the handcuffs, "are necessary." The guard opened Tracy's restraints and left the room. "Thracius," Ken said softly.

"Father." They embraced. "How did you find out?"

Ken indicated for Tracy to sit and he took a chair. "I was attending a Jesuit conference in Hissilek. I thought I'd look you up. I found your father's shop and he told me what was happening. I was surprised to hear this, and... well, disappointed."

"I didn't do it, Father. Any of it."

"It did seem out of character."

"But you believed it," Tracy challenged.

"I thought there was a chance your anger and resentment might have gotten the better of you."

"No, it was my other sin—pride—that brought me here." Unable to sit still Tracy stood and paced away to the table. Stared down at the wax drips that had congealed on the metal. "That and trying to do the right fucking thing. Like they say—no good deed goes unpunished."

"Tell me."

"I've told too many people already. People who I'm afraid have been hurt, and people who might get hurt. I don't want to add you to the list."

"I have the seal of the confessional. I'm no threat to whoever it is that you fear."

Tracy dug at the wax with his thumbnail. A faint scent of frankincense replaced the stale smoke odor and left the pad of his finger feeling oily. Tracy desperately wanted someone to say he'd done the right thing. Someone other than a damn alien with a personal interest. His father had been worried and shocked, but only worried about Tracy and not thinking about the broader implications. The journalists had just wanted a juicy story with ties to the crown. Mercedes only considered the politics of the thing. The lawyers only looked at the rules of evidence, and what had happened on Dragonfly wasn't useful and therefore they didn't care. *Maybe*, Tracy thought, *I could bear this and what's to come if someone tells me I did good.* He was no longer sure he believed that he had.

Returning to the priest Tracy dropped onto his knees in front of Russell. "I did something, Father, and I'm not sure anymore if I did it for the right reasons or so I could feel superior and important."

A hand brushed softly through his hair. "Tell me, my son."

Drawing a deep breath Tracy began. When he was finished he lifted his head and looked up into Ken's eyes begging for approval. After a long silence the priest asked, "Would you take the same actions today knowing where it would lead?" He gestured at the spartan room.

Tracy stared down at his folded hands. Thought about all the points along the way where he could have turned aside. Thought about the eyes of that child who had clung to his leg. Finally he responded, "Yeah, I would."

"Then you have your answer. You don't need to hear it from me."

A rueful smile touched his lips. "It would still make me feel better."

"All right. I could not have taken direct action against those soldiers, but I would have placed my body between their guns and those children."

His eyelids stung from unshed tears. Tracy whispered, "Thank you, Father."

28

DIAL UP A MIRACLE

Tracy didn't need a law degree to know things weren't going well. Clancy just sat in his co-counsel chair and didn't say a word. Gurion peppered the judge with objections, most of which were overruled, and the five officers on the jury panel were stone faced. There was a plain-faced man in civilian dress watching the proceedings. A faint glow showed a ScoopRing was activated. Technically a violation of court rules, but Tracy knew how to recognize a SEGU agent. The spies were streaming the court-martial, and Tracy assumed it was going back to the palace. He pictured Mercedes watching his railroading and humiliation. Did she feel the smallest bit of guilt for destroying him? Fury and sadness warred for primacy. Sadness won.

His father, Malcomb, and Father Ken were a constant presence, as was Donnel. Tracy was oddly touched by the creature's loyalty, but also depressed by the fact he had no other supporters. He supposed it was normal. The friends he had made were all in the military, serving on distant ships, but it didn't help the sense of isolation. Sukarno's request for leave was taking forever to come through. Cipriana was serving on a distant star base, and the commander of the *Estrella Avanzada* was dragging his feet as well. The forces arrayed against Tracy seemed determined that he have no one to speak on his behalf.

The only bright spot was that the trial itself was being held on Ouranos and Tracy was in the brig on the military base next to the spaceport. It meant his father could visit every day instead of twice a month.

Thus far only the prosecution had been making their case. The prosecutor, Commander Lord Etienne, had VR-star good looks, a resonant voice and the stature to make his statements seem like holy writ. Etienne entered damning documents into evidence with the speed of a blackjack dealer. He then called a seemingly unending line of Tracy's enemies who managed to blacken his character with every utterance. The three lieutenants from the *Triunfo* (now commanders) discussed his laziness and lack of readiness.

"Thanks to them," Tracy whispered in Gurion's ear.

During cross-examination the old lawyer masterfully lured them into revealing their resentment over Tracy's assignment as adjutant to the XO, but weighed against the computer record of missing supplies and Tracy's presence when they went missing he wasn't sure it did much good.

Captain Carson was next on the stand. He spoke of Tracy's generally bad attitude and insubordination. He baldly lied saying that Tracy resented having to lead *fusileros*, leaving the impression that Tracy thought he was too good for such assignments and that he was too lazy to keep up with the rigorous physical demands that leading marines required. He then produced the usual faked documents showing missing supplies and Tracy's retinal signature on the inventory lists.

Etienne finished and Gurion rose and strolled up to the witness box. He leaned an elbow on the railing to Carson's evident discomfort. "So, according to these records one of the items stolen was a Delphi generator."

"That's right."

"Valuable piece of equipment."

"Sure as hell is."

"Have you ever calculated the value of the supplies Lieutenant Belmanor is accused of stealing, Captain?"

"Not precisely, but it was a lot of Reals."

"Combined with the goods he stole while he was aboard the *Triunfo* that must be a sizable amount of merchandise that he could sell."

"Definitely."

"Probably brought a good price."

"Yeah."

Tracy couldn't help it—he leaned over to Clancy and whispered, "What's he doing? Why's he making the prosecution's case for them?" The young JAG officer just shrugged and looked as confused as Tracy felt.

Moving back to the defense table Gurion lifted a flimsy. "We offer into evidence Lieutenant Belmanor's bank records and those of his father as well. As you can see, at the time of his arrest the lieutenant's bank account held only 1753 Reals." Gurion activated his ScoopRing and referred to a document. "According to Jaynes auction house the going price for a Delphi generator is 65,000 Reals." The old man's voice softened to a murmur. "So where's the money?"

Carson gaped then blustered, "How should I know?"

"Leaving that for the moment. Where do you think Lieutenant Belmanor sold the generator?"

Carson's lip curled. "Probably on one of those repatriated planets. Those chiseling Hidden Worlders are always trying to get around League laws." Carson then added, "Or he sold it to aliens. He was always an alien lover."

Gurion pounced. "Why would you say that, Captain? Was there some action taken by Lieutenant Belmanor that would support that belief? An action taken on Dragonfly, for example?" Gurion rushed out the final sentence as the judge drew in a breath and the prosecutor leaped to his feet.

"I've warned you about this, counselor," the judge said. "The events you are trying yet again to sneak into evidence are not relevant to the matter before us, which is the theft of government property."

"I would argue that the witness opened up that line of inquiry, your Honor, with his statement regarding my client's attitude toward aliens."

"Well I don't agree. Watch it or I will have you removed from the defense."

Gurion bowed his head in acquiescence and turned back to Carson. "So we have this Delphi generator."

"Yeah."

"How much does one weigh?"

"Huh?" Carson's eyes flew questioningly to the

prosecutor. Tracy noticed that the commander had stiffened.

Etienne leaped to his feet. "What is the relevance of this question, your Honor?"

"I was wondering the same thing," the admiral drawled.

"Bear with me, your Honor. One more question will make the relevance quite clear."

"All right, you may proceed."

"How much does it weigh, Captain?"

"I… I don't know."

Gurion tapped his ring and a page of specs appeared in the air. "There are the specs on a Delphi generator. They weigh 1224.699 kilograms or 2700 pounds. How did Lieutenant Belmanor move the generator?"

"I presume he used a crane and a forklift."

"So let me understand. Lieutenant Belmanor used a crane to load this large and unwieldy object onto a forklift and then drove it through the corridors of *your* ship, with no one noticing, to a secret location where he then hid this 1224-kilo object." Carson had the look of a rabbit caught in a spotlight. "Assuming he accomplished all that, Lieutenant Belmanor then removed the generator from its hiding place on the ship, drove the forklift carrying said generator to the shuttle bay, loaded it onto a shuttle and delivered it to a planet with no one logging the shuttle flight or noticing that a shuttle had left without an authorized co-pilot. Or perhaps your security is so lax they didn't notice the launch?" The silence stretched on and on. "Perhaps you should have given more thought to your fabricated list of stolen items, Captain," Gurion said softly.

"Objection!" Etienne roared.

"Sustained," said the judge.

"Nothing further." Gurion flapped a dismissive hand. "I won't waste any more time on this lying witness."

"Objection!"

Gurion returned to the defense table. For the first time a look of excitement lit Clancy's face and he gave the old lawyer a buffet on the shoulder. Tracy glanced over at the panel of five officers who would decide his fate. The impassive faces of the men gave away nothing.

"Redirect," Etienne said. The judge nodded in acquiescence.

"The defendant has a Cara'ot batBEM, correct?"

"Yes."

"So it's possible that that individual might have arranged for the generator to be smuggled off the ship."

"Absolutely," Carson agreed. "I mean whoever heard of an officer with a Cara'ot?"

"This witness is excused," the prosecutor said quickly, trying to keep Carson from *helping* any further. Carson left the stand and the prosecutor's gaze swept across the panel and the judge. "The prosecution calls to the stand Commander Mark Wilson."

Commander, he's a fucking commander, Tracy thought. Mark walked past the table where Tracy sat with his lawyers and gave Tracy a triumphant and venomous look.

He took the oath with a pious air and sat down. "So, Captain Carson established the fact that the defendant has a Cara'ot batBEM. When did he acquire this particular servant, Commander?" Etienne asked.

"When he entered the High Ground."

"And what was their relationship at that time?"

Both Tracy and Gurion were surprised when Clancy took to his feet. "Objection. Is there some relevance to this line of questioning?"

"A good question, Commander," the admiral said.

"Give me just a bit of leeway, your Honor. As Caballero Gurion said earlier—the relevance will soon be apparent."

"Very well, but it should become apparent… soon."

Etienne bowed his head and returned to Mark. Clancy beamed a bit as Gurion gave him an approving nod and a pat on the shoulder.

"So back to the question, Commander. What was the relationship between Lieutenant Belmanor and this," he glanced at his tap-pad. "This… Donnel?"

"The Cara'ot helped Lieutenant Belmanor skirt the rules and regulations. The alien unlocked doors, interfered with security cameras, intervened when upper-class men attempted to discipline and correct Belmanor's behavior."

That brought some shifting from the five men on the panel. Looks stabbed Donnel who shrank down. His lack of a neck made it look like the stubby body was trying to swallow his head.

"So you are a procurement officer, isn't that right, Commander?"

"Yes, sir."

"Can you explain where the missing goods were sold and where the funds from those illicit sales might be held?"

"The Cara'ot are master traders selling mostly to the

other alien races. Their ships move throughout League space but because of the treaty that ended the Expansion Wars, their ships are not subject to search by League authorities. It seems logical that the batBEM arranged to have the goods transferred to Cara'ot ships, sold as legitimate and the monies have been held for Lieutenant Belmanor."

"In other words the perfect laundering operation?" Etienne suggested.

"Exactly."

Gurion heaved to his feet. "Objection, your Honor. I could state that all these missing supplies sprouted wings and flew away and it would have as much credibility as this witness's speculations."

"There's an easy way to find the answer," Etienne said. He pivoted on a heel and gazed at Donnel. "The creature is in the room. We could pull it into custody—"

Gurion spun and almost ran to where Donnel was sitting. "Do you want me as your lawyer?" he demanded.

"Oh hell yeah!" Donnel said.

Gurion turned back and gave the judge and the prosecutor a bright, false smile. "My client may be an alien, but he does have due process rights. I want to see probable cause before you bring him in, and if you do bring him in I'll counsel my client to say nothing."

Donnel made a zipping motion across his mouth with one of his four hands. Etienne looked frustrated, the judge annoyed.

"I think it best that we take a recess. Counselors, consider your arguments. I'll meet you in chambers in thirty minutes."

Tracy found himself in a room with his lawyers and

Donnel. His father and Malcomb had tried to follow them into the small conference room, but Gurion had held them back with an upraised hand. "Just give us a few minutes to thrash this out." The door closed and Gurion whirled on them. "So what the fuck?"

"The lieutenant didn't steal anything, and I never fenced anything. However…" the alien's voice trailed away.

"What?"

"It would probably be best if the League doesn't take a close look at my personal finances. They'd get the wrong idea."

"Meaning what?" Gurion's tone was low and dangerous.

"A lot of money moves through my accounts."

"Accounts?" Tracy yelped. "The hells? I've been paying you a salary but all the time you had money?"

"Where did it come from?" Clancy asked.

"Cara'ot business that I can't discuss."

"Well, you bloody well better discuss it and have a damn good explanation or your master is going to spend the next thirty years in Leavenworth!" Tracy was startled by Clancy's vehemence. He'd always assumed the young man had been selected to put on the barest of defenses. It seemed he'd been either shamed or inspired by Gurion. Or perhaps he was beginning to realize Tracy was innocent.

Donnel drooped. "I'm sorry. No one regrets this more than me, but I can't."

Donnel's four eyes slid warily toward Tracy, who raised a hand. The Cara'ot cringed and Tracy saw fear and sorrow reflected in those dark eyes. The bubble of rage that had been rising in his chest collapsed. Tracy sank into a chair and covered his face. All the times he had cuffed the creature or shouted at him came back to haunt him, especially when weighed against all the times the alien had helped and protected him. Shame lay like a bad taste on the back of the tongue. Tracy looked up and forced a smile.

"Well, that's it then." He stood and gripped Gurion's shoulder. "Don't let them hurt my dad, okay?"

"I won't." The old lawyer turned to Clancy. "Okay, when we go into chambers we're going to throw as much dust in the air as possible. Use the Alien Act of 2314, also the Treaty of Ingolf."

"Okay, but it's probably not going to work," Clancy said.

"I know that, I'm just trying to buy us some time in the hope of a miracle."

The lawyers headed for the door. Clancy paused and looked back. "You really didn't do it, did you?"

"No." Tracy watched belief die and cynicism be born.

The opening door revealed a guard. Tracy sank back into the chair. "I'm sorry," the alien repeated. "I was just a conduit for money. I couldn't use any of it."

"Doesn't matter."

Donnel drew himself up to attention, a ludicrous sight. "It has been an honor to serve you."

"You're a pain in the ass, Donnel, but you've done right by me. Mostly. Hope your next officer has better luck, and… and treats you better."

"Yeah, I'd like to have been an admiral's batBEM," the Cara'ot said with a return to his usual insouciance. "Could have lorded it over all the other batBEMs." He headed for the door.

"Where are you going?" Tracy called.

"I'm gonna try to dial up the miracle the old man wants."

"They aren't going to let you leave."

"How can they stop me? I'm not under arrest. Yet."

He pulled open the door. The *fusilero* glared at him. "Get back in there."

"I gotta go to the john."

"Hold it."

"I got a right to leave," Donnel said.

Tracy wondered what the Cara'ot had in mind. The creature had proved to be cunning and resourceful. He decided he may as well be hung for a sheep as a lamb. He joined Donnel at the door.

"Let him go. That's an order."

"I don't think you're in any position to issue orders… sir."

The man had his hip cocked, stance casual and relaxed. His hand rested on the butt of his rifle nowhere near the trigger. Mentally Tracy thanked him for being a fool. He then sucker punched the guard in the gut. When the man doubled over Tracy brought his knee up into his chin.

Donnel hadn't waited. The moment the first punch had been thrown he was galloping away on the ceiling of the corridor. Tracy dragged the *fusilero* into the room, propped him in a chair, leaned the rifle against the wall well away from him and sat down to wait.

The call had come through on Tracy's ScoopRing. Mercedes had stared at the identification with the air of a rabbit faced with a snake. Tracy was incarcerated. His ring would have been taken. The signal stopped and a tap indicated she had a message. A few seconds later another call from Tracy's ring. Then another and another. Mercedes finally keyed her ring and listened to the message.

"Hey, Princess, this is Donnel. Remember the trousers?"

Memory flooded back; standing in Tracy's quarters at the High Ground with his hand on her thigh as he altered the absurd long skirts they had been forced to wear into practical trousers. His strange Cara'ot batBEM staggering through the door carrying a portable sewing machine. She shook away the past.

Donnel's voice continued. "We need to meet. Figure it out and call me back."

The creature's tone and peremptory command put her back up, but the threat was implicit. She called back.

"What do you want? And how do you have Tracy's ring?"

"He gave it to me just before they arrested him, and I'll tell you what I want when I see you."

She paced to her office window and gazed out at the garden. Three children went darting across the grass heading for the boxwood maze. They were servants' children since none of her sisters or their broods were currently in residence at the palace.

"I can't bring you to the palace," she finally said.

"Then get your royal ass to someplace where we can meet."

"How dare you take this tone!"

"Yeah, well you haven't exactly earned my respect with the crap you've pulled."

"I'm doing what I had to. And what if I say no?"

"Here's an incentive to say yes, Princess. What makes you think I don't have a record of all those clandestine meetings between you and Belmanor? If I were to pass those on to say your cousin or maybe whisper it to Father Jose… I bet he's not all that scrupulous about keeping the seal of the confessional when the family fortunes are at stake."

Her chest tightened. "All right, but it has to be someplace where I won't be recognized."

"There's an alien bar between MonkeyTown and Stick Town. Got everything a BEM might want – water, light, coffee, sezlac. Pretty much just aliens there."

"Which means I'll stand out like a sore thumb," Mercedes snapped.

"Not if you're there to meet with an unsavory and unscrupulous character who's going to do a little job for you. Something about a philandering husband, I think."

A prickle ran down the back of her neck, ghost claws cold and frightening. Shrewd guess or did the alien actually know about Boho's parade of lovers?

The Cara'ot went on. "Of course you'll be veiled for such an assignation. Take a table and I'll join you."

"All right. When?"

"Now. Or as close to now as you can make it."

She glanced around the office. At the calendar that seemed to glare at her with its long list of appointments. "I have responsibilities. I can't just leave. I can clear my schedule for part of tomorrow."

"Tomorrow's going to be too late." He softened his tone.

"Look, Highness, if you care for him at all do this."

A vise closed on her heart. "Okay. Fine. You better be there."

"I will be."

She ended the call and buzzed her assistant. Jaakon was a sleek young man of twenty-five from a well-to-do caballero family. "I'm… I'm not feeling well. Cancel the rest of my appointments and reschedule."

"Yes, ma'am. Do you need the palace physician?"

"No. It's not that serious. I just don't think I can concentrate." She touched her fingertips to her forehead. "Headache. I'll see you tomorrow."

She hurried to her quarters and dug out the veil she'd worn all those long years ago when she'd gone to a whorehouse for advice on how to avoid getting pregnant. Now she wished she could go there and learn how to conceive.

29

A DUTIFUL SON

It was a part of town she'd never visited. Not surprising this was the domain of aliens. The only humans she saw on the street were four very drunk and very loud young men who ogled and laughed at everything.

"What do you want to bet that they'll end up in one of the alien brothels feeling very wicked for flouting the sexual congress laws?" Mercedes said to her driver.

Commander Caballero Davin Pulkkinen, wearing civilian dress rather than his uniform, glanced over his shoulder and gave her his crooked grin. "And I'll raise that bet that they won't be able to perform once they are faced with a Hajin or Isanjo hooker, but will lie their asses off to their less adventurous comrades about their awesome sexual prowess."

They shared a laugh, and Mercedes was glad he was with her. Coming alone was never an option. SEGU, SPI and Captain Rogers would have lost their minds if she had tried. She proposed Davin and they had finally agreed. Rogers and her guards would form a perimeter around the neighborhood in case there was an attempt to kidnap her, and she would go armed. She also lied and told them this had to do with high level but unofficial negotiations with the Cara'ot. It wasn't strictly true, but Donnel *was* a Cara'ot.

She considered taking Rogers, but preferred to have someone who had been a classmate of Tracy's, been his friend and knew Donnel. That might help reduce the tension. She was also sure that with Davin she could be certain that the press or other members of the FFH would not get wind of her little jaunt to a seedy alien bar.

The electric impulses in Davin's artificial hand flickered blue through its milky plastic casing. Mercedes wondered why he had never had the arm and hand coated with a skin substitute. Did he want to remember the events of that chaotic day when they had saved the *cosmódromo* from supposed terrorists? It had been a horrible and exhilarating day. She had proved her prowess as a pilot and Tracy his brilliance as a tactician. At the cost of a boy's life, she reminded herself, and Davin's arm. Mercedes had been surprised when Davin chose to complete his five-year commitment, but the class clown had proved to have the soul of a patriot. After his first tour had ended he had re-upped and then re-upped again. Word from the high command was that despite his injury he was clever, hardworking and well liked by his subordinates and superiors alike. The prediction was that he would continue to rise through the ranks.

The flitter slowed and dropped to the ground in front of a very seedy and rundown building. LED lights in the front windows offered a choice of beers and pool.

Davin looked back at her as she arranged her veil. "So

what's my play? Dutiful, bored servant? Concerned and devoted servant? Lovesick servant?"

"I don't think it really matters since we're just meeting Donnel."

"There are going to be other critters in the bar. We have to sell it to them too."

"Oh, all right. You'll never sell lovesick. You're smirking right now. I'd try for perv with a taste for alien flesh."

He clutched at his heart. "Mercedes, you wound me!"

"If only."

They shared another smile and she flipped the material over her face. As her skin brushed across the lace she remembered Tracy's father, the conversation with Tracy where she'd almost said something indiscreet. There were too many connections. Davin opened the door, bowed and offered his hand to assist her out of the flitter. The building was stained tan stucco with a terracotta tile roof. Several tiles were missing. A veranda ran across the front of the building, a holdover from a time when this was the outskirts of the city and this porch might have offered a view across the chaparral. Now it looked at a payday loan operation and a tattoo parlor.

It was dim inside, the only light provided by more LED signs touting Two Crowns beer and several kinds of tequila. Shadows lurked in the corners and offered secrecy for the tables and their patrons. There were ropes strewn across the ceiling for the comfort of Isanjo patrons. A couple of rough-clad construction workers lounged among them. Three Flutes stood swaying in tubs of water while a red tinged light shone down on them. Whether their listing was due to inebriation or was part of their complex language Mercedes couldn't be sure. Their breathy tweets and twerks clashed with the music. A drunk Hajin beat his palm on the bar, maybe to attract the attention of the Hajin bartender or trying to keep time with the music. In either case he was failing. Two more Hajin played pool. With every clack of the balls there would be either a curse or a shout of laughter.

Davin leaned in and whispered in her ear, "This is great. I feel like I'm in a Dirk Steel novel," referencing a popular stream series about a hard-edge private detective.

Mercedes didn't share his enjoyment because she realized that she hadn't heard a single word in any human language since they'd entered. This was a realm where humans didn't matter. Nervous now, she scanned the room. There was no sign of Donnel. She approached the bar.

The blandness of the bartender's gaze was as telling as open disdain. "I'm… I'm here to meet someone." She allowed her voice to quaver a bit. The Hajin kept washing glasses. "He's going to do… something for me?" She turned it into a hesitant question.

"Through the door by the johns," the Hajin grunted.

They went down a dark, narrow hallway. The sewer smell indicated old pipes or maybe even a septic tank. It was possible this old building had never been hooked up to city services. Staying in character, Davin knocked then opened the door and preceded Mercedes into the darkened room. Donnel was seated at a game table in the center of the room. She moved to him, Davin following in her wake. The alien didn't stand at her approach and indeed all four eyes studied her with contempt.

"Huh, back room poker game? Maybe I can buy in some night," Davin said.

"I wouldn't count on it," Donnel said. Davin gave a delighted laugh at the alien's dry tone.

"Maybe you should wait by the bar," Mercedes said to Davin.

"What, Princess, you don't want him to hear how you fucked over Belmanor?" Donnel said.

"So that's what this is about," Davin said.

"Yes, and since I think Donnel is about to blackmail me I'd prefer you not be present for that," Mercedes replied.

"Okay. Guess I'll go find out if they serve *my kind* in here." Davin shut the door behind him as he left.

"He's charming enough, he'll probably win them over," the Cara'ot grunted. Mercedes pulled out a chair, sat down and threw back her veil. "I'm a bit surprised you showed up. Or didn't show up with the troops you've left at the edge of the neighborhood."

"You're smart enough to know I left word that will be read if I'm not back by midnight. And you're not stupid enough to kill me because you know hell would rain down upon your people," Mercedes said. "So let's get to it. What do you want?"

"You know what I want. Don't let them destroy Belmanor."

She traced a pattern in the felt on the top of the table. It raised a smell of old booze and human and alien tobacco. "He brought this on himself."

Donnel leaned forward, all four arms resting on the table. "Yeah, he's a stiff-necked pain in the ass. He has a bad temper, resentment gnaws at him like bark beetles on a pine tree. He's also honorable and he did a good thing saving those kids, and if you're honest with yourself you know that." The alien paused and took a pull on his beer. "He also fucking loves you and I think you love him too so for fuck sake *help him*."

Agitated she stood and paced. "I can't. It's too late. It's gone too far. He had his chance—"

"And of course he blew it because he's a better person than you or me. He wouldn't take your bribe." He stood and joined her as she paced. His skittering movements on his three legs were disturbing. He grabbed her arm and she flinched. "You need to find a way to keep him out of Leavenworth."

"If I do he'll talk and the peace we've built with your people could be shattered," Mercedes argued.

"Not if you threaten his dad. He'll protect the old man," the alien said. The blunt coldness reminded her of her father and probably herself as well.

"And I'll bet if I have you arrested or killed all of it goes public," Mercedes said. She had an overwhelming desire to laugh.

"You can bet your royal ass. And not just about Dragonfly. I've got all your little adventures documented."

She ripped free of his grip. "Did your people put you at the High Ground to spy on me?" The alien didn't answer. "All right," Mercedes finally said. "I can't reinstate him. Not after all this, but I'll see to it he's just cashiered."

"That'll do." He held out one of his four hands with its six long fingers. "Your word on it?"

"Not yet. You turn over to me everything you have about my dealings with Tracy." With four eyes it was easy to see the mental wheels turning. Finally the creature nodded that absurdly round head.

"Okay. Should have asked for more than just one human's skinny ass," Donnel grumbled as he handed over a data spike.

Mercedes smiled. "Too late." She walked the spike through her fingers. "I trust there are no other copies?"

"My word on it, Highness."

Mercedes extended her hand. "Now you have *my* word on it."

They shook. Mercedes replaced her veil and started for the door. His voice froze her. "You ever stop to wonder how this is going to play for my people? To us Tracy's a big goddamn hero."

Whirling, Mercedes asked sharply, "Do you know something?"

"Nah, I'm just a flunky, but I'm not a stupid flunky."

"The only people who know are your diplomats. We've managed to cow or sequester anyone who was there and might talk."

"Like you were going to *sequester* Tracy."

"We're doing the best we can," she pleaded. "Can you imagine what might happen if your people learned that some of my people massacred a bunch of children?"

"Yeah, I see your point."

The door closed behind her and Mercedes walked to the bar to collect Davin. He had managed to score a drink and he was chatting with the bartender. She envied the man his breezy gift of the gab.

"Ready, my lady?" Davin said, falling once more into his role as dutiful servant.

"Yes."

"Everything handled?" Davin asked quietly as he held open the front door for her.

After the dimness in the BEM bar the streetlights, even through her veil, felt too bright. Or perhaps it was just the headache that had begun to throb. She felt virtuous and relieved but also sad. She would probably never see Tracy again.

"Yes, all settled," she finally answered. "I do wonder how Tracy will react."

"What's your guess?" Davin asked as he keyed open the door to the flitter.

"I'd like to hope for grateful and relieved, but I'm betting he'll be bitter and resentful."

"That's our boy. Well, you did your best. Now it's up to him."

They stood before the judge. Gurion on one side, Clancy on the other as if they feared Tracy would collapse. It irritated him, but he also wasn't sure it wasn't true. The panel was not in place and Tracy couldn't decide if that was hopeful or ominous. As usual his father, Malcomb and on this day Father Ken were in the gallery. No Donnel today.

After the threat to arrest him the alien had vanished. Tracy couldn't blame him. The other spectators consisted of a few low-level reporters looking for a story about the one-time O-Trell hero, though Tracy had to assume that vein had been tapped.

After one brief glance Tracy brought his eyes back to the judge. The rear admiral was frowning. The angle of the track lighting flared off the medals on his uniform coat and threw his face into stark relief. He seemed diabolical in the glow. His clenched jaw and frown added to that impression. Etienne was just finishing.

"…Given the defendant's service to the crown it was felt that merely cashiering Lieutenant Belmanor will be sufficient."

The admiral leaned over the bench and hissed, "I'm starting to feel like a fucking yoyo, counselor. You bring me an overwhelming amount of evidence that this defendant has stolen millions of Reals' worth of equipment from the organization he swore to serve and now you want to let him off with a slap on the wrist?"

"There's been new… um… ah… issues have arisen." Etienne almost seemed to whine.

"Pressure from the palace, I presume?" the judge whispered.

"I wouldn't presume to say, sir." The words were whispered through lips stiff with embarrassment.

While the judge and Etienne were arguing, Tracy leaned in to Gurion. "Cashiered versus thirty years in military prison? Bet your ass I'll take that," he whispered. Of course he would be a disgraced former O-Trell officer with no job and no real civilian skills, but he wasn't going to cavil.

"It's agreeable to us," Gurion said loudly, interrupting the argument.

The admiral flung himself back in his chair, tugged at his upper lip and frowned. "Well, it's not agreeable to *me*."

"Oh shit," Clancy muttered and a stone lodged in the pit of Tracy's stomach.

The admiral lifted his tap-pad. "This man stands accused of stealing over four million Reals' worth of equipment from O-Trell, and he walks away with nothing more than a dishonorable discharge? An *hombre* accused of being intoxicated and flashing his dick at passing women would get that. I'll let him walk, but only if he pleads guilty to a felony, and signs an agreement that he, his heirs and assigns have to repay the money owed to the crown and the service."

There was an audible gasp and Tracy realized he had made it. It was one thing to burden him with this impossible debt. It was another to lay it on his father. Blind rage swept through him, closing his throat, choking off words. He coughed and gave a furious head shake.

"No! I'll do the thirty. You are not laying this on my father. He's blameless. I'm blameless too, but fuck it, you're not going to destroy us both!" Clancy had grabbed his arm and seemed to be trying to say something, but the young JAG officer's words seemed distant and muffled.

There was a thud and a commotion from behind him. Malcomb's voice bellowing, "Tracy!" He whirled to see his father being eased onto the floor by Father Ken. Tracy spun away from the bench and ran down the aisle to where his father lay. Drool was running down Alexander's chin, the right side of his face was drooping, and his eyes were staring off to the left. The priest was loosening Alexander's collar.

"Looks like a stroke," Ken said.

"Dad. Dad. Can you hear me?" The eyes didn't move, continuing to stare grotesquely off to the side. His father's mouth worked and grinding, garbled sounds emerged.

"I'm calling for an ambulance," Malcomb said.

"We're on a military base. Our response will be much quicker." It was the admiral who had left his high seat between heaven and earth and had joined the mere mortals. "Call for the medics," he ordered Etienne.

Tracy sat cradling his father in his arms while agonizing seconds turned into endless minutes. Then the medical personnel were there, loading Alexander onto a float, inserting an IV, giving him an injection. Tracy started to walk out with the float only to be grabbed by an MP. He spun, kicked the man's leg out from under him, grabbed the restraining hand and bent it backward. The guard bellowed and sank to the floor. Father Ken grabbed Tracy's shoulders, trying to pull him away.

"Calm down. He's in good hands. You go biblical on this guy you won't be visiting your father." The priest's lips were pressed against his ear, breath hot and hurried, words tumbling out. Tracy released the MP, nodded and stepped back.

Gurion, talking fast, walked with the judge as the admiral headed back to the bench. "Perfectly understandable… great deal of strain… his father…"

Malcomb grabbed Tracy's arm hard enough to bruise. "Take the deal!" His voice was low but crackled with command. "Your father needs you."

"I'll be a criminal. He'll be so ashamed."

Malcomb gave him a shake. The guards stepped forward only to be held back by Father Ken's upraised hand. "He knows you're innocent. But you refuse this plea you get sent off world. He can't see you. That will kill him. Think, lad!" Tracy stared into Devris's red, sweat-bathed face. Tracy's emotions were too complex to analyze. He was frozen with indecision. "Eat their FFH shit and say thank you and you walk out of here. I take you to your dad. Come on, boy." Tracy finally nodded and Malcomb released him.

Clancy was at his side as they once again approached the bridge. "You're making the right choice," the young JAG officer said.

"Shut up."

Ten minutes later it was done. They took his bars and stars right then. The journalists drifted away. One was whispering into his ScoopRing as he went, as was the SEGU officer. Tracy paused where the man sat in the gallery and leaned in. "Tell her for me that if my father dies I'll never fucking forgive her." The man's look was impassive.

The bailiff wanted to take him back to the station to collect his personal effects. Since that consisted of a handkerchief, the lip balm, an ear piece and a credit spike with maybe forty Reals on it, Tracy couldn't fucking care less and he said so. Flanked by the businessman and the priest he left the courtroom.

30

GHOSTS AND SHADOWS

Through the door came the muffled sounds of a hospital at work—hushed voices, the soft beeps of monitors and the occasional shriek of a medical alarm, moans from post-surgical patients being forced to walk the halls, PA calls for doctors. Sounds of living and dying. The doctors had assured Tracy that his father would be among the former not the latter, but right now he felt only fear. His father lay stiffly on his back, IVs running into his arms, nasal cannulas aiding his breathing. Because the oxygen mask had been removed Tracy could see the ravaged face, the drooping mouth, the sagging eyelid. Alexander slept but he was so still it seemed more like a coma than normal sleep.

Tracy sat by the bed, hands folded between his knees. It was late. He knew in a vague sort of way that he was hungry and he should probably go to the hospital cafeteria and find something to eat, but he didn't want to leave his father's side. He didn't want him to wake and find himself alone with his last memory of his son definitely demanding to be sent to prison.

There was the question whether Alexander would even remember the events leading up to his collapse. The doctors had said they wouldn't know the full extent of the damage for a few days, but Tracy knew this was his fault. He had caused this. Through bull-headed arrogance he'd brought his father to this bed in this hospital room.

He reached out and gripped his father's hand. The skin slipped beneath his fingers, and he felt every bone. "I'm sorry, Dad," he whispered. "But it's okay now. I'll be with you. Just like the old days. We'll be okay."

There was a murmur of excited conversation outside, the rap of booted feet on tile. A grinding certainty washed over Tracy. He went to the door, drew in several deep breaths searching for calm then stepped outside. Mercedes, dressed in highborn-lady elegance, stood inside a wedge of *fusileros*. Medical staff were gathered at the edges of the palace contingent, dropping curtsies and offering bows. A few ScoopRings were grabbing pictures. Every face had an expression of awe. Emotions roiled through Tracy causing him to expel all the air he'd sucked in. Mercedes held out a hand.

"Señor Belmanor, I came to check on your father's condition." Her accents were pure FFH. Tracy knew his role from the position of her hand, and the way her eyes brushed across him as if he wasn't truly there.

Tracy executed a deep bow, but refused to touch the outstretched fingers or offer the fantasy kiss that left lips hovering an inch above that gloved hand. It was a mark of condescension that she would offer her hand for the kiss. A public snub that he had refused. Realizing she looked foolish Mercedes pulled back her hand.

"Highness. How very…" He sucked in a breath. Chewed at the word, fought it. Speech finally emerged as a throttled wheeze. "…kind."

"Your noble father made my wedding gown." For a moment Tracy was confused, then he realized the statement was for the benefit of the star-struck staff and the few patients who had emerged from their rooms. Cover for why the heir to the Solar League was here to visit an ailing tailor. "Something I have not forgotten."

"I haven't forgotten either." He raised his eyes, met hers in a challenge. "And my father isn't noble. Or important."

"Every League citizen is important and valuable to us."

It was the royal We and they were having a conversation in code. Tracy felt whipsawed from the conflicting emotional currents. "There are moments when one does not feel that way, Majesty," he gritted.

"I understand." Silence hung like a cobweb between them. "Might we see him?"

"He's sleeping."

"We will not disturb him."

"I think that ship has left orbit."

A couple of the guards shifted at the evident discourtesy and there were indrawn breaths from the staff. Mercedes would not lower herself to beg, but the dark eyes pleaded. He relented even as an inner voice railed that he was *stupid, stupid, stupid*. He gave a jerky nod and gestured at the door. He wanted to stalk through forcing her to follow, but despite the rage, and the sense of betrayal, he couldn't bring himself to do it. He held the door for her, but jerked his head at the guards. "I don't—"

Mercedes cut him off. "Of course not." She nodded to the squad leader. "Remain in the hall, Captain Rogers. We won't be long."

The door closed behind them. His father's soft breaths and the beeps from the monitor were the only sounds. Tracy stood at a stiff parade rest, hands clasped behind his back. His fingers began to go numb from the force of his grip.

"Say it!" Mercedes commanded. Her voice was low, throbbing with emotion.

"Say what, Your Highness? What would you like me to say? Please instruct me. Having learned the error of my ways I'm only here to serve."

"Oh for Christ's sake, Tracy. Why do you have to be…" She gestured as if shooing away a swarm of bees. "So… impossible?"

"I'm sorry if I have displeased Your Highness."

"You brought this on yourself!"

His eyes slid to his father's supine form. "Yes… yes, I did."

He stiffened as she grabbed his shoulders and gave him a furious shake. "Oh God, just yell at me. Something!"

"I would not presume."

She thrust him away, paced. "You could have been brilliant. Had anything."

"Not everything." It was hard to unlock his jaw enough to get out the words.

"I had to marry him," Mercedes said. Tracy didn't trust himself to answer. She walked to the bed and looked down at Alexander. "What will you do?" He shook his head. "My advice. Get off world. Use your skills."

"I'm not abandoning my dad."

"I don't mean right away, but once he's recovered. I'll see to him."

"That's what worries me."

"You're cruel," she said.

"I'm an amateur compared to you."

Mercedes walked back, got within an inch of his face. "I'm not going to apologize."

"Yeah, why would you?" He studied the way the light reflected in her eyes. Normal moisture or a hint of tears? Her hands opened and closed spasmodically. For a brief moment he thought she was about to kiss him. For one wild moment he considered begging her to come away with him. He didn't. She didn't. The moment passed.

"Goodbye, Tracy."

The door whispered shut behind her. Tracy knew he had seen her for the last time. The room felt empty. His father was a fragile shell barely holding life. And Tracy—a ghost.

The apartment felt unfamiliar. It had been nearly seven months since he'd last stood at this front door. It was also hot and stuffy. Tracy kicked on the air conditioning. Fans whispered. There was no other sound. He called out for Donnel and got no answer. Even though it was stupid, Tracy found himself searching through the apartment. He went to the small bedroom that had housed the servant, thinking perhaps Donnel would have left some kind of message. The room was as anonymous as a hotel room.

Unbuttoning his now bare uniform jacket, Tracy went into his bedroom. His ScoopRing rested in the center of his pillow. There was no sign of his medal. He cupped the ring in the palm of his hand then tried contacting the batBEM. Four calls got nothing, then on the fifth call he got a response. An automated message that *this user is no longer in system*. Tracy could understand why the alien had been AWOL when the court-martial was still underway, but it made no sense now. The trial was over and the alien stood in no danger of arrest. There would be no interrogation about the money he'd handled, at least not from the authorities. Tracy, however, damn well intended to get answers from his batBEM.

Which brought Tracy up short. He was no longer an O-Trell officer. He had no right to a batBEM. Would Donnel want to work in the tailor shop or would he return to the High Ground to serve some new, young, hopeful (and hopefully) luckier cadet?

Out of morbid curiosity he called Mercedes' private number. Like the batBEM's that number had also been dropped from the system. He seemed to be shedding people like a tree sheds leaves in autumn. Tracy toed off his boots and stripped down to his shorts, collapsed on top of the covers and let the cool air from the vents play across his bare skin. He should get down to the shop and see what orders were pending. Help out Bajit and the little Isanjo seamstress. Alexander's next stop would be a rehab center. How soon he returned home would depend on his progress there, and they couldn't afford to fall behind on the work.

Get off world. Mercedes' advice. Yeah, how the fuck was he supposed to do that? He should talk to Malcomb. Maybe he could get a job at one of the flitter dealerships; there were a number of them on various League worlds so he wouldn't have to stay on Ouranos. Tracy pushed aside the brief flare of excitement. He couldn't and wouldn't leave his father. Maybe he'd meet someone. Marry. Have kids. Where there should be emotions there was nothing. Flinging an arm over his eyes Tracy wished Donnel had left the medal. It could have reminded him that once he had been somebody.

He awoke from a sleep he hadn't intended to take. His tongue felt coated with fuzz and his stomach gave a growl. He couldn't remember the last time he'd eaten. Maybe that cup of coffee and a fruit bar from the machine at the hospital? He padded on bare feet into the small kitchen and opened the refrigerator. There was a carton of cottage cheese, half a muffuletta sandwich, and a couple of bottles of beer. He snapped the cap off the beer and grabbed the sandwich. He found a bag of chips in the cabinet and made a meal. His immediate needs having been met Tracy paced through the small apartment. There were holos of him as a kid, pictures of him in the circle of his grandfather's arms. The old man looked angry. Tracy thought this younger him looked scared. More photos from his graduation from the High Ground.

He pulled on a shirt, slacks and a pair of sandals and fled the sullen, grave-like quiet of the apartment. Maybe in the streets and cafés he could feel like life still went on.

He found himself back in the old neighborhood. The tailor shop had become a beauty shop. In the window was a display of cheap and gaudy costume jewelry and rhinestone-studded barrettes and combs designed to hold a lady's long hair, and multi-colored bangle cords to decorate a Hajin's mane. The BELMANOR & SON sign had been painted over with a picture of a woman with flowing red tresses, but in places the paint had worn away and he could see shadows of the letters below. His dad hadn't taken the sign to the new shop because that neighborhood didn't allow for hanging signs. Too déclassé for the upper-middle class trying to pretend they were FFH.

The sparkle of the rhinestones gave Tracy a sudden idea. It did seem the Cara'ot had a communication network. Maybe they could put him in touch with Donnel. He caught a tram down to the warehouse district on the south side of the spaceport. During his three years at the academy Donnel had brought him to the Cara'ot warehouse to pick out presents for the classmates he didn't actively hate. Because of Donnel he got discounts on the goods. He hadn't been back in years, but perhaps it hadn't moved.

It was broiling hot between the big buildings and the air was redolent with the scent of rocket fuel and softened asphalt. Forklifts floated past, loaded with containers off the ships, most manned by humans. Stevedore was a well-paying union job and aliens weren't welcome. Especially since the Isanjo with their clever hands, feet and tails had pretty much taken over most of the construction jobs both for buildings and ships. *Maybe I should apply to be a stevedore*, Tracy thought with bitter humor. *Puts me at least in the* vicinity *of starships*.

Most of the alleys between the buildings looked the same, but after a couple of wrong turns Tracy found the right door. At least he hoped it was. He knocked on the metal door and stepped back in surprise when it swung open. Since he knew the value of many of the items in the warehouse and the kind of locks that protected the facility this was, to say the least, surprising.

He stepped inside. "Hello?" No answer, just the whisper of the air conditioning and humidifiers. "Anybody here?"

A camerabot floated past. Tracy moved deeper into the warehouse. Items rested on sorting tables—objets d'art, medicines and jewels. Not the normal gemstones—those could be found on almost any world, and could be artificially created and were therefore valueless. These were Phantasm gems that could only grow in the gizzard of an extremely truculent flying female lizard that only existed on a particularly poisonous world in the Sidone system. They were incalculably valuable. On a table where it appeared that medicines were being loaded into syringes, Tracy found a shattered syringe, and broken bottles. He also found a clean room suit that looked like the wearer had torn it off. It was puddled on the floor like a cast-off skin.

Tracy moved through the rest of building. In the security office he found a nearly full coffee cup and a half-eaten funnel cake. Powdered sugar was strewn across the desk as if the diner had dropped the pastry. He clicked through the camera feeds. The entire facility was deserted. A plan began to form.

Typing quickly, Tracy erased his entrance into the building and his movements thereafter. He then set the cameras on a loop and headed back downstairs.

He found the correct aisle, grabbed up a soft leather pouch and swept the pile of Phantasm gems into it and stuffed the pouch inside his shirt. The leather was soft against his skin, the gems hard and sharp. It wasn't theft. Not really. They were aliens. They were gone. If he didn't take them someone else would. Once the workers realized that the Cara'ot warehouse was empty and unlocked there would be a looting frenzy.

The justifications continued to tumble through his head as Tracy's gaze darted around considering what else to take. He had always wanted a knife like the one he had bought for Mercedes that first Christmas, now so long ago. He found the area and snatched up one of the morphing boot knives. He thrust it into his waistband. What else? What else. *Don't get greedy*, he admonished himself. He turned away then on an impulse he snatched up an exquisite rapier. The hilt was a work of art of twining colors—bronze, silver and gold. A single Phantasm gem glittered on the top. Tracy wrapped it in the discarded clean suit and slipped out of the building. He thought about closing the door, but decided he wanted his DNA mixed with as many other humans as possible. He left the door standing wide open.

Dodging dock workers, he quickly made his way to the boulevard and caught a passing tram. On a tram you were anonymous. Cabs kept records. Better that no one know he had been at the spaceport. He felt a flare of contrition. There was something off about the way the Cara'ot had decamped. He should probably tell someone. A moment's reflection and his attitude changed. Fuck 'em, he decided, the powers-that-be had thrown him away. He wasn't going to do them any favors.

31

SO WILL YOU BE JUDGED

It wasn't often that Kemel DeLonge emerged from SEGU headquarters, but now he was standing in Mercedes' office. The fact he hadn't just Scooped her was a very bad sign. As usual his expression gave away nothing. His physical presence said it all.

The years had not been kind to the head of imperial intelligence. The wiry hair had gone steel grey and gouges framed his mouth. For such a spare man he had lush lips. Mercedes wondered whom he kissed. She didn't recall meeting a wife or husband at any of the palace social events. Not that DeLonge attended many. Perhaps he kept all of his passion for secrets and for ferreting them out.

DeLonge was not alone. Rohan had accompanied him. It seemed an odd pairing—secrets and money. Upon reflection Mercedes decided maybe it wasn't all that odd.

"Kemel, Rohan, welcome." She indicated chairs.

"You won't say that once you hear my news," the man said as he folded his long frame into the chair.

Mercedes moved to the bar. "Drink? You look like you need one."

"We all do," Rohan said. "You should get one for yourself too."

She spun away from the cabinet. "Okay, now I am worried. And if something really serious has happened, why are you in my office and not my father's?"

"Because we wanted to discuss with you how we best present this information. You know how your dad can be," Rohan said.

Kemel spoke up. "I don't want to have him overreact, but something…" his voice trailed away.

Mercedes splashed brandy into two snifters and carried them to the men. Watching the way the abstemious SEGU chief grabbed the glass like a drowning man on a bit of flotsam added to her disquiet. She returned for a glass for herself, perched on the edge of her desk and took a sip. The liquor exploded on the back of her tongue and left a trail of fire down her throat and into her gut. "All right. I'm fortified. What's happened or is about to happen?"

"You understand we can only monitor so much. Too many worlds. Too many people. Too many cameras. We try to liaise with local law enforcement to give us heads-up about potential problems, but…" Kemel's voice trailed away.

"Okay, I'm getting the idea that you missed something."

Before the SEGU chief could answer, Rohan sipped his brandy and gave the snifter a respectful glance. "Hmmm, very good. Kronos?" he asked, suggesting the source.

"Yes, a new vintner. Branching out from just wine," Mercedes replied.

"Well, very nice. I must make a note of the label." He

snapped a picture with his ring. Kemel shifted in his chair. For this man it was a sign of great irritation. Rohan cleared his throat. "Yes well, going on. Naturally we pay more attention to alien comings and goings," Rohan said.

"Naturally." Mercedes decided to match the men's laconic tones.

"Flight control at all spaceports and space stations monitor alien ships," Kemel added.

"And I'm assuming the Cara'ot come in for the most scrutiny?" Mercedes suggested. Kemel nodded. "So what have they done? Up-armored the ships? Mounted missiles?" She kept her tone light.

The man looked up from his study of the amber liquid that swirled and coated the sides of the glass. He had yet to take a sip. "They've vanished." He then drained all the brandy in one long gulp.

Mercedes shot off the desk. "What?" Her voice had gone shrill and unrecognizable to herself.

"Scheduled landings never occurred. The ships that were dirt side requested early launches. We didn't see the pattern until the early hours of this morning. I wanted to be sure so we waited to verify. No need to alarm the crown if it was just an anomaly or delays in reporting. But it's the same story everywhere. The Cara'ot ships are gone. More than that, the shops and warehouses have been abandoned. Looting has already started, but best we can tell the Cara'ot took nothing when they left. I came immediately, but with time dilation and distance…" He shrugged.

"Oh God." Mercedes sank back onto the desk. "Is this the

beginning of a new war?" The men seemed to understand it wasn't a real question, just her speaking her fear aloud. They stayed silent. She lunged to her feet. "We need to alert the fleet. Put the sentry platforms on high alert. And we need to tell the Emperor. Why didn't you go to him first?"

"Because I wanted to know if you might have some insight into this," Kemel said bluntly.

"Me? Why would I—" The look he gave her backed the words into her throat, almost choking her. "Because I had you monitoring that court-martial."

"Exactly." He drew out the word. "SEGU dealt with many of the parties who were privy to the events on Dragonfly."

"You met the young man in my office and failed to... convince him," Rohan added.

"And..." Kemel gave her a lowering look from beneath frowning eyebrows. "You met with the Cara'ot batBEM who served that young man not two days ago."

Mercedes set down her glass with such force that it shattered. Rohan flinched. Brandy pooled on the desk, rippling under the lights. Mercedes paced madly back and forth across the room. "This is insane. Why would this one man, one low-level officer, matter so much?"

"Maybe it was less him than how we treated him," Rohan said softly. "What it said about the League. As for your father, I've known Fernán for forty years. Stood up with him at his wedding to your mother. I know how he'll react and I wanted us to have a full grasp of the situation before we... upset him."

She leaned over the desk and keyed the intercom.

"Jaakon, get me the Cara'ot ambassadors."

"Yes, ma'am."

Minutes ticked by. Mercedes got a napkin off the bar and mopped up the spill, then swept the broken glass into the trash can. She rang Jaakon again. "Damn it, what's the holdup?"

"There's no response, Highness. Do you want me to send police?"

"No, I'll go myself. Tell Captain Rogers to have a squad waiting for me." She turned back to the men. "Don't go to my father until I report back."

"I should go with you," Kemel said as he unfolded from the chair.

"Fine."

Rohan settled more deeply into the high-back chair. "I'm going to stay here and enjoy another glass of this very fine brandy."

Mercedes dithered, but finally decided against wearing armor like the *fusileros* who accompanied them. She and Kemel were both armed, but he seemed to agree that having the heir to the throne arrive in full battle armor might not send the best message. She did change into her O-Trell uniform.

Embassy Row was a relatively short dead-end street that culminated in the Cara'ot embassy; the largest building anchored the center position in the cul-de-sac. Each of the alien races had an embassy and in an act of supreme arrogance, Earth herself kept an embassy rather than accepting the fact that while the planet may have been the origin of humankind it was now a climate-ravaged world in a backwater of the galaxy.

They were in three flitters and soared in over the top of the ornate wall. The human guards on the front gates craned their necks to follow the progress of the vehicles. They seemed insectile in their helmets with the sun gleaming off the faceplates. Once landed Mercedes went to the gate and returned the salutes.

"Anything to report?" she asked the guards.

The helmeted heads turned toward each other. She could read the confusion. "Uh, no, ma'am."

"Nobody in or out today."

Mercedes glanced over at the SEGU chief. "Well, at least we know they're home." She turned back to the two guards. "Carry on."

"Odd that the Cara'ot choose to have human sentries rather than their own kind," Mercedes mused.

"They have to, Highness. They're not permitted to have troops under the treaty."

"Ah, I hadn't considered that."

They approached the tall metal doors, flanked by the troops. Mercedes rang the bell. Listened to the echoes go running away into the building. There was no response. She nodded to Rogers, who stepped up and banged on the door with the butt of his rifle. Still nothing. Another glance to Kemel, then Mercedes shrugged and grabbed the door handle. It turned and she pushed the door. It swung back with a sigh. The smell of incense, spicy and sweet, swept out.

Mercedes stepped back and Rogers signaled the *fusileros* to enter and fan out. They rushed through, rifles at the ready and began to search. The SEGU chief gave her an approving glance.

"Glad to see you didn't decide to take point."

"First, I'm not wearing armor. Second, smart officers always lead from behind," she said with a wry smile. Fading calls of *clear* floated back to Mercedes and Kemel from the soldiers.

"Hmm, I seem to remember that time you stole an *Infierno* and took on an armed frigate on your own."

"First, I didn't *steal* the fighter, I *commandeered* it. And I was only a cadet and therefore expendable cannon fodder."

Ian returned and snapped off a salute. "All clear, Your Majesty. The place is deserted, but it looks planned."

"What do you mean?" Kemel asked.

"Easier to show you, sir."

They followed him inside. The furnishings were elegant and mostly human normal, but there were a few anomalies, chairs that were either too large or too small for a human frame. The staircase had been modified so there were three types of steps, each one with a different tread height. There was also a lift built onto the bannister.

Rogers led them into the ambassadors' office. The overhead lights had a strange red cast and were quite dim. The captain snapped on his helmet light. Shadows fled to cower in the corners. The drawers on the credenza stood open. There were dividers but no folders or files in the drawers. The room smelled faintly of smoke. Mercedes peered into a trashcan. Taking a pen off the desk she stirred the ash in the bottom.

"Sometimes the oldest methods just can't be beat," Kemel remarked. "Fire is a pretty comprehensive data wipe."

Mercedes picked up an abandoned teacup. The chai had congealed into a brown sludge in the bottom.

Rogers pressed a hand to his ear. "The soldiers report that the closets in the bedrooms are emptied. Toiletries gone," the captain said.

"They had this planned." Mercedes set down the cup. "Any idea how they all decamped without the *fusileros* seeing them?" she asked Ian.

"Not yet, ma'am. I've called for sounding equipment and X-ray. There's got to be a tunnel."

"Keep us informed, Captain," Kemel said. He took Mercedes by the elbow and guided her to the door.

"Yes, I suppose we can't postpone the music any longer," Mercedes said quietly. A hand seemed to be pressing down on her chest. "Boho's out there," she added and couldn't find enough breath to make it more than a whisper. And following close on that thought was relief that Tracy wasn't.

32

WHAT WAITS IN THE DARK

The great ship lay on its side. Airlocks open to the void. The surface of the tiny world was formed by ripples of stone and frozen methane. Which added to the sense that the ship was not a construct of metal and composite, but a lifeless creature washed up on a dark, forgotten shore. The system possessed seventeen lifeless worlds. It had been briefly surveyed and marked as a low-priority mining site. It was sheer luck that a scout vessel had decided to swing through, thinking it might be a gathering place for the Cara'ot fleet. Instead the scout had found the derelict.

Mercedes swung her head so the helmet light and camera could record and send the images to her father waiting at O-Trell headquarters back on Hellfire. The light illuminated sections that glittered where escaped atmosphere from the ship had frozen on the exterior metal. She dropped her head to the ground looking for footprints. There were none. She waited but the Emperor offered no comment.

Boho, a hulking figure in his battle armor, shifted from

foot to foot. "Are we going in?" He sounded both uncertain and unenthusiastic.

"We have to. See if there are bodies."

She walked up the gentle incline toward the ship. The washboard of frozen gas crushed beneath her boots and sprays of ice rose up to swirl around her like dancing dervishes. The position of the ship put the airlock some four and a half meters above her head, but it posed no problem in the negligible gravity exerted by the dwarf planet. Mercedes bent her knees and jumped up and forward. Her aim was good and she landed a few meters inside the airlock. She felt the vibration as Boho landed just behind her. His breaths were loud as they came over the radio and into her helmet.

It was going to be easy to enter the main body of the ship since the inner airlock door was also open. The rest of the squad joined them and they entered. Unlike the embassy there were no cold cups of chai or signs of a hurried departure. This seemed carefully planned. Equipment had been dogged and stored, personal effects had been carefully hung or folded in closets in crew cabins and in the hold were crates filled with trade goods. She tried to calculate the value of the massive ship and the expensive goods that she carried in her belly. It was an absurd amount of Reals. No sane creature would simply abandon such an asset. But apparently that was exactly what had happened.

"Where have they gone?" Boho asked.

"I have no idea."

"Why did they—"

"I don't know the answer to that either."

"Is this war?" Boho said faintly.

Carried across the void her father's voice was cold as death. "Yes."

ACKNOWLEDGMENTS

This book could not have been written without the invaluable help of my friends Sage Walker and Eric Kelley. My editor Miranda Jewess who has made every book better with her insights. And finally my agent Kay McCauley who is my biggest cheerleader and who believes in me more than I believe in myself. Thank you guys for everything.

ABOUT THE AUTHOR

Melinda Snodgrass is the acclaimed author of many science fiction novels, including the *Circuit* and *Edge* series, and is the co-editor with George R.R. Martin of the *Wild Cards* series, to which she also contributes. She has had a long career in television, writing several episodes of *Star Trek: The Next Generation* while serving as the series' story editor, and has written scripts for numerous other shows, including *Odyssey 5*, *The Outer Limits*, *Reasonable Doubts* and *Seaquest DSV*. She was also a consulting producer on *The Profiler*. The first book in the *Imperials* series was published in 2016, and was described as "entertaining and briskly paced" by *Publishers Weekly*. The third book will be *The Hidden World*, published in 2018. She lives in Santa Fe, New Mexico.

THE HIGH GROUND
MELINDA SNODGRASS

The Emperor's daughter Mercedes is the first woman ever admitted to The High Ground, the elite training academy of the Solar League's Star Command, and she must graduate if she is to have any hope of taking the throne. Her classmate Thracius has more modest goals—to defy his humble beginnings and rise to the rank of captain. But in a system rocked by political division, where women are governed by their husbands and fathers, the poor are kept in their place by a rigid class system, and the alien races have been conquered and subjugated, there are many who want them to fail.

A civil war is coming and the machinations of those who yearn for power threaten the cadets. In a time of political intrigue, class conflict, and alien invasion, they will be tested as they never thought possible…

"Snodgrass just keeps on getting better"
George R.R. Martin

"Entertaining and briskly paced"
Publishers Weekly

NEW POMPEII
DANIEL GODFREY

In the near future, energy giant Novus Particles develops the technology to transport objects and people from the deep past to the present. Their biggest secret: New Pompeii. A replica of the city hidden deep in central Asia, filled with Romans pulled through time a split second before the volcano erupted.

Historian Nick Houghton doesn't know why he's been chosen to be the company's historical advisor. He's just excited to be there. Until he starts to wonder what happened to his predecessor. Until he realizes that NovusPart have more secrets than even the conspiracy theorists suspect. Until he realizes that NovusPart have underestimated their captives…

"Tremendously gripping"
Financial Times (Books of the Year)

"Irrestistibly entertaining"
Barnes & Noble

TITANBOOKS.COM

EMPIRE OF TIME
DANIEL GODFREY

For fifteen years, the Romans of New Pompeii have kept the outside world at bay with the threat of using the Novus Particles device to alter time. Yet Decimus Horatius Pullus—once Nick Houghton—knows the real reason the Romans don't use the device for their own ends: they can't make it work without grisly consequences.

This fragile peace is threatened when an outsider promises to help the Romans use the technology. And there are those beyond Pompeii's walls who are desperate to destroy a town where slavery flourishes. When his own name is found on an ancient artifact dug up at the real Pompeii, Nick knows that someone in the future has control of the device. The question is: whose side are they on?

Praise for Daniel Godfrey

"The page-turning style of Michael Crichton" *Sun*

"A remarkably promising debut"
Morning Star (Books of the Year)

TITANBOOKS.COM

THE RIG
ROGER LEVY

Humanity has spread across the depths of space but is connected by AfterLife—a vote made by every member of humanity on the worth of a life. Bale, a disillusioned policeman on the planet Bleak, is brutally attacked, leading writer Raisa on to a story spanning centuries of corruption. On Gehenna, the last religious planet, a hyperintelligent boy, Alef, meets psychopath Pellon Hoq, and so begins a rivalry and friendship to last an epoch.

"Levy is a writer of great talent and originality."
SF Site

"Levy's writing is well-measured and thoughtful, multi-faceted and often totally gripping."
Strange Horizons

For more fantastic fiction, author events, competitions, limited editions and more

Visit our website
titanbooks.com

Like us on Facebook
facebook.com/titanbooks

Follow us on Twitter
@TitanBooks

Email us
readerfeedback@titanemail.com